PRAISE FOR THE NOVELS
OF DAVID BELL

The Hiding Place

"An artfully constructed tale that charts the devastating, life-changing effects over twenty-five years on the people most affected by the murder of a four-year-old boy . . . a powerful, provocative novel."
—*Publishers Weekly*

"David Bell does a masterful job of crafting a crime story, with the guilty and innocent existing next to each other, whether they realize it or not. He has also created a tense drama of emotions and relationships. It is a riveting book with surprising but believable twists on every page." —*Suspense Magazine*

"A truly fascinating novel, involving far more than its mysterious elements . . . an intriguing and complex plot that will keep the reader guessing up to the last chapter." —I Love a Mystery

"I highly recommend *The Hiding Place* to fans of suspenseful, character-driven mysteries . . . I . . . cannot wait for [Bell's] next masterpiece." —Caffeinated Book Reviewer

"An incredibly engaging, emotionally investing read. What David Bell does exceptionally well is maintain a heightened level of suspense from beginning to end." —S. Krishna's Books

"Love that this book keeps you in the dark to the end, full of twists and turns, but still believable to keep you riveted to your seat."
—Once Upon a Twilight

"A vivid portrait of a family and their community coping with pain and loss, and the uncertainty that can bubble to the surface when questions are raised—a chilling story of the worst that can happen to a family." —Thoughts in Progress

"Another amazing book going on my 2012 favorites list. It's a haunting story of a terrible crime, and the family secrets and lies surrounding it that finally surface over two decades later." —Book of Secrets

continued . . .

"A gem of a book. . . . Bell has written another winning thriller that is certain to entertain, frighten, and swiftly climb bestseller lists."

—*Bowling Green Daily News*

Cemetery Girl

"*Cemetery Girl* is more than just an utterly compelling thriller—and it certainly is that. David Bell's stellar novel is also a haunting meditation on the ties that bind parent to child, husband to wife, brother to brother—and what survives even under the most shattering possible circumstance. An absolutely riveting, absorbing read not to be missed."

—Lisa Unger, *New York Times* bestselling author of *Heartbroken*

"*Cemetery Girl* is my favorite kind of story because it takes the familiar and darkens it. This story is essentially about a missing little girl, but trust me: you have never read a missing-persons story like this one. The reader is taken down the rabbit hole in this novel and when he comes out at the end—just beyond that mysterious and hopeful last page—he is all the better for having been invited inside Bell's disturbing, all-too-real world. . . . A fast, mean head trip of a thriller that reads like a collaboration between Michael Connelly and the gothic fiction of Joyce Carol Oates, *Cemetery Girl* is one of those novels that you cannot shake after it's over. A winner on every level."

—Will Lavender, *New York Times* bestselling author of *Obedience*

"Grabbed me by the throat on page one and never let up. An intense, unrelenting powerhouse of a book, and the work of a master."

—John Lescroart, *New York Times* bestselling author of *The Hunter*

"*Cemetery Girl* is a smasher. It twists and turns and never lets go, and . . . it could happen just this way."

—Jacquelyn Mitchard, *New York Times* bestselling author of *The Deep End of the Ocean* and *Second Nature*

"A smart, tense, creepy take on the story of a missing daughter, told by her far-from-perfect father. If you think you know this tale—from all too familiar newspaper accounts, from lesser movies and books—then this terrific novel will make you think otherwise."

—Brock Clarke, author of *Exley*

"[Bell] writes with a clarity of both vision and purpose, and his characters are eerily familiar because they are just like you and me."
—Thomas F. Monteleone, Bram Stoker Award–winning author of *Night of Broken Souls*

"With the psychologically twisted *Cemetery Girl*, Bell stakes his claim as a writer to watch. . . . Consider me a fan."
—Jonathan Maberry, *New York Times* bestselling author of *Extinction Machine*

"Every parent's worst nightmare carries the story on a tense and terrifying journey that brims with emotional authenticity. Bell manages not only to build suspense effectively but also tell a story that goes way beyond simple thrills. Anyone with children who reads this will think twice about security and what is best for young people on the road to adulthood."
—*Booklist*

"The story is engaging and tugs at the reader's heartstrings immediately . . . fast-paced and compelling."
—Fiction Addict

"Suspenseful [and] disquieting."
—*Publishers Weekly*

"A nail-biting page turner. . . . David Bell has delivered a first-rate thriller that provides the reader with enough sketchy characters to engage and challenge even the most seasoned reader. Followers of the genre can celebrate the addition of another gifted storyteller."
—LitStack

"A gripping and intense novel, keeping the reader on their toes until the end. Spellbinding and filled with angst, this absorbing story proves to be a page-turner."
—Reader to Reader Reviews

"Smart, stark, and haunting. This is perfect reading for a spooky autumn night, but be forewarned you might have to later sleep with the light on."
—*Tucson Citizen*

"Disturbing, brilliantly engaging, and a must read for thriller fans."
—*Suspense Magazine*

NEVER
COME
BACK

David Bell

 NEW AMERICAN LIBRARY

New American Library
Published by the Penguin Group
Penguin Group (USA) LLC, 375 Hudson Street,
New York, New York 10014

USA | Canada | UK | Ireland | Australia | New Zealand | India | South Africa | China
penguin.com
A Penguin Random House Company

First published by New American Library,
a division of Penguin Group (USA) LLC

First Printing, October 2013

REGISTERED TRADEMARK—MARCA REGISTRADA

LIBRARY OF CONGRESS CATALOGING-IN-PUBLICATION DATA:

Bell, David.
Never come back/David Bell.
p. cm.
ISBN 978-0-451-41751-0
1. Mothers—Death—Fiction.   2. Family secrets—Fiction.
3. Murder—Investigation—Fiction.   4. Suspense fiction.
I. Title.
PS3602.E64544N48 2013
813'.6—dc23   2013017842

Printed in the United States of America
10 9 8 7 6 5 4 3 2 1

Set in Apollo MT STD
Designed by Alissa Amell

For Mom

NEVER
COME
BACK

Chapter One

I saw people in uniform first—two cops, two paramedics. They were standing in the living room of my mom's small house, their thumbs hooked into their belts, muttering to one another. Small talk and jokes. One of them, a cop about my age, laughed at something, then looked up and saw me in the doorway.

"Ma'am?" he said. A question. It meant: *Do you have any business here?*

The other cop nodded. He understood who I was and what I was doing there.

"Are you . . . ?" he said.

"I'm Elizabeth Hampton," I said. "This is my mother's house."

"Of course," the second cop said. He held up his index finger. "Just one moment."

"My mom," I said. "I got a call from a detective. He said—"

I didn't feel well. My body felt liquid and loose, as if my joints were made of rubber and water. Everything shook. I was scared. I leaned against the doorjamb, trying not to collapse.

The cop left, went down the hallway toward the bedrooms. One of the paramedics, a thick, barrel-chested guy, his arms bulging against his short sleeves, came over and steadied me.

"Here," he said. "Sit down."

I didn't move of my own volition. He moved me. Gently. And then I was sitting on the familiar couch, the one my mother had owned for close to fifteen years, more than half my life.

"Is that better?" the paramedic said.

"A detective called," I said. "He said my mom . . . He said there was a problem, and I needed to get over here right away."

"Just sit back," the paramedic said.

"Is she okay?"

"The police will talk to you."

But I knew. I knew. They didn't call you to the scene. They didn't stand around talking—laughing even. They didn't do those things unless there was nothing else to do.

Unless someone was dead.

I said the words to myself: *Mom is dead.*

I looked around the small, familiar living room. I grew up in that house, lived there until I was eighteen and left Ohio for college. Everything was neat and orderly as always. Vacuumed and dusted. No clutter on the entertainment center. It never changed. Next to Mom's chair sat one book of her crossword puzzles, a pen, reading glasses. Next to the chair a shelf with family pictures. My dad when he was alive. A wedding photo of the two of them, looking both nervous and happy. Also a photo of me and my brother.

"Shit," I said. "My brother. Ronnie. Is he here? He must be here."

"He's fine," the paramedic said. "He's in his room with one of the officers."

"Is he okay?"

"He's doing fine."

A man and a woman emerged from the hallway. The man was middle-aged, almost bald, fit, and quite tall. He wore a suit coat over a polo shirt, and his movements seemed nervous and imprecise. His head turned from side to side, checking out everything in the room, the people and the objects. He was birdlike, an intelligent but edgy bird. The woman looked young, not much older than me. She was black with a short afro. She wore pants and a button-down lavender shirt. She wasn't very tall, and even though she walked with confidence, she stayed a pace behind the man and let him do the talking. Next to him, she looked centered and calm. Even.

"Are you Elizabeth Hampton?" the man asked. He didn't meet my eye. When he spoke, his hands moved through the air, turning over and over as though trying to crank something to life.

"Yes. I want to know what happened to my mother."

"I'm Detective Richland," the man said. "This is Detective Post." He made a gesture that pointed somewhere in the direction of his partner. "I'm the one who called you earlier."

"Is my mother dead?" I asked.

"When's the last time you spoke to her?" Richland asked. He seemed more focused when he asked me that question. His eyes landed and held on mine for a moment.

"Is she dead?" I asked. I heard the edge in my voice, the sharpness. I reached for that tone with my students when I needed to. I doubted it would work with cops, but I tried anyway. "I just want to know what happened and why I've been called here. Is my mother dead?"

Richland took a moment to answer. Then he nodded his head. "I'm sorry for your loss," he said. His words sounded practiced and routine. Did he stand in front of a mirror and run through them?

But I'd known all along. Even still, hearing the words from a stranger brought it home. A gasp escaped from my mouth, an exhalation of disbelief. I felt as if I were sinking into the couch. I stared at the floor, then at those glasses next to her chair. The glasses, such a simple object, so representative of her, suddenly seemed unmoored and cut off from the rest of the world. They looked like an artifact from another time. She was gone. *Mom is dead.*

"Can I get you some water, Ms. Hampton?" Post asked.

I couldn't answer. I didn't say anything. I kept staring at the glasses, then the photo of my dad. He was gone. She was gone. *She's gone.*

Like magic, Post was at my side, handing me a glass of water, one of Mom's familiar, dated orange glasses. I took a long gulp. It helped. I gulped some more, then took two deep breaths.

Richland moved closer to me. He stood over me, his head almost reaching the ceiling. He must have been close to six feet eight inches tall. Could a cop be that size and still do his job? "I'm sorry, Ms. Hampton," he said. "But we need to ask you some questions."

He still sounded robotic. Programmed.

"Did she have a stroke?" I asked. "She had high blood pressure, but she always took her medicine."

"When is the last time you talked to her?" Richland asked again.

I held my water glass tight. I sensed Richland's anticipation. An easy enough question, but I couldn't answer it.

I stumbled over my words.

"I don't . . . I'm not sure . . . it's been . . ."

"How long?" Richland asked, his voice flat. "Just a rough guess."

"I guess . . ." I took another sip. "We had an argument."

I looked up at the two detectives, hoping for sympathy, maybe even a reprieve from the questions. They both looked back at me, impassive, endlessly patient.

"It's probably been about . . . six weeks," I said.

Their faces remained the same, but Richland asked, "Six weeks since you've *seen* your mother?" His hands fluttered. "Or six weeks since you've *talked* to her?"

"Both," I said.

"And you live here in Dover, right?" Post asked.

I liked her better. She seemed calming, encouraging. She seemed to understand that my mother had just died.

"Yes, I do. I grew up here. Then I came back last year to go to graduate school."

"You go to Dalton U?" Post asked. "Here in town?"

"Yes. I'm studying history."

"I went there too," Post said. She looked at Richland. "We both did, didn't we, Ted?"

There was a pause. He ignored her attempt to make a connection, or else he just didn't pick up on her cue. Richland then asked, "Do you mind explaining the nature of this argument you had with your mother?"

"Why are you asking me these questions?" I asked. "You say my mother is dead. She's sixty-nine years old. She lived like a monk. She didn't go anywhere. She didn't do anything except take care of my brother. Why are you saying these things? What happened to her?"

Richland and Post exchanged looks then. Something unspoken passed between them, and Richland nodded, as though giving his approval to a task they needed to do.

He looked at me again. His eyes settled on mine and didn't waver. It made me think all of it—the fluttering hands, the nervous gestures——was some kind of act, something to keep the people he spoke to off balance. Because his voice sounded steady and sure as he delivered the next piece of news to me.

"We're treating your mother's death as a possible homicide," he said. "That's why we need to ask you these questions."

The glass slipped out of my hand and hit the carpet with a dull thunk.

Chapter Two

"The paramedics who responded to the 911 call noticed some irregular bruising on your mother's body." Richland continued to speak in a flat, even tone, as though he were telling me what the weather was like or relaying the score of an unimportant sporting event. His hands fluttered less. "They contacted us to perform a preliminary investigation."

His words flew past me like flung rubber bands. Post came in from the kitchen with a paper towel and dabbed at the water by my feet.

"I can clean that up," I said.

"It's fine," Post said. "You've had a shock."

"What kind of bruises?" I asked. "Was she beat up? Did someone beat her to death?"

"I really can't talk about that—"

"She's an older woman. A mom. Who would hurt her like that?"

"We haven't confirmed a cause of death yet," Post said. "We're not even sure it's a homicide."

"Homicide," I said. The word sounded offensive to my ears, brutal and nasty. I wasn't ready to associate it with my mother.

"It's early still," Richland said. "Give us time to sort things out." He did something with his mouth. His lips moved, and some of his teeth showed. I think he was trying to smile at me. "Let's all be patient."

"I want to see my brother," I said. "I need to see him, to make sure he's okay."

Post stood up, the limp towel in her hand.

Richland nodded, the smile-thing still on his face. "He's in his room."

"And I want to see Mom. I want to see her before they take her away."

"I'll take you to your brother," Richland said.

He waited for me to stand up.

Detective Richland led me to the door of Ronnie's bedroom and stepped aside. But before he did, he said, "We're going to have to do some additional processing of the house. We started before you arrived, but we have some more to do."

"Processing?" I asked.

"Photographs of the scene. Fingerprints."

"Okay," I said, although I wasn't sure what I was even referring to.

Ronnie was twenty-seven, just one year older than me. He was a high-functioning adult with Down syndrome. Before I went in there, I looked to the end of the hall, to my mother's bedroom. I saw the back of someone wearing a Harris County Medical Examiner Windbreaker. I couldn't see anything else.

Ronnie kept his room immaculate with a militarylike efficiency. His bed was always made, his clothes and things always put away and out of sight. Part of this came from my mother and her lifelong quest for order and cleanliness in her house, but part of it came from Ronnie's dedication to routine, his determination to master any task handed to him. He controlled his living space. It was his entirely.

Ronnie sat on the side of the made bed, his hands folded in his lap. Down syndrome kept him shorter than me—only about five foot three—and he possessed the characteristic short neck and flattened facial features common to those who have the condition. He also had the dark brown hair and dark brown eyes that could only have come from our father, whom Ronnie resembled a great deal. He looked up when he saw me, his face expectant.

"Oh, Ronnie," I said.

He didn't move from his spot until I sat down next to him on the bed. Then he let me fold him into my arms. He pressed his face into my neck, and I pulled him tight.

"Mom's gone," he said.

"I know."

We sat like that for a long time. Then he said, "They won't tell me anything. They won't tell me what went wrong."

"Me either."

Ronnie could hold a conversation with just about anybody, despite having a slight impairment that forced him to wear hearing aids in both ears. He worked a part-time job at a local store, bagging groceries and stocking shelves. He managed to get himself there every day by riding the bus or walking when the weather was nice. But he still lived with Mom, which was more her choice than his. She protected him—hovered over him, really. I knew her death would hit him harder than I could imagine. He didn't like disruptions to his routine. He didn't respond well to emergencies or sudden changes. I had no idea what would become of him.

I waited as long as I could before I asked another question. "What happened, Ronnie?" I said. "Did she collapse? Did she say anything?"

He didn't answer.

"It's okay if you don't want to talk about it yet."

"I found her on the floor in her room," he said.

"She was unconscious?"

"I wasn't home," he said. "I came home and she was on the floor."

I looked at the large digital clock next to Ronnie's bed. Ten forty-five p.m. The police had called me about twenty minutes earlier, which meant—

"You weren't home? Where were you? Were you at work?"

He sat up and shook his head. He used his thick fingers to reach into his pants pocket and draw out a neatly folded handkerchief. He wiped his nose and eyes. "I was at Mrs. Morgan's house."

Mrs. Morgan was the elderly—*very* elderly—widow who lived two doors down. She sometimes "watched" Ronnie when Mom had things to do, although Ronnie was perfectly capable of being left on his own for long stretches of time.

"Why were you there?" I asked. "Did Mom go somewhere?"

Ronnie shrugged, still holding the handkerchief. "I don't know. She told me to go to Mrs. Morgan's house around six o'clock. She didn't call for me, and Mrs. Morgan fell asleep. So I walked home . . ." His voice trailed off.

"And you came in and found Mom?"

He nodded. "I called 911 like I was supposed to. I did it right away."

"Of course," I said. "You did the right thing."

Before I could dwell too long on the horror my brother must

have felt when he found our mom unresponsive on the floor, Detective Post stepped into the doorway of Ronnie's room.

"Ms. Hampton?" she said. "Could I speak with you?"

I looked at Ronnie. He seemed withdrawn. Sad.

"Sure," I said.

I hugged Ronnie, pulling him close to me again. His body felt stiff under my embrace. I let him go and stood up. I followed Post into the hallway, and again my eyes tracked to Mom's bedroom. Someone had closed the door.

"We're ready to remove your mother's body from the house," Detective Post said. "I wondered if maybe you wanted to close the door to your brother's room or take him out of the house while we do it."

"I want to see her before you take her away."

Post pursed her lips. "Are you sure about that?"

"Is she damaged in some way?" I asked. "I thought you said she wasn't beaten."

"There are bruises, but they're not consistent with a beating," Post said. "It's just . . . it can be upsetting." She looked me in the eye and I didn't waver. "But if you want to, I think you should."

The detective walked down the hallway to the door of Mom's bedroom and knocked lightly. She looked back at me. "Would you like me to sit with your brother?"

"He's fine," I said. "He's not a child."

Someone opened the door of Mom's room, and Post stuck her head in. She said something, then stepped back, leaving the door open.

"Okay," she said. "They're finished in there. You can go on in."

Chapter Three

As I approached the door to my mother's bedroom, a handful of people filed out, including the person wearing the ME Windbreaker. None of them looked me in the eye or said anything as they passed. Perhaps they thought I was radioactive. When everyone was gone, I stepped into the room.

Both the overhead lights and the bedside lamps glowed, almost hurting my eyes. Like the rest of the house, Mom's bedroom was the picture of order. Bed made, clutter absent. The décor looked out-of-date, as though nothing had been changed or revamped in more than a decade. Only one thing looked out of place.

In the narrow space between the bed and the dresser stood a stretcher with my mother's body lying on top of it. Her eyes were closed, and a sheet covered everything except her head and shoulders.

"Are you sure you're okay?" I jumped at the sound of the voice. It was Detective Post, and she reached out her hand and placed it on my shoulder. "Do you need anything from me?"

"I'm fine," I said. I always told people I was fine. Okay. No problem. No worries. It wasn't always true, but I said it. I'd never been less fine, looking at my mother's dead body.

"You don't have to see her like this if you don't want to," Detective Post said. "The funeral will be a different environment, if you want to wait."

"Has somebody told my uncle?" I asked.

"Your uncle?"

"My uncle Paul," I said. "My mom's brother. Her only relative besides us. I guess I can call him and tell him what's happened."

"What's his full name?" Post asked. "We can make the notification."

"Paul McGrath," I said, happy to be relieved of the burden. I gave the detective his phone number. "He's very close to Mom and Ronnie."

"But not you?" she asked.

"Me too," I said. "I'm just not around as much these days. Why don't you let me make the call? He should hear it from me, not from a police officer."

"I think you have enough on your mind," Post said. She nodded in the direction of Mom's body, then stepped back, leaving me alone in the room.

I hesitated a moment, then moved forward until I was sitting on the bed next to the stretcher. Mom's mouth was pulled back in a tight line, something just short of a grimace. She didn't look, as the cliché has it, peaceful in death. She looked like someone who had died in pain. Mom wasn't a fashionable woman. Everything I learned about clothes and hair and makeup I read about in magazines or heard about from my friends. But Mom always looked good for her age. She remained thin and fit as she aged, and only a few streaks of gray ran through her hair.

I leaned forward and placed my hand on her shoulder. I avoided contact with her skin. I didn't want to feel it if it was cold. That would be too much—too real and harsh. I wasn't ready for that yet. I didn't know what else to do, so I said what I wanted to say.

"I'm sorry, Mom. I'm sorry I couldn't just say what you wanted to hear me say."

I squeezed her shoulder, then cried as I hadn't cried since Dad died.

I don't know how long I cried for, but twice I thought everything had come out of me only to find a new round of sobbing rising up from my chest and shaking my whole body. When it finally seemed to have stopped for good, I removed my hand from Mom's body, pulled some tissues from a box on the nightstand, and wiped my face. I took two deep breaths before pushing myself off the bed and stepping back into the hallway where Detectives Richland and Post waited with a few of the others who had been in the bedroom. They could no doubt tell I'd been crying, had no doubt heard me, and they all shifted their feet uncomfortably and averted their eyes as I passed.

Detective Richland cleared his throat. "We're just finishing up here, Ms. Hampton."

I knew what he meant. They needed to remove the body from the house.

"There's some paperwork you'll have to go over with the medical examiner," he said, his hands moving again as though he were turning a crank. "It's pretty routine. Your mother's body will be transported for an autopsy, and then it will be released to the funeral home of your choice. Did your mother specify any plans for her funeral?"

"I don't know," I said. "Probably. She was a careful planner."

"We contacted your uncle and told him what happened," Post said.

"Is he okay?" I asked.

"He was shaken," she said. "But he seemed to be holding it together."

"I'll have to call him. He'll be good with Ronnie."

"Speaking of that—" Richland leaned over and looked into Ronnie's bedroom. He tilted his head toward the living room, indicating I should follow him, which I did. When we were there, he asked, "Do you know why Ronnie was at this Mrs. Morgan's house tonight?"

"No," I said.

"Did your mother have plans?" he asked.

"I don't know. She never went anywhere."

"Mrs. Morgan isn't answering her phone."

"She's ninety," I said. "And deaf as a stone wall."

"Had your mother been having any problems?" Richland asked. "Money trouble? Disagreements with anyone?"

"I don't know."

Richland appeared to sense my impatience with his questions. He scratched the top of his head, then said, "Make sure you and your brother are around. We may have more questions to ask you both."

"We have a funeral to plan," I said. "I don't think I'll be going on any cruises."

When it was time for them to bring Mom out of her bedroom, I went and sat with Ronnie. I placed my arm around his shoulder again and held him tight. But I didn't close the bedroom door. We sat next to each other, watching in silence, as the two paramedics wheeled the stretcher past Ronnie's bedroom door, the sheet pulled up and covering Mom's face.

Chapter Four

I felt better when Paul showed up.

After the police and the paramedics—and Mom—were all gone, having finally finished with their endless photographs and poking around the house, I called Paul. He answered right away. I didn't have to say anything to him. I couldn't. Just hearing his voice made me want to cry again.

"Paul . . ." I managed to get out. Just that. My voice sounded as if I had swallowed a bullfrog.

"I heard," he said. His voice was hollow and distant. He was sitting in his house, absorbing the blow all alone.

I waited for him to say more, but he didn't. I expected him to be stronger than me. I *needed* him to be stronger.

"Can you—?" I tried to ask. The words were caught in my throat.

"Are you— Do you want me to come over now?" he asked.

"Yes."

"Are they . . . the police and everything . . . ?"

"They're gone," I said.

"Let me get dressed," he said.

Paul was two years younger than my mom and also her only sibling. He'd been divorced a long time, since before I was born, and he didn't have any children. I suspected Ronnie and I filled that role in his life. He treated us like adults, as if the things we said were important. And I know Mom leaned on him a lot.

When he came through the door, just thirty minutes after they'd removed Mom's body, I couldn't have been happier to see anyone. We hugged a long time, and when we finally separated, I saw the tears in his eyes. He looked all of his sixty-seven years. He ordinarily seemed so youthful, so energetic. But that night, he suddenly looked like an old man.

"Ronnie?" he said.

"He's in his room," I said. "He seems okay. But he was the one who found her. He called the police. They told me they think—"

"It's okay," he said. "You can tell me in a few minutes."

But he didn't move. He stood in the living room looking around the house. I couldn't tell what he was doing. Absorbing the scene? Remembering Mom? He looked lost. Confused. Overwhelmed, I guess, would be the best word. I reached out to touch his arm, to tell him he didn't have to stay if he didn't want to, but just as I did, he went down the hall and into Ronnie's bedroom.

While Paul was in there, I gathered my wits. Like most twenty-six-year-olds, I had never planned a funeral. I'd only attended a few, and one of them was my dad's. Mom planned that one, and I assumed hers would be similar—simple, small, low-key. Dad didn't even have a viewing. We just went to the church and then to the cemetery. Some relatives came back to the house with us and ate cold cuts and cake. That was it. Ashes to ashes and all that.

I sat on the couch and used my phone to send a few e-mails. I had just started my second year of graduate school, studying

American urban history. Cities and immigrants and neighborhoods. I had always imagined myself learning about the topic somewhere else—New York or Chicago—but we had an excellent program right here in little Dover, Ohio. And Columbus was just an hour away if I really needed to see a city. I wrote to my advisor and told him what happened. I also wrote to a few friends at school. I didn't stay in touch with a lot of people from Dover. I occasionally ran into them around town, and when I saw them I didn't know what to say. A lot of them were married already and having children. Things went that way in Dover, but not for me. I might get married someday, but not before I was thirty-five. Hell, maybe I'd wait for forty.

Once my messages were sent, I didn't know what to do. I looked around the room. The order, the neatness. The plan. There had to be a plan. My mother *always* had a plan.

I took a slow walk down the hallway. When I passed Ronnie's room, I looked in. Paul was talking to Ronnie in a low voice, soothing him. Ronnie looked tired, his eyes half closed. They seemed so close—my mom, Paul, Ronnie. But not me. I always felt like the outsider, and I knew it was by choice. I had opted for a different life, but that didn't mean I didn't feel the loss of that closeness sometimes. I hadn't planned to move back after I received my undergraduate degree in Illinois. I worked for two years, and then when it was time for graduate school I applied to Dalton only as a backup plan, my safety school. As the fates would have it, they offered me the best graduate assistantship and tuition waiver. I moved back to Dover, Ohio, with my teeth clenched. But, privately, I hoped it would work out. I hoped I'd get along with Mom better, that we'd become closer somehow as adults. What's the word for that—doing the same thing over and over again and hoping for a different result? Insanity?

I went into the bedroom. The death room, as I suddenly thought of it. My dad had died in there after a two-year fight with stomach cancer. And Mom died there too. *Enough of that*, I thought.

I went to the bedside table, the one on Mom's side of the bed. A dark, dusty powder covered the handle on the drawer. I looked around. It was on all the drawer pulls in the room. It took me a moment to figure out what it was. Fingerprint powder? I got it all over my fingers as I opened the little drawer. It held some pens, another crossword book, a Bible, and a manila envelope. I saw Mom's neat handwriting across the front.

To be opened in the event of Leslie Hampton's death.

I knew it. *The plan.* And of course Mom had made sure it was easy to find.

I slid my finger under the flap and pulled out the papers inside. The top sheet informed me—or whoever might have found it first—that Mom had, indeed, prepaid for a funeral with the Myers-Davis Funeral Home in downtown Dover. The phone number was listed at the bottom of the page, as well as a contact person's name. Myers-Davis had handled my father's funeral as well, so it was no surprise that it would handle Mom's. Knowing Mom, she probably paid for her funeral at the same time she paid for Dad's, using the funeral insurance they had purchased. I set that paper aside, making a mental note to call the funeral home in the morning.

Then I turned to the small packet of stapled papers. Mom's will. Across the top I saw the name and address of Mom's attorneys—Allison and Burns, who were located downtown. They had handled Mom and Dad's minor legal affairs over the years. I had never met Mr. Allison, but I remembered seeing him in church when I was a child. He seemed like somebody's grandfather, the kind of man who would probably ruffle your hair with a big callused hand when he saw you.

I skimmed the first page of the document. Legal jargon written in tortured and convoluted sentences danced past my eyes. I turned the page and skimmed the rest. I knew what it said. Mom had once, offhandedly, mentioned that she intended to leave everything to Ronnie and me. She didn't have much—just the house, a ten-year-old Toyota Corolla, and the life insurance. I didn't expect to see much. I figured whatever there was would go to Ronnie's care, and I was fine with that despite my life as an impoverished graduate student.

"Are you . . . ?" Paul looked like he thought he was interrupting something private and personal. He stood at the doorway of Mom's room as though an invisible barrier were keeping him out.

I looked at him and held the paper up. "The plan," I said. "Information about the funeral home. And Mom's will."

"The will's there?" he said. He still didn't come into the room. He looked around again, just as he had in the living room. Absorbing? Remembering?

"It looks pretty standard," I said. "Ronnie and I get everything."

"Good."

"And it names you Ronnie's guardian," I said. "But I guess you knew that."

I felt emotion welling in me again. I clamped my lips tight, biting against it. Everything seemed so final, so certain. So finished. I looked up at Paul. His face was ashen, his lips slightly parted. For a moment, I thought he might faint or fall over. Was he sick?

"Paul?" I said.

I dropped the will and started to get up. But he waved me back.

"I'm okay," he said. "Really. Things are just sinking in, that's all." He let his body sag against the doorjamb. He lifted his hand to his head and rubbed his temple. "Ronnie went to sleep."

"Is he okay?" I asked.

"He's okay. He didn't say much. I think he's wiped out."

"Me too," I said. I picked up the will again. I stared at the stupid papers. My vision started to swim. "Paul, I hadn't talked to her in six weeks."

"I know."

"The last time we talked we had a huge fight."

"Don't do this to yourself," he said. His voice sounded weary and hollow. "She knew."

"Knew what?" I asked.

"That you love her. That you love Ronnie. She knew that."

"Are you sure she did? I never said it. Not since I was a little kid. I probably didn't even tell her when Dad died."

"She knew. Mothers know these things."

"You know what we fought about, right?"

"About Ronnie?"

"She wanted me to promise that I would take care of him if anything happened to her. She wanted me to promise he would live with family and never have to go to an institution or a home. She was adamant, more adamant than ever."

"She always worried about that," he said.

"Why couldn't I just say it, Paul?" I asked. "Why couldn't I just tell her what she wanted to hear?"

"Stubbornness," he said.

"What?"

"Stubbornness. Good old-fashioned stubbornness. We can't

make other people do things for us, no matter how much we want them to."

He seemed to be talking about something I didn't know about, and I didn't ask.

I folded up the papers and slid them into the envelope, then put it back into the drawer. I would make the appropriate calls in the morning.

"And," I said, "here I am tearing myself apart over it, and the fucking will gives you guardianship of Ronnie. Why did she need to ride me so hard?"

I caught myself. Why was I worrying about these things now? She was gone. Mom was gone. Who cared about anything else?

"I'm not getting any younger either," he said. "Look, you're of a different generation than your mother. She's sixty-nine. You're twenty-six. You want to have a career. You worked after college in Illinois and supported yourself. You're independent. She never thought about those things. Her whole life was her kids, especially Ronnie. She lived to make sure he was okay. That's why he's doing so well. She spent so much time with him. Talking to him, reading to him."

I tried to collect my thoughts, tried to be logical and calm at the most illogical time of my life. *My mother is gone.*

I swallowed hard. "So why was she so adamant about getting a promise from me now?" I asked.

"Maybe she felt the clock ticking," he said. "She knew time was passing. She knew this day was coming. Let's face it, kiddo, getting old fucking sucks. It might be the only thing worse than being alone."

He rarely cursed. Given the circumstances, it didn't surprise me that much. I needed to tell him about the police and their questions.

"They don't think she died of natural causes," I said.

He barely moved. "What?" His voice sounded hollow.

"They're investigating to see if Mom's death was a homicide."

Whatever color had returned to his face and lips left them again. Color even seemed to have drained from his eyes. "That's crazy," he said.

I stood up, placed my arm on his, and guided him inside the bedroom. He resisted a little, but I continued with the pressure on his arm. I closed the bedroom door. We stood face-to-face, and I spoke in a low voice just in case Ronnie had woken up. I said, "The police were asking some strange questions before they left."

"Like what?"

"First they wanted to know if Mom had been having any troubles," I said. "I don't know what they meant. I told them she's an old woman who takes care of her adult son. She doesn't do anything else." I paused. I wasn't sure about the next part, but I thought it needed to be said. I hoped Paul could talk me down more than anything else. "Maybe I'm just being paranoid or emotional or something, but they were asking me about Ronnie. About his whereabouts. Like they needed an alibi for him or something."

"Jesus." Paul raised his hand to his mouth and chewed on his thumbnail.

"I know. It was weird."

"Maybe that's just routine."

"They didn't ask about me. I was just sitting at home studying. Alone. Did they ask you?"

He shook his head. "They barely said anything to me when they called."

"See?"

24

"It seems kind of strange . . ." He looked at the floor, his head lowering.

"They said there were bruises on her body." I felt the emotion rising again, almost choking me. My eyes filled with tears, and I wiped them away. I cleared my throat. "I didn't see them. I didn't really look. But that's all they said. Bruises."

"Maybe she bruised herself when she fell."

"And they wanted to know where Ronnie was. He says he was at Mrs. Morgan's house, but he doesn't know why Mom sent him there. Do you know?"

"Where would she go on a Saturday night?"

"Exactly," I said.

Paul didn't stop chewing at his nail. He really worked at it, like a dog with a bone. The color hadn't returned to his face, and he looked worse. Stricken almost.

"If this is upsetting you, we can stop," I said. "I know it's a big loss for you. Your sister—"

"I have something to tell you," he said. His voice sounded leaden and ominous.

"What?" I asked.

"About Ronnie," he said, still chewing that nail. He finally stopped but didn't look directly at me. "Something happened about a month ago. I don't think your mom told you about it."

"Something with Ronnie?"

"We were supposed to go fishing, he and I. But Ronnie did something that got him in trouble. I don't really know what exactly. I think he refused to see his speech therapist, something like that. So Leslie said he couldn't go fishing. You know how she is—rules are rules. Obligation and reward." He sounded a little angry as he spoke, the younger brother who had faced this catechism before. "She told him he couldn't go, and Ronnie . . . well, there's no easy way to say it. He got a little violent."

"What did he do?"

"I don't think he touched her, but she felt threatened, you know, by his behavior."

"He's always had those temper tantrums," I said, remembering many a kicking and screaming fit when we were growing up. They had certainly lessened over the years, but they still returned from time to time. "She can handle those. And so can you."

"She felt it was different this time. Worse." He held his hands out in a resigned gesture. "She called the police. No charges were filed, and Ronnie calmed down. But it really shook her up."

It was my turn to stare at the floor. I couldn't be certain what disturbed me more—the fact that my brother had grown so threatening that the police had to intervene, or that no one had bothered to tell me about this major family crisis.

Paul said, "I don't think she wanted you to worry about her. Or Ronnie."

"No," I said. "She wanted to punish me. She wanted me to know I was being excluded from her life."

"Don't say that," he said. His voice took on an edge. "Not now."

"You know it's true," I said. "That's how she is." I caught myself, cleared my throat again before I spoke. "*Was*. Oh, Paul— I just didn't think she would ever die. I didn't think it was possible for her to die." I wiped at my eyes again. "First Dad . . . now Mom. I'm not ready for this."

"I'm sorry. I didn't tell you to make you upset," he said. "I told you so you'd know. If the police ask. And they probably will ask."

"This is all so much," I said. "Too much."

I walked around the room, but I didn't know where I was going. The room felt small and cramped, like an aquarium filling with water.

Mom is gone. I felt empty and full of emotion at the same time. I didn't know what to think or do.

"Will you stay here tonight?" I asked. "With Ronnie? Will you?"

Paul didn't offer the immediate agreement I had come to expect from him. He stumbled over his response.

"Stay here?" he asked.

"I don't think I can," I said.

Then I understood his hesitation. He didn't want to stay there either. Not in the house where his sister had died.

"I don't think—"

I cut him off. "You don't have to," I said. "I can."

"No, it's just . . . I guess I don't want to wake Ronnie up and bring him to my place."

"It's weird for you too," I said. "Forget about it. I'll stay."

"No," he said, his voice firm now. He nodded his head. "I'll stay. You go take care of what you have to take care of. I'll be here." He turned and opened the bedroom door. He left the space as quickly as I wanted to. "I'll sleep out here. On the couch."

Chapter Five

Paul helped Ronnie with his coat and tie. My brother managed the shirt and pants with no problem. He even polished his dress shoes with a rag from the kitchen and slicked his hair into place with a pocket comb. The tie vexed him, as it would me, but Paul was there wearing a gray suit with a red tie of his own. He stepped in front of Ronnie and expertly knotted it for him.

I opted for a simple black dress. It wasn't too revealing. I didn't want to look like I was hitting a cocktail party. It was Mom's funeral, after all, and I was going to be doing a lot of talking and hugging. Grad school limited my budget, and I had bought the dress the spring before to attend a party at the provost's house. The dress made me look good, but it didn't reveal too much. I was five-five and thin like Mom. We both had narrow waists and small breasts. I didn't work at staying thin—I just *was* thin. My grad school friends whose bodies had started to go to pot thanks to nights of drinking Mountain Dew and eating cheap fast food occasionally cursed me for it.

The previous two days had passed in a blur of phone calls and e-mails and paperwork. And the occasional break to stop and cry. The smallest thing could set me off. I might remember a scarf Mom once wore, or a time she made me a special meal when

I was a child. Then the floodgates would open and I'd cry until I was empty. It made me feel better for a few moments, as if the tears needed to be purged from my body. But I never stopped feeling sad.

When I was coherent and calm, I dealt with the funeral home. As I suspected, Mom had made a lot of the decisions already, but there were still things for me to handle. The staff at the funeral home made it easy. They phrased all the questions to me as if I were a three-year-old child, which was exactly what I needed. They gave me choices, and I picked between two things. *Graveside service or chapel?* Graveside, I chose. *This reading from Scripture or that one?* That one. None of us was ever particularly religious, especially Mom. When it came to the afterlife, she simply shrugged and said, "Who knows what's going to happen?"

Paul spent a lot of time with Ronnie while I tended to the death errands. I found myself only too happy to have an excuse to leave the house. I liked to tell myself it was because my mother died there, that that was why the place felt too uncomfortable for me to be in. But I knew the truth was something different. I feared being trapped there. I worried that my life would become that house, just as Mom had wanted. Before Mom's death, I could tell myself I was leaving Dover again at the end of the academic year when my degree was finished. I could go on to get a doctorate or a job somewhere else. Anywhere, really. That was suddenly all in doubt.

My mother was explicit in her instructions to the funeral home. No viewing. She wanted a simple service at the small Presbyterian church she rarely attended. I pushed the funeral home to have the service as soon as possible. Mom died on Saturday night, and we were burying her on Tuesday morning. Paul had been spending the nights at the house with Ronnie, and I showed up on the day of the funeral so we could all go together. When I arrived, I found them putting the finishing touches on Ronnie's clothes. It brought me a little comfort, seeing them together, knowing they were there with me.

"Looks good," I said.

"We clean up pretty well," Paul said.

Ronnie didn't say a word or smile. He'd been subdued and morose over the past two days. He hadn't said much about Mom. He hadn't said much about anything. I worried about him. Unlike me, he seemed to be keeping a lot bottled up inside. I knew Paul would try to talk to him, but talk only did so much when it went one way.

Ronnie sat on his bed and picked up a pad of paper and a pencil. He liked to draw, and he drew even more in times of stress. He rarely let me see his drawings. With Ronnie occupied, Paul and I walked out to the living room.

"He seems pretty out of it," I said.

"He's trying." Paul forced a smile. "How are you?"

"Fine," I said. "I keep dreaming about Mom. Nonsense dreams. She's just there all the time, in my head."

"I remember that happening to me when my dad died. Your grandpa. You never knew him, but he was quite a guy. Larger than life in a way. I just couldn't believe the world continued to turn without him in it." He placed his hands in his pockets and adopted a slightly businesslike stance. "You know," he said, "if you want Ronnie to come and stay with me after today, he can. Or if you want me to stay here longer to help out with him and everything else."

"I'm going to deal with the lawyer soon," I said. "Do you know what I have to do?"

"I think you take the will to them, and they file it," he said. "Who's the executor?"

"Me," I said.

"I don't see that there's a huge rush," he said. "It's only affecting the three of us. If you need to get back to your normal life, the will can wait." He showed a genuine smile. "Let's worry about it another day, kiddo. Ronnie's doing fine."

I disagreed, but I also wasn't in any position to make demands. Paul knew Ronnie better than I did. He understood his moods. He had a real relationship with him, and I didn't. Not anymore.

The phone started ringing.

"Has there been a lot of that?" I asked.

"Not too bad," Paul said. "A few old friends, that kind of thing."

I went to the kitchen and answered.

"Hello?" A woman's voice on the other end. "Is this——? I was trying to reach Leslie Hampton's house."

"This is Leslie Hampton's house," I said. "This is her daughter."

"Oh . . ."

There was a long pause. I thought I heard something on the other end of the line, a gasp or a cough. I couldn't be sure. The pause went on so long I thought the other person had hung up.

"Hello?" I said.

I heard the sound of a deep breath. "I read something in the paper, a death notice. I just wanted to call to make sure it was really true."

I didn't recognize the voice, which didn't surprise me. Even though Mom had few friends, I couldn't know them all. And I obviously didn't know a lot about her life, considering what Paul had told me about Ronnie the other night. But just having to tell someone else—even someone I didn't know—brought a catch of emotion into my own throat. I fought back against the tears.

"Yes," I said. "It's true. My mother passed away Saturday night. It was unexpected."

"Oh," the woman said again, and that led to another long pause.

"Were you a friend of my mother's?" I asked.

"I was just getting to know her," the woman said.

"I'm sorry," I said.

"I guess I should be saying that to you, shouldn't I?"

"Thank you. The funeral service is this morning if you're able to make it. It's at First Presbyterian."

"I don't think I can," she said. "I live a little ways away, and I have my grandchildren here today."

"I understand—"

But she hung up before the words were out of my mouth.

Chapter Six

The funeral was, indeed, small. Before the service Ronnie, Paul, and I stood in the back of the church and greeted the arriving mourners. There weren't that many. Maybe forty total, including the three of us. Most of them were women my mom's age, ladies she had known to some degree during the thirty years she'd lived in Dover. If I had ever met or seen any of them, it would have been years earlier, and as they approached me, shaking my hand and hugging me, it amazed me how much they had aged. Graying hair, deeper wrinkles. Funerals do make us think of our own mortality. How much time had flown by for me?

After the service, we proceeded to the cemetery. It was a warm day in late September, and, contrary to popular belief, it didn't have to rain during a funeral. Few clouds interrupted the flat blue of the sky. The trees had just started throwing out their brightest colors. We rode to the cemetery in Paul's car, easing along right behind the hearse. Mom hadn't felt the need to pay for an extra vehicle or anything as extravagant as a limo.

The graveside service passed quickly. A few words from the Bible, all of us standing there with our heads appropriately bowed. Birds chirped overhead and a light breeze ruffled everyone's clothes. I stared at the ground, first at the hole that awaited my mother's coffin. Then I turned my eyes to the space next to her, where my father lay buried. The gauge for my emotional tank showed empty. I'd cried everything out already and just wanted to get out of the cemetery.

The minister announced that everyone was invited back to Mom's house for some snacks and drinks. As the mourners filed out, they took the time to talk to us and wish us well. The women doted on Ronnie, and he bore their fussing with the same blank look he'd worn for the past few days. The women also stopped and talked to me. They offered to bring food to us and to check in from time to time.

Then a woman named Nancy Porter, who volunteered at the library my mom always went to, stopped and leaned in close to my ear. She wore a floral dress with a white cardigan over top.

"I know you'll take good care of your brother," she said, her eyes wide and earnest. "You're going to do what your mom wanted you to do, right?"

I gritted my teeth.

"She wanted you to do this for her, Elizabeth."

Even then, speaking to someone I owed nothing to, I couldn't say what I was supposed to say. Mrs. Porter moved on.

Finally, it was time for us to go. People were on their way to the house, so we needed to get back and open things up. Paul had ordered food from a local deli. It was all crammed into Mom's refrigerator, waiting for the descending hordes of hungry mourners.

I looked around the cemetery. I didn't see Paul. His car was still sitting in the cemetery roadway, the sun glinting off its chrome and glass. But he was nowhere in sight.

"Come on, Ronnie." I took my brother by the hand, and we started for the car.

Then I saw Dan.

He stood in the shade of a big maple, wearing a white dress shirt and a vintage blue and gray tie with a thick knot. He was thirty, almost five years older than me. A few flecks of gray were starting to show in his dark hair, but he still managed to look boyish. A young, handsome intellectual.

"Hi, Elizabeth." He came forward and gave me a hug. It felt good, and for the extra long moment he held me, I relaxed my body and let myself be supported by him, as though I were on the brink of collapse. I needed that. "I'm so sorry," he said.

"Thank you," I said as he let me go. "How did you know?"

"Professor Niehaus told me. I've been calling you for the last two days, and you haven't been responding. Plus you didn't come to class, so I asked if something was wrong. I thought maybe you were sick."

"I asked her not to tell anybody," I said.

"She told me because I pushed," Dan said. "And because she knew we were, or had been, close. Other people from school would have come to the funeral, you know. Why didn't you want them to hear the news?"

"I just didn't want to make a big deal," I said. "I'll be back to school tomorrow."

"Are you okay?" he asked. "Really?"

"This is my brother, Ronnie," I said.

"Hi, Ronnie," Dan said.

Ronnie shook Dan's hand but didn't say anything.

"My uncle is here somewhere, but I don't— Wait. There he is."

Paul stood on the other side of the road, about fifty yards

from the car. He was talking to a man I didn't recognize, someone I didn't think I had seen at either the church or the graveside service. If he had been there, he hadn't spoken to me. Paul threw his hands out to his side a few times, as though exasperated and trying to make an important point that the man wasn't understanding.

"Do you know who Paul is talking to, Ronnie?" I asked.

Ronnie shook his head.

"Do you need anything, Elizabeth?" Dan asked. "Help with school or your classes? Do you just want to get together and have a drink and talk?"

I looked over at Paul again. He made a dismissive gesture toward the other man, as if telling him he was finished with him. The two men walked off in opposite directions. Paul came toward us while the man—short and chubby—walked off the other way. I didn't know where he was going. I didn't see a car or anyone waiting for him.

I turned to Dan. "We have to go now," I said. "We have to open the house for the guests."

"I can't make it to your house," Dan said. "I have class."

"That's fine. It's just some old people my mom knew. Nothing fancy."

Paul used his remote key fob to unlock the car, and I began to head in that direction.

"I have to go," I said.

"Okay," Dan said.

I turned back on the way. "Thanks, Dan. Thanks for coming."

"Call me if you need anything," he said.

I looked back once as we drove away. Dan remained in his spot, waving good-bye.

Chapter Seven

Paul's face was flushed as we drove to the house. I thought maybe it was from standing in the morning sun. Or maybe stress and grief. But I also remembered the way he'd walked away from the man at the cemetery. The big gestures, the dismissal. He gripped the wheel tight as he drove.

"Who was that you were talking to?" I asked.

"Who?" he asked.

"The man at the cemetery. Is he a friend?"

Paul didn't respond right away. His eyes pointed straight ahead, fixed on the road and the traffic.

"Just someone we used to know growing up. He's nobody."

I thought about asking more, then remembered my own awkward encounter with the past in the cemetery. I decided not to press it. Some things were better left alone.

About fifteen people came back to the house after the graveside service. The die-hards, I supposed. They were waiting politely on the porch when we pulled up. The gathering passed with a lot of muted small talk. Comments about the weather were popular, as were compliments about the food. I realized an eternal truth:

death makes people hungry. Either because they've decided to embrace life to the fullest in the wake of another's death, or maybe because they don't know what to talk about at such an event. In any case, the guests made a nice dent in the food. No one held back.

Paul seemed distracted during the gathering. When I was a kid, he would glide from group to group at family functions, talking to everyone with equal enthusiasm and energy. A funeral didn't compare to a Christmas party, and I attributed his lack of energy to the accumulated toll of the previous days' events. He sat on the couch, an empty paper plate balanced on his knee, and nodded thanks to the people who came by to talk to him.

I tried to play hostess. I made sure the bucket was full of ice, that enough napkins and plasticware sat on the small kitchen table. Some of the ladies helped as well, and they never failed to give me a gentle pat on the arm or back. I didn't thank them for the kindness, but I appreciated it more than they could know.

Mrs. Porter came up to me again, and rather than let her dictate the subject of the conversation, I decided to initiate.

"Did my mom say anything to you about her health?" I asked. "Any complaints or worries?"

Mrs. Porter scrunched up her face, as though giving the question a good thinking over. I knew Mom had spent a lot of time at the library, checking out books for both herself and Ronnie. I wondered if she had said something to Mrs. Porter that she hadn't said to anyone else. Something that would make the possibility of murder less real.

"You know, it's been a month since I've seen her," Mrs. Porter said. She was wearing a floral dress with a lot of purple in it. She raised her hand to her chest and said, "I had to read about this in the paper."

"Thanks for coming."

"Had she said anything to you about her health?" Mrs. Porter asked.

"No," I said. "But she liked to play things close to the vest, as I'm sure you know."

"The last time she came into the library she came alone," Mrs. Porter said. "That was unusual. She always brought Ronnie with her. I asked about it because I thought maybe Ronnie was sick." She lowered her voice. "I know his disability can cause other complications. But she said he was fine. She said she had an appointment downtown." Mrs. Porter nodded her head to emphasize the last point. "She seemed to be in a hurry."

"How long ago was that?" I asked.

"I said a month," Mrs. Porter replied.

A month. Shortly after our fight. "And you didn't know where she was going?"

"I didn't ask," she said. "I'm a live-and-let-live kind of person. I figure most things are none of my business."

"Of course."

"This whole thing is terrible. Just terrible."

Yet neither of us had any idea how much worse it would become.

Chapter Eight

After an hour, the guests started to leave. They made their excuses and offered their final condolences. A couple of the ladies, including Mrs. Porter, began to clean up the kitchen. I offered a mild protest, but they ignored me and went about wrapping the remaining food and putting it away. I decided to accept their help and went off in search of Ronnie.

He was sitting on his bed, still wearing his coat and tie. He held an object in his hand, a picture frame or something, but when he saw me coming into his room, he slid the object beneath his pillow.

"Hi, Ronnie," I said.

He didn't answer me, but folded his hands and remained still, staring at the floor. I came into the room the rest of the way and sat on the bed next to him. He had stayed out of the way during the little gathering at the house. I wasn't even sure he had eaten anything.

"What did you have there?" I asked.

No response.

"Was it a picture of Mom?"

"Maybe," he said.

Maybe? Clearly he wasn't up for interrogation, and I couldn't blame him.

"People are starting to leave," I said. "I just wanted to see if you were okay. Do you need anything?"

He shook his head.

"I know you're sad about Mom," I said. "I am too. I know I haven't been around much lately."

"It's because you had that fight with her," he said.

This surprised me, although it shouldn't have. Ronnie knew everything that went on in the house, and even though he was at work when Mom and I had had it out the last time, he would have picked up on Mom's mood and behavior. He would have known something was wrong.

"We did have a fight," I said. "Did she say anything about it?"

He shook his head. "I could tell she was mad."

"Yes, she was. But I don't want you to be scared by any of this. Paul and I are going to figure out where you're going to live now. We were thinking you could either move in with Paul, at his house, or he could move in here and live with you. Paul's okay with either of those."

Ronnie remained silent for a few moments, then asked, "What are you going to do?"

"I'll still live in my apartment," I said. "It's close to school, and all my things are there. But I'll come stay here sometimes." His face showed nothing, so I upped the ante. "In fact, I promise I'll come around more. It won't be like the last six weeks or even the last year when you didn't see as much of me. I promise."

His facial muscles relaxed a little. He almost smiled, and I took that as a moral victory.

"Promise?" he said.

Before I could repeat the word, Paul appeared in the doorway, his face still drawn and tired looking. "There are people here who want to see you," he said. "You should come talk to them."

The little crowd in Mom's house had moved beyond hushed to dead silent. The appearance of two police detectives at the front door tended to have that effect. And make no mistake—even though Richland and Post wore plain clothes, their badges and guns hidden, everyone there knew they were cops. And if the guests weren't fascinated by the fact that they were police, they could have just as easily been entranced by the physical differences between the odd couple at the door.

Richland spoke first when he saw me. "Ms. Hampton. Sorry to intrude, but we have some matters to follow up on."

"Now?" I asked.

"Is there someplace we could speak?" Richland asked. He waved his hand at the perimeter of the room, a gesture that made sense for a change.

I looked around. Everyone except Paul pretended they weren't eavesdropping. Even Mrs. Porter busied herself with wrapping a pie in cellophane. I lowered my voice. "Couldn't this wait?" I asked. "I can come talk to you later this afternoon."

"I'm not sure it can wait," Richland said.

"Maybe you'd like to step onto the porch with us?" Detective Post said, nodding toward the door. Before I answered, she opened it and started to go outside. I felt I had no choice but to follow.

On the front porch, Richland stood to my left and Post to my right, leaving me in between them like a child. My eyes were level with the pocket protector Richland wore on his shirt. I noticed that, in addition to the dark sedan that I assumed belonged to the detectives, a Dover police cruiser was parked on the street. Two uniformed officers sat inside it with the windows rolled down, their faces obscured by the shade of the trees.

Richland said, "We wanted to let you know that the medical examiner's office has reached a preliminary conclusion concerning your mother's death. It looks as though our initial concerns were correct—your mother died as the result of manual strangulation."

At first the words didn't make sense to me. Richland might as well have been speaking to me in another language, and those two words—"manual strangulation"—were some kind of incantation I simply couldn't understand. But they rattled around in my brain and finally came to rest someplace where I could understand them. Reflexively, I lifted my right hand to my own throat.

"Someone killed her," I said. "Mom."

"We're sorry to have to bring you this kind of news," Richland said. "We were hoping to move ahead with some things relating to the case."

"Did someone rob her?" I asked. My mind drifted away from the reality of what they had told me to speculation about why it had happened. "The house didn't look like it had been broken into. She didn't have anything worth stealing really." I tried to think of another explanation besides robbery, but I couldn't. Mom didn't do anything. She didn't know anyone. She didn't owe money or deal drugs. Why would someone come into her house and kill her?

"We were hoping we could spend a little more time speaking to your brother," Richland said.

His words brought me back to the present. And to the conversation from the other night when Richland seemed to be dancing around the edges of accusing Ronnie. No more dancing.

"He wouldn't hurt Mom," I said. "She was practically his whole life."

Post spoke up. "We don't want you to think we're going to

be *interrogating* your brother. We really can't do that if someone has any kind of disability. What we want to do is have him examined by a psychologist, someone who understands these issues."

"What issues?" I asked.

"We need to know if your brother is *capable* of hurting your mother," Richland said. "And then we need to know if he *understands* what that even means."

"He's not an idiot," I said.

"No one said he was," Post said. "But it's best for everyone if we let professionals intervene at this stage."

"And what if I say no? What if I don't let you near him?"

Richland and Post exchanged a look. They'd already discussed this.

Richland's hands fluttered, but it was Post who answered the question. "It's within your rights to deny us access to your brother, especially if you're his legal guardian in the wake of your mother's death. Are you?"

"I think it's my uncle," I said. "We haven't gotten into all of that."

"Be that as it may," Post said, "we would then have to go to court and get an order allowing your brother to be turned over to our custody. It's a lot easier this way."

"Easier for who?" I asked. No one bothered to answer my question, so I said, "I want to talk to my uncle about this. He's right inside, and I think he'd want to understand what's going on."

Post and Richland exchanged the look again, and they both nodded.

"If you don't mind," Richland said, his eyes averted, "try not to take too long."

I stopped. "Maybe I need to call a lawyer," I said. "Is that what I should be doing? Calling a lawyer to protect my brother?"

"That's certainly your right," Post said. "Although no one is being charged here. But you do have the right to talk to a lawyer. Of course."

Richland nodded in agreement. Then he tapped the face of his watch.

I wanted to ask him—and his pocket protector—what the damn rush was, but I kept my mouth shut and went inside.

Chapter Nine

When I stepped back inside the house, every eye in the room turned to me. I felt like the anticipated guest of honor at a surprise party, except no one cheered. No one said anything. Paul waited in the living room, sitting in Mom's chair.

"Can we talk for a minute?" I said to him.

He answered by standing up, his face nervous with anticipation about whatever I had learned, and followed me down the hallway to Mom's bedroom. I closed the door.

Paul stood in the center of the room, his hands resting on his hips. His lips were parted, ready with questions, but he didn't say anything yet.

I didn't sit either. "It's worse than I could have thought," I said. Then I realized where we were standing again: the room where Mom died. It had happened right there. Someone had killed her. My mind raced with the most awful thoughts: How badly did she suffer? What was it like to have a monster of some kind standing over her, squeezing the life out of her? And the police thought that monster was my own brother.

Finally, Paul spoke. "What is it, Elizabeth?"

"They say Mom was murdered," I said. "Strangled."

Paul raised his fist and placed it over his mouth, as though stifling a cough. Or a cry. But no sound emerged.

"It's worse," I said. "They think Ronnie . . . he's really a suspect." My hands fluttered uselessly in the air around my body. I must have looked like Richland. "It looks like they want to take him with them. They want a shrink to talk to him, someone who knows about Down syndrome, I guess, in order to determine if he did it or not."

Once the words were out—the awful words and the awful truth of what the police had told me—I understood with great clarity what I wanted from Paul. With Mom gone, he became the adult. The rock. He needed to put a stop to all the foolishness and restore order. I needed him to back me up and tell the police to take a walk.

"That's just so . . . goddamn terrible," he said.

"I know." A bad taste entered my mouth, something bitter, as if I'd eaten poison or rotten fruit. I thought I might vomit. "I don't know what to do. Should I call a lawyer?"

He took a step back and sat down on the end of the neatly made bed. He hadn't been sleeping there, I knew; he slept on the couch every night. He looked thoughtful, calm. He said, "I'm not sure what a lawyer could do for us."

"Stop them," I said. "They want to take Ronnie away."

"I told you I was afraid of this," he said. His voice remained calm, and while he spoke I saw the remnants of his career as a high school English teacher in the wise, instructive way he spoke. "But, look, maybe this isn't as bad as we think it is. Maybe we're all in over our heads here. Do you believe Ronnie could do this to your mom?" he asked.

"No," I said. "I mean . . . no is what I mean. They put doubts in my head, if I'm honest. And that story you told me—"

"Ronnie hasn't been himself the last few days," he said. "Understandably so. He suffered a horrible loss just like all of us. But haven't you been thinking already that we might have to get Ronnie some counseling or something?"

I nodded. I had been thinking that. I just didn't know where or when to turn to it.

"Maybe this is what he needs," Paul said. "Let him speak to a professional, let him work through his feelings." He sighed. "Hell, we all probably need it now. Some help."

"Fuck," I said. My eyes burned, the hot tears rising again. "This is so fucking rotten. It's all just rotten."

"I know," Paul said.

"You asked me a question before," I said. "You asked me if I thought Ronnie could have done what they say he might have done. Let me ask you the same thing. Do you think it's possible?"

I knew what I wanted his answer to be, no matter what he thought. I wanted him to reassure me.

"I can't even go there," he said. "It's just too far to go."

Not exactly what I wanted to hear, but I took it. I wiped at my eyes and managed not to lose it.

I stepped out into the hallway and stood in the background while Paul gently started explaining to Ronnie about the police and why they needed to talk to him. After just a few minutes of watching that, I decided I might be more useful dealing with the detectives, who I assumed were still waiting on the front porch.

Except they weren't. When I came out of the hallway I saw the last few guests leaving the house. As they went out the door,

Richland and Post were coming in, apparently having seen the breakup of the reception as an invitation to come back inside.

"Can you give us a minute?" I asked, trying to speak to the police the way I sometimes spoke to my students: firm, in charge. "We're trying to get Ronnie ready. To explain to him what's happening. We just buried our mother today, for Christ's sake."

But my words failed to intimidate or even sway the police officers. They both looked at me, their faces professionally stoic. They didn't offer to move, and Richland looked around the room as if he were thinking of buying the house.

But I wouldn't be deterred. I pushed more.

"Why don't you two just leave?" I said. "We can bring Ronnie to the hospital or doctor or wherever you want him to go. You don't have to hover around here. We're not criminals."

"Ms. Hampton," Richland said, focusing his attention on me, "we need to escort your brother. It's just the standard procedure."

"Can one of us ride with him?" I asked. "Me or my uncle?"

"You can come along in a little bit," Post said. "And you can see your brother and visit with him once he's been processed."

"Processed?" I asked, nearly spitting the word. "What is he? A cow?"

"Easy now," Richland said.

"Easy? You show up here telling me my mother was murdered and you want to take my brother away and you say *easy*?"

Neither of them looked at me. Their eyes drifted over my head and past me to the hallway. I turned. Paul and Ronnie came out of Ronnie's bedroom. Ronnie carried his sketch pad in his left hand, and Paul walked by his side, holding on to Ronnie's arm like an escort. Ronnie wore the same impassive look on his face, but his eyes betrayed him. They flickered back and forth, giving Ronnie the look of a skittish child.

"Oh, Ronnie," I said. "I'm sorry."

"He's fine," Paul said. "We talked about it."

But I knew Ronnie wasn't fine, and so did Paul. They reached the police, and Paul let go, his hand slipping off Ronnie's arm and falling back to his own side.

Post stepped forward and smiled. "Ronnie, you know you're going to take a little ride with us?"

"Don't talk to him like he's six," I said.

Post ignored me, and Richland opened the door. "We'll be at Dover Community Hospital," he said.

"Dover Community?" I said.

"Yes," Post said.

"The loony bin?" I said.

"It's a mental health facility," Post said. "It's an excellent hospital."

Post guided Ronnie to the door, and I allowed myself to think that Paul was right, that this was for the best and Ronnie needed the extra attention and counseling a professional could give him. And just as the thought crossed my mind, Ronnie's body froze. Every muscle grew rigid, and if I didn't know any better, I would have thought he was suffering a seizure of some kind. He locked up, refusing to move past the doorjamb.

"Paul!" he cried. "Elizabeth! No. No no no no no no."

"Oh, Jesus, Ronnie," I said.

Paul stepped in. He went to Ronnie and placed his hands on Ronnie's shoulders. "It's okay, bud," he said. "We'll see you real soon. Remember what we talked about? Remember?"

"Elizabeth," Ronnie said, his voice lower and weaker.

"Ronnie?" Paul said. "Remember."

As the words came out of Paul's mouth, the resistance seemed to drain from Ronnie. His body sagged; his shoulders slumped. He allowed Richland to place a hand on his arm and guide him through the door and onto the porch. Richland towered over my brother, practically casting him in shadow. When they were out of sight, I went to the door myself, with Paul right beside me.

Ronnie shuffled down the walk with the detectives on either side of him. A couple of the mourners, Mrs. Porter included, still lingered on the sidewalk, chatting before they headed in their separate directions. They stopped their talk and watched as the police placed Ronnie in the back of the cruiser, which remained parked beneath the trees on Mom's street.

If I'd cared more about what other people thought in that moment, I would have been mortified, knowing the way gossip and rumor and misunderstanding spread in a town like Dover. But none of that mattered to me. All I heard in my own head was the sound of my brother's voice calling my name, saying to me, *How could you let this happen? How?*

Chapter Ten

Paul and I waited for close to an hour when we reached Dover Community. Before we were allowed to see Ronnie we were given a number of forms to sign. Since I was his next of kin, the admitting nurse told me I was able to sign them. I asked what they were for, and she said they gave the hospital and doctors permission to provide care for Ronnie. Medication, counseling, food, everything.

"Medication?" I asked. "Do you mean sedation?"

"Possibly."

I looked at Paul, who shrugged. I turned back to the nurse. "I don't want him zonked out like some zombie."

"I doubt that will be an issue," she said.

I looked at Paul again, and he nodded. So I signed.

When we were finally allowed into his room, we found Ronnie sleepy. He looked as if he'd been sedated. His eyes fluttered and then closed as we talked to him. Paul could tell I was angry, and he told me to trust the professionals.

"Mom would hate this," I muttered. "She'd hate if they put him on drugs. She'd hate him being in the crazy hospital."

Paul and I decided to leave. Before we did, I bent down and kissed Ronnie on the forehead. He didn't stir.

In the hallway, we ran into Detective Richland. He held a cell phone to his ear, but put it away—somewhat reluctantly—when he saw us coming. I didn't bother with formalities or greetings. I simply asked, "How long is all of this going to take?"

He cleared his throat. "The doctor should be by sometime tomorrow to get the ball rolling," he said.

"I don't want anyone coming by and asking him questions without one of us being here," I said. "What time?"

"I can't predict what time," he said. "The doctor has a lot of patients to cover."

"Call us then," I said.

"Don't you have to go back to school tomorrow?" Paul asked me.

"Yes."

He turned to Richland. "Why don't I give you my cell number? You can let me know when something happens. I may be here anyway just visiting Ronnie."

Richland made an elaborate display of taking out his phone and then entering Paul's number into it. When he was finished, he nodded. "You know, Ms. Hampton," he said.

I noticed that his hands had stopped fluttering. The tall detective seemed grounded and centered for a moment, leading me once again to wonder whether the whole thing was an act, a put-on to lull people into a false sense of comfort and security.

"What?" I said.

"I'm sorry about earlier, taking your brother from the house that way. We thought everyone would be gone and . . . we just thought it would be easier."

I knew what I was supposed to do. I was supposed to accept the apology, to see Richland as a well-meaning, overworked public servant, trying to do his best in difficult circumstances. Like all of us.

But I couldn't.

"I guess that can't be undone, can it?" I said.

I walked away with Paul following me.

We stopped next to Paul's car in the parking lot. The late afternoon sun slanted through the trees, and for the first time since Detective Richland called my apartment on Saturday night, no immediate, pressing concerns weighed on me. Mom had been buried. Ronnie was in custody. Paul had his own life to return to—card games with former colleagues, the harvesting of his summer garden, his books, his friends. I expected to feel some measure of relief at that moment, but I didn't. How could I?

"I know I should have just accepted his apology like a nice little girl," I said.

"It doesn't do any good to antagonize the police," Paul said.

"Any other advice?" I asked.

Paul didn't say anything. A sound, something between a deep breath and a hiccup, came out of his mouth, and when I turned to look at him more fully, I saw that he was crying. He raised his fist to his mouth, and his chest shook with a couple of deep sobs.

"Oh, Jesus. Paul? Are you okay?"

And that was enough to start me again. The tears welled up in my eyes, burning them, and I felt them spilling over and stinging my cheeks. But I tried to focus on Paul.

He wiped tears off his cheeks. "I want you to know something," he said when some of his composure returned.

"What?" I asked, struggling to keep my own emotions in check. I wiped my tears away with the backs of my hands, making a smeared mess across my face.

"I'm not going to let anything happen to Ronnie," he said. He swallowed and coughed. A siren sounded and then wound down on the far side of the hospital. A new tragedy arriving. Some disturbed soul who had had enough of the world and flipped out. He said, "I'll be here. Nothing bad's going to happen to him."

"I know you'll look out for him," I said. "We both will."

He brought out a handkerchief and wiped his cheeks and eyes some more. "We're all on the ropes here, I guess."

"Yes," I said. "Are you sure you're okay? Do you want to go get something to eat?"

"I'm okay," he said. "I'm tired. I'm a tired old man. I need to go home and take a nap. The next couple of days could get kind of crazy."

"Are you sure?"

He put the handkerchief away and nodded, regaining his usual certainty. "I should be worried about you," he said. "Are you taking care of yourself?"

"I'm trying to."

"You should take a nap."

"Maybe I will. I have to get back to campus tomorrow. I was going to deal with the will, but it doesn't seem that important now."

"That's good."

"Unless you think the lawyer can help with Ronnie," I said. "Are we being idiots here, Paul? Are we just going to let them put him in there and examine him?"

"Who drew up the will? Frank Allison?"

"Yes."

"I don't know how much criminal law he does in a town like this," Paul said. "If that's what you're thinking. Beyond that, I guess we're all in over our heads. Look, he's more in the care of the doctors than the police now. That might change if the police get more serious, but I take some comfort in thinking about the doctors more."

"Sure," I said, not wholly convinced. "But if more trouble comes down, I'm calling a lawyer. I might do it anyway."

"That's fine," Paul said. "Do what you think is best."

He held out his arms, and we hugged. We held each other a long time. I didn't want to let go. When we finally did, I stepped back and looked up at him.

"Tell me this is all going to be okay," I said.

He didn't hesitate. "Sorry, kiddo, but I just can't do that."

Chapter Eleven

I didn't call Dan before I went to his apartment. I knew that if I called, he'd offer to come meet me wherever I was, and I wasn't sure yet that I wanted to see him. I wanted to still have an out. My escape plan amounted to showing up unannounced, allowing myself the option of turning around and leaving if I wanted.

But when I arrived outside the dingy brick apartment building Dan lived in, I realized I did want to stay. Dan lived on the second floor, alone. Half the lightbulbs were burned out, and with evening coming on, the stairwell was uncomfortably dark, especially for someone whose mother had just been murdered. Music twanged behind one of the apartment doors, and I heard the unmistakable drunken whoop of a college boy. For the first time in my life, that sound brought me comfort. There were people around. And life. I wasn't alone.

Dan opened the door to my knock, his eyes widening in surprise.

"Oh," he said. "It's you."

For a brief, terrible moment, I worried that someone was in the apartment with him. "I didn't call," I said.

"It's okay." He stepped back, opening the door all the way. "Come in."

I knew the place well. He had lived there in the cramped, run-down space for just over a year, ever since we both entered the graduate program in history as members of the same class. For six months of that year, he and I had been a couple. Intensely. Crazily. We burned for each other like two hormonal teenagers, but we also possessed enough brains between the two of us to examine every flaw with our pairing, which meant we fought a lot. We broke up a lot. We got back together a lot.

I followed him into the living room. Ever since we'd broken up—and in the wake of two very temporary reunions and their accompanying breakups—we hadn't known how to act around each other. Do we hug? Do we shake hands? Do we nod at each other like strangers passing on a narrow sidewalk? I bypassed the dilemma by moving quickly to the couch and sitting down. He stopped in the center of the room.

"Do you want something?" he asked. "Coffee? Wine?"

"You know me well enough," I said.

"Beer?"

"Amen."

He left and came back with two opened bottles. He sat on the far end of the couch from me, respectfully giving me my physical space. He'd finally learned to do that on the day I needed him not to.

"Are you doing okay?" he asked. He quickly added, "I know, that's a silly question."

"I don't mind you asking," I said. "And thanks for coming to the cemetery today. It was really sweet."

I took two long drinks from my bottle. It tasted good. Really good.

Dan drank from his too. A flush spread on his cheeks, but I knew it wasn't from the beer. Even when we dated, when we were in our most intense periods of romance, an uncertainty, a nervousness hovered around Dan. No matter how much time we spent together, it still seemed as though he didn't know what to say to me or exactly how to take me. He said, "I know you well enough to know that you don't want to discuss what happened, but I feel obligated to say out loud that I'm willing to listen to whatever you need to say."

"That's what I want to talk about," I said. I jabbed my finger into the space between us, trying to emphasize my point.

Dan jumped a little. "What?"

"That. That quality of mine you just mentioned."

"Are you saying it's not true?" he asked.

"It *is* true," I said. "And I need to talk about it."

"Okay," he said. "But I'm not a licensed therapist."

"You know, I really appreciate the sarcasm today."

"Are you being sarcastic?" he asked.

"No." I drank more of the beer, almost finishing it. Too fast. I suppressed a burp and patted my chest. "Well, get ready for an awkward transition. My mother was murdered," I said.

It felt like the first confession of a long recovery. Something had pivoted in my life. I had gone from being a person who read about families affected by violent crime in the newspaper to being a member of such a family. I no longer needed to understand such things from the outside. I needed to process it from the inside.

"Jesus," Dan said.

"But wait—there's more."

I told him everything, finishing the first beer while I revealed the details about my mom's death. The fact that there had been no sign of forced entry. The violent encounter with Ronnie over the fishing trip. The inability of the police to account for Ronnie's whereabouts. Ronnie's trip to what I could only think of as the mental ward. The fight I had had with my mother and our six weeks of silence.

Dan didn't interrupt. He let me get it all out, and even rose once when I paused to take a breath in order to walk out to the kitchen and get two more beers. I happily started the second while I finished my tale of woe.

When it was all out, Dan said simply, "I'm sorry, E. I'm really sorry."

"I know. And I appreciate it."

"But I get the feeling that's not really what you wanted to talk about," he said. "You said something about some quality you possess . . ."

"I didn't know any of these things were happening," I said. "My family—my mother and my brother—were deep in a crisis, and I didn't know anything about it. I was cut off from it."

"You can't blame yourself for all of this," he said.

I stood up, beer bottle in hand. I paced across the worn wooden floors. "Don't," I said. "I'm not looking to be let off the hook."

"All right. I was just trying to help. Did you come here to flagellate yourself?"

I kept pacing. I didn't look at him. "Did I ever tell you what it was like to grow up with Ronnie as a brother?"

"Tell me?" he said. "Your mother and brother live across town. We dated for six months, more or less, and the first time I ever laid eyes on a member of your family was at the funeral. No, you almost never talked about them, except to say you didn't want to talk about them."

I grunted. I hated to hear my own words repeated to me, even though I knew they were true. I drank from the bottle.

"Let me just say this," I said. "Ronnie took up a lot of mental space."

"Because of his disability," Dan said.

"Because of that, yes. And because my mom was determined, absolutely determined, to give him the best life possible, she devoted herself to him. One thousand percent. I was closer to my dad. I'm more *like* my mom, but I was closer to my dad." I felt like an idiot pacing. Every time I turned around I saw Dan's books, his empty coffee mugs—all the sad remnants of a grad student's life. I took my seat again, my back straight and rigid. I held the beer bottle in two hands. "My mom told me something once."

"Something about Ronnie?" Dan asked.

"Something about me," I said. "This was in high school, the first time Dad was diagnosed with cancer. He beat it then, but it came back and killed him later, when I was in college. When he was first diagnosed, we were all scared. We said the right things to each other, but we were scared. My mom and I were talking about family and caring for each other and how important it was to have children in your life. I was in high school. What did I know? I just listened. And then she told me that it was a tough decision for her and Dad to decide to have another baby after Ronnie, you know? Mom was forty-three when I was born, and that was just a year after Ronnie. The odds of having *another* baby with Down syndrome were still high. She said they almost didn't have me."

"So you were lucky. You were wanted."

"Oh, yes," I said. "Very wanted. Because you know what Mom told me during that conversation? She said the main reason they had me was to take care of Ronnie after they were both gone. Can you imagine telling a kid that?"

I drained the second beer. My head had started to hurt, but I didn't want to switch to water. I felt like getting drunk. I waved the empty bottle around. "Any more where this came from?" I asked.

"There is," he said, but he didn't get up. "I'm sure your mom was just—"

"Don't defend her," I said. "You didn't know her, as you pointed out. You can't take her side."

"I'm not taking sides," Dan said. "I'm trying to understand. Are you saying you never felt close to your family or let them into your life because of this?"

I raised the beer bottle again. "Another round? Then I'll tell you the rest."

Chapter Twelve

Dan came back with two more beers. When he settled back in, he didn't say anything. He just waited for me to go on.

I finally said it: "I used to hate my brother."

Dan didn't respond. He watched and waited.

"When we were kids, people looked at us wherever we went. I knew what they were thinking. 'Oh, that poor family. That poor boy.' And then Ronnie would chew with his mouth open, or he'd grunt when he should have talked, and that would only make it worse for me. I'd want to hide under the table, or just run away."

"A lot of kids would feel the same way in your situation. I'm sure they have."

"I used to wish for something," I said. "After my mom told me why they had me, I used to wish that *she* would die. It would make sense for me to want her to stay alive because then she would be there to take care of Ronnie. But I used to wish she'd die so I could be free of my obligation to her."

"And to Ronnie?" Dan asked.

I nodded.

"You know that's illogical, right?" Dan said. "I mean, he's your brother, so if your mom died—"

"I didn't say it was logical, Dan."

"Right," he said. "Well, just because you have those feelings doesn't mean you would really act on them."

"But I did act on them," I said. "I've been absent from their lives."

"Well, I know all about that," he said.

I turned to him. "What are you saying, Dan?"

"I guess I'm wondering what you're here for," he said.

"Dan, my mother died. She was killed."

"I know," he said. "I know. I'm just saying, E, that you don't exactly let people in, you know? You're not always there for others. At least not for me." He held his hands out before him. "I shouldn't be saying all this now. It's bad timing."

"Go ahead," I said.

"I'm fine."

"Go ahead," I said. "I might learn something."

He reached up and ran his hand through his hair. "I don't know what you're here for. Do you want absolution? Or sympathy? I don't see or hear from you for weeks, and then here you are on my doorstep. I know your mother died, but I had to hear about it from someone else."

I felt my chin quiver. I bit back any tears, holding them in. I looked at the floor again.

"Do you want to hear the truth?" he asked.

"I thought I already was hearing it."

"It's possible if you were more involved with your family's life that you could have done something. But that's assuming your brother really did this, and that's assuming there was anything to be done. You could have been right there, camped out in the living room, and the same thing might have happened." He sighed. "Or maybe you would have been hurt too."

He sounded concerned, as though the thought of me being hurt was painful to him. It was sweet to hear, even if he was mad at me.

"Thanks," I said.

"It's too late for your mom," he said. "You can't do anything to help her. But you can still do what she wanted you to do. You can still take care of your brother."

"I've seen the will. It makes my uncle Ronnie's guardian. And that makes the most sense. Paul and Ronnie get along well. Paul is patient. He understands what Ronnie needs."

"Ronnie still needs you. You can play a role in his life. A big one."

"Unless . . ." I almost couldn't say it. "Unless the worst is true about him, the things the police say."

Dan didn't have any words of wisdom to share about that.

Chapter Thirteen

I woke up between the familiar sheets of Dan's bed. My head felt foggy from the beer and the sleep. I rolled over and found the other side of the small bed empty. The clock read eight thirty.

"Dan?"

He came in the door dressed for school, which meant he was wearing a flannel shirt and ratty jeans. But he'd showered, and when he lay down next to me I could smell the shaving cream and soap. He wasn't as dirty as he looked.

"I have to go in a few minutes," he said. He put his arm around me and pulled me close. I drank it in. "What are you doing today?"

I yawned. "I think I need to get my life in order a little bit," I said. "I'm trying to get back to normal. I've been neglecting school the last few days. I don't want to get miles behind."

"I understand that," he said. "Do you need help with anything?"

"No, thanks. My nose is just above the water. I can keep it there."

"You can always withdraw for the semester, or take an emergency leave. Everybody would understand, and they'd hold your funding for you."

I shook my head. "I don't think that's necessary," I said.

Dan must have heard a hint of irritation in my voice because he said, "You don't like that I said that, do you?"

"This is why I don't like spending time with you," I said.

"Ouch."

"I'm sorry. I just mean . . . you know me too well."

"Well," Dan said, "we can't have any of that, can we?"

"One day at a time," I said. "Okay?"

"Sure. And your brother and the stuff we talked about last night?"

"I'll see him later. And I'll check in with Paul. You know, if my mom wants me to help take care of my brother, I need to stay in school and get a job. I can't help him out if I'm working at McDonald's."

"Then I'll get off your case." He kissed the top of my head and stood up. "I have to go. But we can talk later, if you want."

"Sure," I said. "And, Dan? Thanks. It was good talking to you."

"I'm glad you came by," he said. "And don't worry."

He didn't explain, so I asked, "Worry about what? My family?"

"About me," he said, smiling. "I won't assume that this means anything. You know, you staying here and sleeping with me."

My face flushed. "Dan."

"Hey," he said. "I'm glad you came by because I really needed to get laid."

I had just enough time to go back to my apartment—which seemed smaller and darker than the last time I was there— shower, dress, and grab my things before going to campus. I felt like I'd already missed too many classes. Anyone who has ever been in graduate school would understand what I was experiencing: sheer panic. I assumed the academic world had passed me by, that all the best resources had been given out to my peers, that all the great ideas and themes had been written about, that I was hopelessly behind and would never catch up. Indeed, as I drove the ten minutes from my apartment to campus, I convinced myself that my future did indeed lie in a McDonald's restaurant somewhere, that I would spend the rest of my life wearing a hairnet and dishing up salty fries.

But the reality wasn't that bad.

Everyone had heard the news by then, and everyone understood. My fellow grad students offered their condolences, and I even found a bouquet of flowers sitting on my desk and a card signed by almost everyone I knew, including Dan. My professors were sympathetic and encouraged me to take my time getting my personal life in order and catching up. Even the biggest hard-asses among them expressed sympathy, and I realized a fundamental truth about humanity: we all have mothers, and no one wishes ill on anyone's mother.

Even the students in the introductory section of American History One I taught had heard the news and sheepishly nodded their sympathy to me when I walked into the classroom. I had prepared nothing to teach. Nothing at all. If someone had put me on the spot and asked me to name the first president of the United States I would have been stuck for an answer. But I soldiered through. I reached into the professor bag of tricks, put them in small groups, and let them discuss the day's reading assignment, which was something I hadn't even read yet. It worked, and I made it through my first day back.

When I walked out of that classroom, I felt spent. It was late in the afternoon, nearing four o'clock, and I hadn't checked in with Paul all day for an update on Ronnie's condition. I looked at my phone as I walked through the hordes of students, and the only thing that brought me a measure of relief from guilt was the fact that Paul hadn't called. I would have felt worse if he had contacted me, if he had needed me, and I had missed it.

"Hey, Dr. Hampton."

I stopped. The voice sounded familiar but I couldn't locate its source in the crowd. I had almost started walking away, thinking that maybe I had been hearing things, when the voice called again.

"Over here, Dr. H."

And then I knew the source.

I turned, and as the crowd thinned and parted, I saw my summoner. Neal Nelson. He stood over six feet tall and soaking wet couldn't have weighed more than 130 pounds. He wore a scraggly beard, one that would have looked more at home on the face of a fifteen-year-old than on a college student. And he wore a thick green army jacket even though the temperature remained warm and comfortable. I walked over to him.

"Hello, Neal."

"Dr. H. Good to see you."

"I've told you before you shouldn't call me 'doctor,'" I said. "I'm a graduate student, not a professor. I don't have my PhD yet. I don't even have a master's degree."

"Bah," he said, waving his hand in front of his face. "What's that word people use? Semitics?"

"Semantics."

"That's it," he said. "You're my favorite professor."

"You've only been in my class for a month, and you've only showed up half the time."

"And you're not a dick about it," he said. "That's what I like about you, Teach. I'm sorry I wasn't there today. Something came up, but at least I'm here in the hallway now that class is letting out."

He smiled down at me, one side of his mouth curling up. His eyes were blue, and he knew how to squint them in just the right way that I couldn't be mad at him. He wasn't that much younger than me, probably just five years or so, and I made certain to leave enough space—both physical and emotional—between us.

"Well," I said. "Maybe you'll make it to class again this semester."

As I was turning away, he said, "I'm real sorry about your mom. It's a shitty thing."

I turned back. "How did you hear about that?" I asked. "Did you actually come to class when they announced it?"

"I read the paper," he said. "People need to know what goes on in the world, so I follow the news." He took a step closer and lowered his voice. "I also saw that it was foul play." He shook his head, his face sincere. "I don't know what I can say about that. It's brutal. I'm sorry, you know? Your mother and everything. Shit."

"Thanks, Neal."

"I had an uncle once who met with that kind of trouble." He shook his head again. "It rips your guts out, Teach. Totally out."

On that point, he was onto something—I hadn't heard it put better.

"You're right," I said. "It does."

"If there's anything I can help you with, just let me know. My old man, he knows things."

"Things?"

"He likes to help people," he said. "And so do I."

"Thanks, Neal. But if you want to help someone, help your-self. Come to class more often."

I ran into Dan as I was packing my things and getting ready to leave for the day. I hadn't seen him since he left his apartment that morning, and I suspected he'd been trying to give me a certain amount of space while we both did our work. But he found me just before I left and asked if everything had gone okay on my first day back.

I heaved a theatrical sigh. "Well, I didn't break down crying. And I convinced a roomful of students that I possessed some degree of competence. I'd call all that a success."

"Great."

I knew he wanted to ask me where I was going and what I was doing. But he didn't. He gave me all the space he thought I wanted.

"Have a good night, then," he said and walked away.

He did exactly what I wanted, and I hated it.

Chapter Fourteen

I arrived at Dover Community after five o'clock and signed in at the nurses' station.

On my way through the hallways, I passed shuffling patients, their eyes either glazed by drugs or open wide as though they had just woken up and seen the truth about something. Maybe it was the truth about where they really were, or maybe it was some larger truth about the world we all careened through. Whatever it was, they didn't like it, and their unease figuratively knocked me back a couple of steps.

When I turned into the last hallway, the one where Ronnie was, I heard a woman's voice screaming over and over, "Help me! Help me! Help me!"

I can't, I wanted to yell back. *I can't even help my own brother.*

And I froze in the hallway, just twenty feet from the door to Ronnie's room. My feet felt like concrete, my legs like lead. I couldn't move. I knew it could be bad, seeing Ronnie in there. I lost track of how long I stood there like that, locked in place like a child afraid of entering a dark basement. The spell broke when a nurse came out of Ronnie's room. She was about my age and slim, her legs pumping with controlled efficiency. She was carrying a packet of papers, and when she saw me, she lifted her glasses up to the top of her head, resting them on her thick hair.

"Elizabeth?" she said.

I didn't process that she had said my name. I couldn't imagine how she could have known my name. I figured I looked like a lot of visitors to that ward. Awkward, uncertain. Scared. Probably happened every day.

"Elizabeth Hampton?" she said.

I looked more closely at her face. I did know her, but her name didn't come to me right away.

"It's me," she said. "Janie Rader. Well, I go by Jane now. From Dover East."

It came back. Janie Rader. We went to high school together and hung around occasionally. During junior year we spent a lot of time together, sipping beer in Janie's basement, listening to loud music, trying on clothes, and pretending to be more sophisticated than we really were. We hadn't stayed in touch since then.

"Oh, Janie. It's you. I'm sorry."

"It's okay," she said, smiling. "How are you doing?"

"I'm fine," I said. "I'm here to see my brother."

"I know," she said. She leaned forward and placed her hand on my upper arm. "I heard about all of that. I'm sorry. And your mom . . . I thought of calling you when I heard the news. I didn't even know you were living back in Dover."

"I just moved back. For graduate school."

"I remember your mom from when we were . . . when we hung out together in high school. She was always so nice to me when I would come over to your house."

"Yeah," I said. "I guess we didn't spend as much time at my house as we did at yours. How's Ronnie?"

"Oh, Ronnie," she said, nodding. "He's doing better now. He's calmed down."

"Did he have a rough night?" I asked. "I was worried he would be anxious after he came here."

"Last night was fine," she said. "We gave him something to help him sleep. No, today was the rough day."

"Why's that?" I asked.

She seemed to be choosing her words carefully. Janie had always been easygoing and reluctant to say anything bad about anybody. "I know you're his closest relative, right? There's just you and Ronnie?"

"Yes."

She paused another moment, then said, "You may want to tell the rest of the members of your family to show some more restraint when they come to visit him."

"What do you mean, 'restraint'?"

A phone buzzed somewhere on her body. She pulled it out of her pocket, flipped the glasses down, and studied the screen. "Sorry." She silenced the phone and dropped it into her pocket before looking back at me. "I'm sure you know that Ronnie is in a precarious emotional state right now," she said.

"I know. When Mom was . . ."

Was murdered. Murdered. But I couldn't. I just couldn't bring myself to say that out loud. It seemed too . . . ugly. Too real.

"I know," she said. "And we're trying to keep him calm so the doctors can do their work. But one of your relatives came by today and got him pretty agitated. If that happens, then they have to medicate more, and it makes it more difficult for the doctors to examine him."

"Are you talking about my uncle?" I asked. "He wouldn't agitate Ronnie. It would be just the opposite."

"No, I've seen your uncle here. Paul, right? No, not him."

"Then who? Are you sure we're talking about Ronnie? No one else would visit him—"

"I know it's Ronnie," Janie said. "I've been here all day, working a double shift. I know."

"So what happened?" I asked.

My legs no longer felt so heavy. They felt lighter, but not in a good way. I leaned back against the wall of the hallway. The lights overhead seemed too bright, too piercing. And the cries from the helpless patient started again.

"Help me! Help me! Help me!"

Janie ignored it. "Someone came by to see your brother today," she said. "A woman. At first, everything was fine. They seemed to be visiting. Then, I don't know, things took a turn. Whatever she said to your brother got him stirred up. He became emotional, almost hysterical. When I went in there, the woman was crying a little too, and she left before I could find out what happened. She just apologized and bolted."

"Did she hurt Ronnie?" I asked.

"No, he's fine. It wasn't anything like that. I got the feeling she was asking him things, talking to him about family stuff. Maybe she was talking about your mother. I'm not sure, but whatever it was, it didn't work for him right now. So maybe just spread the word among the relatives to keep everything light when they come here. Just talk about happy stuff, mundane stuff. And bring him flowers or something to add some cheer—"

"We don't have any other relatives," I said, my voice flat and distracted.

"What's that?"

"We don't have any other relatives." I looked into Janie's eyes. Hers were pale blue, the sclera tinted a little red. Tired. But also sympathetic. I welcomed the warmth I saw there, the familiarity and the comfort. It was good to see her. "It's just Ronnie and me and my uncle. That's it. Everybody else is dead."

She didn't know what to say to that. She reached out and placed her hand gently on my arm again. "I'm sorry," she said. "I don't know if this woman was a relative or not. I just assumed, and that's my mistake. I know your family's been through a lot."

"Thanks."

"Whoever it was, relative or friend, just try to, you know, keep it a little on the cheery side for now. This isn't easy for your brother." She nodded toward the door to Ronnie's room. "He's asleep now, but you can go on in."

I didn't move. "This woman," I asked, "what did she look like?"

The phone buzzed again, and this time Janie didn't even bother to look at it. "She was about fifty, maybe a little older. Thin. Dark hair." She shrugged. "I really didn't pay too much attention since I was tending to your brother. Maybe she's a friend of the family?"

"Maybe," I said.

"I do have to go now, Elizabeth," she said. "Duty calls. But you're welcome to stay." She waited a moment. "It was good to see you again."

"Yeah," I said. "It was. Thanks for being so understanding."

"It's part of the job," she said. "And we're old friends, right?"

"Right. Of course."

I started to move on, but Janie said, "You know, if you ever need someone to talk to about all of this, I'm around. We can meet for coffee or something."

"Yeah," I said. "Maybe we should."

"I'm sure you're busy, of course."

"Thanks, Janie."

She walked off, the brisk motion of her legs making the fabric of her pants swish together.

I tried to picture the woman she described in my mind, but it was pointless. I had no idea who Janie was talking about.

I finally did move forward. I traveled the rest of the way down the hall to the closed door of Ronnie's room. I paused again, but immediately thought of what Mom would have wanted. And I knew she'd want me in that room, visiting Ronnie.

I pushed the door open and said, "Knock, knock."

The curtains were drawn, and only a small light burned by the side of Ronnie's bed. As I came into the room, my feet lightly shuffling over the linoleum floor, Ronnie didn't move. He lay on his side, his back to the door. I stopped near the bed and studied him. For a long moment he lay so still I worried there was something wrong with him, and I waited, my anxiety rising along with my heartbeat, until I saw the slightest movement in his body. It rose and fell, ever so slowly, as Ronnie breathed. He must have been deeply asleep thanks to whatever medication they had given him.

I felt the relief, let it ease through me.

Don't be silly, I told myself. *He's fine. He's doped up, but he's fine.*

I moved around to the far side of the bed, the side Ronnie faced. A functional wood-framed chair, its leather back a sickly orange color, sat in the corner. I pulled it out, closer to Ronnie's bed, and sat down. Ronnie didn't move while I did these things. Air whistled through his nose, and a thin ribbon of drool hung from his lower lip. I looked at his bedside table. I pulled a tissue from the box and gently wiped the drool away. When I did, Ronnie stirred a little. He turned his head a couple of inches and scrunched his facial features into a mask of irritation.

I threw the tissue in the trash and said, "Ronnie? It's me. Elizabeth."

He moaned and didn't open his eyes.

I leaned back in my chair, thinking of giving up, of just leaving him alone. But Janie's story had me thinking.

Who had come to talk to Ronnie? Was it someone who worked with him? Someone from speech therapy? But then why would he get so upset?

I leaned forward again, lowering my face closer to Ronnie's. His eyes were still closed. "Ronnie? Can you hear me? Can you talk to me for just a minute?"

He moaned again, but this time his eyes opened a little. "Mmph," he said.

"Good," I said. "Can you tell me who came to see you today? Did someone come into your room and talk to you today?"

His eyelids fluttered. He looked like a drunk losing the battle against unconsciousness.

"Ronnie?" I said.

"Mmph."

"Shit," I said.

"Paul."

"What?" I asked.

"Paul," he said.

"Paul?" I said. "Paul was here?"

"Mmph."

"Okay, I figured Paul came by. Did someone else come by? A woman? The nurse said a woman came by to talk to you. Do you remember that?"

"Mmph."

"Ronnie, stay with me. Who was this woman who came to see you?"

A long pause. Then he said, "Elizabeth."

"Yes?"

"Elizabeth."

"I'm here."

He didn't say anything else, so I said, "Who came to see you today, Ronnie? Please?"

"Elizabeth."

"I'm here, Ronnie. I'm right here. I wasn't here earlier. I was at school. But I came as soon as I could to see you."

He seemed to be gone then. His eyes closed and his breathing returned to the rhythm of a sleeper. I let out a long sigh. I reached out and pushed the hair out of his face. I didn't know whether it brought him any comfort or not, but I wanted to do it. He looked so small and defenseless. I tried not to think of him as a child and to never treat him as such, but seeing him there looking so vulnerable just made me want to protect him. And I was the younger sister, the baby. But he needed it much more than I did, at least in that moment.

"Mmm," he said.

I leaned closer. "What, Ronnie?"

"Mom," he said.

I thought that's what he'd just said, but I wasn't sure.

"What about Mom?" I asked.

He took a long time to answer, but he finally said, "Mom . . . here . . ."

A shiver shot up my back with such force I raised my chin, tilting my head and retracting it into my shoulders. When it passed, and my jangling nerves lost some of their electric charge, I said to Ronnie, "Mom wasn't here."

He didn't say anything.

"Did you have a dream about Mom?" I asked. "Is that why you got upset today?"

"Mom," he said. "Here."

"Ronnie, no. Mom's gone. Remember? You found her. She's gone."

But he didn't say anything else. Whatever had allowed him to come out of the drug-induced sleep closed him in its grip again—if he had even been truly awake in the first place. Maybe everything he said had been sleep-talk and nonsense.

But it wouldn't easily be forgotten.

I leaned back in the chair again. Not easily shaken off or forgotten at all.

Chapter Fifteen

On my way out, I stopped at the nurses' station. Janie was gone, so I talked to someone else. She looked to be my age or even younger, and she was tapping away at a computer when I walked up. She stopped what she was doing and smiled up at me.

"I had to sign in when I came in," I said. "Does everybody have to do that?"

"Yes," she said. "It used to be only after nine, but we have staffing shortages because of state budget cuts, so now all day."

I scanned the names above mine on the sign-in sheet. I didn't recognize any.

"My brother is Ronnie Hampton. Did you see the woman who visited him earlier?"

"I'm sorry. I just started at five."

She eyed the keyboard like it was a juicy steak. I knew I was keeping her from her work.

"I spoke to another nurse—Janie Rader—who said they had to put my brother on something to calm him down. He got a little emotional earlier apparently."

"Okay," she said.

"Is it possible for something like that to cause hallucinations? Or make someone so out of it they might see things that aren't there?"

Her eyebrows went up. "If your brother is seeing things or hallucinating—"

"No, no," I said. "I'm not saying anything is wrong. Not really."

"Then what is it?" she asked, her impatience starting to show. I wanted to get mad at her but couldn't. I would have acted the same way if someone had shown up and interrupted my work with questions. I felt the same way about my students all the time.

"Our mother just died, and Ronnie said he saw her. And this woman came to visit him apparently . . ."

"He probably had a dream about your mother," the nurse said. "And the drug may have made it more difficult to tell the dream from reality."

"Yeah, that's probably it."

"I talk in my sleep all the time," she said, dropping the businesslike air for just a moment. "My boyfriend thinks I'm crazy."

"You're probably right."

She turned to the keyboard and started popping the return key as if it had done something wrong and deserved to be punished. Then she started typing.

"I'll note it in your brother's chart," she said. "It can't hurt to have the doctors check it out. Maybe they can give him something else."

I didn't leave. I took a pen from the top of the nurses' station and found a scrap of paper. I scribbled my e-mail address and cell phone number. "Can you give that to Janie when she comes back? She wanted it."

"Of course," she said. "She'll be back later."

"Thanks."

Walking away, I felt even crappier. Had I just made Ronnie's life worse, consigned him to an even deeper drug-induced oblivion?

Paul called me as I was getting into my car. Visions of my tiny apartment danced in my head. The fluffy couch. The criminally small TV. I had work to do, lots of it. But when I left the hospital, all I could think about was being flat on my back, my brain shifted to neutral. But Paul knew which button to push to change my mind.

"Are you hungry?" he asked. "I know it was your first day back."

"You had me at 'Are you hungry?'" I said.

Besides, there were things I needed to ask him about.

We met at the Downtown Diner, a local institution that had been unapologetically raising the cholesterol and blood sugar levels of Dover residents for nearly fifty years. When I arrived at seven thirty, Paul waved to me from a booth. The dinner crowd had thinned out, and except for the sounds of cleanup—clanking dishes, rattling silverware—the place was pretty calm. It smelled good, though. Very good. Grease hung in the air as thick as humidity, reminding me I hadn't eaten much all day. Not for the past few days in fact. I needed to eat, and Paul knew that too.

He looked better than the last time I had seen him in the hospital parking lot. He looked a little more rested, a little less old and tired. He smiled when I sat down, and only mild strain showed in his eyes.

"I'm surprised you wanted to come here," I said. "You know . . ." I pointed to his chest.

Paul had suffered a mild heart attack a few years earlier, one that required an angioplasty to reopen a clogged artery. In the wake of the procedure, he adopted a healthier diet and started walking or riding a bike a few miles every day.

"Oh, that," he said. He made a dismissive wave of his hand. "I cheat sometimes."

The waitress arrived, notepad in hand, and we both ordered cheeseburgers, fries, and Cokes. Paul even asked for a side of mayonnaise for his burger. "You know," he said when she'd walked away, "you'd think having my sister die would make me take more caution with my health, but instead . . ." He let the thought trail off, but I got the point.

"You want to live it up while you can," I said.

"I guess so. Living it up with my cheeseburger." He forced a smile. "The police paid me a visit today," he said. "Those two detectives."

"What did they want?"

"Who knows?" he said. "I guess they just wanted to ask me some routine questions. Mostly it was stuff about your mom. You know, did she have any enemies? Did she have any friends? A background examination, I guess you'd call it. They want to know if there was anything in her life that might have driven someone to harm her."

"So they're not just focusing on Ronnie?" I asked.

"They asked about him as well. Just more stuff about violent tendencies or whatever. I didn't have anything else to tell them."

"Good," I said, allowing myself to feel relief.

"I have a feeling they'll be coming to you soon," he said.

"I can't wait."

"You need to be prepared for the kinds of things they're going to ask you," he said. A firmness had crept into his voice.

"They're going to— I don't know. They may say things that will upset you."

"Like what?"

He seemed about to say something, then thought better of it. "I don't know. Just be ready for anything they might throw at you. And remember, they're cops. They may push you a little, rattle your cage. Just keep your cool with them."

I wanted to say more but didn't. "Okay." I let it go.

I sensed Paul's mood slipping in the wrong direction. The cheer he'd summoned when I came into the restaurant seemed to be draining away, so I tried to steer him toward something else.

"I made it through my first day back," I said. "No casualties."

He brightened again. "Good."

"I wasn't prepared and I'm light-years behind, but I went."

"Work can be good for that," he said. "Taking your mind off your troubles. I almost wish I was still working for that reason. Almost." The waitress brought the Cokes, and Paul peeled a straw from its wrapper and took a long drink. "You have that practical aspect to your personality. It comes from our side of the family."

"Work through things by just moving on?" I asked.

"Exactly." He looked a little distant, a little lost in his own thoughts. "I don't have that quite as much as Leslie did. I get a little hung up on things, and they turn over in my mind. Over and over sometimes."

I drank my Coke, felt the sugar and caffeine hitting my bloodstream. It was delicious, and I wished they could serve it to me through an IV. "It's because you care," I said.

"Like Ronnie," he said. "I think of him in there, in that hospital." He shook his head. "I worry about that and all the pressures on him."

"I just came from there," I said. "Did you go today?"

"This morning. I guess I was there until about two."

"How did he seem to you?"

Before he answered, our food arrived. The waitress set the thick plates heaped with meat and fries down in front of us, then handed over a sticky bottle of ketchup. I asked for another Coke, and once that was delivered, Paul and I were ready to continue our conversation.

"He seemed fine," he said. "Quiet still, just like he was at home. But not bad, I guess." He sighed. "I guess I expected the police to show up and bug him, but they didn't. Not while I was there."

I considered not telling him about Ronnie's outburst during the afternoon. I didn't want to make him feel any worse or more guilty or conflicted over Ronnie's stay at Dover Community. But I needed to know if he had any guesses as to who else could have gone to Ronnie's room that day, so I told him all about it, relating Janie's story as accurately as I could recall it. While I was telling Paul, he stopped eating. He picked at his fries, lifting them up and setting them back down on his plate without taking any more bites. When I was finished telling him, he didn't look up.

I asked, "Do you have any idea who this woman might be? Does she sound like anyone Ronnie or Mom knew?"

Paul lifted his hand to his forehead and rubbed his temple. "I don't think so. I don't know everybody they knew."

"Could it be someone Ronnie knew?" I asked. "Someone from where he went to speech therapy, or someone from work?"

"Your guess is as good as mine," he said, his voice weary.

"The nurse thought it might be a relative."

"We're short on those," he said. "And getting shorter every day."

I decided not to press him too hard. I turned my attention to my food—which I enjoyed a great deal—and tried to think of non-bothersome small talk. But what was there to talk about? What else existed in the world besides the crisis enveloping my family? I gave up trying to talk about anything else and said, "Ronnie said something strange when I asked him about it."

Paul ate a couple of fries. "What was that?" he asked.

"Well, first he said my name. I asked him who came to see him, and he said, 'Elizabeth.'"

"He was doped up by then?" Paul asked.

"Yeah."

"He didn't know what you were asking him."

"Right. But then he said that Mom had been there."

Paul slumped when I said those words. I could see the energy draining from him.

"Why are you telling me this?" he asked.

"I thought—"

"What does it have to do . . . with anything? He's high as a kite and he's dreaming," he said.

"I know. I'm sorry." I looked down at my plate of food. I wanted to stop myself from saying anything more, but I couldn't. "I just really want to know who this woman is who went to Ronnie's room and upset him so much. Don't you want to know?"

He sighed. "Elizabeth, I'm not sure I want to know anything else about any of this."

We ate the rest of our meal mostly in silence.

Chapter Sixteen

I lived in what might generously be called the graduate student ghetto on the east side of campus. The undergraduates dwelled mostly on the north of campus, where there were larger places to live and share—rental houses and town homes, spaces landlords were more than willing to wedge six or seven students into and charge them an exorbitant monthly rate with the hope that the parents would just go ahead and pay it. Most of them did.

Graduate students tended to live alone or in pairs, and the apartments on the east side of campus were smaller and slightly nicer. And slightly nicer meant the roofs probably weren't falling in, the hot water worked at least half the time, and the chances of the police descending on a residence, lights swirling, to roust a group of underage drinkers was next to none. I lived alone, by choice, in a studio apartment on the top floor of an eighty-year-old building. The railroad tracks ran alongside it, and three times a day or night, freight screamed by. It woke me up the first two nights I lived there. After that, I slept through it without stirring.

I parked in the tiny lot at the back of the building. It was dark by the time I returned home after my dinner with Paul. I was tired. The streetlights were coming on, their yellow glow leaking through the canopy of trees that grew over the back of the apartment building.

I never felt unsafe in my neighborhood, or anywhere in Dover for that matter. The town had its share of small crimes—cars got broken into; apartments and houses were burgled, usually when people forgot to lock their doors. Around campus, we experienced the typical array of drinking and drug arrests, but there were few assaults and almost never a murder.

But Mom's death had put me on edge. On the drive home, I considered calling Dan or stopping by his place, which would inevitably lead to spending the night with him again—and not spending the night alone in my apartment. But a river of complications flowed from that one simple act, and I needed more than anything else to keep things as simple as possible. And I needed to not be a baby, to not let what happened to Mom filter into my mind so much that I started running scared and jumping at my own shadow.

So when I stepped out of the car into a surreally calm night, I told myself that it was my imagination, my own creeping fears and insecurities preying on me rather than any real disturbance or threat. But the area was dead quiet. Dead. None of the sounds that usually dominated the neighborhood—music, conversation, cars—were there. And it was too early for things to be so quiet.

Why?

I looked all around me, swiveling my head like a soldier on combat patrol, as I moved to the side of the building where a rickety wooden staircase led to my apartment at the top. I cursed myself for not carrying pepper spray or having taken a self-defense class—all the things I was supposed to do as a young single woman living on her own in the big world. But my mother had lived the most cautious life imaginable. She locked every door and window and would never open her house to a stranger. Once darkness fell, she did everything in her power to not leave the house. And what had that prudence done for her?

A door slammed somewhere. It sounded as if it had come from behind me, from another building or maybe a car. I turned to look back but saw nothing. I had reached the base of the stairs and started up, hurrying as best I could while carrying my laptop bag and my books. My graduate student tools, the things I carried with me everywhere I went.

The staircase went up three stories, zigzagging up the side of the building like in an Escher drawing. I reached the first landing and heard someone coming down toward me. Enough space existed for two people to pass without touching each other, but unconsciously I moved to the edge, toward the outer railing, when I heard the steps coming. The person was moving fast, faster than would be normal. I expected it to be one of my neighbors, one of the guys who lived below me who were always hustling off to a basketball game or the library. In the darkness the figure coming toward me looked big—short, yes, but hulking and big, his face obscured and turned away from me in the half-light. He brushed past me, his left arm hitting mine and nearly knocking the bag out of my hand. The force of the contact spun me around a quarter turn, giving me a clear view of his departing back.

"Hey!" I said.

But he didn't stop. He thumped down the stairs, his body just barely maintaining control and remaining upright. The body didn't look as if it belonged to a student. It looked . . . older somehow. A professor at our building? Was he slumming?

The man disappeared into the night. I listened for the sound of a car door or engine, but it didn't come.

"Asshole," I muttered, then continued my trek to the top.

And when I made it there, slightly out of breath, my arms weakened from hauling my gear, I understood why the man had been in such a hurry.

My door sat ajar, the wood around the lock splintered into hundreds of shards and pieces.

I didn't enter my apartment, not alone. I turned and went back down the steps, only to reach the halfway point and realize that the man I'd passed—the one who was very likely responsible for breaking into my apartment—could be lingering at the foot of the stairs. Or somewhere in the darkness of the parking lot. I hadn't heard a car start. Hadn't heard anything to indicate he had left the scene.

I had no way of knowing whether he was the one who'd broken into the apartment. I'd been gone all day, and since my unit sat alone on the top floor, no one would have noticed the shattered door.

I went one floor below, to the two apartments beneath mine. I didn't really know my neighbors. I suspected they were grad students just like me, given their ages and monklike habits. They were quiet as well, never disturbing me with loud music or parties. But I had spoken to a guy in one of the apartments. Once. A pipe beneath my kitchen sink had sprung a leak one night during the previous winter, causing water to run all over my floor and cascade into his apartment. Fortunately, he was home, and he came up and found the shut-off valve for the water. We didn't say much to each other—what do you say to someone whose apartment you've just flooded?—but he seemed friendly enough. Polite at least. A little nerdy. A little awkward. Some kind of science grad student, I guessed at the time. Maybe engineering.

I knocked on his door, hoping like hell he'd be home. If he was, he was moving slowly, so I knocked again. I was ready to step over to the next apartment, where God knows who lived, when the door opened.

His brow furrowed when he saw me. I didn't think he recognized me, and maybe he wondered what I was carrying in my arms and trying to sell on a fall evening. He looked ready to object, to send me on my way with a polite but stern "Thanks but no thanks," when some flicker of recognition crossed his face.

"Oh," he said. "Do you live upstairs?"

"I do," I said. "Can I come in? My place has been broken into."

I didn't wait for an answer. I went inside and put my things down. I pulled out my phone and dialed 911, reporting the problem to the dispatcher, who asked me three times if I was someplace safe or in any immediate danger. The third time she asked I turned to my neighbor, who was standing in the same spot, his mouth slightly open, and asked, "She wants to know if I'm in any immediate danger now. Am I?"

He shook his head.

"I'm fine," I said. I told her where I was so the police could find me when they arrived, and we ended our call. "They're on their way," I said to the neighbor, the guy whose name I didn't know.

"Okay," he said.

He didn't offer me a seat or a drink. I didn't care. I asked, "Did you hear anything unusual upstairs today? My lock is totally shattered."

He thought about the question for a minute, then said, "No, I didn't hear anything. But I was gone most of the day. I had a lab. And tonight I had my headphones on."

"Physics?" I asked.

"Astronomy," he said. "I'm a TA for Professor Landon."

Astronomy. Made sense.

"Did you have a friend over here tonight?" I asked. "Right before I came home?"

"A friend?"

"Yes," I said. "A friend. Or an acquaintance. Did you have someone to your apartment tonight?"

"Are you suggesting I know the person who broke into your apartment?" he asked, his back stiffening with indignation. Grad students could be touchy.

"I passed a man on the stairs when I came home," I said. "A stocky little guy. I thought maybe he was here to see you."

His posture eased. "No, he wasn't. I've been alone."

"Is anybody home next door?" I asked.

He looked at the wall as though he could see through it and into the next apartment. "I don't think so. I don't think he's ever home."

"I guess I never see him either."

"He might have a girlfriend," my neighbor said. "I talked to him once. He's getting a doctorate in English."

It was then I realized my hands were shaking. Really shaking. I didn't know what to do with them. I didn't know what to do about anything.

My neighbor said, "So if the guy wasn't here and he wasn't next door, that means you probably passed the guy who broke into your apartment. You must have just missed walking in on him."

"That seems to be the case," I said.

Our conclusion didn't do anything to slow my shaking, so I just waited for the police to arrive.

Chapter Seventeen

I met the police on the stairs outside my neighbor's apartment.
During the short minutes we waited, he and I managed to intro-
duce ourselves to each other. His name was Jeff. I apologized
again for the kitchen flood. He blinked at me a couple of times. I
thought maybe he'd forgotten about it. Then he said, "You're
providing all the excitement for the building."

The police—two young officers, both with crew cuts—told
me to wait in Jeff's apartment while they went and checked out
my apartment. That was fine by me. When they were finished,
they called me up to assess the damage.

Having never been burgled before, I didn't know what to
expect. My laptop went with me everywhere, and it mattered
the most. I didn't own expensive jewelry or rare antiques. My
television was close to ten years old, and I rarely turned it on.
When I stepped into the apartment, I saw a mess. That's the simplest way to describe it. It looked like a small tornado had blown
through, kicking up papers and knocking cushions off my love
seat and chairs. The desk drawers had been yanked out and
dumped. One of the cops emerged from the small bathroom and
announced that the door to the medicine cabinet hung open, its
contents scattered across the floor.

"Meth heads," his partner said. "Do you see anything missing?"

I looked around the room. "Tidiness and order," I said.

"Ma'am?"

"I don't see anything missing," I said.

"The TV and DVD player are there." He looked around. "Phone. Toaster. Do you have a computer?"

"A laptop. It was with me."

"Lucky. They take electronics and sell them to get money for drugs. Or they just steal drugs if you have them."

"I saw the man," I said. "I passed him on the stairs as I was coming home."

"Oh, yeah?"

I told them what had happened—the man passing me, bumping into me. His rush down the stairs. I told them he looked like an older man, not a junkie.

"They come in all ages," the cop said. "Anything else you can tell us about him?"

I thought about it. "It was dark."

"Was he white or black? Anything?"

"I really couldn't tell," I said. "White, I guess."

The other officer came out of the bathroom. They stood side by side, surveying the damage. They were both solidly built, former football players or marines or something. They looked like law enforcement bookends. Giant law enforcement bookends.

The one closest to me said, "Well, we can file a report. If nothing significant is missing, then you probably don't want to bother your insurance company with it."

"I don't have renter's insurance," I said.

"Then you should probably have your landlord get a locksmith over here," he said. "And have them put in a dead bolt this time. That lock you had was pretty flimsy. Especially if you're living here alone."

"There's something else," I said.

Both officers turned to listen to me.

"My mother died—she was murdered this past weekend."

I'd managed to say it out loud. Murdered. My mother. All in the same sentence to complete strangers.

Recognition crossed their faces. They must have heard about it. I was sure everybody in town knew.

"Do you think the two could be related?" I asked. "Someone kills my mother in her home, and then someone breaks into my apartment this way."

The two officers nodded sympathetically. They seemed to be taking my concerns seriously and giving them their full weight. But I don't think they bought into it.

"I understand this is disturbing," one of them said. "Especially in light of such a tragedy. But these meth heads break into apartments all the time. We've had a little rash of them around the edges of campus lately. It happens. I don't think it was directed at you."

The other one said, "They were clearly just looking for something to sell to buy drugs."

I looked around too. I agreed with them about one thing: whoever that man was, he was definitely looking for something.

Chapter Eighteen

Since I didn't have a lock and not even much of a front door, and since someone seemed to think my home was a ripe hunting ground for whatever they were looking for—drugs or something else I couldn't even imagine—I needed someplace to sleep. A call to Dan would provide the easiest solution. I knew he'd be only too happy to open his door—and his bed—to me. But easy didn't always mean simple. And I worried about leading him on too much, making his life as well as mine more complicated.

So I called Paul and asked if I could spend the night in his spare bedroom. He readily agreed, and it was only when I showed up on his doorstep and saw him again, still looking tired and hangdog, that I wished I hadn't bothered him. The stress of my mother's death hung from him like heavy chains. I felt as if I'd just added a couple more links.

But I felt safe in his house. I locked the bedroom door when I went to bed and woke up every hour on the hour thinking someone was smashing the window to pieces and coming into the house after me. And once I woke up because I heard someone yelling from the other room. It was Paul, in the grip of some nightmare. I jumped up and went to his bedroom door, knocking lightly. When I called his name, he stopped yelling, but didn't say anything else.

I stood there in the darkness, feeling very much like a lost and scared child. Two hours passed before I was able to fall back asleep.

Paul, the perpetual early riser, sat at the breakfast table when I walked into the kitchen the next morning. He looked showered and shaved, and some of the color and vitality seemed to have returned to his cheeks. He smiled when he saw me and pointed to fresh bagels and a dish of fruit.

"I have cereal and oatmeal if you want it," he said. "And there's coffee made."

"Thank you."

The bagel and coffee brought me back to life. I needed it. My eyes were raw and aching from a lack of sound sleep. My landlord was supposed to have the new lock—a dead bolt—installed early in the day. I hoped so, so I could take a nap later—if I could manage to sleep in my apartment again.

"Sleep okay?" Paul asked, although I suspected he knew the answer.

"Could have been worse," I said. "How about you?"

"Not too bad," he said.

I told him about his nightmare, and how I'd gone to his door and knocked until he stopped yelling. He listened to my story, his smile turning wry.

When I was finished, he looked more shaken than I would have predicted, and I wished I hadn't told him. He said, "I've had quite a few of those dreams since . . . you know. I think in all of them your mom needs my help, and I can't give it to her. Sometimes we're kids in the dreams. It's weird. The dreams are disturbing, but I almost like having them."

"Because she's alive again," I said. "Even just in your head."

Paul stood up and started doing the dishes. He didn't say anything else and didn't need to. We understood each other.

Paul promised to see Ronnie early that day. Not only did I have a stack of student essays to grade, which had been sitting in my briefcase since before Mom died, but I also woke up to two messages on my phone. One was Detective Richland asking me to call him back. I assumed the two officers who'd responded to the break-in at my apartment had told him about it, and he wanted to get the straight story himself.

The other call was from Mom's attorney, Frank Allison. He too wanted me to call him back about, as he put it, a matter concerning my mother's estate.

Estate, I thought to myself. Such an expansive word for describing the worldly possessions of someone who didn't have that much. I thought Detective Richland's call would be more complicated, so I called the attorney first. I hadn't heard from my landlord about the lock. I opted to head to a local coffee shop and grade my papers there. I was on my way, cautiously driving with one hand on the wheel and holding the phone with the other, when I was connected with Mr. Allison.

"Ms. Hampton?"

"Yes?"

"Sorry to bother you, but I wanted to touch base with you about filing your mother's will."

I skirted the edge of downtown and headed north toward campus and the Grunge, my preferred coffee and grading hideaway.

"I know I have to do that," I said. "Everything's been crazy."

"Oh, no, no," he said. "I'm not calling to put pressure on you." His voice practically boomed through the phone, his tone somewhere between commanding and jolly. "I just wanted to let you know about a phone call I received."

"Okay," I said as I slowed to allow pedestrians to pass in front of me. Classes were changing. It was close to nine, and the intersections around campus swelled with students. Traffic backed up at every crosswalk and corner.

Mr. Allison continued. "Someone called, a woman, asking about Leslie Hampton's will. At first I thought it was going to be you. Your mother named you executrix, after all. But it turns out it was someone asking if the will had been filed yet. Apparently this person thought she might be named in there and wanted to know if she could do anything to speed the process along. I guess she needs the money."

"Who was it?" I asked.

"She didn't leave a name. All I could tell her was that the will hadn't been filed for probate yet. You know, there's no time limit on such things. But you may want to tell your relatives that you haven't gotten around to it yet."

He didn't say why, but I understood. He didn't want to have a bunch of relatives calling to ask him if their ships had come in.

But there was something about the whole thing I didn't understand: who was this woman who thought she would be named in my mother's will?

Chapter Nineteen

I managed to grade a few papers at the Grunge. My mind wandered every chance it got—to Paul's state of mind, the break-in at my apartment, the woman calling about the will. I wondered how anyone functioned in the world when dealing with a crisis. And I answered my own question: you just do it. You do it because you have to.

I'd called Detective Richland back after talking to Mom's lawyer. Richland seemed thrilled to hear from me, as if I'd called to offer him a year's supply of tooth pain. He didn't give me a chance to mention the break-in. He was on his way to a meeting—could I come by the station around noon?

"Sure," I said.

And he hung up.

Which is how I ended up at the Dover police department after leaving the Grunge. It was a deceptively cheerful-looking little building constructed out of red brick in an almost Colonial style. Despite its classic appearance, it had been built only a decade earlier thanks to a property tax increase that most of the citizens of Dover still complained about. They wanted the police to do their jobs—they just didn't want to have to pay for it or give them any additional space.

An officer greeted me at the front desk, then buzzed back to tell the detectives I was here to see them. Detective Post arrived in a matter of minutes and led me down a short hallway and then through a roomful of desks where officers in uniform and plain clothes pecked away at computers and talked on phones. Post turned back to me and said, "We can go into the conference room. It will be quieter."

A heavy oak table dominated the center of the conference room, and the thick carpet and heavy drapes absorbed most of the noise. When Post closed the door behind me, it felt as if I'd been sealed in an airtight chamber. We were the only ones in the room. Detective Richland was nowhere in sight, and I asked about him.

"He's out on another call," Post said. "We're covering a lot of cases, so we divide the labor."

I didn't say it out loud, but I didn't miss him.

Post pointed to a small table in the corner of the room. "There's coffee," she said. "Or I could get you a soda."

"I'm good," I said.

We both sat down near the end of the table closest to the door. Post carried a manila folder, which she placed in front of her but didn't open. Post wasn't wearing a jacket, and her sleeves were rolled up to her elbows as if she was about to do some serious work.

"I hope things have been going okay for you," Post said.

"Aside from my mother dying and my apartment being broken into, things are fine. Oh, I forgot that my brother is the prime suspect in the murder of my mother."

"What about your apartment?" Post asked.

"It was broken into last night," I said. "I thought that's what I was here to talk about."

Post looked puzzled. "Tell me about this."

"Two of your officers responded to my house," I said. "I told them about Mom's death, and that you and Richland were investigating."

Post took a deep breath. I could tell she was trying to project calm and professional cool. She reached into her pants pocket and pulled out a little notebook.

"I'll deal with the communication issues later," she said. "Can you tell me about this break-in?"

"They really didn't tell you?" I asked.

"I mostly work with men," she said. "What happened?"

So I told her about coming home, the still, quiet night. I told her about passing the man on the stairs, the one in a hurry who apparently wasn't coming from any of the other apartments. I told her about the shattered lock and the ransacked apartment, including the violated medicine cabinet.

"The cops who were there chalked it up to meth heads or something like that," I said. "But none of my electronics were missing. Granted, they might be worth up to three or four dollars on the open market."

"Junkies don't make those distinctions," Post said.

"Exactly."

"Still, we've had a lot of these break-ins lately, especially around campus. The meth heads and even just your garden-variety burglar think college kids have a lot of money and are careless with their things. They tend to leave doors and windows open and their toys just lying around. And a lot of that is true."

"I'm a grad student," I said. "I'm poor."

"They also don't understand that distinction," she said.

She scribbled in her book. I waited. She kept scribbling, so I said, "Don't you think it's odd that my mother is murdered and then all of a sudden someone is breaking into my apartment? Doesn't that seem strange to you?"

"But why your apartment?" Post asked. "Why not your mother's house?"

"Maybe they did break in there," I said. "I haven't been back in days."

Post looked at me, the wheels in her head turning. Without saying anything else, she stood up and left the room, taking the notebook and folder with her.

I waited. I stared at the bookshelves filled with law enforcement manuals and textbooks. Quite possibly the world's most boring collection of books. Post came back a minute later and closed the door again. She sat down.

"I sent a car to check your mother's house," she said. "Just as a precaution."

"So you agree with me. This break-in at my house isn't just a random crime."

"Was anything missing?" she asked.

"Nothing that I could see."

"Any important papers? Photos? Anything relating to your mother?"

"I didn't check that carefully," I said. "To be honest, I was too freaked out to stay. I haven't been back yet. They're putting in a new lock."

"Make sure it's a dead bolt. And get a chain." Post tapped her pen against the notebook a few times. "I still think it's a long shot this would have anything to do with your mother's death. Like I said, we get a lot of this kind of crime. If they just ransacked the place, it's not significant."

"It's significant to me," I said.

"I understand. It's a violation. It's unnerving."

"If I hadn't stopped to have dinner with my uncle, I might have been home when that man came into the apartment."

Post watched me for a moment. She made a little noise in the back of her throat. It sounded like "Hmm."

Someone knocked on the door. Post rose and opened it. She stuck her head out, nodded, thanked the person, and came back into the room.

"Well," she said. "Your mother's house is fine. Our patrol car checked it out. No sign of any break-in or vandalism."

I felt a little deflated hearing that news. It was almost as if I wanted there to have been a break-in at Mom's house—then the one at my apartment would have made more sense. It would have all been part of a whole, something that started to form a coherent picture.

"Detective, if this break-in at my apartment is related to my mother's death, then doesn't that prove that Ronnie didn't do it? How could he be locked up in Dover Community and break into my place?"

"I wanted to talk to you about your mother a little," she said.

"You didn't answer my question," I said. "How could my brother be in the hospital and involved with that break-in?"

Post smiled without showing her teeth. "I think you're probably letting the emotion of these two events cloud your judgment. It's very likely you were just the victim of a random break-in. I can show you the charts we have to track these things. Break-ins in that area are up about twenty percent this year. Someone—or a group of people—is doing it. We'll find out eventually, but it won't be connected to your mother's death. As for your brother, I can tell you that it's moving slowly because your brother hasn't been as cooperative as we need him to be."

"Cooperative?"

"I know," she said, holding up her hand to fend off my objections. "I'm not unsympathetic to all the issues associated with him being in the hospital."

"You can't just dismiss them as 'issues.'"

"What I'm saying is, if you have any ability to talk to him, to get him to open up a little to the doctors who want to speak to him, then maybe things will move along more quickly. I don't like the idea of a guy like your brother being cooped up in a hospital either. But we need to find out more from him. We all have the same goal here: to solve your mother's murder."

Her words took the slightest edge off my anger and frustration. Not all of it—just a bit. It was remarkable what treating me as a human being could do.

"I'll try to talk to him," I said. "He doesn't listen to me. He's all doped up. They medicated him yesterday because someone upset him."

"I heard about that," Post said.

"Do you know who that woman was?" I asked.

"No. Do you?"

"No. That's just it. What's going on here? A strange woman shows up at my brother's hospital room and sends him into a fit of hysterics. My apartment gets broken into. And then—" I stopped myself. I realized my voice was getting louder. Post looked at me with the calm condescension usually reserved for mental patients. "I'm going to get some of that coffee," I said, getting up and walking over to the other side of the room.

The act of pouring it into the cup and adding sugar, then stirring and watching the dark liquid swirl around in the cup soothed my nerves just enough. I came back to the table and sat down. Post gave me a moment. I sipped the hot liquid. Despite the generous amount of sugar I added, it still tasted bitter.

Post said, "It's been a few days, and we were just wondering if anything else had come to mind about your mother. Any problems she might have been having. Any relationships that might have been a source of trouble for her."

"I've thought about this a lot," I said. "I don't know who would hurt my mother."

"Anything at all? Money problems? Something else?"

"If there's been a rash of break-ins around town, what's to say Mom's death wasn't the result of one of those?"

"You said your lock was splintered and your apartment ransacked?" Post asked. "You saw your mother's house the other night. There's a difference there, right?"

I didn't answer, but I understood. My attempt to make a connection between the two events, to stretch a link so far between two dissimilar events, made me seem amateurish and desperate. I wanted Mom's death to make more sense than it did, but I couldn't. And neither could Detective Post.

"What about your father?" she asked. "He's deceased, right?"

"He died almost five years ago."

"Was there anything about him that might be relevant to your mom's case?" Post asked. "Any unresolved problems? Any issues?"

"My father?" I said. "That man didn't have any issues. He was peaceful and easygoing." I felt myself smiling just thinking about him. "I got along with him much better than with Mom. I guess Mom and I were too much alike in a lot of ways."

"Did your mother date anyone since your father died?" Post asked.

The question—no, the idea of the question—almost made me fall out of my chair. "Date someone? My mother?" I laughed, and the expression on Post's face didn't change. "No, she didn't date anyone. You wouldn't ask that question if you knew my mother at all."

"But you didn't know everything about your mother," Post said. Her voice was flat. She didn't add any "gotcha" inflection. She didn't need to. She had, indeed, made her point and proven my argument to be vulnerable.

But I wouldn't be so easily swayed, at least not on the point in question. "I don't think my mom even dated any other man *before* my dad. I know, I know—we all find it hard to think about our parents as sexual beings."

"It can seem like parents didn't have lives before their children were born."

"My mom especially," I said. "I know you didn't know her, but she was so . . . closed off to the world. So rigid and uptight. She didn't let anybody in. I don't know how my dad ever got through to her."

Post leaned back in her chair, stretching her thin body out and trying to adopt what might look like a more casual posture. Was she trying to suggest we were just two girls chatting? That I could tell her anything? Anything at all about the murder of my mother?

"You never really told us about this argument you were having with your mother," she said. "Things were chaotic that night, of course. But could you tell me what it was about?"

I told her about Mom's insistence that I promise I would always be there for Ronnie and always take care of him. I explained that Mom's biggest fear was what would happen to Ronnie if she were ever incapacitated or died. "My uncle says

Mom was really worried about it because she was getting older and my uncle is getting older. I guess she saw me as the last, best hope."

"So what was the fight about?" Post asked, still not getting it.

Or was I the one not getting it? I thought the problem was clear as day, but apparently the detective still didn't understand.

"I didn't make the promise," I explained. "I just didn't."

Post raised her eyebrows. She didn't say anything. She didn't need to. Her expression said it all.

"I would think you would understand," I said. "If you're trying to have a career, you can't be caring for someone. Not someone like Ronnie."

"Some people would say family always comes first," Post said.

"I know, but we had family. My uncle . . . and my mom was fine then. It's not like she knew—" Post and I locked eyes. Again, she didn't reveal anything. She let me reach the conclusion. "She couldn't have known anything was going to happen to her. Could she?"

"There'd already been one incident with your brother," Post said. "One serious enough to warrant the police being called."

I didn't know where to look. I let my eyes wander around the room, past the stupid books, the coffee machine, anywhere but on Post. What she was suggesting didn't make sense. If Mom felt her life was in danger from her own son, why would she insist on making me a participant in his long-term care? She'd be endangering me as well. Right?

Unless . . .

"She might have thought, or hoped, I wouldn't turn him over to an institution or something like that. She must have thought a family member wouldn't do that."

"Would your uncle?" Post asked.

"Never. He loves Ronnie. He's better with Ronnie than I am."

Post didn't respond. She tapped her pen against the notebook a few times, a slow metronomic beat. She waited. Was she keeping something from me? I wondered.

"Do you know something about this I don't know?" I asked. "Did Paul say something to you about all of this?"

Finally, she said, "Your mother apparently didn't tell you about a lot of the things that were going on in her life. She kept these things to herself."

"So?"

"So I'm just saying that if there's one thing I've learned from doing this job, it's that people possess an infinite capacity to surprise."

"Are you trying to suggest something?" I asked.

"What I can tell you is that your brother remains a suspect in your mother's death." She flipped her notebook shut. "As far as issues between your uncle and your mother, or between you and your uncle, those are for you to figure out."

Chapter Twenty

That afternoon, after my class, I went to Dover Community to see Ronnie. When I arrived, a nurse intercepted me and told me I couldn't go in because a doctor was examining my brother. I had never seen the nurse working there before, but it seemed like every time I went to the hospital a different one was working. There must have been an unlimited supply. I had hoped to see Janie. A friendly face was always welcome.

"You can come back later if you want," the nurse said. "Or you can wait."

"How long?" I asked.

"It could take an hour or so."

I thought of the bag in my car, the one filled with thirty ungraded essays. I needed to tend to them.

Then the nurse said, "Your uncle went to the cafeteria. You could go wait with him if he's still there."

I selected a tea bag and added hot water to my mug. I grabbed more than enough sugar packets and paid. Paul sat alone at a table in the corner. The day had turned overcast as a cold front passed through, bringing with it a hint of fall. Mom and I both loved autumn, even the cool gray days. Sometimes I liked those best of all.

Paul had a newspaper spread out on the table, and he smiled when I approached and took the seat across from him. My face must have betrayed my feelings because right away he asked me what was wrong.

"Is it something with Ronnie?" he asked.

I put my tea down on the table. "I was at the police station with Detective Post."

"Oh," he said. "Was it rough?"

"I'm trying to understand some things."

Paul took off his reading glasses and laid the newspaper aside. "Anything I can help with?"

In that moment, I didn't like him. He seemed too helpful, too fatherly. I had a father and a mother. They were both gone, but I had them. I remembered them. I didn't want or need someone else to fill that role. Not right then. I wanted to know the answer to something.

"Did you tell Mom to send Ronnie away?" I asked.

To his credit, he didn't try to tap-dance around the question. He held my gaze and answered without hemming or hawing.

"Yes," he said. "I did, right after Leslie had to call the police about him."

"Why?"

"Isn't it obvious?" he asked. "I felt that Ronnie was having some problems—emotional and anger management problems—that would best be addressed by professionals in a controlled setting. It didn't have to be permanent, but I thought that intervention was needed."

"But you know that's not at all what Mom wanted," I said. "To say that to Mom would be like spitting in her face. You knew that."

"Sometimes if you care about someone, you have to—and I'm using your indelicate metaphor—spit in their face. I thought I was doing the right thing, the best thing, for everybody."

"What did she say when you suggested that?"

"About what you'd expect." He rubbed his hands together. "She was angry—very angry. I think she took it as a criticism of her. Criticism of her parenting ability and criticism of her ability to take care of herself. People our age start to get testy when others suggest we may not be in full control of our lives. She said, 'No. Never.'"

The tea was still too hot to drink. I hadn't even tried it yet. I shouldn't have come down to the cafeteria. I shouldn't have brought anything up. I remembered that Paul said the police would say a lot of things to me, that they might say things meant to upset me. Was this what he'd been talking about?

"Why are you so worked up about this?" he asked.

"Because . . ." But I didn't have anything else. I couldn't say why I was angry. I gave it my best shot. "It feels like a betrayal."

"A betrayal? Of whom?"

"Of Mom," I said. "And Ronnie."

"And you?"

"In a way, yes."

A smirk crossed his face. He could be condescending when he wanted to be. The teacher amused by the confusion of the pupil.

"Don't do that," I said.

"What?"

"Smirk at me like that," I said. "You look just like Mom when you do it. But she was never as condescending as you can be."

I didn't like where any of this was going, but I also felt powerless to stop myself. It was as though I were outside myself somehow, watching myself have an argument with my beloved uncle during the worst week of our lives.

"Okay," he said. He picked up his glasses and slipped them into his shirt pocket. Then he reached out and started folding up the newspaper. "You're obviously upset, and I understand that. I'm just going to go. I've been here all day anyway. There's no use in both of us being here, especially when they have Ronnie doped up to his eyeballs."

I sat still while he gathered his stuff and pulled his coat on.

Before he stood up, he asked, "What would you do with Ronnie?"

"What do you mean?"

"If Ronnie were placed in your care, what would you do with him? Would you quit school? Hire a babysitter? What?"

"I could make it work. Mom wasn't tied to Ronnie all day. He worked. He was independent."

"Ronnie is who he is today because your mom gave up her life for him," he said. "She was his everything. I don't think anyone else could do that. I know she wanted me to do that for him, to be his guardian. But I don't know if I can really do it. And I'm not sure it would be healthy to live that way." He stood up and zipped his coat. "But I think you knew that without me saying it, right? After all, you didn't make that promise to your mom, did you?"

The words entered me like a needle, sharp and stinging.

He paused a moment. He seemed to be thinking of something else to say. I just wanted him to go. "I'm sorry, Elizabeth," he said. "I just don't think you're in a position to judge anybody."

And with that, he left the hospital.

Chapter Twenty-one

I almost left as well. I only wished I had left before talking to Paul.

When I returned to Ronnie's floor, I saw someone talking to the nurse who had sent me to the cafeteria. As I came down the hall, the nurse made a nodding gesture toward me, as though the man wanted to see me. I assumed he was Ronnie's doctor.

"Ms. Hampton?" he said.

"Elizabeth," I said.

We shook hands. He was a white-haired man in his early sixties. He wore a tie and a sharply pressed shirt and told me his name was Dr. Heil. He placed his shiny gold pen in his shirt pocket.

"Is Ronnie okay?" I asked.

"He's doing fine," he said. "Better than yesterday, as I understand."

"Is there anything I should know?" I asked.

"Well," he said. He pointed to a door that opened off the hallway. It looked like any other patient room, but once we were inside, I saw that it was a consultation room, a place families gathered with doctors to hear bad news about their loved ones. Dr. Heil closed the door and we sat in the upholstered chairs.

"There really isn't much for me to say right now. My role is to examine your brother and make a report available to the police. I'm going to write that up in the next day or two."

"A report about what?" I asked. "If Ronnie is a killer?"

"That's not my job," he said. "I'm not a police officer. No, I'm just here to offer my medical opinion on your brother. And I pass that on to the police. How they decide to act is up to them."

"Is there anything you can tell me?" I asked. "He's been in here a few days already. I don't know what's been happening."

He smiled at me, a comforting grandfatherly smile. He wanted to put me at ease without saying anything he wasn't allowed to say. "As I'm sure you know, your brother is quite high functioning for someone with Down syndrome. It's obvious that someone has taken a great deal of care with him over the years. I'm guessing that's your mother?"

"Yes."

"That's what Ronnie said as well. He's smart, and a good communicator. And understandably, he's a bit overwhelmed by all of this." He leaned forward. "He needs you to be his sister right now. He needs someone just to talk to him and treat him normally. I think you'd be good for that. He thinks very highly of you."

"Does he?" I asked.

I assumed Ronnie didn't think much of me at all, mainly because I knew I had my own wall up with him. I'd let him be Mom's concern over the years and kept my distance, even going so far as to withdraw and stay far away whenever Ronnie had an issue of any kind. I figured he'd picked up on that—he was too smart not to—and took the same approach with me.

"He spoke glowingly of you today," Dr. Heil said. "I think he recognizes what has happened to your family and the position that puts the two of you in." Then he made the simplest state-ment of all, and perhaps the one I most needed to hear. And maybe I heard it better because it came from someone outside the family, an independent authority figure. "You're his closest relative."

I nodded, letting his wisdom sink in.

"I understand what you're saying," I said.

"Good," he said. "You never know how bumpy the road ahead is going to get."

When Dr. Heil was gone, I went in and sat with Ronnie. He was asleep, either as the result of the medication or just because being examined by a head shrinker was enough to wear anyone out. And Ronnie's reserves must have been pretty low at that point.

Even though he didn't know I was there, I felt an obligation to stay a while. But "obligation" wasn't the right word. I *wanted* to stay. I wanted to know he was safe, that no one else was go-ing to come in and bother him or interrogate him. Not as long as I had anything to say about it.

I graded papers while Ronnie slept. The time passed quickly. My phone rang not long after I started grading. It was my land-lord informing me that I had a new door and a dead bolt.

"You should be fine," he told me. He agreed to come by the hospital and bring me the new key, which he did, meeting me at the front door.

Was it just that easy? Bolt the door and sleep tight? My moth-er's house had more locks than Buckingham Palace and look what they had done for her. Sure, I wanted to be there for Ronnie. But I was avoiding something as well. I wasn't looking forward to going home and sleeping in that apartment. I couldn't imagine closing my eyes and not dreaming of someone breaking in again. I wanted to protect Ronnie, but who was going to protect me?

I kept on grading. They brought a tray of food for Ronnie. Some processed meat smothered in gravy, mashed potatoes, sliced pears, and a chocolate milk. Ronnie woke up, probably because he smelled the food. He wasn't a picky eater. I knew he'd love the meat and potatoes, even though the thought of it made my stomach turn a little. And I hadn't eaten much all day.

Ronnie looked surprised to see me. He looked groggy, his eyes heavy lidded and bloodshot. His hair stood up in a swirl as if someone had given it a going-over with an electric mixer. I decided to comb it down for him, but I let him eat first.

We didn't say much to each other initially. As Ronnie ate, he reached for the remote control and turned on the TV. A news show played, a recap of all the disasters in the world. Ronnie watched it while he plowed through the meat and potatoes. He could be like that sometimes—intently focused on the task in front of him, a little removed from the people around him. I don't think it had anything to do with the Down syndrome. I could be the exact same way.

At the first commercial, he turned to me. "You look tired, sis."

"I am."

"You need to sleep," he said.

"I will. I'm trying to get caught up on paper grading."

"Work, work, work," he said, smiling a little. It was good to see that. "Is Paul coming back?" he asked.

"I think he went home for the night," I said. "He was here while the doctor was with you."

"I know. I saw him."

"Did you like talking to the doctor today?" I asked. "Dr. Heil?"

"He was nice."

"What did you two talk about?" I asked.

Ronnie shrugged. The news came back on, a story about wildlife in Africa. Ronnie's eyes were glued to the screen.

"What did he ask you about?"

"A bunch of questions."

"Were they about Mom?"

Ronnie didn't answer. He watched the TV. I thought about reaching for the remote and turning it off. If we were teenagers, I would have done that very thing. But I didn't want to get him angry or upset. He'd had a hellish day as well. But still, I wanted to know what they'd talked about. I felt I had a right. And I remembered what Dr. Heil had said to me just a little bit earlier. It could be a bumpy ride ahead.

Did Ronnie know that?

"And that's it?" I asked. "Nothing else?"

Agitation crept into his voice. "He was nice, sis. I liked him. It's fine."

He turned his attention back to the TV and drank his milk.

I wished I could believe him.

Chapter Twenty-two

I thought of calling Paul as I left Dover Community. It felt too much like those last six weeks with Mom—something unresolved hanging between us. But I was still angry. Just thinking about it—thinking about him—stirred the anger almost to a boil. I trusted him, and so did Mom. Would he really just hand Ronnie over to an institution or a home? Is that why he had been so cavalier about sending Ronnie to the hospital? And when I'd suggested we get a lawyer, that we work to get Ronnie out, Paul was dismissive of the idea.

The sun was setting as I drove to my apartment. The clouds from earlier in the day had parted. A band of orange marked the horizon, and flocks of birds, black specks against the darkening sky, swept past in the distance. Halfway home, I almost picked up the phone and called Dan. I told myself I didn't *need* him. I just wanted him—or someone—to be there with me when I went to the apartment. I tried to convince myself I would have settled for Jeff, the astronomy nerd downstairs. But I knew the truth. I really did want Dan to be there. After the whole long day and the fight with Paul, I wanted Dan to be around.

But I didn't call him. I put the phone down.

I needed to go in alone.

I hurried to make it home before darkness fully fell. I parked the car, but before climbing out I looked all around me. Two runners jogged by. The night looked normal, and when I stepped out, it *felt* normal. Cool and crisp, but normal. I hustled up the stairs. I felt some comfort when I passed Jeff's apartment; a light glowed in the window. I wasn't completely alone. There were other people in the world, people sharing the spaces I inhabited. I just needed to notice them.

The key the landlord gave me worked like a charm. I slipped inside as quickly as I could, locking the dead bolt behind me before I even hit the light. When I turned it on, I saw the mess. I hadn't been home since the night before. I'd forgotten about the condition of the place, the things strewn around, the upended drawers.

I dropped my bag to the floor, overwhelmed by it all.

I'd proved my point to myself. I'd made it home. I felt tears coming again. I didn't want to give in to them.

But I also needed help. I found the phone and called Dan.

True to form, Dan arrived about thirty minutes after I called. And he didn't arrive unarmed. When I undid my new dead bolt lock and opened the door for him, he stood there on my stoop carrying a bag of food from our favorite Thai restaurant. Why did I think I didn't have room in my life for this man? Why did I think I couldn't balance a career and a love life?

He stepped inside and assessed the damage. "It's not as bad as it looks," he said.

"Nothing is as bad as this looks."

First, we ate. He knew what to get me—shrimp fried rice, spring rolls—and I loved every bite. I went to the kitchen and opened beers for us. It was easy to find the opener with the contents of the drawers scattered across the linoleum.

For a few minutes, the food and the drink and the company helped me forget the crappy twenty-four hours I had been through. Dan gave me my space. He didn't ask me a lot of questions, and he avoided the subject of my family and all of their drama. He avoided it so much and so skillfully that I found myself wanting him to ask. As I finished my last bite of food, I tried to send telepathic messages to his brain encouraging him to ask me about my day. About Ronnie. About Paul.

But he didn't know those people. Dan was right. I'd kept the two halves of my life—school and family—separated as if they were warring factions. Yet they weren't—they couldn't be, because they didn't know each other. And if they had met, it would have been fine. My family—especially my mother—would have been thrilled if I'd brought a nice, normal-looking guy home to meet her. She would have been glad there was a chance I might not spend my life alone. Mom was a little old-fashioned and worried about those things. But it didn't matter to me. I tried to keep things simple and easy. For me, if not for anyone else. Now Mom would never meet that man, whoever he turned out to be. I tried not to think of that either.

When we were finished eating, Dan, ever the chipper taskmaster, stood up. "Want to get started on this mess?" he asked.

He didn't wait for a response. I suspected he was trying to keep the evening's momentum moving forward. He probably feared a pause, a moment in which I could turn to him and announce that it was time for him to go. He didn't know how happy I was to see him there.

And he had been right about the mess. It wasn't as bad as it looked. It was a mess, but it was a simple mess. Hardly anything was broken. Things just needed to be put back in their places, which we managed to do, working together. We still didn't say much, except when Dan asked me questions about where to put things. It took about an hour. A lamp I had purchased from Goodwill had its bulb broken. An old calculator I used to figure grades was smashed. And near the end, right when everything was pretty much put back in order, Dan handed me a framed photo. It showed Mom, Paul, Ronnie, and me. The glass was shattered. It looked as if someone had dropped a brick on it. I shook the shards of glass loose. We all looked happy for some reason. I remembered the photo being taken about three years earlier, not long after I had graduated from college and a couple of years after Dad had died.

"Be careful," Dan said.

I stared at the photo a long time, felt the tears starting to come, and fought them off. But I couldn't hide it from Dan.

"It doesn't look like the photo's damaged," he said. "And we can buy a new frame for it."

We, he said. Always willing to share the load.

"It's not this," I said.

"What isn't?" he asked.

"Everything." I put the photo down. "Remember that talk we had on the night of the funeral? The one about how cut off I was from my family?"

"Sure," he said.

"I'm not getting any better," I said. "I'm getting worse."

"In two days? You can't expect—"

I cut him off. I didn't want to be encouraged or placated. I took him by the hand, and we went over to the couch. After we sat down and got settled, I told him about Paul encouraging my mom to have Ronnie put somewhere and how that led to the argument I had with Paul at the hospital. Dan listened patiently, nodding as I went through blow by blow. When I was finished, he didn't say anything. He sipped from his beer.

"Well?" I said.

"You're both under a lot of stress," he said. "It's no surprise you might blow up at each other. Families fight."

"You're not getting it," I said.

"Okay. What am I not getting?"

I started to say it, then stopped. Then I went ahead and said it. "This is something else about my family I'm learning after the fact. Isn't that crazy?"

"Like I said, it's only been a couple of days you've been thinking about this."

"That's not true," I said. "I've been thinking about this a long time. Maybe since I was in high school. Or when my dad died."

"Thinking about what?"

"About being alone," I said. "Do you realize my mother died alone? I know she had Ronnie. And she had Paul."

"And you."

I ignored him. "She didn't have friends. She didn't share her life with anyone."

"She was a widow," Dan said. "Unfortunately, that's not unusual for someone her age. Especially women."

"But she'd always been alone. Few friends. Just her family. My dad was a little better, but he didn't have much of a life. And now I'm turning into them. If I died today, who would care? If I'd been home when that man broke in here, and he'd put a pillow over my face while I slept, who would care?"

"Aren't you being a little dramatic?" Dan asked. "Lots of people would care."

"Really care?" I asked. "Really?"

"I would," he said. "Remember? I'd miss the sex."

"And I've cut you out of my life, right?" I said. "Until I needed something? And now Paul, my only family left besides Ronnie. Everything with him is screwed up."

"It's one fight. Families fight."

"You're so logical. And calm."

"Somebody has to be."

I stood up and walked over to the kitchen. I opened the refrigerator and stared at the beer, but I didn't take one. I didn't feel like it just then. I wanted my head to remain clear. It held enough clutter at that moment. I didn't need to add to it.

I came back to the couch and sat again.

"I don't want to die alone," I said.

"I don't think you're the only person who feels that way."

"But I'm in danger of having it happen to me, right? You're not. You have a ton of friends. And family. Everybody likes you."

"You shouldn't feel like you're just turning to me because you've had a crisis in your life."

"Why not?"

"Well, okay, you should recognize that you're doing that. After all, we both know you only came by the other night because of the crisis, right? And, really, I'm only here because someone broke in."

"Are you trying to make me feel better or worse?" I asked.

"What I'm saying is, just because that led you to call me doesn't mean it isn't a real change. Sometimes it takes a crisis to drive us in a certain direction. Right?"

I let his words sink in. He looked so calm saying them to me, so rational and smart. So comforting. I felt better. Not a lot better, but better.

"You're saying there's hope for me?"

"Always," he said.

"Thanks," I said.

Dan looked around the apartment, surveying the work we had done. He nodded his head in satisfaction.

"I'm glad you have the real lock now," he said. "That helps."

"You don't think anyone can get through that?" I asked.

"No way. Maybe the Incredible Hulk could, but not a petty thief."

"Good."

"Well," he said. "I know you have papers to grade."

He started to stand up, but before he could get all the way, I reached out and took his hand in mine.

"You don't have to run off," I said.

"Really?"

"Really."

He eased back down onto the couch. "I was hoping you might say that." He patted his pocket. "I even brought my toothbrush with me."

Chapter Twenty-three

A knock on the door of the apartment woke us up the next morning. Our bodies were entwined along with the sheets, and it took several moments for me to figure out what the noise was. Then I dug my way out of the tangle.

"Who's that?" Dan asked.

"I don't know."

And I didn't. No one ever came to my door. Even Girl Scouts selling cookies and Jehovah's Witnesses peddling salvation didn't bother to make the trek up the stairs to where I lived. Which helped make the junkie break-in theory all the more implausible to me. I was out of the way. It would take an ambitious junkie to find my door.

I checked my phone. Seven fifty-one a.m. And I had a message.

But the knock came again. First things first. I found a robe and pulled it on.

"Do you want me to go?" Dan asked.

He was naked, his skin pale and goosefleshed in the morning chill.

"If I scream, come out there," I said.

"Do I have to get dressed first?"

"That's up to you."

I trudged through my newly clean apartment to the front door. I looked out the peephole. The morning light was bright and my vision was still blurry from sleep. It took a moment for the figure to resolve into something clear and coherent. When it did, I saw a young guy not much older than me, wearing a coat and tie. His hair looked to be thinning, and he held an envelope in his hand. He looked familiar.

Cop? I thought. *No. Doctor? No.*

Who else had I been dealing with? Then I remembered—he was from the funeral home. And unless he was going door-to-door to create new business, I was probably safe.

I opened the door. He looked me over from head to toe. The disheveled hair, bare feet, and robe. His face flushed.

"Oh, excuse me," he said. "I'm sorry. I called."

"It's okay," I said. "I always look like this in the morning."

He held the envelope toward me. "This is your mother's death certificate. I was on my way by here . . ."

"Oh."

I took it from him.

"You need it to file the will and send the estate into probate. We thought you'd be moving along with those things."

I hadn't been, of course. But hearing him say that made me think of the whole list of tasks that needed to be addressed. The will, the house, Mom's car. I remembered the call from Mom's lawyer. Clearly other people were eager to move forward as well. Who they were I didn't know, but it might make sense to start the process.

"Thanks," I said.

"Was there anything else we can help you with?" he asked.

He looked so eager to serve, so happy to be doing his job. Not the stereotype of the grim mortician at all. I wanted there to be another task, something else that needed to be done on Mom's behalf.

"And we don't owe you anything?" I asked.

"That's all been taken care of as part of your mother's pre-planning," he said.

"Right. Of course."

We stood there, the two of us, in the bright morning sunshine. The air was cool. I could feel it on my bare feet.

"So there's nothing else?" he asked.

"I guess just this," I said, holding up the envelope.

"Your lawyer will take you through all of that," he said.

I couldn't think of anything else to say, and he took that opportunity to turn and head back down the rickety steps. The formal process of burying and saying good-bye to Mom was basically over. It was time to move on.

Dan needed to leave. He needed to go home and get ready for his Friday classes. When he said he'd brought his toothbrush with him, he was lying. He hadn't anticipated spending the night at all. I told him about the delivery of the death certificate but not the feelings it evoked inside me. I didn't have to. Dan read my moods as easily as stepping outside to see whether it was night or day.

"What would your mom want you to do?" he asked.

"What do you mean?"

"Would she want you to keep delaying things? Or would she want her estate wrapped up as quickly as possible?"

I knew the answer. When Dan was gone, I called the lawyer. Mr. Allison had an appointment available that afternoon, after I was done with school.

I agreed to it. Then I got ready and left for campus.

Chapter Twenty-four

I arrived right on time for my four-thirty appointment with the lawyer. The school day had passed uneventfully. I faced my class and told them once again that I didn't have their essays graded. They grumbled a little, and I realized that the shelf life of students giving their teacher a break because the teacher's mother had been murdered was getting shorter and shorter. Moving on with the estate business and putting everything to rest would be good, for my own psyche and for my professional career. I couldn't do much of anything about Ronnie, but I could take care of the things I still had some measure of control over.

Mr. Allison's elderly secretary, her hair pulled into a tight bun, told me to wait, so I sat in an uncomfortable leather chair. I didn't read any of the magazines or play with my phone. Instead, I watched the secretary at her desk. She looked to be my mother's age or older, and I silently questioned the universe, asking it why this woman lived while my mother was gone. My anger grew—a slow churning in my chest—and I knew I had started down an unproductive and hurtful mental path. Just to distract myself, I picked up the first magazine I could reach, a copy of *Sports Illustrated* with a hulking football player on the cover. I flipped through it, past ads to help men with erectile dysfunction and high cholesterol. The phone on the secretary's desk buzzed, and she stood up and asked me to follow her.

I had never met Mom's lawyer. I knew that when Dad died everything had gone to Mom. It wasn't much. The house, the car, and a life insurance policy. Mom kept information about her finances to herself, so I never knew how much the life insurance policy paid out. Mom certainly didn't change her lifestyle once Dad was gone, so I assumed that the money sat in a bank account somewhere accumulating a safe, steady return.

Frank Allison waited for me just inside his office door. He had a broad face and thinning white hair, which he combed back. His cheeks were a little ruddy, as if he'd just been out in a cold wind, and he wore a white shirt, dark tie, and suspenders. He shook my hand when I came in and offered his condolences while he guided me to a seat. He was over six feet tall and built solidly, and when he sat down behind the desk he let out a little grunt as though the very act of returning his butt to the chair required a lot of effort. The secretary closed the door when she left.

"I know this is a difficult time," Frank Allison said. "But you're smart to get the ball rolling on this." He pulled out a pair of rimless glasses and set them on the end of his nose. "This death business can be a little like getting nibbled to death by ducks, but my job is to help you get through it."

"Thanks."

"We'll get this all square for you in a couple of shakes."

Before I'd entered his office, I wouldn't have believed folksiness could be a cure for anything, but just a few minutes in the presence of Frank Allison, and I started to calm down. It didn't hurt that the wall behind him was covered with pictures of his children and grandchildren and even one of Mr. Allison himself in a Santa suit, the beard pulled down to reveal his smiling face.

"I have a copy of the will," I said. "It was in among Mom's personal effects when she died."

"Your mother was very practical," he said, spreading some papers out on his desk. "She didn't want to burden her children with anything, so she tried to make it easy. You have the death certificate, right?"

I handed it over. Mr. Allison studied it, his lips pressed together. He shook his head.

"I just don't know where we're headed when these kinds of things happen," he said, tapping the certificate with a big finger. "Your mother was a nice lady, very warm."

He looked up at me and smiled, his lips spreading across his broad face.

"Thank you," I said. No one had ever described my mother as warm, but I knew he was trying to be nice, so I accepted it. Superficial comments were welcome, even encouraged.

Mr. Allison lifted a packet of papers backed by a light blue piece of cardboard. "Here's the will," he said, handing it over to me. "It's all pretty cut-and-dried. I'll give you a moment to look it over if you'd like."

"I already have one," I said, holding up the papers.

"Oh, that's right. You did say that." He adjusted his glasses. "Well, you don't have to doubt those were her most recent wishes. If you look at the last page, you'll see she updated the will just about a month ago."

I froze. "She did?"

"Indeed," he said.

"Did she change things?" I flipped through the copy sitting

in my lap and checked the date on the last page. It was old. "This one is from two years ago," I said.

"You don't say," Mr. Allison said. He chuckled a little. "Well, maybe your mother has a surprise or two inside of her. Can I see that?"

"She changed it a month ago?" I asked. The volume of my voice had dropped. When I handed the copy of the will—the old will—over to Mr. Allison, my hand shook ever so slightly. It felt as if those few pages of white legal paper weighed twenty-five pounds.

"That's right."

A month. Right after our fight. Mr. Allison had possession of the last words my mother would ever speak to me in the form of her bequests, and I had no idea what she might have to say—if anything. Would I finally find out what she really thought about my refusal to care for Ronnie? Would she cut me out entirely?

"Is it changed a lot?" I asked.

"Oh, she rearranged the furniture a little." He must have noticed my shakiness, because he pointed to a copy of the will on his desk, then said, "Would you like me to explain what all this means?"

"Yes, please."

"All righty," he said, adjusting the glasses again. He took the old will, the one I had brought, and tossed it onto the table behind him. "We don't need that." He picked up the new one and handed it over to me. "The first page there just says all the typical gobbledygook that we have to say. Your mom's of sound mind and body and a resident of this county and that this will supersedes any previous will she might have made. That's how we know this one will stand up. The latest one signed by the person is the one that counts. Everything else is null and void."

"Okay," I said. I took the copy of the new will and scanned the first page. The words all ran together and meant nothing to me.

"Then, on the second page there, you see that your mom directed that all of her property and assets, including any insurance policies she might have, be divided into three equal shares. Again, all pretty standard. If you go to the next page . . ."

But I wasn't listening to him anymore. My eyes were stuck on the second page and the section where it named the recipients of the equal shares of Mom's estate.

"Hold on," I said, raising my index finger.

"What is it?" Mr. Allison asked.

"Who is this person?" I asked.

He looked up from his copy of the will. "Which person?"

I saw three names listed. Mine, Ronnie's, and one more. I was relieved to see my name listed. I hadn't been cut out. But someone else was included. Added, I should say. A name that wasn't in the will Mom had in her drawer at home, the one I found the night she died.

"This," I said. "Elizabeth Yarbrough. Who's that and why is she in Mom's will?"

"You don't know who she is?" he asked.

I sat back in my chair and tried to think. I ran through the names of every relative I could think of—and there weren't that many. Dad was an only child. My grandparents were dead. And then there was Paul and Ronnie and me. As far as friends . . . I think every single one of them was at the funeral, and I didn't remember that name—Elizabeth Yarbrough—although it could have slipped past me.

"Is she a friend of my mother's?" I asked.

Mr. Allison frowned a little. He dug around on his desk and

pulled out a manila folder. "You know what I do now that I'm getting older? I take notes whenever I talk with a client, just in case something like this comes up." He flipped the folder open. "Here we go." He read over something in the folder. "It just says here your mom came in and made this change to her will, adding this Elizabeth Yarbrough woman as one of her beneficiaries."

"Did my mom say why?" I asked.

"No, ma'am. It says here that I asked your mom who this Yarbrough woman was. A friend or a relative. Your mom just said she was somebody close to the family, and I let it go at that." He closed the folder. "You know, I've handled your parents' wills and things since you were born. Neither one of them was very rash or impulsive. If your mom said she wanted to make a change like this, I figured she meant it. I try not to argue with women who know their minds."

"Doesn't she have to tell you who she's leaving money to?" I asked. "You're the lawyer drawing it up."

"She's under no obligation to tell me anything, even if I am her lawyer. It's a family will. It's not the Magna Carta. Now, if someone wants to contest it, that's another matter."

"No, no," I said. "I'm not saying that." I stared down at the paper again, at that name. My first name too. My chest felt hollow. Here was something else I apparently didn't know about Mom.

Mr. Allison said, "It says right there Elizabeth Yarbrough of Reston Point, Ohio. That's about an hour from here. Does your mom have any people there?"

"No," I said. "She's from Haxton."

"That's the other way," Mr. Allison said. He scratched his chin. "You know what I'm thinking, don't you?"

"That Elizabeth Yarbrough is the person who called you on the phone the other day?"

"Exactly," he said. "She must have known, or suspected, that she was going to be named here. Your mother must have told her about that, and she must have known your mother had died. Of course, anyone could find that information out."

I remembered the phone call, the one that had come on the day of Mom's funeral. The woman said she was just getting to know Mom but couldn't make it to the service. She didn't give her name.

"I guess we'll hear from her again," I said.

He tapped the will with his index finger. "Do you want to look at the next page? There's a provision for custody and care of your brother, who I believe has some special needs." I turned the page, and he said, "As you can see, your mother named you guardian of your brother and placed his share of the estate in trust to be managed and controlled by you. A little farther down, you'll see she named you as executrix as well. She certainly had a lot of faith in you, and I bet that gave her a lot of peace."

"But—" I stopped myself. I knew Mom didn't have much faith in me, which is why she needed to beg for my promise to care for Ronnie. In the end, it didn't matter. She had given that responsibility to me whether I wanted it, or even felt up to it. "This is a change as well. My uncle was supposed to be Ronnie's guardian. That's how it was in the other will."

Mr. Allison opened the folder again. He read off the paper, his lips moving ever so slightly as he did so. "It is," he said. "Your mom transferred the guardianship from your uncle to you. And your mom was pretty clear about that, according to my notes. She said she felt her brother was getting on in years, and she wanted the peace of mind of knowing someone would always be around for your brother. So that's you."

"You know my uncle, right?"

"Paul? I do. He's a good man. Schoolteacher, right?"

"Retired."

"I guess he's about that age. What about him?"

"I don't . . . I guess I need to talk to him about all this."

"You don't *have* to," he said. "He's not named anywhere in this document. Of course, you're welcome to explain things to anyone in the family if you so desire. But like I said, your mom knew her mind."

"My mom didn't tell me she was naming me Ronnie's guardian," I said. "Why didn't I have to sign anything or fill out any forms? Wouldn't I have to do something like that?"

"I figured she told you," he said. "Usually the person making the will hashes that out with the guardian before coming in here. Besides, you're his sister, right? There's just you and your uncle. Who else would be taking care of him?"

"Right. I've even thought about how I could make it work. I'm in school full-time. Graduate school. It's going to require some juggling."

"Most things do." He scratched his chin again. "Your brother is over eighteen. He's an adult. A disabled adult, but an adult. He doesn't have to live with you. You don't have to be his full-time caretaker. There are homes where folks like your brother live pretty independently."

"I know. I'm aware of that."

"All I'm saying is that you have options. Part of the reason you didn't have to sign anything or write your name down in blood is because your brother is an adult. This isn't like someone left an infant on your doorstep."

I put the will back on his desk. I sat still, letting it all sink in. Paul had been cut out. If he'd suggested to Mom that she send

Ronnie away, I could see Mom taking that step. Maybe. Even for Mom, it was pretty harsh, but still. She had little tolerance for anyone who crossed her about Ronnie. And I had no idea who Elizabeth Yarbrough was, but at least I hadn't been disinherited. "Is there anything else in there?" I asked. "I mean, did she leave any notes or letters? Any instructions?"

"If she did, they're not with me," he said. "You can check for a safe-deposit box or something like that. Maybe she said something there. But I just handled the will."

I let out a deep breath. I hadn't even known I'd been holding it in.

"It's a lot to take on," he said.

"Yeah," I said. "You know, my brother . . . he's in the hospital right now."

"I'm sorry," he said. "I heard about that too."

"He's in Dover Community being examined."

"I see."

"The police ordered it," I said. "They have some questions about Ronnie's behavior as it relates to my mother's death. They're trying to determine if it's possible that Ronnie was involved in some way."

Mr. Allison was a professional who had probably heard all manner of strange admissions coming across his desk. "I see," he said again.

"Did my mother ever mention being afraid of Ronnie?" I asked. "Did she ever try to . . . I don't know . . . have something done for him?"

Mr. Allison was shaking his head before I even finished the question. "Never," he said. "Didn't even hint at it. Again, that's just what I know, but she never said any such thing."

His words brought me some relief. But they also left me standing on square one. "Do you have any advice about the situation?" I asked.

"I don't do criminal law," he said. "With someone like your brother, someone who has those special needs, the police have to tread carefully. They don't always, but they're supposed to. Chances are the medical exam is a pretext to give them cover. They know where your brother is, they can watch him, and, yes, they want the shrink to look him over and see if he does have any violent tendencies. But, really, they're probably trying to make a case. Bottom line—they can't just keep him there forever. Once the exam is over, they have to release him or charge him. You should keep an eye on what they're doing, and if they sit on the pot too long, insist he be released. If it comes to that, I'd be happy to help you. Did they examine him yet?"

"A doctor did yesterday," I said. "He said he was writing up a report for the police."

"Then there you go. I'd expect you'll know something pretty soon. If you don't, then call me and we'll give the police a little goose." He punctuated the sentence by jabbing upward into the air with his thumb.

"Thanks," I said.

"In the meantime, I'll file the will and get it into probate. As the executrix, you should start going through your mother's things. Bank records, insurance policies, all of that. Find out what she has to divvy up."

"Is that all I have to do?" I asked.

"You have to make sure it all ends up in the right hands," he said. "Meaning you have to find this Elizabeth Yarbrough."

"Do you have her address?" I asked.

He shook his head. "Your mom didn't leave it. I figured it was a family member or close friend."

"What if I don't find her?" I asked. "She could be anywhere."

"I suspect she's nearby," he said. "It's a bit of conflict of interest, right? You could say to yourself, 'Hey, let's not look for her too hard. More for me.' Right?"

"I hadn't thought of that," I said.

"I'm teasing," he said. "But some people do think that way. Look, take it from me—if your mother put this woman's name in the will, then she's probably expecting something. Someone called here asking about your mother's will. Don't you think that's our mystery woman? I suspect she'll turn up. Go through your mom's things. Address book. Computer files. You know this woman lives in Reston Point. If all else fails, I'd open up the phone book."

Chapter Twenty-five

I drove away from the lawyer's office with that name tumbling around in my head. Elizabeth Yarbrough. Something about this woman drove my mother to show up at her lawyer's office just a month earlier and include her in the will. And Mom did this shortly after I refused to give her the promise about Ronnie's care that she wanted. Were the two events linked somehow?

I wanted to call Paul. I figured there was a good chance he knew who Elizabeth Yarbrough was. If he didn't know, I wasn't sure anybody did. And I suppose I wanted to tell him about the changes to the will, the differences between the one we read at Mom's house and the one she'd updated with Mr. Allison. More than anything, I wanted to hear the sound of his voice again. I couldn't even say who needed to apologize to whom. I didn't care. I just wanted things to be back to normal.

Humility and apology didn't come easy to me. It should stand as a measure of how much I cared for Paul that I dialed his number. While it rang, my heart thumped.

But the call went straight to his voice mail, my uncle's polite, Midwestern tone asking me to please leave a message. It made me feel weak to experience relief at the sound of the greeting, but I did. I even considered—briefly—not leaving a message.

But the cell phone didn't allow us to hide from people. He'd still receive a missed-call notification with my name attached to it, so I plowed ahead.

"Hi," I said. Then I was stuck. Apologize? I shook my head. *No*, I told myself, *just be normal*. "I'm driving away from the lawyer's office. I thought you might want to know some of the things we talked about with the will and everything. So . . . okay. I'll talk to you soon."

I hoped he'd call me back.

My mother once cleaned my room for me when I was seven. Admittedly, I liked messes as a child. I threw my clothes and toys on the floor with no regard for a system. I grew to hate messes as I became a teenager and then an adult, but back then—look out. My bedroom resembled a yard sale. So Mom insisted on cleaning it for me. And I suffered for it, in the way only a kid could suffer. Mom developed a simple system: She picked up a toy or an article of clothing and asked me the last time I had used it or worn it. If it had been more than a year, she put the item in a box. I didn't catch on fast enough because when we were finished—and the room was clean to Mom's standards—she took the box to the Salvation Army. I cried to my dad about it that night. He was always the softer of the two, the more tolerant of the emotional torrents of a young girl's life, and he held me in his lap while I soaked his neck with tears.

But when I was finished, when I had cried it out, he asked me a simple question: "Why are you crying over things you really didn't want anymore and had probably outgrown?"

He stumped my seven-year-old brain back then, but as I got older the wisdom of what he said sank in. He really wanted me to not let the past control me, to not stop forward progress for the sake of looking back. And Mom taught me that as well. When something outlived its usefulness, she let it go without regret. Without emotion. I had even allowed myself, just for a few moments in the lawyer's office, to think she might have extended that philosophy to me and cut me out of her will.

But I was foolish to think Mom would ever do that to Ronnie or me. She was a great mother, and she loved both of us far too much.

Mom's house reflected her streamlined, unadorned philosophy of existence. It was almost six, and the route back to my apartment took me right past Mom's street. I hadn't planned on going there, but the thought of looking through some of Mom's things—and maybe, just maybe, getting a clue as to who Elizabeth Yarbrough was—proved to be too tempting. If Mom changed the will just one month earlier, then it stood to reason there might be recent evidence of interactions with this woman. A phone number. Letters. A gift or a card.

I turned down Mom's quiet little street and pulled into her driveway. I sat in the car for a moment, contemplating the scene. The police told me I could go back inside if I needed but to not spend a great deal of time in there. They had finished with it as a crime scene but could require access to the house for follow-up at any future point in the investigation. I remembered so many things about that house. Mornings being hustled off to school, the smell of pancakes and bacon in the air. The little swing set in the backyard, which was taken down when Ronnie and I became teenagers. I sneaked out the back door more than once in high school, meeting up with friends in the middle of the night, even though we really didn't have anything to do.

In the wake of Mom's death, the house looked, for lack of a better word, dead. The blinds were closed, the flowers on the porch wilting and dying of neglect in the early fall. It wasn't that my mother kept the most vibrant or ostentatious house—quite the opposite in fact—but without anyone living there, without any life inside, the house seemed noticeably deflated. It reeked of absence.

I didn't know whether I could will myself to go in. I knew officers had checked the house the day before while I sat with Detective Post, and just sitting there in the driveway, with the sun starting to set and the shadows lengthening, I couldn't see any sign that anything had been disturbed. It seemed fanciful and even childish to think that some kind of boogeyman waited inside, hiding behind a door or inside a closet, eager to spring out at me and club me over the head. Fanciful and childish except for the fact that a boogeyman had already visited this house and killed my mother. At least I hoped it had been a visitor and not someone who already lived there. Add to that the break-in at my own apartment and it started to seem unwise for me to enter the empty house alone.

But just enough daylight remained. I carried my cell phone with me, ready to call for help at the first sign of trouble. If the doors were still locked, if there were no signs of disturbance, why shouldn't I go in? I remembered what Dan had said the night before: *What would your mom want you to do?* She'd want the matter resolved, and she wouldn't want to have a daughter who was afraid of her own shadow. Besides, she had left the gaping mystery right there in her will, and named me the executor of the whole thing. If she didn't want me to dig around and investigate after her death, she should have told me herself what was going on.

Maybe she would have if the two of you had been speaking to each other . . .

"Shut up," I said to the little voice in my head. To all those voices.

I paused on the front porch. My keys jingled at my side, the spare to Mom's house separated from the rest and held between my thumb and index finger. I looked up and down the street, realizing as I did so that I was making myself look as suspicious as a burglar. I didn't see anybody or anything. The sun's rays were elongating, stretching through the trees and into the back of Mom's yard. Soon, I knew, we'd likely have to put the house on the market. I doubted that my small graduate stipend could even pay the taxes, let alone what remained of the mortgage. And if the house was gone, what sense of my mother would be left? Between that and Ronnie's hospitalization and my fight with Paul, it felt as though everything was slipping away. For so long I'd held my family at arm's length, only to find out how much I wanted them near me once I risked losing them.

I slipped the key into the lock, still stained with fingerprint powder. The lock turned with only a little resistance, and I stepped inside the darkened living room. I went directly to the windows that looked out onto the street and pulled the blinds up, letting in the light that still remained of the day. It was a fair amount, and immediately the house felt less stuffy, less claustrophobic and close.

I stood by the front door and called out, "Hello?"

There was no response. But what had I expected? Would a burglar or a killer hiding in the dark really answer me?

Undeterred, I said it again. "Hello? Anyone? Hello?"

It made me feel good to hear my voice rattling through the house. Any human sound, even one generated by me, brought a small measure of ease and comfort. I didn't know where to start. I wasn't even sure what I was looking for. Mr. Allison had said that at some point I would need bank statements and insurance policy information, a total accounting of Mom's assets and liabilities. But I was less interested in that. I thought I needed to find something more personal.

"Okay," I said to no one in particular. "Let's do this thing."

I eased down the short hallway, the one that led back to the bedrooms. When I passed the open door to Ronnie's room on my left, I looked inside. Nothing seemed out of place or disturbed. I resisted the temptation to go in there and peek in the closet or drop down on all fours and check for monsters under the bed. I went past the bathroom on the right, then reached Mom's room. I stood in the doorway, waiting and staring, before I went in. I knew I had been in there the other night, talking to Paul, but being in there alone raised a chill on the back of my neck. If ever I was going to turn and run and leave my investigating for another day, it would have been then. But I fought back against the anxiety and stepped into the room where my mother died.

I started in the most obvious places. I went through the drawers of her dresser, finding mostly clothes. As I pawed through them, I realized they had no use anymore, not for my mother anyway. They needed to be gathered together, boxed up, and sent to a charity. I added that task to my mental list of things to do. And I knew Mom would have wanted it done. Within a week of Dad's death, his clothes were out of the closet. Life moves on, Mom would say.

I found more of the same in her closet, which is to say— nothing. Clothes. Lots of clothes. Simple, unadorned, old-lady clothes. I saw shirts that my mother had been wearing for close to twenty years, ever since I was a child. The closet held a few more personal items, mostly relating to Ronnie or me. Old report cards, silly drawings we made and brought home to her. There were a few photos in a box—all stuff I'd seen before. And no mention of anyone named Elizabeth Yarbrough. I checked the nightstand again, the place where I'd found the will. There was nothing else.

I stopped and stood still in the middle of the room. Something else occurred to me. Not only was I not finding anything about Elizabeth Yarbrough, I wasn't finding anything about my mother's past at all. *Nothing* about the years before she met my father and gave birth to Ronnie and me. No high school yearbooks, no letters from old friends. Nothing even about Paul. I'd never seen those things in the house. Mom never talked about the past. She acted as if the world began the day she married Dad. As I looked around the house, it seemed to be true.

I moved my search out to the living room, to the coat closet in the entryway. As I dug around in there, finding nothing but heavy winter clothes and a box of scarves and gloves, I reflected on how little I really knew about my mother. As a teenager, I'd assumed what all teenagers assume—Mom and Dad just didn't have lives before I was born. Now I realized how silly that was. Mom didn't give birth to Ronnie until she was forty-two. She'd married Dad at forty. She'd mentioned having jobs and never finding the right guy until she met Dad, but in those years she'd obviously lived a life of some kind. And judging from what I was seeing, it appeared my mom hadn't documented it.

Having my face buried in the closet made me hot, so I took a break and sat on the couch. My anxiety about being in the house alone had eased. Other concerns had taken over my mind, but as

I sat still on the couch some of those fears crept back over me. The house—even with the curtains open, even with me inside it—felt like a tomb, an abandoned, used-up space. And I felt like an intruder, violating that space as I dug around. Why should I feel that way in my own mother's home?

I pulled out my phone and checked the white pages for "Elizabeth Yarbrough" in Reston Point, Ohio. No listing, so I tried a Google search for "Elizabeth Yarbrough." A lot of stuff came up, but nothing of use. High school girls on MySpace and Facebook. An obituary for a ninety-three-year-old woman in Kansas. I tried "Elizabeth Yarbrough Reston Point." Again, nothing promising. As a last resort, I entered Mom's name and Elizabeth's name. Still nothing.

I looked up another phone number, this one right in Dover. She was easy to find, and I dialed. When she answered, I said, "Hello? Mrs. Porter?"

"Yes?"

"This is Elizabeth Hampton. Leslie's daughter."

"I know who you are," she said. Her voice sounded a little haughty, as though my clarification had insulted her intelligence. Maybe so, but I was just trying to be clear.

"I'm sorry to bother you, but—"

"It's no bother," she said, her voice brightening. "I wanted to tell you I was thinking of starting a little memorial fund at the library in your mom's honor. She loved the library so much."

"That would be very nice." I held my tongue and didn't mention that Mom's obituary instructed any memorials to be made to the local chapter of a Down syndrome support group. I needed Mrs. Porter on my side. "I was wondering if my mom ever mentioned someone named Elizabeth Yarbrough to you."

"Is this a friend of hers?" Mrs. Porter asked.

"I'm not sure," I said. "I thought maybe you'd know."

"Did you find her name in your mom's things?"

Who's asking the questions here, you or me? I wanted to ask. "Something like that," I said instead.

"What's the name again?" she asked.

"Elizabeth Yarbrough."

A long pause. "Hmm. That doesn't ring a bell with me," she said.

"Well, thanks. And thanks for the memorial for Mom."

"I did think of something else after your mom's funeral," Mrs. Porter said.

"Yeah?"

"Remember I told you I hadn't seen your mom in about a month? She liked to come in once or twice a week with your brother."

"I remember," I said. "You said she came in alone and was in a hurry to get to an appointment."

"Right. Well, I remember something else we talked about that day. I remembered it last night as I was dozing off."

"What's that?"

"You know your mom liked to educate herself. She read every book she could get her hands on about Down syndrome. And when she'd read all of ours, she requested them from other libraries around the state. She read every new book that came out on the subject."

"She was thorough," I said.

"Well, that last time she came in she asked for a book on a different subject. Not Down syndrome. I can't remember the name of it, but I thought it was an odd thing for her to be looking for."

Something tingled at the base of my skull. "What was the book about?" I asked.

"Something to do with childhood trauma," Mrs. Porter said. "I know . . . it was something like helping an adult deal with childhood trauma. Does that mean anything to you?"

I sat forward on the couch. The phone shook in my hand. I answered Mrs. Porter with complete honesty.

"I have no idea why she'd want that at all."

Chapter Twenty-six

I sat on the couch holding the phone in my lap. *Helping an adult deal with childhood trauma?* Who could the book be for? Ronnie had Down syndrome, but he hadn't suffered trauma. Not that I knew of. Those five words seemed to be the qualifier I needed to add to everything I said or thought about my mother since her death. *Not that I knew of.* Had Ronnie been abused or subjected to something awful that I didn't know about? A kid with Down syndrome—or any disability—was ripe for being preyed on. My grip on the phone tightened just thinking about it.

Could it have been something else? Had Mom been abused or traumatized? Her generation didn't talk about those things as much. Could she have just started to come to grips with it before she died?

The possibility of those things twisted inside me like a rusty knife. If someone hurt one of them . . . if someone had taken advantage of or abused a member of my family . . . I just couldn't imagine. My chest felt compacted, as if someone had placed me in a vise and squeezed, pressing the organs together, crushing bone against flesh until I had no air.

I sat there with my head down, squeezing the phone between my hands, until the pressure in my chest eased. I took deep breaths that sounded close to sobs. They broke the stillness of the house like shattering glass.

What do I do with this knowledge? I asked myself.

I tried to tame my emotions. I tried to let the logical part of my brain have its say.

Just because she wanted the book didn't mean it was about her. Or Ronnie. Maybe she was just curious. Maybe she had heard about it on TV. The logic didn't help much. I knew Mom. She didn't pursue knowledge just for the sake of knowledge. She pursued knowledge in order to *apply* it. She *used* what she learned.

I looked at the phone. Paul. Would he know? And if he did, why had *he* kept it a secret from me?

I dialed his number. Again I heard his voice mail greeting. I didn't leave a message. The truth was, I just didn't know what to do.

I went out to the kitchen. In a drawer next to the telephone, Mom kept stacks of mail. Mostly, it was stuff she hadn't gone through yet. Credit card offers, coupons, magazines, occasionally a bill she hadn't paid. Things cycled through that drawer pretty quickly thanks to Mom's thoroughness, but if something had arrived in the house in the days before she died, there was a chance she hadn't tended to it yet.

I grabbed a handful of the mail. I flipped through it, my eyes not really registering the things as I did so. I was still thinking about my conversation with Mrs. Porter and that book she mentioned. It was eating away at me, a slow scratching at the base of my skull. I was so distracted I almost missed the bank statement the first time I passed by it. Some part of my subconscious must have registered the name of the bank because after I'd paged through a few more letters, it clicked. I stopped, flipped back, and found the bank statement. I dropped the other mail without thinking.

I slid my finger under the flap, tearing the envelope as I moved along. Mom would have chastised me for not using a letter opener and making a neat, narrow slit in the envelope. But I was rushing, so much so that my hands shook. I pulled the statement out of the envelope and flipped the folded paper open.

I scanned the numbers quickly. Mom maintained a decent minimum balance—at least decent in the eyes of a poor graduate student—of about two thousand dollars at all times. Her checks and debit card payments didn't look unusual. Small to moderate amounts that I imagined went for food, utilities, Ronnie's speech therapy, and things like that. I flipped to the second page and then the third. Still nothing.

Then I saw the last page. Mom's savings account. The balance surprised me—just over thirty thousand dollars. I hadn't realized Mom had so much cash at her disposal. I assumed most of it came from Dad's life insurance policy. I wasn't sure how much the policy was worth when he died, but I assumed it was at least one hundred thousand or so. It only made sense. I thought, looking at the balance, that Mom must have kept a certain amount in a savings account in the event of emergencies, and I hoped the rest had been invested somewhere safe. I'd find out soon enough when I began digging through the rest of her things.

But before I folded the papers and returned them to the envelope, another number caught my eye: $14,550. That number appeared in an entry at the bottom of the page under "Yearly Debits to Date." So far that year Mom had withdrawn over fourteen thousand dollars from her savings account.

What for?

I thought back over the previous year. Had Mom encountered any difficulties? Had the house needed a new roof? Had there been car repairs? Had there been a crisis with Ronnie—medical or otherwise—that required a large outlay of cash? I couldn't think of anything.

My mother didn't travel. She didn't gamble. She didn't even buy clothes for herself. What had she done with $14,550?

I looked through the drawer for anything else of note and found nothing. There were no other bank or credit card statements, just coupons and pens, rubber bands and paper clips. I shut the drawer.

I decided to look one more place before I left Mom's house—Ronnie's room.

Ronnie didn't like anyone going into his room when he wasn't there. On the day of Mom's funeral and the night Mom died, he'd let me come in there because he was there already. He kept his room neat and orderly, with some but not much help from Mom. He lived in fear that someone—like his little sister—would come in and wreck things, which I'd done on more than one occasion when we were under the age of ten. Given the extreme circumstances of the moment, I had to believe he would forgive me if I entered his private space.

I didn't expect to find much. Ronnie kept jigsaw puzzles and sketchbooks stacked neatly on a shelf by the room's lone window. He shared that analytical, logical side of his personality with Mom and not really with me. I opened his closet. Everything hung neatly on hangers, and the shoes were lined up on the floor, two by two, like animals ready to enter Noah's ark. I didn't see any loose papers or cards. I closed the closet door.

I was ready to leave when I saw the photo next to Ronnie's

bed. Ronnie used a small nightstand, one made out of cheap particleboard. It had a drawer and two shelves, and on the top sat a lamp, an alarm clock, and an empty water glass. The framed photo rested on the bottom shelf, almost obscured by a box of tissues.

I went over and picked it up. My heart flipped when I realized it was a photo I had never seen before. In the shot, Ronnie and Mom stood behind two small children about three and five years old. Everyone smiled big and goofy, the kids hamming it up like performers. Everyone looked happy. More than happy. Ecstatic. And I had no idea who the kids were.

I guessed it was a recent photo. The four of them were standing outside near a lake, and the trees in the distance were thick and green—it must have been summer. Just a couple of months ago? Was it possibly the last photo ever taken of Mom?

I traced my finger across the glass in the frame, right over her face. I swallowed hard. Who were these goddamn kids? And who had taken the photo?

"Okay, Mom," I said. "You're coming with me."

I threw the photo—frame and all—into my purse and left the house.

Chapter Twenty-seven

Ronnie lay with a sheet pulled up to his chin, his eyes closed. I stood and watched him sleep, his chest gently rising and falling with each breath. The air made a soft whistling sound as it passed in and out of his nostrils. He looked peaceful.

I thought about the new will and my guardianship of Ronnie. If all this ended the right way—*when* it all ended the right way—and Ronnie was released, he would be in my care. He needed a place to live, structure, and stability. My graduate school life provided none of those things. Still, my mind ran through the possibilities. I could schedule my classes and teaching for a few days a week and stay home with Ronnie on the others. With Paul's help and understanding from my professors . . .

But then, when I graduated? When I went looking for a job, one that might send me anywhere in the country to teach? I had refused to promise Mom for the very same reason. I wanted a career, a life. I didn't see how the two went together.

Ronnie's eyes fluttered open. He blinked against the light from the bedside lamp, then looked over and saw me.

"Hi, Ronnie."

He smiled. "Hi, sis."

I went to the side of his bed and sat down. I ran my hand over his arm, which was still beneath the sheet. I remembered when Dad was first in the hospital. Nothing makes a person seem more vulnerable and weak than being wrapped up in a hospital bed.

"How are you?" I asked. "Are you feeling okay?"

"I'm okay," he said.

He seemed less morose than he had before. I couldn't be sure how much of that had to do with whatever drugs they were giving him to even out his moods.

"Are you getting enough to eat?" I asked. "Shoot. I should have stopped and got you a sandwich or something. Do you want me to go out and do that?"

"I ate my dinner here," he said. "Not too bad."

"Good."

Then he said, "I don't want to be here anymore."

His words hit me in the chest, as if someone had taken a two-by-four and whacked me there. I struggled for air. "I know, Ronnie."

"I miss home," he said. "I miss Mom."

"I know," I said. "I do too." I rushed to speak before he could say anything else that would break my heart. "Look, I'll talk to the doctor in a minute. I'll find out what's going on. You'll probably just have to stay here a little longer."

"That's what Paul said. He wouldn't take me home either."

My brother didn't sound angry or emotional. Just resigned. I think the resignation in his voice, the defeat, made it even worse. I decided to change the subject as fast as possible.

"You know what I found today?" I asked, trying to sound chipper. To my own ears, my voice sounded high-pitched and a little crazy, laced with false cheer. I might have found myself on the receiving end of a visit from the men in white coats. "Do you remember Peppy?"

Ronnie's face brightened a little. "Of course," he said.

Peppy was a white poodle. Someone Dad knew had found him abandoned on the interstate when he was just a puppy. This person asked Dad if he'd like to take the dog, since he knew Dad had two kids. Peppy lived with us for more than ten years, until he had to be put to sleep when I was in high school.

"Do you remember that picture Mom took of him?" I asked. "The one where he's wearing the Santa hat?"

Ronnie nodded. "He used to jump on us in the yard when we came home from school. Every day he came running out to us."

"Mom let him out so he could do that," I said.

"He used to sleep in my bed sometimes," Ronnie said.

"Sometimes? He slept in your bed all the time. He wouldn't sleep with anyone else."

"I know."

"You know? Then why did you say sometimes?"

He tried to suppress a grin. "I didn't want you to feel bad."

I laughed at his slyness. "I was mad then. I wanted him to be my dog, but he was yours. He lived with the whole family, but he loved you the most. He was your dog."

"He went to Indiana Beach with us," Ronnie said.

"That's right."

We'd rarely taken vacations when I was growing up. We weren't poor by any means, but we didn't have an excess of anything. And Ronnie's extra schooling and medical bills took a bite out of the family budget. In fact, Mom didn't have any real sense of financial security until Dad died and she collected on his life insurance policy.

But one summer when I was eight, the vacation bug bit my parents. All four of us piled into Dad's Ford Taurus and we drove across the state line to Indiana Beach, a cheesy, family-friendly resort area someone had built on the shore of a man-made lake in west central Indiana. We spent five days there, going on the rides on the boardwalk and swimming in the small roped-off enclosure they'd made for kids in the lake. I could still smell the cotton candy and the popcorn, the elephant ears and the hot dogs they grilled along the midway. Ronnie loved it. We all loved it, but for some reason we never went back.

"Peppy got carsick," Ronnie said. "He puked in the backseat."

"He did. That's right." It didn't sound like fun, riding down the interstate in a hot car with a puddle of dog puke at my feet, but I couldn't think of it any other way. "Dad was furious," I said.

"He said he didn't want to bring Peppy in the first place."

I laughed. "Oh, my God." I closed my eyes and the memories were all right there, as vivid as anything on a movie screen. Dad in his Ohio State baseball cap. Mom in her sunglasses. The green car, the passing scenery, the fishy smell of the lake. I closed my eyes tight, squeezing off tears.

Something touched my arm. It was Ronnie, reaching out for me. "It's okay, sis," he said. "It's okay."

"Thanks, Ronnie." We clasped hands. His skin was warm and a little clammy from being tucked inside the sheet, but I didn't mind. We held on to each other, and I gathered myself.

"You're welcome, sis."

"I wanted to ask you about something else," I said.

I bent down to my purse and took out the photo. Ronnie and Mom and the two mystery children weren't at Indiana Beach in the picture. I had no idea where they were standing, and I was counting on my brother to straighten it out. I handed the photo to him.

"Ronnie, who are these kids in the picture with you?" I asked.

He took the photo, and his brow creased. "You took this from my room," he said.

"Yes, I did, Ronnie."

"Why?"

"I'm trying to find some things out about Mom. I had to go in there." He didn't look mollified, but I pressed on. "So, who are these two little kids with you and Mom?"

"You know them," he said.

"No, I don't. I've never seen them before."

"They're our cousins. That's what Mom said."

"Cousins?" I leaned forward and looked at the photo again. We didn't have any cousins. Dad was an only child. Paul had no children. We were it, the whole generation. "I don't think that's right."

"Mom said."

"I heard you. Do they live in Dover?"

Ronnie shrugged.

"What are their names?"

Ronnie thought for a minute, then pointed at the children one by one. "That's Skylar. And that's . . ." He scrunched his face in concentration. "Vanessa."

"And their mom or dad? Did you meet them? Who are they?"

"The police think I hurt Mom," Ronnie said.

"I know. They told me all about it."

Ronnie didn't say anything else. He lay there, still holding the photo. He stared up at the dingy gray drop ceiling.

"Ronnie, you didn't hurt Mom, did you?"

He took his sweet time answering me. I let him have all the

time he wanted. I wasn't sure I wanted to hear the answer. It disturbed me more than anything that I wasn't sure what the answer would be.

Finally he said, "I got mad at her. Really mad."

"You mean the time the police came? The fishing trip with Paul?"

It took me a moment to realize that Ronnie was shaking his head, ever so slightly. *No,* he was saying. *Not that time.*

Had there been another time?

"What happened, Ronnie?" I asked, keeping my voice low. I had no idea who might be lingering in the hallway outside his room.

"She didn't want me to go to speech therapy," he said.

"Again?"

"Yes."

"When was this?" I asked.

He shrugged. "I don't remember."

"Ronnie, this is important. Was this before the police came that time or after?"

"I'm tired, sis. Tired."

"I know. Just answer that question."

But he turned away. He tucked the photo against his chest and rolled over, turning his back to me.

"Ronnie? Are you going to answer me?"

Silence. He'd totally withdrawn. I asked one more question, but he didn't answer that one either.

"Ronnie?" I said. "Who is Elizabeth Yarbrough?"

I wandered down the hallway and out to the parking lot, lost in my own thoughts. The sodium vapor lights were coming on, casting the lot in an artificial glow. I pulled my keys out and heard my name called.

"Elizabeth. Hey."

I turned. It was Janie. She was wearing her scrubs under a lightweight jacket. She was carrying a canvas tote bag that looked like it was holding a brick.

"Hi," I said.

Janie came over. "How's Ronnie doing today?" she asked.

"He has moods. Sometimes he doesn't like to talk."

"I've noticed that," Janie said. "He's probably overwhelmed."

"Yeah."

"Are you heading out?" Janie asked. "Or home? I just got off, and if you want to get coffee or something . . ."

I looked at my car. Then I looked at the darkening sky. What waited for me in my apartment? Ungraded essays?

"If you're busy . . ." Janie said.

"I think there's a Starbucks across the street," I said.

We settled with our drinks. The place was half full. Teenagers laughed at one table. An elderly man worked a crossword puzzle next to us. A family of four occupied another table. They seemed to be trying to set a world record for looking wholesome and happy.

Janie wore her hair piled on top of her head. I noticed that she used a number two pencil to hold it in place. She seemed the same as in high school—an open book. No secrets. No dodging or sugarcoating. She explained how she'd stayed in Dover after high school and attended Dalton for her nursing degree.

"It took me an extra year and a half," she said.

"Were you paying your own way?" I asked.

"No. I had too much fun when I was a freshman," she said. "I partied. I didn't go to class. You know, the usual."

"Sure."

"I was a student nurse at a local general practitioner's office. One of my professors came in and saw me there. The poor guy. He probably thought to himself, 'How is this dummy who couldn't come to class going to check my blood pressure?' I couldn't blame him for thinking that."

"But you have your act together now," I said.

"Well enough." She sipped her drink. "You seem to be doing well. That's no surprise. I always thought you'd be the type to study abroad or go to grad school. I figured you'd be living in New York or someplace like that."

"Not yet."

"Did you come back for your mom and Ronnie?" Janie asked.

"No, it just worked out that way. I got an assistantship here. It's a good program. I'm going to move on after I get my master's." As I said the words, I realized that I wasn't sure I believed them anymore. Could I move on? What about Ronnie? What about all of it?

"I saw your dad died too. In the obituary. I'm sorry. I remember he was sick when we were in high school."

"The cancer came back when I was in college."

"Shit," Janie said. "Fuck cancer. You know?"

I had to laugh. It reminded me of the stupid things we used to say when we were seventeen. *Fuck cancer. Yes. Fuck it.*

"Are you married?" I asked.

She held up her left hand. No rings. "Most people we went to high school with are married. And have babies. I'm in no hurry for that." She made a dismissive wave with her hand. "I have a boyfriend. We've been seeing each other for six months, but who knows? He's nice. What about you?"

"Single," I said. "Well, there's a guy. It's casual. Off and on. He's nice. A good guy. Too good sometimes, you know?"

"A good boy?" she said.

"A loyal pup," I said. "I'm lucky. He treats me well. But it's hard with school and trying to focus on a career. And now my family."

"You used to say you didn't want to have kids."

"I know," I said. "I still feel that way."

"You've got time to decide," Janie said. "We can have kids when we're in our thirties."

"That sounds so old. Thirties."

Janie laughed, and I did too.

I said, "I just looked at Ronnie when we were growing up, you know? My parents had him, and they were . . . I don't know, trapped, I guess. I didn't want to be trapped. By anyone. I wanted to have a career and get away from Dover." Janie was listening intently. "Not that there's anything wrong with staying here."

"I get it," she said. "I still think I might move away. I can go anywhere and get a job as a nurse. I can make good money. There are shortages of nurses in some places. I could name my price."

"Better than being a history professor," I said.

Janie smiled. "I do like it here, though. It's home. There are memories." She rolled her eyes. "My parents are here. My sis-ter." She looked at me. "I'm sorry. I hope that didn't upset you. I'm saying, 'My parents are here and it's great.' And you just lost your—"

"It's okay," I said. "I understand."

The family across the way laughed together. I remembered Janie's house. It was small and warm, and her mother always hugged me when I came and went. So unlike my mom. And so unlike my family.

I'd said I understood, but I didn't. I really didn't understand that kind of life at all.

Chapter Twenty-eight

The phone woke me the next morning. It was Saturday, and normally I slept with the phone off on weekends. But I was still waiting for Paul to call me back, so I'd left it on. Maybe, I figured, if he called while I was half asleep it would be easier to talk to him, to get past the awkwardness of our fight and move on. And the sooner we moved on, the sooner he might be able to answer the questions raised at the lawyer's office.

But the phone call that woke me wasn't from Paul. I reached for the phone and looked at the display screen. I saw a local number, one I didn't recognize. I wondered if maybe it was the hospital, but I didn't answer. My mind was too foggy, my brain and body too tired from the week. *If it's important,* I thought, *they'll leave a message or call back.*

A few moments later the phone chimed, letting me know I did have a message. But I rolled over and closed my eyes. I kept them shut, trying to drift back to sleep. I had slept surprisingly well, considering that it was my first night alone since the break-in, and my body and mind wanted more. Only, when I closed my eyes, everything from the day before tumbled through my mind.

Elizabeth Yarbrough. Ronnie wanting to leave the hospital. The bank statement, the picture, the "cousins"—

The phone rang again.

"Okay," I said.

Maybe it was important. A message and a call back.

I rolled over and picked up the phone. The identity of the caller made my heart jump.

It *was* Paul. I held the phone in front of me, staring at the screen. My strategy hadn't worked—I was plenty awake. And nervous to talk to him. For a split second, I thought about ignoring it, but I knew I couldn't. He had reached out. And with everything going on, I couldn't make it the way I always made it. I couldn't do it all alone.

I needed help.

"Hello?" I said.

"Elizabeth . . ."

He sounded tired, almost as if he too were still half asleep.

"Paul? Are you okay?"

"I'm here," he said.

"Where?"

"I'm here. On the phone."

"What's the matter?" I asked.

"Did the police call you?" he asked.

I knew—the message I hadn't listened to. The call I hadn't taken.

"Someone just called. But the police? What's wrong? Are you hurt?"

"No," he said. "It's Ronnie."

"Oh, God."

A burning pain crossed my midsection. It felt as if someone

had placed a hot poker there, just rested it against my flesh and didn't move.

Ronnie. What happened to Ronnie?

"Is he dead?" I asked.

A long pause. I heard Paul breathing.

"Paul?"

"He's not dead," Paul said. "It's worse. He confessed, Elizabeth. This morning he told the police he killed your mom."

Chapter Twenty-nine

I expected to walk into a scene of chaos at Dover Community—police officers talking into phones and radios, doctors and nurses scurrying to and from Ronnie's room. Maybe even television cameras, a reporter in front of the building with a news van and a live remote. Wouldn't a murder confession, especially the confession of a man with Down syndrome to the crime of murdering his own mother, warrant all of that activity?

But the hospital corridor looked just as it did any other day. An elderly patient shuffled by me, muttering about the condition of her slippers. The nurses worked at their stations. The only addition to the scene was Detective Richland. He stood outside Ronnie's room, talking on a cell phone. He didn't move his eyes toward me as I rushed down the hallway. I was wearing the first clothes I had found on the floor of my apartment—a sweatshirt and a pair of jeans, running shoes without socks. I hadn't brushed my teeth and had only smoothed down my hair with my hand while I drove.

I tried not to make eye contact with Richland. I angled for Ronnie's room, and as I did, he stopped his call and held his hand out to me, a traffic cop's gesture.

"You can't go in there," he said. His hand was huge, the size of a dinner plate.

"Why not?"

"You just can't," he said, sounding a little petulant. He didn't meet my eye either. "We're working on your brother's case."

"Is he in there?" I asked. "Is my brother still in that room?"

"Why don't you wait in the lounge?" He pointed with his phone toward the consultation room where I had spoken to Dr. Heil.

"Did you take my brother away?" I asked.

"Please wait in there," he said. "I'll be with you in a minute."

I stood in the hallway, hanging between two impulses. As a good girl, one who was raised to respect authority and always do what I was asked to do, I felt compelled to just slink off to the room and wait. My mother was gone and Ronnie in custody—did my family need any other drama, like a run-in with the police?

But I wanted to see my brother. It was bad enough for him to be left alone in that hospital for the past week, away from everything he knew, everything that brought him comfort, even at the time he mourned the loss of the most important person in the world to him.

Richland made another gesture toward the consultation room, his body language more insistent. He indicated that I wouldn't be getting many more warnings from him. So I took the out he offered me. Why? Because I wasn't sure how much I wanted to see Ronnie right at that moment after all. What would I say to him? And what would he have to say to me?

What if what he had confessed was true?

I turned away and entered the small room. As I did, I heard Richland go back to his phone call. I tried to listen to what he was saying, to pick up on some sense of what he was talking about, especially if it related to Ronnie, but he spoke in a low, muffled voice so I couldn't hear.

Inside the room, I sat alone. There weren't any magazines to read and no television. This room meant business. If you were in there, you weren't supposed to be distracting yourself from whatever difficulties you were facing. I had my phone, though. Paul said he was coming to the hospital as well, but I hadn't seen him anywhere. I texted him, asking where he was. I started to text Dan, but what would I say? *At hospital. Brother confessed to murder. LOL.* I thought about calling, but even then, how would that work? What would I want from him? Dan would insist on coming, on sitting by my side and riding the rapids with me. I wasn't sure I could ask anyone to do that, not when things were getting as deep as they were.

I waited, my hands folded in my lap.

Why, Ronnie? Why?

And, Mom—why? Why did you let things get so far out of control?

I rested my elbows on my knees and brought my hands up to my face. I buried my face against my palms, which were sweaty and warm. I closed my eyes and tried to absorb it all.

Why?

I don't know how long I sat that way. It felt like hours, but it must have been only a few minutes. I looked up when I heard the door open. Detective Richland came into the room, still holding his phone and nothing else. He didn't make eye contact with me or offer a greeting. He took the seat across from mine, folding his extended frame into the compact chair. He didn't pull out his little notebook or anything. I wasn't sure why he was there.

"Are you doing okay, Ms. Hampton?" he asked. He met my eye this time. He seemed to be trying.

"No."

"Do you need some water?" he asked.

"Why do you cops always offer me water?" I asked. "Do you think that's going to make anything better?"

"No," he said. "But I'm trying to be nice." His hands fluttered a little, then quickly stopped.

"Why don't you tell me what's going on?" I said. "My uncle called me this morning and said Ronnie confessed to killing my mother. That has to be a mistake."

"Just to be clear," Richland said, "we tried to call you first. You're the next of kin, of both the victim and the perpetrator. We did call you, and you didn't answer. That's when we called your uncle."

"What happened?" I asked.

"I'll tell you what I can right now," he said. "We're still putting things together and tying up some loose ends. But this morning I came by here to consult with Dr. Heil about your brother's situation. I had some follow-up questions about the report Dr. Heil had submitted after he examined Ronnie. And let me just state this up front—Dr. Heil's report assured me that Ronnie is capable of understanding the difference between right and wrong and understanding the consequences of his actions. The report spoke very highly of his intellectual capabilities."

"I could have told you that," I said.

"You understand we need to hear it from a professional."

"How did all of this lead to a confession?" I asked.

"When I arrived here at the hospital, Ronnie told the nurse on duty that he wanted to speak to me. I went in, and he told me that he had killed your mother."

"He just told you that."

"He did." Richland raised his right index finger as though to emphasize a point. "Dr. Heil was present when I spoke to your brother, and after he made that declaration—what we call a spontaneous declaration—I informed him of his Miranda rights. In fact, I went over them three times with him. He understood them. Dr. Heil felt Ronnie understood them and understood what he was telling me."

"And he just said it to you, just like that."

"He said, 'I killed my mom.' Clear as day he said it. And he repeated it when I followed up."

I closed my eyes. I tried to lose myself in the darkness behind my lids, to drift away and out of that room and that space. But I couldn't. I could still hear the soft hum of the hospital's heating and cooling system, could still hear the occasional footsteps in the hallway, the voices over the loudspeaker paging nurses and doctors to more trouble. I couldn't escape it.

"Why?" I asked, opening my eyes.

"What's that?"

"Why did he do it?" I asked. "What did he say caused . . . this to happen?"

Richland paused. "At this point, I don't want to get into any of these details. Like I said, we're working some things out."

"So you won't tell me anything except that my brother confessed to killing my mother?"

"You know what the issues were we already had," he said. "We haven't been able to account for your brother's whereabouts on the night your mother died. We have a history of violent behavior. And now . . ."

He didn't say it, but I knew what he meant. *Now, a confession.* And I couldn't help but think back to the night before, when I had spoken to Ronnie in the hospital. I had asked Ronnie directly if he'd hurt Mom—and he didn't answer me. He didn't confess, but he didn't deny it either. And I wondered, sitting there with Detective Richland, if my question from the night before had set Ronnie on the path to confessing to the crime. Had he wanted to do it for a while, but couldn't bring himself to say it to me?

"What happens now?" I asked.

"I'll hand everything over to the county attorney's office. It will be in their hands from here on out. They'll decide the best facility to hold your brother in short term and then long term."

Long term?

"How long?" I asked.

"I can't say. That's out of my hands."

"Are we talking about life in prison?" I asked.

Richland raised his hands as though to say, *I don't know. And please don't ask.*

"Can I go see him?" I asked.

Richland shook his head. "Not now. No one can see him now. Everything is at a crucial point. We can't risk having someone else in the mix."

"Do you understand that disabled people have a strong desire to give in to and please authority?" I asked.

"I told you he was informed of his Miranda rights—"

"He might have confessed just to do that," I said.

"To do what?"

"To please you because you're in a position of authority over him."

"What about your mother?" he asked. "Isn't—or should I say *wasn't* she in a position of authority over him? She was his mother, right?"

He looked at me, waiting for an answer. I didn't give him one.

"He didn't respect her authority that night he went after her and she had to call the police, did he? And he didn't respect her authority when he killed her." He waited another moment. "Did he?"

I didn't answer. I didn't have anything to use against him. He had completely deflated my argument. He unfolded himself from the chair and left me alone in the room. Alone with the knowledge that my family was disappearing—and one of them had very likely killed the other.

Chapter Thirty

I waited in that little room for a long time. It felt as if that little room existed on its own plane of the universe, cut off and separated from everything else happening in the world. It was hard for me to imagine that Ronnie lay in a hospital bed less than a hundred feet from where I sat. He might as well have been on the moon. If I opened the door, it wouldn't have surprised me to see not a hallway but a steep cliff, something that separated me from everything else in the world.

I had thought Mom's death was bad enough. But I was suddenly living through something even worse.

I had to do something. Something for Ronnie. It did none of us any good for me to sit and stew.

I pulled out my phone and dialed a number. Frank Allison wasn't in on Saturday, so I told his answering service what I wanted. I didn't spare the melodrama.

"He needs to call me back right away," I said.

"I'll pass it along, dear," the efficient voice said.

I stood up and paced. It didn't take long. About two minutes later the phone rang in my hand. It was Frank Allison, and I gave him the rundown on Ronnie's situation.

"He confessed, huh?" he said, his voice low and distracted.

"I don't know where that came from," I said. "It's crazy talk."

"Sure, sure," he said. "And you say you're at the hospital? Is it Dover Community? And he's still there as well?"

"Yes."

"I'll get there as soon as I can," he said. "And, Elizabeth? Don't let him say anything else if you can help it."

"Got it."

I felt a momentary shiver of relief pass through my body. I wasn't being completely worthless. I started toward the door to go down to Ronnie's room. I intended to keep the police away from him if I could. I didn't know how, but I meant to try. But Paul came through the door before I left the room. We almost bumped into each other, and when I saw him I didn't care about the fight or the things he had said to me. It didn't matter. I was just glad to see a friendly face, a comforting face.

But the strain showed on him again. He looked as ashen and grave as he had in the wake of Mom's funeral. He entered the room and came right over to me. He sat in the chair next to mine and draped his arm over my shoulder. He pulled me close. I smelled shaving cream and mouthwash, smells that reminded me of my dad. I let him hold me. We didn't say anything to each other right away. We just sat like that. I closed my eyes.

When he finally released his grip, I straightened up. Paul's eyes were red rimmed, either from crying or a lack of sleep or both.

"I'm sorry," he said.

"It's not your fault," I said. "The police . . . and Ronnie . . ."

"I mean the other night," he said. "I said some awful things. I shouldn't have said them."

"It's fine," I said. "I got my back up. I do that sometimes. You know that."

"You've been very good to your mom and Ronnie," he said.

"Not as good as I could have been, but thanks."

"I think we've all been negligent here," he said.

He reached up with his right hand and wiped a tear from his eye. His hand shook as he did it. That combined with the poor color of his skin made him look older than I'd ever seen him look. It was as though the past week had accelerated his aging process like a time-lapse film. If things kept going the way they had been going, he'd look like a centenarian soon.

"What did the police say?" he asked. "Did they tell you anything?"

I related my conversation with Richland, leaving out the shitty comments he'd made at the end about Ronnie not respecting my mother's authority. Paul didn't need to hear about that. Then I told him about my conversation with Ronnie from the night before, how he hadn't answered when I'd asked if he had hurt Mom.

"Why wouldn't he answer me, Paul?" I said. "I know Ronnie can be moody just like anybody else. Lord knows moodiness and reticence run deep in this family. But he brought it up. He said, 'They think I killed Mom.' And when I asked him if that was true, when I gave him a chance to put my mind at ease and deny that, he wouldn't take it. He didn't say anything at all. He didn't admit it, but he didn't deny it either."

"I don't know," Paul said. "I bet they pressured him or coerced him. Hell, they've had him cooped up here, alone basically. Anyone would say anything to get out of here. Or he might just say something to get people off his back."

"That's what I said. I told the detective that people with disabilities might say anything to please an authority figure."

"You wouldn't have to have a disability to do that," Paul said.

I knew he was right. And yet there remained unspoken things between us, things I didn't dare bring up. I didn't bring them up because I didn't want to risk having another fight at a time when we needed each other the most. I didn't want to bring them up because, on some level, I didn't want to know whether he harbored the same doubts about Ronnie that I did. I suspected he did. Why else would he have advised my mother to have Ronnie sent away after one of his outbursts? He saw Ronnie more than I did. He must have understood him better in some ways. And I just wasn't ready to see into all of those dark corners.

"I'm going to see him," Paul said.

"I was just about to. They wouldn't let me before, but I called Frank Allison. I want a lawyer here to deal with this."

"Good." Paul looked at me a long moment, his tired eyes growing angry. "That's bullshit," he said. "We can see him if we want."

"Richland said no," I said. "He said everything is too delicate right now. I guess he means the case, but Allison said to not let Ronnie talk."

Paul looked away. "He's in the hallway—Richland. He didn't even look at me when I walked down here. He just pointed to this room. You know, he waves those hands around like he's corralling butterflies or something. He was talking to a nurse or doctor."

"I wish Detective Post were here," I said. "At least I could talk to her a little. At least she seems human."

"She's a woman," Paul said. "She has a lighter touch. She listens. Or pretends to."

"Come on," I said. "Let's both go down there."

As if his ears were burning in the hallway, Detective Richland came through the door. He nodded at both of us as though we were friendly acquaintances, then took a seat. I'm sure he didn't notice, but I didn't grant him the courtesy of eye contact. I looked at a spot on the wall above Richland's head. I bit back on my anger.

"I want to see my nephew," Paul said. "Something isn't right here."

"I've already explained to Ms. Hampton that I can't let you do that right now. I was just on the phone with someone from the county attorney's office. They certainly don't want any family members going in there and confusing the story your nephew has to tell."

"Confusing it?" I asked. "Are you saying we'd try to get him to lie?"

"It's best to just keep things simple right now."

"Our lawyer is on the way," I said. "He requests that you stop talking to Ronnie."

"Detective," Paul said. "I need to talk to you." His voice sounded level and calm, strangely so given the circumstances. It fit Paul's demeanor since Mom's death—sober and a little detached. He'd really only showed a full spark of life when he yelled at me in the cafeteria. "Could we speak somewhere?"

"We can speak right here if you have questions," Richland said. "I don't want you all to feel this is adversarial. I'm aware of the issues surrounding your nephew's condition—"

"It isn't a condition," I said.

"Well—"

"'Condition' suggests an illness," I said. "Ronnie doesn't have an illness. He has a disability."

"Okay," Richland said. He reached up and adjusted his shirt collar. "I understand that. I'm trying to be sensitive to the issues that come up."

"I was hoping we could speak alone," Paul said.

That sentence landed in the room like a lead weight. Richland looked at me, and I looked at Paul. Paul had his eyes steadily placed on Richland, waiting for a response. He acted as if I wasn't in the room anymore.

Richland took a long time to answer. Then he said, "Sure. If you would like to, we can speak alone."

But I wasn't going to be cut out of the conversation. I wasn't going to get up and leave the room, not if they were talking about the fate of my brother. I had no idea what Paul wanted to say to the detective that I couldn't hear, but I didn't intend to make it easy for him. I remained rooted to my spot, as obstinate and stubborn as a child.

Richland read my body language. He said to Paul, "Would you like to speak out in the hallway? Why don't we do that?"

They both rose from their chairs and went through the door, trying to leave me alone in that little room again. Paul turned back to me before he walked out. "Just wait," he said. "I'll take care of this, okay?"

But I decided not to sit still for being banished. I pushed myself up out of the chair and followed them into the hallway. Paul and Detective Richland were standing just a few feet away from each other, the difference in their heights striking. Paul looked like a child. When they heard me come through the door, they looked up. Disappointment crossed Paul's face, but I didn't slow down. I brushed right past him, heading for Ronnie's room.

"Ms. Hampton?" Richland said behind me.

I was tired of being called "Ms. Hampton." I was tired of his forced and overly formal public servant manners. I didn't stop. My shoes squeaked on the hospital tile. I yanked open the door to Ronnie's room.

He lay in there alone, the TV playing. His eyes opened wide when he saw me. Not in fear or shame, just surprise. Maybe the police had told him he wouldn't be having any visitors, or maybe he knew how strange it was for his sister to be showing up anywhere so early in the morning.

"Ronnie?" I said. "Why? Why did you tell them that? Tell them the truth, Ronnie. Tell them."

Before Ronnie could say anything, the door opened again and Detective Richland was there behind me. Then he moved in front of me, blocking my view of my brother.

"You can't—"

"Ronnie. Tell them. You don't know what they're going to do—"

"That's it," Richland said. "You have to go. You can't be here."

"Ronnie?" I said.

Paul took me by the arm, applying gentle pressure. "Come on, honey," he said.

"No," I said. "He has to know. He has to understand this."

"Mr. McGrath," Richland said. "Please, can you take her out of here?"

"Elizabeth," Paul said.

I turned away from both of them. I turned toward Ronnie.

"Ronnie?" I said. "It's not true, is it? Tell them it's not true, or you'll get in trouble."

He looked at me, his eyes focused and clear. But he didn't say anything. He turned his head to look at the TV screen again, and that was all the fight I had in me. My body wilted, physically and emotionally.

I let Paul lead me out of the room.

Chapter Thirty-one

Paul sent me away from the hospital. He walked me down to the front door and told me that I wasn't doing any good there, especially if I was losing my cool.

"Losing my cool?" I said. "If anyone deserves to lose her cool, it's me."

"I'm not disagreeing with that," he said. "But the days ahead just grew a lot darker, don't you think?"

I couldn't argue. The days ahead had just turned as black as night. I wasn't sure we could even call them days anymore.

"We're both going to need to be at our best," he said. "Why don't you go home and rest? I'll stay here with Ronnie, and you can come back later."

What he said made sense, and I could feel the logic of it seeping into my brain. But I still didn't like it.

"No," I said. "My place is here. There's so much more to talk about—"

"I know. And we'll talk about it."

"What did you want to talk to Richland about?" I asked. "I don't like there being secrets. If you had something to say, you should say it in front of me."

Paul's face flushed, as if he'd been caught in a lie. I don't know what I liked least—the fact that he might have tried to keep something from me or the fact that I'd exposed him for it. Had he been planning to tell Richland that Ronnie really did need to be put away? And he just didn't want me to hear him say that in the wake of our fight?

"It wasn't anything about Ronnie," he said. "Not directly."

"Then what?" I asked.

He let out a deep breath. "Look, just . . . I wanted to talk to Richland about our legal options with Ronnie. And I didn't want to say it in front of you because I thought you were running out of patience with the whole thing. And I was right."

I started to object, and he stopped me.

"I'm not saying you didn't have a right to. I'm just saying you were on the verge of losing your cool. And that's why I think you should go now. Go home. Regroup. If anything changes, I'll call. When Frank Allison gets here, I'll deal with him. I know him a little. Otherwise, you can come back later." He paused and looked at me a long time. His eyes contained a message, some significant meaning I was meant to understand but couldn't. "Who knows? Maybe some things will be clear then."

He gently guided me through the glass doors of Dover Community and into the midmorning sun.

"What could possibly be clarified by then?" I asked.

But Paul just waved at me and turned to go back into the hospital.

I didn't like being dismissed and shunted aside. I didn't like having my emotions questioned, as though I were a hysterical woman who couldn't stand the pressure of a big moment in the life of our family.

I didn't like not knowing everything that was going on.

I also had no idea of what I could do about those things unless I went back into the hospital demanding answers from the detectives, the doctors, or even my uncle. And if I did that, if I pitched one more fit or made one more scene, I might have ended up doing more harm than good.

Then I remembered the person who might be able to help me in the way a lawyer could not, who might be able to hold my hand while I stepped through the minefield.

I didn't have his phone number, but I did have his e-mail address. And I knew how to reach him through Facebook. I tried both approaches sitting in my car in the hospital parking lot.

As soon as I sent the messages, I felt empty again. It was a Saturday morning. What were the odds he would write back? And what were the odds he could help?

It took only thirty seconds for me to hear something. My phone chimed with the new e-mail message, and I read it with a little bit of a smile on my face.

Good to hear from you, Teach. Want to have coffee at the Grunge?

I arrived at the Grunge first. I ordered coffee, black. I didn't feel like messing around with anything as dainty and polite as tea. As I sipped the coffee and felt the first jolt of the caffeine hit my bloodstream, I wished I carried a bottle of whiskey with me. I could have used a shot of that to go along with it. But I settled for ingesting the only drug it was really acceptable to ingest so early in the morning.

I drummed my fingers on the table while I waited. The Saturday morning crowd in the Grunge consisted of locals, mostly professors, who came in for a coffee, a bagel, and a copy of the

New York Times. A few students occupied tables in the corners, their eyes still droopy from sleep, their bodies still recovering from the previous night's debauchery. I downed half my cup before Neal came through the door. He smiled when he saw me and came straight to the table without ordering anything.

"Hey, Dr. H."

"Neal," I said. "You know you can call me Elizabeth. We're outside of class, and I'm asking you for a favor."

"Elizabeth," he said. "Whoa. What's that one book? You know, the one about the guy sleeping with his female professor? *Lolita*?"

"That's not what that's about. And neither is this meeting."

"Still. Okay, Elizabeth. What do you need from me?"

He was wearing the army jacket again, and his beard looked a little fuller, a little less scraggly. He wore a gray shirt open at the collar with nothing on beneath it.

"Are you going to drink anything?" I asked. "Coffee?"

"I don't touch the stuff when it's fresh," he said. "Besides, I have enough energy."

"Okay," I said. I leaned forward a little. Despite the noise around us, I still felt worried about everyone hearing our conversation. "I'm not even sure if you can help me. I just . . . Some things are beyond my control and understanding right now."

"Is this about your mom getting offed?" he asked.

Offed?

"Yeah, it is."

"Tell me all about it," he said.

"You need to tell me something first," I said.

"Shoot."

"What exactly do you do?" I asked. "I mean, outside of school? What is it you spend your time doing?"

"Why do you want to know about this stuff?" he asked, half smiling.

I had to admit the smile was charming. He wasn't my type. He was too scruffy, too unwashed. I could imagine whoever lived with him spent a lot of time picking up dirty socks and putting the toilet seat down. But he had a presence, an energy that I suspected drew a certain kind of undergraduate girl to him like a magnet to iron.

"You said something to me in the hallway the other day, something about your dad working to help people. I just wanted to know what you meant."

"Oh, that," he said. "It's true. My old man's a lawyer. Well, he was a lawyer at one time. Are you looking for a lawyer?"

"I have one of those."

"Who?"

"Frank Allison. He practices here in Dover."

"Never heard of him," Neal said. "But my dad doesn't do the law stuff so much anymore. You know?"

"Then what does he do?"

"Like I said, he helps people. Say somebody suspects their husband is cheating on them, and they need to know for sure in order to go to court. Or maybe somebody has an employee, and they think the guy's doing drugs and is in danger of ruining the company. My old man checks that stuff out. He helps people."

"He spies on them?" I asked.

"He investigates," Neal said. "Like a PI, I guess. But without all that Tom Selleck shit. Sometimes I help him, especially if it's a matter involving the campus. Look, we can get the job done for you. Just tell me about it, and we'll figure something out."

I hesitated. I didn't know that he could really do anything for me. I stood up and went to the counter, where I refilled my mug.

When I came back, Neal sat with his face eager and open and expectant.

"Okay," I said. "You read the stuff in the paper about my mom, right?"

"I did."

"There's something else to it, something that hasn't had time to be in the paper yet, but believe me, it's going to be there tomorrow or the next day."

I told him about Ronnie's confession as well as the reason the police had suspected Ronnie in the first place. I told him about the scene at the hospital that morning, and Ronnie's refusal to answer my questions about whether he'd committed the crime or not. Neal listened to all of it attentively, his eyes fixed on my face as though I were telling him the most important story in the world.

When I was finished, I said, "Well?"

He stood up. "I'm hungry. I need a bagel or something."

I waited while he went through the line. He came back with a bagel smeared with peanut butter. He took a big bite and started chewing with his mouth open. He didn't say anything.

"Well?" I asked. "What do you think of what I just told you?"

"I'm kind of wondering what you think we can do to help you," he said. "You have a lawyer, like you said. It's always good to have a lawyer on your side if you're charged with something. That's what Dad's always told me. He first told me that when I was eight."

"I guess I don't know what I want you to do," I said. "That's what I thought you would figure out."

He nodded his head, chewing the whole time. He wiped his mouth with the back of his hand. "You want to know if it's possible that someone else killed your mother, and you want us to help you find that out. You think the cops are taking the easy way out, letting this confession thing fall into their laps. Right?"

"I guess so."

"And you think this lawyer guy you have— What's his name?"

"Frank Allison."

"Frank." Neal laughed a little. "You think he's too old-school for the case. I mean, he'll do his job and everything, but you don't think the legal wheels will turn as fast as you want things to turn. Right?"

"Sure."

"I have to say, if you want my professional opinion—"

"Are you a professional?" I asked.

"I get paid, don't I?" he said.

"Okay. Go on."

"Anyway," he said, "I have to say it looks pretty rough for your brother. I mean, the lack of an alibi, the violent past. And, hell, a confession. Looks like a slam dunk."

"I know."

Just hearing the facts recited back to me weighed me down. My shoulders dipped as though someone had placed bricks across my back.

Neal must have seen the slump in my posture. He leaned forward, leaving his bagel alone for a moment. "Hey," he said. "I'm sorry."

"I know Ronnie," I said. "There's just a part of my mind that can't accept he would do this."

"But a part of your mind does?" he asked.

I didn't answer.

Neal pressed on. "Is it typical for people with whatever it is your brother has—"

"Down syndrome, Neal."

"Right. That. Does it tend to make people violent?"

"No more than anyone else," I said. "I guess if you have a disability that limits some aspects of your life, you might tend to get frustrated easily."

"That makes sense." He stuck a finger into his mouth and dislodged some peanut butter. "And was your mom pretty tough on him? I mean, did she ride his ass about things?"

"She was tough. She expected a lot from him. And me."

"Sort of like you in class," he said. "A hard-ass."

"She loved Ronnie. She'd do anything for him."

"I hear you, Teach. We all love our moms. Right?" Neal shook his head. "My mom. Sheesh. She's a tough lady. I bet your mom was like that too. I can see it, Teach."

"Can you do anything?" I asked. "Or can your dad?"

He chomped on the bagel again. This time he didn't bother to wipe the peanut butter and crumbs from out of his beard. I wanted to grab a napkin and reach across the table myself, but I knew better.

"I'll poke around a little bit, see what we can find out." He threw the last bite of the bagel into his mouth. "Hell, I'll do it pro bono. That means free, right?"

"Yes, it does," I said. "But you can't just do it for free. If you're working, you should get paid something."

He nodded, a large smile spreading across his face.

"What?" I asked.

"I know what my fee will be," he said.

"What?"

"Have you graded my paper yet?"

He laughed and winked at me.

Chapter Thirty-two

Dan called while I was driving home from the Grunge. I answered as I drove, one hand on the wheel and the other on the phone. I hoped no cops saw me.

"I was just seeing how you were doing," he said. "If you need anything."

Do I need anything? I thought. *Where do I begin?*

I opted for a simple statement of fact. "I was at the hospital already this morning."

"That's an early start," he said, trying to sound light. It didn't work. His words hit my ear like a lead weight.

"There's a lot going on here, Dan," I said. "A lot."

"Oh," he said.

I understood where he was in his approach to me. He wanted to be cool and coy. He wanted to give me space, but he also didn't want to miss the chance to help me if he could. It was impossible, and I couldn't blame him for fumbling it.

"Do you need anything?" he asked, trying to keep it simple.

My apartment building came into sight. I cut down the small alley and pulled into my designated spot. The sun was bright, the air still cool. I'd cracked the window and let the breeze blow against my face.

"Look," I said, "this is all going to be in the news soon, so you might as well know. Hell, everybody at school is going to hear about it too." That realization just hit me. My life would become an even bigger soap opera, the kind of story passed along to each new class of graduate students. *Yeah, her mom was murdered. And her mentally handicapped brother did it.* "It's Ronnie," I said. "He confessed to killing my mom this morning."

There was a long pause. I thought the call had dropped. Then I heard an intake of breath. "Jesus," he said. "I'm so sorry."

"So am I," I said.

"Jesus," he said again. "Where are you? Are you at the hospital?"

"I'm home now," I said. "Or almost home. I'm in the parking lot of my building."

"Do you want me to come over?" he asked.

"No," I said right away. I knew my voice sounded sharp, almost harsh. I didn't want to dismiss him. I just needed a moment to . . . I don't know what I needed to do. I just didn't think I needed Dan there right then. "I'm okay," I said. "I have some calls to make. I've already talked to a lawyer for Ronnie. My uncle's going to call and let me know what's happening. And I have to go back to Dover Community later. I'll call you, though. In a little bit, I'll call you."

"Okay," he said. "Sure. Call me when you want."

He put on a brave face, but I could sense the edge of disappointment in his voice. He wanted to be Johnny-on-the-spot for me.

"I'll call you," I said. "I promise. You know how I am. I have to sort through this first. Give me a little bit of time to absorb all of this."

"Sure," he said. His voice had some starch back in it. "I'll let you absorb. I understand."

"Okay," I said. "Bye."

As soon as my right foot hit the bottom step, I heard someone call my name from behind me.

"Ms. Hampton?"

A man's voice. *Ms. Hampton.* A cop? Richland?

But the voice sounded gruff and older.

I turned around, taking my foot off the step.

"Elizabeth Hampton?" the man said.

The man who faced me was short, almost squat. He looked to be as tall as me, about five feet, five inches. And he was squarely built, his body bulky and thick through the stomach and chest. His legs were short. He wore a dark sport coat and matching pants, a white shirt open at the collar, and no tie. I guessed he was about seventy years old, maybe older. But despite his age, his body gave off a sense of power and strength.

He smiled at me. "I'm sorry," he said. "Sneaking up on you like this."

He looked familiar. I had seen him somewhere before, but I couldn't place it. And I didn't know his name.

"Do I know you?" I asked. I backed up a step, returning my foot to the bottom step. I placed my hand on the banister. My phone was in my hand.

"Could we talk?" he asked. "Maybe in your apartment?"

I shook my head. "No," I said. "And if you don't tell me—"

He smiled but didn't show any teeth. He had a small mouth and a weak chin. "I get it," he said. "After what happened to your mother, you're cautious. I understand—I really do."

When he mentioned Mom, the connections in my brain sped up. That was how I knew him. He had something to do with Mom.

"Were you—?"

I stopped. I saw it in my mind. At the cemetery, the man Paul was talking to while I was with Dan. The man who seemed so agitated with whatever Paul was telling him. That was the man standing before me.

"You were at the cemetery," I said. "You were talking to my uncle."

"Paul," he said. "I've known Paul most of my life."

"Were you friends with my mother?" I asked.

"More than friends," he said. "Are you sure you want to do this out here?"

"Yes, I'm sure," I said. "And what do you mean you and my mom were more than friends? Did you date her?"

He smiled again, but his eyes looked sad. It seemed put on, forced, as if he wanted to play the role of sad puppy dog.

"What do you mean?" I asked again.

"Your mom and I were high school sweethearts, and we were married for more than fifteen years."

Chapter Thirty-three

I remained frozen in place, one foot on the stairs, one foot on the ground. I might have blinked a few times or shook my head, like someone confronted with something that simply didn't make any sense.

"My mother was only married once," I said. "To my father."

The man in front of me, the man whose name I still didn't know, only smiled. And his smile looked self-satisfied and smug. Even as I said the words and issued the denial about my mother's past, I understood that I was stepping out on a limb. I thought of my trip through her house looking for documents after my meeting with Mr. Allison. I remembered the lack of pictures from the past, the lack of mementos or artifacts that might explain her life to me.

But that was just because Mom was private, right? Or because she simply didn't have much of a life before I was born?

She didn't even tell me about Ronnie . . . About the police coming . . . About any of it . . .

The man's smile loosened. "I'm sorry that I'm the one who has to tell you about this," he said, although he didn't look sorry at all. "I know it would have been better coming from your mother or your uncle."

"I don't believe you," I said, my voice quiet from lack of conviction.

The man sighed a little. I was the thickheaded and exasperating child who refused to see the lesson right before her eyes.

"It's all true," he said. "Are you sure we can't talk somewhere? Somewhere more private maybe?"

I looked down at the phone. "I'm calling my uncle," I said. "I'm calling Paul."

"You can do that," the man said. "But he and I don't exactly get along. He may say some awful things about me."

"What's your name?" I asked.

"Gordon," he said. "Gordon Baxter."

Paul's phone rang. It rang and rang and then went to voice mail. I didn't know if I wanted to leave a message or not.

Then the man said, "Really, I'm happy to tell you whatever you want to know about me or about my relationship with your mother."

Relationship?

The word froze me. My mother didn't have relationships. She was married, yes. Once. To my father. But that was a marriage. It was simple and clear-cut. They married and they had children and then Dad died. And Mom lived her life until she was murdered. That was it.

Relationship? No, my mom had relationships only with Dad and her children and her brother.

I hung up the phone.

"Have you been to my apartment before?" I asked, thinking of the robbery. The man before me possessed the same short, squat figure as the man who'd brushed past me on the stairs the night my apartment was broken into.

He didn't bat an eye. "I came by a day last week, but you weren't home."

"Did you let yourself in?" I asked. "And trash everything?"

"That sounds pretty brazen, doesn't it?"

But you haven't denied it, have you?

"How did you find me?" I asked.

"Your name was in the obituary online," he said. "And you're listed in the phone book. I'm a curious man, that's all. Curious."

I was in the phone book. As "E. Hampton." Why did women think using an initial protected them?

I brought my foot down off the step again. "You can't come in my apartment," I said. "I don't know you. I won't be alone with you."

"I understand," he said. "But I don't bite."

"Do you have a car?" I asked.

"Yes." He pointed to the street. "It's that blue Ford over there."

"Do you know the McDonald's on Grant Street?" I asked. "The one by campus? It's always crowded."

"I know where it is," he said. "I don't live in Dover, but I've passed it."

"I'll meet you there in ten minutes," I said.

As I drove the short distance to McDonald's, I called Dan. "I need you to do me a favor," I told him when he answered.

"Sure."

"I also need you to not ask me a bunch of questions about it."

"Okay," he said, his voice cautious.

"I'm going to call you in an hour," I said. "If you don't hear from me in an hour, call me back. Or just come to the McDonald's on Grant. One hour."

"What the hell is going on, Elizabeth?" he asked.

"Okay," I said. I couldn't just keep him in the dark. "I'm going there to talk to someone who says he knew my mother. I don't know this person, and he might be a lunatic, but he might also know things I need to know. That's why we're talking in a crowded restaurant, and that's why I need you to check in with me later. If you don't hear from me, assume he's an ax murderer."

"Great," Dan said. "What a relaxing hour this will be."

"I need you to do this for me," I said. "I know I can trust you."

"You know I'll be your loyal pup," he said.

"Something like that."

The restaurant came into sight. The parking lot was full, and through the large windows I saw a number of diners sitting at the tables. I wouldn't be alone, not by a long shot.

"Are you sure you don't need to call the police?" Dan asked.

I guided the car into an empty space. I looked around and didn't see Gordon Baxter anywhere. For all I knew, he wouldn't make the trip. He could have been a crazy coming out of the woodwork just to antagonize a crime victim's family.

"It's okay," I said. "But make sure you check in with me in an hour." I paused. "I appreciate it. Really. I know I can be a pain, but I need you to do this for me. Please?"

"Of course," he said. "One hour. Got it."

I hung up and climbed out of the car.

Chapter Thirty-four

Gordon Baxter sat at a table near the door of the McDonald's. A Styrofoam cup of coffee rested in front of him, the steam rising toward his face. I bypassed the counter and went to the table, but I didn't sit. I didn't know what I was going to hear from this man. I didn't know whether I wanted to hear it at all.

He looked up at me, his face benevolent. He pointed at the empty chair across the table. "Have a seat," he said. "Or are you getting something to eat?"

I sat down. I kept the phone in my hand. I wanted it to remind me of my deadline with Dan. One hour.

It was lunchtime, and the tables on either side of us were occupied. The chattering buzz of conversation went on all around us, punctuated by the occasional scream of a child or a shout from an employee in the kitchen. Gordon Baxter sipped from his cup.

"What would you like to know?" he asked.

"You're the one who showed up on my doorstep," I said. "You must have something you want to say to me."

"Fair enough," he said. "But in order to tell you why I came by your apartment, I'm going to have to give you some background. Maybe we'll both get the information we want."

I didn't say anything. I waited for him to go on.

"Like I said, your mom and I were high school sweethearts."

I interrupted him before he got going. "And just so you know, I told my friend where I am right now. He's going to come looking for me in an hour if I don't call him."

Gordon Baxter considered me. Some of the benevolence drained out of his face, and he tilted his head to the left. "Your mother wasn't very trusting either," he said. "She had that streak in her, that quality that told her a person had to prove their trustworthiness to her."

"That's fine," I said, standing up. "I don't want to hear this stuff."

"So you don't want to hear about your mother's past?" he asked. "You don't want to know her?"

His questions stopped me. I hated that it had worked. I settled back into my chair.

"Your mom told me that about you," he said. "She thought you were tough to get through to."

"You talked to my mother about *me*?"

"Sometimes."

"You were in touch with her recently?"

"I'll get there," he said. "But you're going to have to let me get there the way I need to."

"Fifty-five minutes now," I said, looking at my phone.

"Okay," he said. "Like I said, we were high school sweethearts. And we got married around graduation. We were young and dumb, but young and dumb people used to get married back then. Our generation did that a lot. We were living over in Haxton, where we both grew up. That's how I know Paul as well. We all grew up over there and went to school together. It sounds really quaint and all-American, and I guess it was."

"Why didn't Mom ever tell me about you?"

"I have my guesses."

"There's no shame in being divorced," I said. "You got married young and you split up, right?"

"It's more complicated than that."

"Why did she hide that from me?" I asked, pushing him for the truth.

"You would have to ask her, but I guess you can't do that now."

"How do I even know you are who you say you are?" I asked. "I see no proof."

"I know about you being in graduate school," he said. "I know about your brother, about Ronnie. I know your mother had high blood pressure. I know about Paul and how he's retired and has a bit of a heart condition."

I was already shaking my head. "Most of that stuff you could learn in the newspaper. This is a small college town. Everybody knows something about somebody. So what?"

"You're right," he said.

He stopped with that simple statement, and I didn't know what he meant.

"Right about what?" I asked.

"What I'm saying," he said. "It doesn't prove anything." He reached into the inside pocket of his jacket. He brought out a small white rectangle, and only when he held it up did I realize it was a photograph. A fragile, yellowing snapshot. He held it in the air between us, the plain white back facing toward me. "You could wait and ask your uncle," he said. "Or you could look at this."

I lifted my hand, but he pulled the photo back from me.

"Not so fast," he said. "I want you to look at this, and if you accept it as proof, then I want to know you're really going to listen to everything I have to say."

"Just show it to me," I said. "And you're down to fifty minutes."

He held the photo out, and I took it.

My hand shook a little as I turned it around. I didn't know what I would see. The photo showed a man and a woman. She wore a plain wedding dress, short sleeved. It flared at her waist. The man wore a dark coat and tie. They stood close to each other near a three-tiered wedding cake, each holding a glass of champagne. I recognized both of them despite the passage of time. The man was a younger and thinner version of Gordon Baxter. His hair was fuller and darker, the face less round. But it was him.

And the woman was Mom. Unmistakably. She looked young, even stylish. Her skin smooth, her eyes bright.

She looked like me.

She wore a half smile, one that spoke of something between insecurity and fear. Gordon had his arm around her, pulling her close to him with his free hand. She wasn't hugging him back. She couldn't—her upper arms were squeezed close to her body, her free hand clutching the champagne.

It was Mom. So young, so beautiful. I'd never seen her quite like that before.

"What do you think?" Gordon asked.

I kept staring at the photo. I tried to keep it together despite the emotion that slowly rose in my throat. My vision started to swim a little. I blinked my eyes a couple of times, fighting off my feelings.

Gordon reached out and took the photo.

"Do you believe me?" he asked.

I couldn't speak. The photo confirmed everything I had been thinking—that I really didn't know my mother. Not only had she not told me about her recent life, but she hadn't told me about any of her life. She was a stranger to me.

But why?

Gordon slipped the photo into his pocket. I wanted to reach out for it and take it back. I wanted to study it longer. What if there was something there that told me what I needed to know about my mother?

"So you'll listen now?" he asked.

"I still don't know if whatever you tell me is the truth," I said.

"You can confirm it all with your uncle," he said. "I'm sure you called him on the way here, right?"

I didn't answer. I looked at the top of the table.

"Do you want to remind me of how much time I have left now?" he asked.

"What happened with you and my mom?" I asked.

"You're not married, are you?" he asked, but didn't wait for an answer. "You're not. I know your mom was worried about that, about whether you'd ever settle down and have a normal life."

"Jesus," I said. "I'm only twenty-six."

"Your mom worried about it. I could tell. When you're married to someone and you share certain experiences, a bond forms that really never goes away. You're tied to that other person whether the relationship is the same as it once was or not. That's what happened with your mom and me. Even after all those years, there was still something there. A connection, something we shared. That was there for us, even in the time before she died."

"You were in touch with her?" I asked. "Recently?"

"Yes. We stayed in touch off and on over the years. Even

during the time you were growing up. Like I said, we're from the same place. We know many of the same people."

"Did my dad know about you?" I asked.

"He did. He had to. When you get married, you have to disclose any previous marriages you may have had."

"Did you ever meet my dad?" I asked.

"In passing once," Gordon said. "I even met you one time, although I'm sure you don't remember."

"When was this?" I asked.

"You must have been about five, maybe six. You were out with your mother and your brother. It was in the shopping mall here in Dover. I was there, and by chance we all ran into each other. Your mother introduced me to you as an old friend. Do you remember?"

I thought about it but couldn't summon the memory. Who knows how many times I went out with Mom? And even though she didn't have a lot of friends, she still knew people. As a child, I always felt as if I was being introduced to some new person, usually with my mother gently nudging me to remember my manners, look people in the eye, and say, "Pleased to meet you."

"I don't," I said.

Gordon took a sip of his coffee, apparently draining the cup. He pursed his lips as though the dregs of coffee at the bottom of the cup were particularly bitter.

"That was tough for me," he said. "Seeing your mother with her children."

I didn't immediately process what he was trying to say. Then I thought I understood. "Is this because you and Mom didn't have any kids?" I asked.

He looked into his empty cup. "I should really get some more coffee."

"Is that it?" I asked.

He didn't say anything. I knew he wanted me to think he wasn't saying anything because whatever was on his mind was too troubling to talk about. But I sensed there was something else at play as well. There was a practiced quality to his reluctance, something that told me he wanted me to ask the question. That he needed me to press more.

I gave him what he wanted only because of my intense desire to know.

"Did you try to have children?" I asked.

"We had a baby girl," he said, his voice low.

I tried to let that sink in. "A baby?" I said, repeating the word, my voice low and husky.

Gordon nodded. "Yes."

"Did—" I stopped. Then I went on. "Did you lose the baby?"

"She wasn't a baby," he said. "Not anymore. I think of her that way, though. As my baby."

"How old was she?" I asked.

"She was fifteen years old," he said. "She was fifteen when she was taken away and murdered."

Chapter Thirty-five

Gordon Baxter took his empty coffee cup and stood up. He carried it with him to the counter, leaving me to sit alone at the table and digest the bombshell he had just dropped on me.

A child. My mother had had another child. Which meant I had a half sister.

Had a half sister. She was dead. Murdered. Just like Mom.

But I couldn't fix my mind on my dead half sister for very long. Instead, I found myself thinking of my mother. Not only had there been something else I didn't know about her—she'd been married and she'd had a child before Ronnie and me—but she had lost that child. Violently. My mother had carried around with her one of the gravest losses a person—a mother—could suffer.

And yet she had never told me about it. She had never mentioned it, talked about it, not even hinted at it. Not with me. She'd carried that burden with her silently, suffering in secret.

I looked around the restaurant. A couple two tables down fussed over their baby. College kids laughed and joked as they inhaled French fries and hamburgers. Life went on. People were just living their everyday, mundane lives. Could any of them imagine the things I was finding out, the truths that were being revealed to me?

Out of the corner of my eye, I saw Gordon returning. He held his fresh cup of coffee as he deftly weaved between the people coming and going. He sat back down at the table, then added a sugar packet to the cup and stirred it with a small red straw.

"She was fifteen," Gordon said. He removed the straw and sucked a drop of coffee off the end. "Just started her sophomore year of high school."

"Was she your only child?"

He nodded. "Yes. We tried to have another but couldn't. Your mother really wanted more. I guess it makes sense that she had children when she married your father."

"What happened to this . . . to your daughter?" I asked.

"Beth," he said. "Her name was Beth."

"No, it wasn't."

He nodded. "Elizabeth, but we called her Beth. Your mother liked that name, I guess. Or she felt she was naming you as a tribute to her lost daughter."

"You're lying to me."

"Remember, you can verify all of this when you have the chance," he said. "If you wanted, you could take your phone, the one I know you have in your hand underneath the table, and call your uncle. You could call him right now, and he would verify all of this. It's true. I'm not making anything up."

My mom, my whole family had always called me Elizabeth. Never Beth. Never Betsy or Betty or Liz. Elizabeth. And when anyone tried to shorten my name—a friend, a teacher, a neighbor—my mother corrected them. "Elizabeth," she would say. "She goes by Elizabeth."

Was that why? She had named me after her deceased daughter, but couldn't go all the way and call me by the same exact name?

Was that why I was always Elizabeth? My mouth felt dry, almost cottony. I swallowed, trying to bring moisture back to my mouth.

Gordon said, "Beth didn't get along very well with your mother. *Her* mother. She was a teenager, and she had some problems."

"What year was this?" I asked.

"Beth died in 1975." He sipped the coffee. The baby at the table near ours started to cry. I watched the mother lift it from its high chair and pull it close, gently soothing it with whispered words. "It wasn't that unusual to be a rebel back then, at that time. And there were a lot of things for young people to get involved in. I'm sure you can imagine."

"Are you talking about drugs?" I asked.

"Drugs, yes."

"That wasn't unique to the seventies," I said. "Kids can still do that now."

"Sure," he said. "Of course. But there was something in the culture then, something that almost required it of young people. A lot of them were getting high and dropping out. Kids ran away. You know, they'd just up and quit school and decide to move somewhere else, somewhere more exciting than Ohio. Oregon. California. Who knows? Beth was becoming one of those kids. She was troubled. And she was a troublemaker. She had some run-ins with the police. Minor stuff up to that point. She ran with the wrong kind of crowd. Certain kids from the school who were also into the drugs and the drinking and the partying. Some of the kids were older. I knew that on a few occasions she came down here and hung out on campus, going to parties with older kids and who knew what else."

"I'm sorry, but I'm not sure that behavior is that unusual for a teenager whether it was in 1975 or today. Some kids party and run around with a faster crowd. It's normal teenage rebellion. I did some of those things in high school and certainly in college."

"About two months before Beth was killed, your mom found something in her room."

He paused, letting the words hang in the air.

"What did she find?" I asked.

"She found a bag of drugs and a couple of hypodermic syringes," he said. "Real, hard drugs. Heroin."

I didn't say it out loud because I didn't have to, but I understood his point. Heroin was a major step up. It wasn't just teenage rebellion and mischief.

"What did Mom do?" I asked.

"We did what any parent would do," he said. "We sat her down and we confronted her. We told her, in no uncertain terms, that she was not to bring that kind of thing into our house ever again. We laid down the law, the way parents are supposed to in a case like that." His voice took on a firmness, a conviction that hadn't been there before. It sounded like these were the words he truly believed. "You know, back then parents were much more comfortable laying down the law like that. We could say to a child, 'It's my way or the highway.' It was a better way to raise a child."

"Did you try to get her help?" I asked.

"Help?" he said, his voice dismissive. "We didn't used to believe people with drug problems needed help. We used to believe in an application of will. If the kid couldn't do it, then the parents did. I *still* believe that."

"She was fifteen," I said. "Don't you think she deserved a break?"

"I knew her," he said, his voice cold. "She was my daughter. I knew how to raise her."

I sensed a dead end, a point at which Gordon Baxter and I were not going to agree. And I really didn't care to push him—I hadn't come for a debate about parenting styles. I wanted to learn about my mother's life.

"So what happened?" I asked.

"She ran away," he said.

"I thought you said—"

"She came back," he said. "She was gone for a few days, probably crashing at a friend's house. Or God knows where. It drove your mother crazy with worry. I don't think Leslie slept the whole time Beth was gone. When Beth came back, things just got worse. She was skipping school. Coming home late. If we grounded her, she snuck out." He sighed. "One night the police brought her home. She had snuck out and gone to a party. When the police broke up the party, they found out Beth was under-age, and they brought her home to us. What could be worse for a parent than to have the police bring your child home in the middle of the night?"

"I'm guessing the murder part was worse," I said.

He studied me from across the table, his eyes growing flat and glassy. I imagined having him for a father was a laugh riot. I suspected that if he could get away with it he probably would have slapped me right there in McDonald's.

"Children shouldn't talk to adults like that either," he said, his eyes still flat. "It shouldn't matter whether the adult is your parent or not."

"I suspect you and I have some philosophical differences that we really can't solve here. Do you want to tell me the rest of your story?"

"Aren't you going to remind me of my time limit again?" he asked.

I looked at my watch. "You have twenty-five minutes left."

Gordon sipped his coffee and didn't say anything for a long moment. I started to wonder whether he was going to go on with his story at all, or whether he'd decided he'd had enough of me. Then he cleared his throat.

"She disappeared one night," he said. "She went out with friends. We let her go out that night. You mom did anyway. Leslie thought like you, I suppose. She thought if you loosened the reins a little bit things might get better. So Beth went out one night with her friends and she never came back. At first, we thought she had just run away again. If someone does something like that once, then it's certainly likely they would do it again. But after a few days when she didn't return, we started to think something really had gone wrong. Maybe she had overdosed. Maybe she'd been taken against her will. So we finally called the police."

"After a few days?"

"It's easy to judge, isn't it?" he said. "Especially with the hindsight of—what, thirty-seven years?" He let that sink in for a moment. Then he said, "The police investigated the disappearance. They talked to her friends and all of that. People at school. They didn't find anything, nothing that would tell them what happened to her. Pretty quickly, they seemed to turn their attention to other things."

"But a fifteen-year-old girl?" I said. "How could they just let her go so easily?"

"Like I said, it was a different time. People didn't get all weepy over missing kids the way they do now. Kids weren't the center of the world."

"She could have been in danger," I said. "She *was* in danger." I found myself getting worked up over what seemed to me an injustice. This was my sister, my family. It must have ripped my mother's heart out. How could anyone let such a thing happen? So casually? "You said she was murdered. Did they at least convict the guy responsible?"

"No," he said.

"No?"

"They didn't convict anybody," he said, shaking his head. "They never even found her body."

"Then how—?"

"The police decided she had run away again," Gordon said. "We told them about the drugs, about the wild crowd. Kids from the town and the college ran off from time to time. They'd come back, but their parents would be worried sick. But it happened. This was before the Internet, remember. Before CNN. Before all those crime shows on cable TV. Kids ran away, and the police let them go."

"But you say she was murdered."

"A police officer gave me his theory once," he said. "It was off the record, of course. Just something he'd concluded on his own. Are you familiar with the name Rodney Ray Brown?"

I shook my head.

"He's a serial killer. *Was* a serial killer. They executed him in 1984 in Ohio. Apparently, Brown was in Haxton around the time Beth disappeared. He ran with some girl whose grandmother lived there. There's no proof he committed the crime, and the police aren't even sure he was here the day Beth disappeared. But Brown liked certain kinds of girls. He liked them young— high school age—and he liked them with long dark hair. That's Beth." He paused. "I think he got her."

"But he wasn't charged in her death?" I asked.

"Never. They convicted him of killing six other girls. There are other murders and disappearances they suspect him of, but we'll never know for sure. He took those secrets with him."

I sat back in my chair. The couple with the baby had gone, and a group of teenagers, probably the same age as my dead half sister, took their place. They all held phones and talked and texted while they ate. I felt overloaded by the things Gordon told me, as if a great gust of wind had come at me suddenly, knocking me onto my butt.

I had questions. Lots of questions.

But one rose to the top of my mind.

"Why exactly are you telling me all of this?" I asked.

He worked his tongue around in his mouth. I saw it bulging against his cheek. Then he said, "I thought you'd want to understand what happened to your half sister, especially since I know your mother hadn't told you about it. I also wanted to make sure you understood some things about my relationship with your mother. I wanted you to know that even though we weren't together and hadn't been for quite a number of years, we still shared something."

"The memory of your daughter," I said.

"The memory. The pain. The bond that created."

"But if you were so important to her, why didn't she ever tell me about you? You said you were in touch with her right up until she died. How do I know that's true? Or are you just going to tell me to ask Paul?"

"No," he said. "Not that. Your mother had been . . . helping me recently. From time to time over the past year or so."

"Helping with what?"

"My life hasn't been the same since Beth died. I never really had my feet on the ground again. Losing a child, it's . . . it's just something I never could have imagined. Things never went right after that." He looked me right in the eye. "I was glad your mom found someone else and had more kids. It was tough seeing her that way, but I knew she'd moved on. Maybe that's why she didn't tell you about it."

I thought of my mother—her no-nonsense approach to living, the way things were cut-and-dried for her. She didn't waste time looking backward. But this man—my mom's ex-husband—wanted me to believe that my mother, my very loving mother, could just move on from the loss of a child as easily as someone could move on from the loss of a piece of jewelry or a car.

"If what you're telling me is true," I said, "I doubt it. How could she just move on?"

"Well," he said, "it's not for me to speculate."

His passive-aggressive tone made me uneasy. He was trying to say something about Mom, to plant some seed of doubt within me, as though I hadn't had twenty-six years of my life with the woman. I knew her strengths. I knew her weaknesses. A man I talked to for less than an hour wasn't going to change that. There were things I didn't know about her, but I did know her. I reminded myself of that—*I knew her*.

I pointed to my watch again. "What is it you wanted?"

He smiled. "Again, so much like her. So eager to cut to the heart of the matter."

"I learned from the best," I said.

"Beth was like that too," he said, his smile turning wan. "Anyway, your mom was helping me out from time to time with a little money. Like I said, I haven't had the best of luck, and my health has also had some ups and downs."

"You want money?" I asked. "I don't have any money. I'm a graduate student."

"But your mom has some money," he said. "I think it's from the insurance policy when your father died."

"But her will is set—"

I stopped. If my brain were run on wires and plugs, that moment would have been when it felt like someone had flipped a switch, sending a burst of light to the right part of my head. I hadn't thought it before, but once I did, it made perfect sense to me.

"Elizabeth Yarbrough," I said. "The woman named in my mother's will. Everything my mother owned is to be divided three ways between me, my brother, and this woman named Elizabeth Yarbrough. I don't know her, and neither does the lawyer. But you're telling me my mother had another daughter named Elizabeth, right? And there's a woman in the will named Elizabeth. Is that her?"

Gordon was already shaking his head. "Didn't you hear the story I just told you?" he asked. "Didn't you listen to any of that? Beth is dead. Our Beth is gone."

"But there was no body. No conviction. How do you know?"

"I'd know my own daughter, wouldn't I?"

"You've met her? You've met Elizabeth Yarbrough?"

"We're getting off track here," he said.

"So you *have* met her?" I asked. "Is she your daughter?"

"No," Gordon said. "She's not. Absolutely not."

"So why did Mom leave a third of her estate to her?" I asked.

"Your mother fell prey to a . . . a con artist. Yes, that's the only term that applies. A con artist. That woman, that Elizabeth Yarbrough, has taken advantage of your mother. She preyed on her and convinced her that she is really our Beth. I had no idea about the will," he said. "But it doesn't surprise me in the least. Elizabeth Yarbrough is fleecing your family."

Chapter Thirty-six

Just then my phone rang. I knew who it would be. I checked my watch. Still ten minutes to go until the deadline I'd given Dan, but I knew he wouldn't wait the entire time. He'd grow impatient and nervous, and then he'd call.

I wanted to continue the conversation with Gordon Baxter. I wanted to hear what he had to say about Elizabeth Yarbrough. But I knew if I didn't answer the phone, Dan would think the worst. The Dover police would be at the door of the McDonald's almost as fast as he would be.

"Are you going to take that?" Gordon asked.

"I have to," I said.

I lifted the phone and saw it wasn't Dan on the other end of the line.

It was Paul.

I had a lot to say to him. A lot. But not at that moment. I answered, though, intending to make sure I could see him sooner rather than later.

"Are you at home?" Paul asked right away.

Something sounded off in his voice. There was an urgency in it, an edge that made it seem on the brink of breaking.

"What's wrong?" I asked. "Paul?"

"It's Ronnie."

"What happened?"

What else could *happen?* I wanted to say. *What else could possibly happen?*

"He got ahold of some pills in the hospital," Paul said. "Elizabeth, he tried to kill himself. I think you better get over here. I'm in the emergency room of St. Vincent's. That's where they brought him."

I was standing before I could say another thing. And I didn't say anything else—nothing that I could remember anyway. And I don't remember what Gordon Baxter said to me before I left either. I rushed to the car in a daze.

I cried on the way to St. Vincent's Hospital. Not sobbing or hysterics, just quiet tears. They ran from my eyes as I drove, and I spent most of my time wiping them away. As I pulled into the parking lot, the phone rang. I parked the car before I answered. I considered not answering and just running inside, but I thought it might be Paul again.

But it was Dan, checking in.

In the mad rush to get to St. Vincent's—the *other* hospital in Dover, the one for *physically* sick people—I had forgotten all about him. I gathered myself and tried to sound collected and calm when I answered. I didn't want to have Dan worrying about me any more than he already was.

"Hello?"

"Are you okay?" he asked.

Had he heard something in my voice? Or was he really just making sure I was okay?

"I'm fine," I said. "I'm not with that person anymore."

"Where are you?"

"I'm at the hospital," I said. "I have to see Ronnie."

"Is something the matter?"

I must not have been able to hide my feelings as well as I thought I could. Or I just didn't care anymore. How much good had it done my mother and me to hide everything from each other? How many messes could have been avoided if we'd just talked to each other?

"Ronnie . . ." I couldn't say it. Just as I couldn't call my mother a murder victim, it was difficult to choke out these words about Ronnie. I took a deep breath and then said it as clearly as I could. "It looks like Ronnie tried to kill himself."

"Jesus," he said. "Do you need anything?"

And then, as hard as it was to admit I needed help yet again, I said yes.

"What can I do?"

"Can you just come to St. Vincent's and sit with me? I'd like to have you here."

"I'm on my way."

I found Paul in the waiting room of St. Vincent's. He was sitting in a plastic chair among the other families and victims of random Saturday afternoon mayhem and maladies. He didn't notice me until I came within earshot of him and called out his name.

He jerked his head up, his face startled. Then his features relaxed a little and he said, "Elizabeth, it's you."

He stood up, but didn't offer me a hug. He seemed particularly distracted.

"What the hell happened?" I asked.

As I said it—and I'm sure I wasn't the first person to say that in the emergency room that day—several heads turned in our direction. A middle-aged guy two seats down from Paul held a bloody cloth to a cut on his knee. And a kid in the row behind him hacked with a cough that would give a coal miner a run for the money. They all watched, not even hiding their curiosity.

Paul placed his hand on my right arm and guided me to the other side of the room, where no one was sitting.

"Wait," I said as we moved. "Is he okay? Is he even—?"

"He's alive," Paul said. "They're treating him right now."

"Have you seen him?"

"Not yet. But the nurse came out and updated me. She said he's unconscious but stable. That was all she said."

"What happened? What did he do?"

"It's not entirely clear," Paul said. "What I know is that a nurse went into Ronnie's room late this morning, after you left Dover Community, and found him unresponsive. Frank Allison had arrived at the hospital, I guess, and started talking to one of the detectives. They went off somewhere, and they were gone for forty minutes or so. No one was allowed in Ronnie's room. When the nurse went in, his breathing was shallow. He showed all the signs of having suffered an overdose. They think it's possible he's been hiding his pills for the last few days, maybe longer. Not swallowing them when the nurse brings the medication around."

"Don't they check that?" I asked.

"I'm sure they try," Paul said. "But the place is understaffed. Every nurse and every aide looks dead on their feet. Ronnie's smart enough to sneak something past them."

"And he just confessed," I said. "Do you think it's because he feels guilty? Hell, it makes him look guilty. Doesn't it?"

Paul simply reached out to me, his hand shaking, and took my hand in his. He didn't say anything else. We sat like that for a while. My tears had stopped, at least for the moment. Paul squeezed my hand. His skin felt cold, clammy.

"I should have seen this coming," he said. "I should have known."

"We both should have, I guess."

"No, no," he said. He squeezed my hand a little tighter. "Earlier this morning, at the hospital, I wanted to talk to the police. Remember?"

"Did you want to warn them about this?" I asked. "Ronnie's never done or talked about anything like this. Has he?"

"No, of course not."

He didn't say anything else. He stared straight ahead, his hand still in mine. A nurse came out carrying a clipboard, and my expectations rose. But she summoned another patient, the guy with the gash on his knee. I watched him limp behind the nurse.

Maybe the distraction of other people's problems brought my mind back into focus. "Paul?" I said.

"Hmm?"

"I met someone today. A man named Gordon Baxter."

Paul continued to stare straight ahead, but I saw him swallow, his Adam's apple bobbing up and down as though he were passing a peach pit through his throat.

"Do you know him?" I asked.

Paul nodded.

"He was at the cemetery, right?" I asked. "At Mom's funeral?"

"Yes, he was. But he wasn't supposed to be."

"So it's all true, then? Mom was married to him? And they had a daughter?"

Paul still didn't look at me, but he said, "There's so much more to the story than anything that man could tell you."

Before I could ask for more of an explanation, Dan came through the doors of the emergency room and headed over to us.

Chapter Thirty-seven

I stood up as he approached, and he folded me in his arms. He held me for a long time. When he let go, he looked at Paul, and I remembered that the two of them had never met. I introduced them, calling Dan my friend from school. They shook hands, formal and a little stiff, and then we all sat down again.

I could tell Dan wanted to ask a bunch of questions, but he didn't. He sat next to me, and the three of us were in an awkward little row, nobody knowing what to say or do.

I knew what I wanted to talk about, though. I wanted to ask Paul all about Gordon Baxter and the story he'd told me. Paul had said there was more to the story. I wanted to hear it all.

But I didn't want to get into it with Dan there. And I was glad he was there. I leaned in close to him in our uncomfortable waiting room seats. He took my hand.

"Do you want anything?" he asked. "Something to eat or drink?"

"No, thanks," I said. "I'm fine."

"If you need help covering your classes next week or anything, I can do it."

"I know," I said. "Thanks."

"I'm glad you called," he said. "I mean, I wish you didn't need to, but I'm glad you did."

"It felt like I *needed* you," I said.

"Is that a problem?" he asked.

"No," I said. "I'm okay with it."

I didn't know how much time passed with the three of us sitting mostly in silence. It must have been twenty minutes or so before a nurse came through the swinging doors and called out for the family of Ronald Hampton. We all perked up, and Paul and I moved quickly toward the nurse.

"The doctor is coming to speak to you," she said. "You can wait in this room here."

She pointed us toward a door. Paul went through. I asked, "Is my brother okay?"

The nurse smiled without much joy. "The doctor is on his way. I don't know anything about his condition."

Paul and I waited with the door closed. I was glad Dan hadn't tried to follow us. He could have come into the room and heard the news from the doctor. But was it his place? Were we there as a couple? My heart started to thump as we waited. I tried to read the tea leaves. Would they have left us here to wait if Ronnie was dead? Would they tell us he was dead in a room like the one we were in? Is that how things worked?

"Your friend seems nice," Paul said.

"He is."

"It's thoughtful of him to come."

"Yes. Paul, do I really have a half sister?" I asked.

"*Had,*" Paul said. "She's dead."

His voice sounded cold and flat as he said the words. Almost angry. Was he angry with me for bringing it up? Or was he angry about something else?

"I never told you about the will—"

The door opened, and a middle-aged woman in scrubs entered the room. She reached out and shook hands with us, introducing herself as Dr. Something-or-other. I didn't catch her name. I didn't care what it was.

She didn't beat around the bush.

"Ronald is stable now," she said. "We're moving him to a bed in intensive care for a while, probably the next twenty-four hours or so. After that, we'll move him to a regular room and continue to monitor him there."

"He's alive?" I asked, my voice sounding like a child's in the small, cramped room. A child pleading with an authority figure. *Please tell me my brother is alive.*

"He is," the doctor said. "Very much so. Like I said, we'll watch him and make sure there isn't any long-term damage. It doesn't look like the dose he took was that high, so there's reason for optimism."

"How did this happen, Doctor?" Paul asked. "He has Down syndrome, and he's been in Dover Community."

"They'll be figuring that out over there in the coming days, I'm sure," the doctor said. "But my guess would be he's been holding pills back and not swallowing them. Maybe everything they give him. Your brother takes a variety of medications, which is not unusual for Down syndrome. He could create a pretty good cocktail over there. But like I said, thankfully not enough to do the job he wanted to do." She stood up. "You'll be able to go up and see him in about an hour if you want to go home or get something to eat. Someone will let you know when it's time."

She nodded at us and left the room.

I felt relief. A small measure, but it was there. I also felt something else. I turned to Paul and said, "I think I'm hungry."

Chapter Thirty-eight

Dan was still there when we came back into the waiting room. He looked at us expectantly, and I suspect he could tell simply by the looks on our faces that we hadn't received terrible news.

"He's okay," I said to him. "I mean, as okay as he can be, considering."

"Good," Dan said.

"We're going to get to see him in ICU soon. They're moving him up there now."

"Good," Dan said again.

Paul said, "We were going to go get something to eat, if you'd like to join us."

"He can't," I said.

Both Dan and Paul looked at me. I sounded edgy and firm, like someone giving commands to a small dog. I could read the look on Dan's face. He seemed a little hurt. I knew he thought all the progress we had made—my *needing* him—had evaporated with one sentence barked out by me.

"Can you excuse us just a moment, Paul?" I said.

He nodded and walked away, heading to the cafeteria.

I turned back to Dan. "Look, I'm sorry," I said. "But I need to talk to my uncle. Alone."

He still looked hurt, but he put on a brave face for me. "I understand."

"It's about that person I was talking to today," I said. "And a bunch of other things."

"Okay," he said. "Family stuff. You know, someday we are going to have to talk about all of this . . . and you're going to have to tell me what's going on." He paused. "If we're going to be in any kind of relationship."

"I will," I said. "I wish I could tell you all about it today. Right now. But I just can't. I have to get some other answers first. Believe me, I'd rather be with you than doing any of this."

He nodded. "Call me when you can."

I leaned up and kissed him. Right in front of everyone.

"Later," I said. "I promise."

I selected a lot of food as we went through the St. Vincent's cafeteria line. I took a plate of roast beef and gravy with a side of mashed potatoes—and more gravy. I also grabbed a piece of chocolate pie. I hadn't eaten all day, and it was well past lunch. I didn't even care that the pie looked like it had been sitting on the cafeteria line since the Reagan administration.

Paul was more controlled. He picked a salad and a turkey sandwich. When we reached the cash register, he paid. I made a token offer to pick up the tab, but he refused. I doubted I had more than a few dollars in my wallet.

We found a table out of the way. The cafeteria wasn't very crowded on a Saturday. People in Dover seemed to be falling ill and having accidents mostly during normal business hours. I dug into my food as soon as we sat down. And I started with the questions right away.

"So, it's all true?" I asked. "What this guy told me?"

"I don't know everything he told you," Paul said. He picked at his salad with a plastic fork.

"I'll give you the gist," I said. "Mom was married to that guy—and not just for a short amount of time. They had a daughter. Oh, and her name is Elizabeth, same as mine. That's not creepy at all, Paul. Not at all. And on top of that, this daughter, this other Elizabeth—my namesake apparently—ran off and was murdered, possibly by a serial killer. And Mom never told me about it. Neither Mom nor Dad—or *you*—ever told me about it."

Paul looked as though he didn't know what to say. He concentrated on his food, his head drooping a bit between his shoulders. My little rant had brought something home to me, something I hadn't fully comprehended before. This was no longer just about Mom. Sure, she had kept things from me. But so had Dad—and I thought he and I had understood each other in ways Mom and I didn't. And Paul. He was supposed to be the cool one, the favorite uncle.

Why didn't anyone tell me?

"For the record," Paul finally said, "I think your mother should have told you. I encouraged her to."

"Why didn't she?"

He laid the plastic fork aside. "Honestly, I think she was embarrassed. You know what she was like. Private, closed off. Strong. She didn't admit weakness very well, and here she would have had to tell someone very important to her, someone whose opinion she valued, that she had made a horrible mistake in marrying Gordon Baxter. But she had her reasons for doing it."

Paul's response seemed to miss the point. I mostly wanted to understand why I had never been told about having a sister who'd been murdered. Paul seemed more concerned with Mom's marriage.

"Why was marrying him a horrible mistake?" I asked.

"You met him," Paul said. "What did you think of him?"

I summoned a mental picture of Gordon Baxter. An odd man, that was for sure. Yes, a little creepy. I couldn't imagine my mother marrying or spending time with someone like that, but then I couldn't imagine my mother spending time with any man. I knew she and my father loved each other, but their marriage sometimes looked like a relationship between platonic roommates.

"I think I'm missing something," I said, taking another couple of bites of my food.

"He's a criminal, Elizabeth," Paul said.

"What do you mean?" I chewed, trying to concentrate on what Paul was saying.

"He's spent time in jail."

"And Mom married him?"

"This was after he and your mom split up," Paul said. "Several years after. But make no mistake: the guy's bad news. I never liked him. He was an asshole back in high school, and I'm sure he hasn't changed."

Asshole? Paul rarely cursed.

"Mom was a good judge of character," I said. "She didn't tolerate anything. She acted like leaving the toilet seat up meant you were going to hell."

"They met in high school," Paul said. "Your mom was quiet. Bookish would be the polite way to put it. A nerd, I guess, is what young people would say now. She didn't have a lot of friends. She certainly never dated. She didn't even go to the dances we had at the school. And Gordon . . . he was something of a big man on campus. He played sports, football and baseball.

He had a lot of friends. I guess he was handsome in his own way, even though he was short."

Again, I visualized the man I'd spoken to in McDonald's, the man who'd been married to my mother. "Handsome" didn't come to mind. "Toadish" was more like it. But I was meeting him fifty years after the fact. In the wedding photo, he had looked only okay, but I wouldn't say handsome.

"Go on," I said.

"He took an interest in Leslie," Paul said. "I don't know why. She was a pretty girl when she was young, even if she was reserved and quiet. You've seen the pictures of her. It would be easy to see, given her looks, that a young man could be taken with her. I suspect her quiet nature, her refusal or inability—I'm not sure which it was—to reveal anything of herself to the world made her seem even more alluring. You know, the power of mystery. So he pursued her. Asked her out on dates. Took her to dances. He fell for her, and she for him."

"What did she see in him, then, if he was such an asshole?"

"You remember high school," Paul said. "What would it be like to have a popular guy show an interest in you? Everybody wants to feel special, to feel pursued and desirable. Right? Your mother was different, but she wasn't that different. Inside, she was a teenage girl who wanted the things teenage girls want."

"She wanted them enough to marry him?"

"They got married during their senior year in high school and settled in Haxton."

"Wait—*during* their senior year. They got married while they were still in high school?"

"Yes."

"Was Mom . . . ?" I couldn't bring myself to say it. The whole idea seemed so crazy to me.

Paul nodded his head. "She became pregnant with Beth during her senior year and had her when she was just seventeen. Your mom's birthday is late. July. She didn't turn eighteen until after graduation. After Beth was born in June."

"Jesus," I said. "Mom? Mom got knocked up?"

"Don't be crude," he said.

"Was it a scandal? Didn't they used to send girls away for that?"

"They did. Sometimes. But your mom got married to Gordon as soon as they realized what had happened. They cut it close. I'm sure people did the math and figured it out, but they got married so fast it couldn't really become an issue. Some couples just got married during high school back then, pregnant or not. This was small-town Ohio. Kids got married young. Girls started having babies young."

"And Mom didn't want to go to college?" I asked. "Even once she had the baby?"

"This was 1960," Paul said. "Do you think women from Haxton, Ohio, went off to college, baby or not? Hell, the guys barely did. I was one of the few. When I told my father, your grandfather, I wanted to go to Ohio State and get a college degree, he laughed at me. It was another time."

"But you said Mom was different."

"She was. But even she couldn't fight the combined societal forces of sexism and low expectations for girls. She did what she was supposed to do. More so, really. Do you think my parents ever expected her to get married? They probably looked at her all those years and imagined she'd end up an old maid, living at home with them until they died. Not only did she get married, she married a good guy. In their eyes. And in the town's. She snagged a prize. Gordon had a respectable job as a salesman. He made a comfortable living. And . . ."

"And?" I prompted him.

"And they had a baby. Right away, they had a baby."

I reached for my glass of milk and took a big gulp. "This is Elizabeth."

"Beth," Paul said. "We always called her Beth."

My voice rose for the first time in our conversation. "Why the hell did Mom name me after a dead girl? If she's really dead. Why did anyone let her do that? Why did Dad?"

"Leslie felt guilty about what happened to Beth," Paul said. "Any parent would. She felt responsible. You know, she and Beth had a rocky relationship. It was the seventies. Beth was a strong-willed teenager."

"I heard," I said.

"Gordon told you all this?"

I nodded. "She had a rough time with her daughter. With my half sister. I still don't know why she named me after a dead kid."

"I know it's strange," Paul said. "I thought it was strange too. But I tried to understand where she was coming from. That name told me how much she valued you because I understood how deeply she was affected by losing Beth. You were a second chance, especially with Ronnie . . . you were her best chance. You really were."

"I thought she had me just so I could take care of Ronnie."

"Who told you that?"

"She did. She said it right to my face."

Paul sighed. "That's not the only reason they had you. And you know it."

"Do I?"

"Yes. Your mom was practical. She did think that way. She devoted her life to making sure Ronnie was cared for. But she also desperately wanted to have children. She loved being a mom. That was her whole life, you and Ronnie. She wanted you very much, just for you."

A cafeteria worker pushed a big cart full of empty and dirty trays past us, the wheels squeaking against the tile floor. We couldn't talk for a moment, and I took the opportunity to gather my thoughts. Had she really *wanted* me? Or was I a caretaker for Ronnie? A do-over for the first Elizabeth?

Would I ever really know?

Chapter Thirty-nine

I returned to my food for a few minutes. We both did. Maybe Paul hoped the conversation had run its natural course, that all of the questions I had come armed with as a result of my conversation with Gordon Baxter had been answered. Of course, that wasn't true. Not by a long shot.

"Damn," I said. "Mom got pregnant and got married in high school."

"She did."

"The girl," I said.

"What?"

"The girl. Elizabeth. Gordon says she was murdered. Is that true?"

"She ran away. That's the first thing you need to know," Paul said. He looked down at his food and jabbed at the salad with more intensity than before.

"Out in the waiting room, you said you thought she was dead. Gordon said the same thing."

"I'm sure she is," Paul said, still not looking up. "I'm sure she fell in with the wrong crowd. She was doing drugs. Hard drugs. You can't expect a life like that to turn out well."

He sounded cold, dismissive. His voice carried no empathy or understanding for Elizabeth. It didn't seem like the Paul I knew, and I called him on it.

"Running away," he said, "is the worst thing you can do to a parent. She put Leslie through hell when she was here, but once she ran away, that was the worst thing of all. To not let your mother know where you are? I can't imagine."

"Do you know about the will?" I asked.

He stopped jabbing at his food and looked into my eyes. "You said you had something to tell me. I'm afraid I know what it is."

"What?" I asked.

He put his fork down and picked up his napkin. First he wiped his mouth, slowly and methodically. Then he balled the napkin up and tossed it onto his tray.

"It's that crazy woman, that Elizabeth Yarbrough. Are you telling me your mom left her something in the will?"

"A third of the estate," I said.

Paul closed his eyes. He looked as if he had just been struck by a heavy blow that knocked the wind out of him. "Jesus," he whispered. "Jesus."

"You agree with Gordon?" I asked. "You think this woman is a con artist?"

His eyes remained closed. "The alternative is to believe that woman is my niece who's been missing for thirty-seven years."

"Why is that hard to believe?" I asked.

He started shaking his head. "I didn't want to say this to you."

I waited. I didn't know whether I wanted to hear anything else from him. But I couldn't not hear it. That was the problem. After being kept in the dark for so long, I needed to hear everything.

"Say what?" I asked.

He rubbed at his eyes with his knuckles, then opened them, blinking several times. "For several months before . . . before your mom died," he said, "I worried about her. About her mental state. I thought she might have been . . . slipping a little bit."

"Dementia?"

"Not severe. Not yet. But she might have been heading that way. Did you notice anything?"

"I didn't—"

But I stopped myself. Who was I to say? I wasn't speaking to my mother in the weeks before she died.

"I've seen this happen to elderly friends of mine," Paul said. "And their parents. They become susceptible to believing just about anything that they may intensely want to believe. That's why con artists prey on the elderly. They can't make the same judgments they once made. They can't judge character as well." He tapped his index finger against his temple. "I don't know when this woman, this Elizabeth Yarbrough, showed up. I'm guessing it was close to a year ago. You know your mom. She wasn't always eager to reveal anything to anyone until she had to."

"I know."

"It was just a few months ago she told me about it. She called me over and told me that she had been reunited with Beth. *Her* Beth. She was thrilled, of course. Overjoyed. She said they were getting to know each other, and that Beth had apologized for running away. Your mom seemed . . . happy about it. Relieved, almost. I guess she always thought she was going to die without ever seeing Beth again, without ever knowing what really happened to her."

"Is that when you saw Beth yourself?" I asked.

Paul's eyes widened. "I never saw her," he said. "I've never laid eyes on this woman. That's part of my concern. I started to feel that Leslie was hiding Beth from me. At first, it was under the guise of the two of them just needing to spend time together and get reacquainted. And I could understand that and give them their space. But I think Leslie started to see that I had doubts, and rather than introducing me to Beth and easing those doubts, she kept me away from her. I never met her. When your mom died, it was all a mystery to me."

"But don't you think Mom would know her own daughter? Wouldn't she recognize her?"

"People see what they want to see," Paul said. "And after thirty-seven years, who can say what anyone would look like? I look at old pictures of myself, and I think I'm seeing a stranger."

"But there must be some resemblance," I said. "Something."

"I wouldn't know," he said. "I never saw her. Not even a picture."

"And you think somehow this woman weaseled her way into Mom's life and got into the will?" I asked. "How many people even knew Mom had a daughter who disappeared?"

"Everybody who was alive in Haxton in 1975," Paul said. "I kind of figured it was somebody's kid or relative, someone who had heard of the case and saw an opening."

"Maybe it's even someone who went to school with Beth and knew her," I said.

"Good point."

Other things started to click into place. It was true—Mom's will seemed to have changed suddenly, out of the blue. And then there was the call from a woman to Mr. Allison's office inquiring about the estate. Who would do that unless they knew they might be getting something—and didn't want to wait very long to have it? And there was the mystery woman at the other hospital, the one who'd gone to Ronnie's room to speak with him, leaving him in some kind of unexplained emotional turmoil.

"And Mrs. Porter," I said.

"Who?"

"Mrs. Porter. You know, Mom's busybody friend from the library?"

"I know her."

"She told me Mom came in looking for a book on . . . I can't remember it exactly, but it was something about dealing with an adult child who has suffered trauma. Something like that. I had no idea why Mom would be looking for that, but it might make sense if this woman gave her a long sob story about what she'd been through. Right?"

"That's a sure sign," Paul said. "Her answer for everything was to go read a book about it."

"Do the police know about this woman?" I asked.

"I didn't tell them."

"Why not?"

"I didn't think . . . I don't know who this woman is. I don't even know if she's real. It didn't cross my mind."

"Jesus, Paul. Do you know what I'm thinking?"

He didn't say anything, but he nodded his head ever so slightly, as if the movement required a great deal of effort.

"If this woman got into the will, and then Mom ends up dead, doesn't this make her a suspect?"

"But Ronnie?" Paul said. "What he told the police?"

"You don't believe that, do you?" I asked. "His confession? Do you really believe that bullshit?"

"He tried to kill himself, Elizabeth. Why else are we here, in this place, except that he couldn't live with himself for whatever he did?"

I wanted Paul to take a firm stand—and for that firm stand to be on the side I wanted him to be on. But he refused to do so.

It required an effort for me to let it go. I wasn't going to fight with him again. I wasn't going to turn against anyone who should be my ally. Instead, I shifted my attention to the tasks I saw ahead of me, the things I needed to take care of.

I needed to contact the police and tell them about the will.

And then I needed to find out all I could about Elizabeth Yarbrough.

Chapter Forty

In the ICU of St. Vincent's, Paul and I were allowed to spend fifteen minutes with a still unconscious Ronnie. He looked like hell, make no mistake about it. An IV line dripped a clear liquid into his arm. His skin looked ashen, his cheeks sunken. If not for the steady beeping of the heart monitor and the slow rise and fall of his chest, I would have thought he was dead.

I leaned in next to his bed. I gripped his hand in mine. His skin felt cool and clammy, giving me a chill of my own. I remembered touching my father's hand as he lay in his casket. His skin felt rubbery and fake. So did Ronnie's.

But I didn't let go.

I grasped Ronnie's hand and squeezed, exerting just a small amount of pressure. I didn't want to hurt him or startle him. I had no idea what effect the contact might have on him. Nothing happened, so I squeezed again. This time he returned the gesture. I felt the slightest bit of pressure returned against my hand. He was there. Ronnie was still there.

Paul walked out of the room by my side, his arm around my shoulder. No matter what, I had the two of them. A long road stretched ahead, but at least the three of us were still there.

I asked Paul if he minded staying at St. Vincent's for a while so that I could take care of some other things. He told me he didn't mind at all.

"What else is an old retired guy going to do on a Saturday?" he said.

He was clearly just as relieved as I was that Ronnie was alive. Maybe more so.

"You know, we need to remember . . ." He didn't finish the thought, but I knew where he was going.

"He's not out of the woods yet," I said. "I get it."

And we didn't say what really hung between us about Ronnie: even if he got through this, he still faced the prospect of a murder charge.

Some things were better left unsaid.

In the hospital parking lot, I pulled out my phone. I hadn't had any luck searching for Elizabeth Yarbrough. But now I had a different name to try.

I typed in a search for "Elizabeth Baxter" in Haxton, Ohio.

Nothing came up.

I tried again, adding the word "missing" to the search. Again nothing. I added "missing person" and then "disappear." Still nothing.

Was it possible for someone, a fifteen-year-old girl, to disappear and for there to be no trace or record of it in the world? Did people just forget?

I sent a text to Neal Nelson. It took just seconds for him to call me. When I answered, he didn't say hello or ask me how I was doing. He just jumped right in.

"I knew you'd need me," he said. "What can I do for you, Teach?"

"I need you to find somebody," I said. "And if you can, find out *about* somebody."

"Teach, I love a good caper," he said. "I imagine this has to do with your mom."

"It does," I said.

"Glad I can help. Just give me the name and whatever you happen to know about this person."

"You know what?" I said. "Now that I think about it, I'm going to need you to look into two people for me."

Chapter Forty-one

I remained in the car for a few minutes longer. The weather had been milder than everyone had expected, and people had emerged from their homes, blinking in the sunlight, deciding that they'd better hurry up and enjoy it because it might be the last day like that for a long, long time.

I cracked the window, letting in a little air. I called Detective Richland. It was late on Saturday afternoon, and I had no idea whether the detective would still be on duty after the events of the morning. He didn't answer his phone, so I left a message explaining that I had new information about my mother's case and to please call. I called and left a message for Detective Post as well, under the assumption that she would be more likely to call me back than Richland.

I started the car and headed for downtown.

If the Internet didn't have the answers I wanted, I knew a place that might. The Dover Public Library sat two blocks off the courthouse square downtown. It was a boxy limestone building with small windows and heavy doors. It looked like a place constructed to withstand a siege.

I mounted the front steps and went into the dark, silent space. I loved being inside the library. Mom and Dad had brought us there all the time when we were kids. I'd been to libraries in other towns, and I liked the Dover one best. I applied the same theory to libraries that I did to churches. I didn't want them to look modern and bright and welcoming. I was more comfortable in them when they were heavy and foreboding.

I hadn't been to the periodicals room in years. I used to go there when I was a teenager and read music magazines, thinking to myself that I would run off someplace where all those cool bands hung out and played: Austin, London, Los Angeles. I hadn't run off, of course, but I did associate the library with the freedom to dream.

As the fates would have it, a friendly face waited for me in the periodicals room. Mrs. Porter stood behind the counter. She held a paperback novel in her right hand, her eyes glued to the pages. She didn't see me right away. But as I approached the desk, she looked up and greeted me with a big smile. She marked her place with a piece of paper and put the book aside.

"Well, well," she said. "Elizabeth. To what do we owe this honor?"

"I'm here to do research, I guess."

"Is this for school?" she asked. "You know, I don't ordinarily staff the periodicals desk. The woman who normally works here, her daughter had a baby so she went to Cincinnati to help out. I'm just filling in."

"I'm looking for newspapers," I said.

"They're all right there," she said, pointing. "Local, state, and national. Although how anyone can read the *New York Times* I'll never understand. Too liberal for my tastes."

"Do you carry the newspaper from Haxton?" I asked.

Mrs. Porter scrunched up her face. "Oh, honey. The *Haxton Herald-Leader* ceased publication five years ago. Nothing ever happens in Haxton."

"I'm looking for old papers," I said. "From, say, the seventies. Do you have those on microfilm?"

"Oh, those. See those big things over there?" She pointed to a large filing cabinet with elongated drawers. "They're all in there, chronological by date. See, I do know something." She winked at me. "Say, didn't your mother grow up in Haxton? I think she mentioned that once."

"She did," I said.

Mrs. Porter looked suspicious. "So this isn't a school project, I gather?"

I shook my head. "Actually, Mrs. Porter, I was wondering if I could ask you something about my mother. Something strange."

Mrs. Porter's eyebrows rose halfway up her forehead when I said the word "strange."

"You can ask me anything," she said, barely concealing her anticipation.

I almost didn't say it. I knew how rumors and stories could spread in a town like Dover, and Mrs. Porter had to be at the white-hot center of the gossip wildfire. But I needed to find out whether she knew anything.

"Did my mom ever mention anything to you about being married before she was married to my dad?" I asked.

If you looked up the definition of "taken aback" in the dictionary, you would probably find the look Mrs. Porter showed on her face. The corners of her mouth turned down in an exaggerated frown. She appeared almost offended.

"I never heard any such thing," she said.

I worried that I had crossed a line, that Mrs. Porter would see my question as unseemly and somehow besmirching the memory of someone recently deceased. I couldn't necessarily blame her.

But then she leaned forward, placing both her elbows on the counter. She brought her face close to mine and spoke in a low voice. "Is that true?" she asked.

I kept my voice low as well, entering into the conspiracy with her. "I think it is."

"Are you researching marriage records?" Mrs. Porter asked.

"Something like that," I said.

"Well," she said, the single word an expression of surprise and also some kind of judgment. "People do surprise you."

"Indeed they do."

"But Leslie Hampton? I guess she's the last person I would expect to surprise me. That woman was as steady as a rock."

"I agree. Well, I'm going to get to work over here."

"Elizabeth? Did you ever figure out why your mother wanted that book she was in here looking for?"

"No," I said. "I'm still figuring that one out."

Mrs. Porter looked at me suspiciously.

"Heck," I said, "maybe after all those years of reading about Ronnie, she decided she really needed a book to figure me out."

Mrs. Porter didn't laugh. "Your mother was very proud of you," she said. "She talked about it all the time."

I hadn't expected those words, nor did I expect my response. I felt tears welling in my eyes. I don't know whether Mrs. Porter noticed or not, but I turned away as fast as I could and headed for the microfilm drawers.

The task of making sense of the microfilm filing system gave me time to collect myself again. I blinked the tears away as I went through the drawers that held the *Haxton Herald-Leader*. It took a few minutes to work my way down the length of the filing cabinet. Then I had to run through the dates until I came across the right time frame. I found 1975, but that didn't narrow things down much. A daily newspaper left me 365 days to choose from.

Then I remembered what Gordon Baxter had said about Beth. She had just started her sophomore year of high school. So I decided to begin with the microfilm for the month of September.

I threaded the strip through the machine, turned the viewing light on, and began. I immediately felt overwhelmed by the impossibility of the task. I wasn't even sure what I hoped to find.

The front pages of the daily editions of the *Haxton Herald-Leader* scrolled by, making me dizzy. I worried important information would fly by without my noticing. In the first few minutes, only key words jumped out. "School tax levy" went by a lot. "President Ford" passed a few times. The high school football team, the Haxton Raiders, was apparently off to a good start. I stopped on a few photos, all in black and white. The men wore checked sport coats and wide ties. Most of the women had long straight hair, usually parted in the middle. It didn't look like just another time; it looked like another planet. Did I really have a sibling who grew up in that world?

I approached the end of the month. Twenty-third, twenty-fourth, twenty-fifth. Maybe I missed it. Or maybe I just needed to keep looking further through the year.

Had anything happened the way people had been telling me?

Both Paul and Gordon Baxter had told me—emphatically— that this Elizabeth Yarbrough woman was a con artist. But was Gordon Baxter one as well? Paul called Gordon a criminal and said he'd been in jail. Were Gordon and Elizabeth working together? The large withdrawals from Mom's bank account, the appearance of Elizabeth in the will . . . Was Paul right? Had Mom lost her sharpness and been taken advantage of? Had they played on her intense desire to see her daughter again?

Then something caught my eye. I scrolled past it accidentally since my hand seemed to be moving faster than my brain. I rewound until I saw the page I wanted again.

There it was. A headline read, "Local Teen Missing for Three Days."

Three days? Did it really take three days for something like this to become a news story?

There were no pictures, just a story I skimmed through. It repeated the same fundamental details Gordon Baxter had told me in McDonald's. "Fifteen-year-old Elizabeth Baxter went missing from her home . . . a sophomore at Haxton Senior High . . . no information about her whereabouts . . . police aren't sure whether to call her absence a crime yet."

What had the police known that they weren't saying? At that point they would have already talked to Mom and Gordon Baxter. The police would have known about the troubles they were having with Elizabeth. Gordon specifically said they'd mentioned the drugs to the police. How hard were they really looking for her?

I skipped ahead to the next day. No story. And the same for the two days after that. September was over at that point. I reached down and brought out the roll of film for October, switched the reels, and started looking again. On October 1 a longer story ran—and for the first time, I saw a picture of my half sister, Elizabeth.

She looked just like my mother. If I hadn't known my sister existed, I would have thought it was a portrait of my mother taken when she was a teenager. They shared the same eye and nose shape, the same high forehead. I didn't know—or care—what Gordon Baxter contributed to the young woman. I saw only my mother. And, yes, even pieces of me. I lifted my hand and brought it to the screen. I touched the image gently, as though I expected some emanation to come through, some information that would explain everything that was going on. But of course it didn't.

I leaned back a little and read the story. The police reiterated that they weren't ready to call the missing girl the victim of a crime. In fact, this story reported that the girl's father, Gordon Baxter, had informed them that the girl was "troubled" and "high-spirited."

High-spirited? I knew what that meant. It was code for "strong-willed girl." Not only could Gordon not control his daughter, he couldn't even begin to understand her. So he labeled her a troublemaker in the newspaper, for all to see. The article ended with Gordon saying, "She started to run with a bad crowd. Maybe she just didn't want to be here anymore."

So the consensus had been reached even back then, from her father—Mom wasn't quoted in the article—as well as the police: Elizabeth Baxter had run away. But Gordon insisted to me that she had been killed, probably by some serial killer the state had put to death. I remembered the name: Rodney Ray Brown.

I took out my phone and searched the Web. I entered "Rodney Ray Brown" along with "Elizabeth Baxter." Just a few hits came up. One of them was from a Web site devoted to serial killers. A small note at the end of the entry on Brown mentioned that he was suspected in more killings, and it listed Elizabeth's name as one of the possibilities. Beyond that, little seemed to tie the two together. Brown had killed in Ohio and Indiana during the 1970s. Elizabeth had run off in Ohio during the 1970s. That was about it.

"Who's that?"

I jumped. Mrs. Porter had managed to sneak up on me and was looking over my shoulder. I reached for the on/off switch.

"Is that your mother?" she asked.

"It's—"

I don't know how bad her eyesight was, or whether she just didn't look closely enough to see the headline, but she patted me on the shoulder and said, "It's amazing how much you two look alike."

Chapter Forty-two

My phone rang just as I was leaving the library. My heart jolted. I'd told myself to expect the same shock every time the phone rang while Ronnie was in the hospital. Any call coming in could be good or bad news.

But it wasn't Paul. Or the hospital. And it wasn't even Dan.

"Hello?"

"Elizabeth," he said.

"Who is this?" I asked.

"It's Gordon Baxter."

"How did you get this number?" I asked.

"You gave it to me before you left McDonald's. Remember?"

I thought about it. I might have. Those moments were a blur.

"You were upset when you left, Elizabeth."

Just hearing him say that name gave me the creeps. He had called his daughter that name all those years ago. He might have even wept while he said that name or dreamed about her and called her name in his sleep. To have him call me by that name—even though it was my name—added a layer of weirdness to the whole enterprise.

"What do you want?"

"I hope your brother is okay," he said.

"He's okay."

I didn't like the idea of revealing anything to this man about my family, even though it was apparent he already knew far more about my family than I did. In a way, he was *part* of my family, whether I liked it or not.

"I'm glad to hear it," he said. His voice sounded oily and insincere, even more than it had in the restaurant. I'd have to wipe the slimy residue of his voice off my ear. "I know our conversation got cut short earlier, so I was just calling to see if you had talked to Paul."

"As you can imagine, we were a little more concerned about my brother's health than your story."

"Oh," he said, sounding almost surprised not to be the center of attention.

"I talked to Paul," I said, "and maybe he did confirm some aspects of your story."

"See?" He sounded very pleased with himself.

"Yeah. I guess I'm still wondering what you want from me. Are you still asking me for money?"

"We didn't really get to finish our discussion."

"Right. You said you'd had some ups and downs. Some bad luck, as you put it."

"Health problems too. I have a heart condition. A lot of medication."

"Does your bad luck also involve being in jail?" I asked. "I understand that was part of it."

I heard his breathing through the phone. It was heavy, but not from exertion. It sounded like the low huffing of an animal, the rhythm of a predator gathering his strength.

"That would be your uncle talking," he said.

"It would be."

"Well, he has his own side of the story to tell. Don't we all?"

"I think I need to go, Mr. Baxter. As you can imagine, I have a lot of other things on my mind right now."

"So your answer is no?"

"I don't know why my mom gave you money, but I can't afford to. I have a brother to take care of. I just became his guardian, and that's enough for me. If you don't mind—"

"You're the guardian?" Gordon asked. He sounded surprised and knowing at the same time.

"I am. It's in the will."

"Hmm," he said.

I expected him to say more, but he didn't. He just left the conversation hanging there. I was tempted to hang up, but I also wanted to see how this would play out.

"Is something wrong?" I asked.

"I thought for sure your uncle would be the guardian," he said.

"I thought so too," I said. "But he's getting older. Mom was worried about having someone here for Ronnie, someone who would be here a long time."

Gordon made a low, dismissive sound—the beginning of a laugh, bitten off and truncated.

"You're such a good girl," he said. "Believing whatever they tell you to believe."

"What do you mean—?"

Without saying anything more, he hung up.

Since the police station was so close to the library, I took a chance and stopped by there, hoping to find Richland or Post hanging around. The station was quiet. It was getting on toward sundown, and I supposed the Saturday evening mayhem hadn't kicked in. Everyone was resting up and saving their craziness for later.

The desk officer seemed indifferent to my presence and mustered a halfhearted "Help you?" when I stepped up. I asked for either one of the detectives and the desk officer asked me the nature of my problem.

I decided to use my mother's death—murder—for whatever it was worth. If I was going to be the victim of a crime and be seen that way by the world, I might as well take advantage of that status when it could do me some good.

"They're investigating my mother's death," I said. "Leslie Hampton? She was murdered a week ago."

The invocation injected some life into the officer's movements. His neck straightened and his eyes opened wider. "Did they ask you to meet them here?"

"No," I said. "I called them. I wanted to see if they were in."

"You called them here?"

"Cell phone," I said. "Is one of them here or not?"

"I doubt they're in today," he said. "It's Saturday, and I haven't seen them. I can leave them a note, or you can call them back. Or you can talk to someone else."

"Might they be back there?" I asked, tilting my head in the direction of the door behind him.

He stared at me for a long moment, as though considering whether to get up and look for the detectives or not.

I decided to give him a little push. "I have information for them about my mother's case."

He nodded. "Okay. I'll check. But if they're not here, you have to talk to someone. You can't let that information go."

He went into the back, letting the heavy wooden door swing shut behind him. I felt tired. It had already been a long day. A long week. My neck hurt and my eyes felt as if they'd been scrubbed with sandpaper. I remembered that I hadn't showered, that my body had taken on that greasy, gritty feel of not having been washed. I surely smelled.

The door opened again, and the officer held it open for me. "You're in luck," he said. It was a strange turn of phrase to direct at someone whose mother had been murdered, and the officer seemed to realize that as the words came out of his mouth. A flush rose on his cheeks and he looked at the floor. "I mean, Detective Post is back here, and she wants you to talk to her."

Post sat at her desk typing on her computer. She didn't look up as I approached; she appeared to be getting down one last thought before she stopped. I reached the side of her desk and waited. I knew she sensed me there, and she hit the last key with more force than normal, the punctuation to something important. Then she stood up and reached out to shake my hand.

"Hello, Elizabeth," she said.

It always felt weird for me to shake another woman's hand. But I didn't want to hug her or peck her on the cheek either. A handshake would have to do. My hand felt small in hers.

She pointed to a chair, and I sat. Post was wearing jeans and black boots. The sleeves of her navy blue shirt were pushed up to her elbows. She smelled good. Unlike me.

"I was going to call you back," she said. "I got your message. I just wanted to finish here." She pointed to the computer screen.

"Paperwork?" I asked.

"School," she said. "I'm getting a master's in criminology. Sometimes I study here on Saturdays because it feels like a place to get business done. You know, I can't just turn on the TV. Or talk to my boyfriend."

It was the most personal conversation we'd had. The notion that she led a life, that she had friends or parents or pets, hadn't really occurred to me. I wanted something very simple from her: to make sense of my mother's death, preferably in a way that didn't land my brother in jail.

"Right," I said. "Well, I'm sorry to just barge in on you like this. And I'm sorry to call you when you're off."

"It's no problem," she said. "The officer who showed you back said you had some information you wanted to share about your mother's case."

"I do," I said.

"By the way," Post said, "how is your brother doing?"

"He's in ICU right now. I guess I'll be going back later—"

"ICU? What do you mean?"

"At the hospital," I said. "He's at St. Vincent's Hospital. He tried to kill himself earlier today."

Post's mouth opened. I saw her white teeth, a flash of dental work. She was silent a moment, then said, "Are you kidding me? I'm so sorry."

"No. I figured they would have called you. Both of you."

Post turned and reached for her cell phone. She checked it, shaking her head, then set the phone back down. "They didn't call both of us," she said, still shaking her head. "They called *one* of us. And he didn't tell me." She used her thumbs to send a quick text. Then she put the phone facedown on the desk and asked me to explain what had happened. I did, sparing no details about Ronnie's suicide attempt. Post didn't take notes, but she seemed absorbed by what I told her. As I spoke, her cell phone buzzed, but she ignored it and asked a few follow-up questions about Ronnie's condition and his state of mind the last time I saw him before the attempt.

Once I'd told her everything—which wasn't much—she picked up the phone. Whatever she read there didn't make her any happier. If head shaking were an Olympic sport, she'd take the gold.

"Is that what you wanted to tell me about?" she asked. "Your brother's suicide attempt?"

"No, it really isn't," I said. "I wanted to tell you about a few other things. Should I be telling them to both of you?"

"No," she said. She clamped her lips tight. I saw the muscles in her neck clench as well. "You can tell me, and I'll share the information with my partner."

"Okay," I said. I trusted Post more than Richland. I liked her. She maintained some semblance of a professional wall, but she also came out from behind it from time to time. I sensed she was doing that then. "I found out that my mother was married once before," I said. "Her first husband came by to talk to me."

Post tilted her head a little. "What do you mean, 'found out'?"

"He told me all about it," I said.

"But you didn't know that before?"

"No, I didn't. Did you?"

Post looked uncomfortable, as if maybe she'd sat on a nail. "We do background checks on anyone who has been the victim of a crime like the one involving your mother. It's standard procedure during the investigation. We saw that she had married this—" She leaned forward and opened a manila folder, leafed through a few pages. "Gordon Baxter? Is that the man you spoke to?"

I nodded.

"She was married to him for a while," she said. "And he came to see you? Why? How did he find you?"

"I'm in the book."

"You know—"

I held up my hand. "I know, I know. It doesn't matter. He found me. I didn't let him in. We talked in public."

"You should probably avoid contact with him in the future." Post reached for the folder again. She brought it back and opened it in her lap.

"My uncle says he's a crook."

Post nodded. "He's done time for larceny and assault. Make that twice for assault. And these are just things he's been convicted of. Chances are there's more. He didn't threaten you at all, did he?"

I considered the word. *Threaten*. He didn't threaten me. But . . .

"He wants money from me."

"For what?"

"He says my mother was giving him money, helping him out. Now he wants me to keep doing it. I'm the executor of the estate. My mother got some money when my father died. A life insurance policy. And I'm sure there's a policy on my mom as well. Gordon Baxter wants some of whatever money my mom had."

"How much?"

"He didn't say. But I found my mom's bank records in her house. She'd withdrawn fourteen thousand dollars over the last year. That's totally unlike her. She wouldn't even eat at a fast-food restaurant. She wore the same clothes for the last twenty years. I have no idea what she took that money out for."

"But he didn't threaten you?"

"No," I said. "He didn't say, 'Give me the money or else.' Nothing like that. He seems shady. In some way, his presence is threatening. He showed up out of the blue on my doorstep. I wondered if maybe he was the one who broke into my apartment."

Post nodded. She made a note in the open file folder.

"But," I said, "I can't imagine what he'd be looking for there. I don't have anything. And he doesn't know anything about me."

"I'll keep it in the back of my mind," she said.

Post's phone buzzed again.

"Do you need to get that?" I asked.

She shook her head.

"So," I said, "if you know all about her marriage to Gordon Baxter, you must know about their daughter, right?"

I knew professional police decorum meant never showing surprise when presented with unexpected information. Post mostly concealed her reaction, but her eyes moved just enough—a twitch or a tic—to tell me that she not only didn't know about the other Elizabeth, but was quite surprised to hear it.

She didn't answer. So I said, "You didn't know, then? Wouldn't you find out if you ran some sort of a background check on my mom?"

"A juvenile that long ago might not show up in the system. We haven't had computers forever."

"Okay. Well, now you know."

She hesitated. "I'm not sure how it's relevant to the case."

"Not relevant?" I asked. "My mother's ex-husband has a criminal record, and they also have a daughter who went missing years ago and now has managed to get herself into my mother's will. And that's not relevant?"

Post considered a moment. She closed the folder in her lap and placed it back on the desk. "Is there something I need to know about this daughter?"

"A few things," I said.

I gave her the whole rundown, from Elizabeth's disappearance in 1975 to her apparent reemergence into my mother's life sometime in the recent past. I made sure to include the stuff about the will, including Elizabeth Yarbrough's call to the lawyer, as well as my uncle's and Gordon Baxter's assertions that Elizabeth Yarbrough was some kind of grifter taking advantage of my mother and not the rebellious teenager who walked out of their lives thirty-seven years earlier. Post asked a few questions as I went along, mostly just clarifications of minor points. She still didn't take any notes, but she was attentive. When I was finished, she leaned back in her chair, the springs squeaking as she moved.

"You've never met this woman?" she asked. "This Elizabeth Yarbrough?"

"Never."

"And where is she?"

"She lives in Reston Point, according to the will. That's all I know."

"Hmm," Post said.

"Look, you're trying to hang this all on my brother—"

"Nobody's hanging anything," she said. "We're dealing with the evidence."

"Okay. Fine. But you have someone with a criminal record who was getting money from my mother, and you have someone else—someone who was given up for dead long ago—suddenly showing up and working her way into the will. She gets a third now that Mom is gone. Are you telling me that isn't suspicious?"

"One of your sources against this Yarbrough woman is the guy you also say is a crook. Gordon Baxter," Post said. "Who knows why he's smearing her? And you don't know that *this* woman called the lawyer. And even if she did, I'm not sure what it proves. People call lawyers. Maybe it shows she was after the money. Maybe. But maybe she just had a legitimate question."

I accepted the dousing of cold water. But I wasn't finished. "At least admit it's hard to believe Ronnie killed my mom. Can you just admit that for me?"

"Can you admit it?" she asked. "Do you have any doubts about it?"

"I do."

"You mean you have them now?"

I didn't answer. But she was right, and she knew it.

"People kill for all sorts of reasons," she said. "And you'd be surprised at who ends up doing the killing. You may not expect it from them, but they do it. And the one constant, the almost ninety-nine percent answer to the puzzle is—the killer knew the victim and, in their mind, had a very good reason to do it. So far, I only see your brother fitting that bill. And I have to be honest—this suicide attempt doesn't make things look any better for him. We're still looking at other options, and maybe Elizabeth Yarbrough and Gordon Baxter will factor into that. No charges have been filed yet, of course. But your brother has confessed."

"He didn't do it," I said. "Okay, you're right. I have my doubts. Little moments of doubt about Ronnie. Sure. He had outbursts. Apparently Mom felt scared enough to call the police once. That's there. I can't change it. But I know him. I know him. He didn't do it." I felt I'd been convincing, that I'd stated my case so clearly and strongly no one could refute it.

But Post didn't show much on her face. It was as if I hadn't spoken. Her phone buzzed. This time she picked it up and read the text. She thumbed a quick reply, then turned back to me.

"I have to go to the hospital now," she said. "I'll follow up over there and put my head together with Detective Richland. We'll see where we stand."

"So you believe me, right?" I asked. "There's something to all of this stuff I've been saying."

She stood up and offered me her hand. "Thanks for coming by, Elizabeth. We'll be in touch."

Chapter Forty-three

I left the police station and went to Dan's house. I'd started driving in the direction of St. Vincent's, but the day's events had left me wiped out. I called Paul to check in, and he told me that Ronnie's condition was the same. He was resting comfortably.

"You rest too," he said. "You can come here and relieve me later. If anything changes, I'll call."

I felt guilty about not going to the hospital, but I saw the wisdom in what Paul had said. If I rested just a little, I could be at my best later that night.

I went to Dan's because I didn't feel comfortable returning to my apartment with Gordon Baxter roaming around town. I doubted I could sleep there even if I wanted to.

Dan gave me my space. I was happy to see him and happy to not really have to talk much. He circled around me while I undressed and slid into his bed. In the living room, his computer sat open on his desk, surrounded by an obscenely high stack of library books. The apartment smelled like scorched coffee and frozen pizza. I hoped Dan wouldn't want to crawl into bed with me, not even just to sleep. I really was tired.

"I'll leave you alone," he said.

"Thanks."

"But just one question. Is there anything else I need to know? Any other revelations?"

"Too many," I said. "I'm sorry. I'm just a little overwhelmed by it all now. And I'm tired."

He pulled the bedroom door shut, and I was asleep before my eyelids closed. I dreamed of my mother. I was inside a house, and she stood outside. Rain poured down, blurring my sight. Mom was drenched. I worried about her because she was so old. I thought she might get sick. Her hands waved around, trying to communicate with me. But I didn't know what she wanted. None of it made sense. I thought, *Just knock on the door. Just come in.*

Then someone was knocking. The light from the other room came through the crack as Dan opened the bedroom door. I didn't know where I was or who he was right away. A yelping noise escaped my throat.

"It's okay," he said. "It's just me."

I sat up, tried to clear the cobwebs away. I looked at the clock. I'd been asleep for forty-five minutes. Ronnie. I needed to go see Ronnie. Is that why Dan woke me up? To go back to the hospital?

"I'm awake," I said.

"Good. There's someone here to see you."

"Someone to see me?"

"Yes," Dan said. "He's being insistent."

I still wasn't fully awake. "But how does anyone know I'm here?"

"I don't know. It's some guy."

I pictured Gordon Baxter, his heavy bulk leaning against the door of Dan's apartment, pushing through it. Coming after me.

"Who is it?" I asked, hearing the alarm in my own voice.

"He says he's a student of yours," Dan said, barely concealing his disdain. "Some tall dude. He says he's your favorite student. Elizabeth, I can get rid of him if you want."

Then it clicked. I was surprised he hadn't yelled "Hey, Teach" from the front door.

I threw the covers back. "I need to talk to him."

I started toward the door, and Dan pointed at me.

"What?"

"I think you should wear pants," he said, his voice dry.

I'd stripped down to my underwear and a T-shirt when I'd crawled into bed. I found my jeans on the floor and pulled them on. Yet Dan was blocking the doorway.

"Who is this guy?"

"He's helping me out," I said. "He's doing research."

"Is he a grad student?"

"Not that kind of research. He's looking into Mom's case."

Dan looked at me without speaking, then finally moved out of the way.

I walked out to the living room but didn't see Neal.

"Where is he?" I asked.

"He's outside. Obviously I didn't just let a stranger in." Dan went to open the door, revealing the tall figure of Neal Nelson. He wore a goofy grin, as though it had been fixed to his face the entire time the door was closed.

"Is it safe to come in, Teach?"

"Yeah, come on in."

He stepped across the threshold. As he did, he gave a sidelong glance at Dan. "Your bodyguard was suspicious of me."

"He doesn't know what a fine, upstanding citizen you are." I pointed to the couch. "Want to sit?"

"Sure."

But before he could move, I said, "Wait a minute. How did you find me here? This isn't my house."

Neal flung himself down on the couch. "Hey, Teach, I told you we were good at what we do."

"But—"

"You have a boyfriend," he said. "I looked up his address. Come on—I have more goodies for you."

I went over and sat next to him. Dan closed the door. He looked lost, not knowing whether to stay or go.

"Do you want to sit and listen?" I asked. "It might not all make sense."

"Do you want something to drink?" Dan asked.

Neal looked at me, then at Dan. "I smell coffee. Burnt coffee. I love burnt coffee. Can I have some of that?"

"I think I have some dregs left in the pot," Dan said, disappearing to the kitchen.

"Nice guy," Neal said when Dan was gone. "He really likes you. Dude, I thought he was going to fight me over getting in the door."

"He has no idea who you are," I said. "And I thought you didn't drink coffee."

"I shouldn't. But when it gets that scorched taste, I can't resist it."

"Okay. Did you find something out already?"

"Of course."

"In a day?"

"Teach, we have this thing called the Internet, and it has these things called databases. They tell us most of what we need to know. A few phone calls to some well-placed friends, and we're there."

"Okay," I said. "So get to it."

"Just like in class. All business. Which lovely do you want to hear about first? Elizabeth Yarbrough or Gordon Baxter?"

"Yarbrough," I said.

Just then Dan came back into the room with a mug of coffee. He set it on the table in front of Neal.

"Thanks, boss," Neal said.

"I'm assuming you don't want any cream or anything," Dan said.

"No, no. That would ruin it." He leaned forward and took a gulp. He smacked his lips. "Perfect. I love that burnt taste." He put the mug down and pulled out his phone. He tapped it a few times until he found what he wanted. "Okay, one Elizabeth Yarbrough." He looked at me. "A naughty, naughty girl. Two convictions for drug possession and one for DUI. And, lo and behold, once she even took a fall for solicitation. You know what that means, right, Teach?"

"You mean . . . ?"

"That's right," he said. "She tried to sell her lady parts to an undercover cop." He scrolled through the phone. "Looks like she went through some sort of rehab or diversionary program at some point."

"Are these arrests recent?"

"Nothing in the last five years," he said. "She must have cleaned up or slowed down. But I bet she was fun to party with when she was in her prime."

"Does it give any other names she may have used?"

"She's used a lot of names," Neal said. "She's had a lot of husbands. Three at least. She's been known as Elizabeth Hayward, Elizabeth Fontroyal—I like that one the best—Elizabeth Stiegerwald—"

"What about Baxter?" I asked. "Elizabeth Baxter?"

Neal nodded. "That one too."

Dan cleared his throat. "Who is this person? Did she hurt your mom?"

I hadn't told Dan anything about Elizabeth Yarbrough. Not the will, and certainly not about her—maybe—being my half sister. I hadn't explained it to Neal either.

"We're trying to find that out, Dan," I said.

"Yeah," Neal said. "Have a seat, chief. There's a lot to learn here."

Dan looked at me, and I shrugged a little. Dan sat down in a chair, his body oozing reluctance.

"So she did go by Elizabeth Baxter at one point," I said. "And did she live in Haxton?"

"Sure did."

"So do we know that this is the Elizabeth Baxter I'm looking for?"

"We know she was born in 1960 and lived in Haxton. We know she's Elizabeth Yarbrough now and lives in Reston Point."

"So it is her?"

Neal shook his head; now he was the teacher. "Not really. All we know is that the woman in Reston Point is using the same social security number as the woman in Haxton. At some point, the only way to tell for sure is to go ID this woman in Reston Point. Technology can only do so much. Without a picture or DNA or something, it could just be someone using someone else's identity. That happens, you know."

"Sure."

"You want to hear about this old dude? Gordon Baxter? I'm assuming these two are related, although not married. That would be sick—he's ancient."

"I think he's probably sixty-nine," I said.

"Seventy," Neal said. "He's been a bit of a son of a bitch too. A couple of arrests."

"Larceny and assault," I said.

Dan looked at me, surprised. Neal started laughing.

"Hey," he said. "Sherlock Holmes got the jump on me."

"The police told me about it."

"The police," Neal said, waving his hand. "Those guys are so slow."

"Hold it," Dan said. "Who are these criminals we're hearing about? Are you in trouble?"

Neal ignored the question. "And it's not larceny. It's grand larceny the old man committed. That means he took control of someone else's property, and said property had a decent value. In Ohio, that means more than twenty-five hundred bucks. Could be a car. Could be jewelry. Either way, he's a bad boy. And not just assault—aggravated assault. That means he probably used a weapon."

"Jesus," Dan said.

"There are some cool people in the world," Neal said.

"Is that it on Baxter?" I asked.

"Pretty much," Neal said. "Last known address in Columbus. Only been married once." He turned and looked at me. I could see what he had pieced together. "A woman named Leslie Baxter. Also known as Leslie Hampton. Now deceased."

"Hold it a minute," Dan said. "This guy, this criminal . . . your mom?"

"Pretty wild, isn't it?" Neal said.

"You knew this?" Dan ignored Neal and looked directly at me.

"No," I said. "I just found all this out today. I asked Neal to dig into these people a little more. I wanted to know what I was dealing with."

"Jesus," Dan said again.

Neal said, "You're hoping that these people—one or both of them—killed your mom. If they killed her, then your brother is off the hook. Right?"

"Doesn't it make more sense?" I asked. "Look at them and look at Ronnie."

"What's the motive?" Neal asked. "People don't off people for no reason. Unless they're in love with them or something."

"Money," I said. "This Yarbrough woman showed up and got in the will. My mom is dead and Ronnie is accused. She gets a big cut of what my mom had."

"Pretty slick," Neal said.

"I think I'm missing a few steps," Dan said. He looked at Neal. "How did you find these things out? Couldn't Elizabeth or I have found them on the Internet?"

"Not really, chief," Neal said. "I mean, you can pay for some background-check stuff online, but it's second-rate. And the Teach here is a poor grad student. She doesn't want to go through all that expense." He wiped his nose. "Besides, you have to know how to interpret the data. That's what my old man does. He took a look at this and helped me analyze it."

"Your old man?" Dan asked. "Is he a cop?"

"Not even close," Neal said.

"Dan," I said. "It's okay."

"Then tell me how this woman could convince your mother to let her into her will. What did she tell her?"

"It's a long story," I said. "It's—"

"Yes," Neal said, cutting in. "A very long story. And we don't have much time."

"Why is that?" Dan asked.

Neal held up his phone. "I have a full tank of gas and directions to her house. Since Elizabeth likes to party and it's Saturday night, she might be going out. I think we need to get to Reston Point as soon as possible, before she decides it's time to hightail it out of there."

Chapter Forty-four

"Wait a minute," Dan said. "You're not really going to go up there and confront this woman, are you?"

I didn't answer. I didn't have to. He knew what I was thinking.

Neal jangled his car keys.

"Hold it," Dan said. "Don't you think you should call the police? If there's reason to think this woman harmed your mother, then the police need to know."

Neal shook his head. "Not happening, chief. Not that way. You have to understand people like this, which you probably don't since you're a professor type. People like this spook easily. Hell, they can tell when a cop gets within five miles of them. She'll run off. She'll turn ghost and run. And even if the cops find her, she isn't going to tell them anything. I think Teach here needs to go."

"Dan," I said, "the police already know all of this. I just talked to them today. I told them about both of these people."

"And what did they say?" Dan asked. "Did they suggest you go find them?"

"They acted like they'd look into it, but I can tell they won't. They think they know who did it already. Ronnie. That's it for them."

Neal stood up. "Besides, this woman could really be Teach's—what, half sister? Is that what she is?"

"She could be dangerous," Dan said. "You think she might be working with this guy, this Gordon guy. What if they are in it together?"

"I know what I'll do," I said. "I'm the executor of the will. She's eager to get her share, right? If I have to, I'll just tell her that's what I'm there for."

"Works for me," Neal said. He pointed to my bare feet. "You better put shoes on. It's getting chilly out."

"I'm going too," Dan said.

His words didn't surprise me. I knew he'd insist on coming along and making sure nothing happened to me. I appreciated it.

"Look," I said. "I just—" I turned to Neal. "Do you mind waiting in the car?" I asked. "I'll be right there."

"Sure," he said. "I'll get it warmed up, pick out the CDs, all that stuff."

When he was gone and the front door closed behind him, I turned to Dan. I couldn't tell him the truth about why I didn't want him to come. The truth was, it just didn't seem like the kind of place for Dan to go. I knew Neal could take care of himself if he needed to, but I wasn't sure Dan could. It wouldn't be for lack of trying. I knew he'd lay down his life for me if the situation called for it.

But that was just it. His focus would be on me. Helping me. Protecting me. Catering to me. I didn't need that. I didn't need all that pressure. I had a job to do, and I wanted to concentrate on that.

"I need you to stay here," I said.

"Who is this guy?" Dan asked. "He just shows up. He's doing all this Sam Spade stuff. Who is he?"

"He's a student of mine," I said. "And he works doing this type of thing."

"What type of thing? Stalking?"

"I don't really know what he does, but I asked for his help. And he provided it. The police haven't done it. I needed someone to step in."

"Why don't you want me to go?" Dan asked.

I stepped closer to him. I raised my right hand and brushed it along his cheek. He had shaved that morning, and his skin felt smooth and new. "I need you to do me a favor," I said.

He didn't return my affection. He averted his eyes. I saw a vein twitch in his neck. I knew he was mad. Once I was gone, he'd gear up for an epic sulk, which is why I gave him a job to do.

"I need you to go to St. Vincent's for me," I said. "Go there and find Paul. He's expecting me to show up and see Ronnie. They're going to be moving him to a regular room soon if every-thing is okay. Just go there and tell Paul that something came up. Don't tell him any details so he doesn't worry. But let him know I'm fine and see if he needs anything."

Dan's eyes moved back to mine, but he didn't speak.

"Do you mind?" I said. "I'll call you when I know some-thing."

"Are you sure about this?"

"I am. It has to be this way. I'll be fine. Really."

He reached out and took my hand in his. "Do me a favor," he said. "Keep in touch. Text me as much as you can so I know you're okay. Or have Encyclopedia Brown out there do it for you."

"I will," I said.

"Okay," he said. "I'll go see your uncle."

"Thank you."

We stood close to each other for a long moment. I leaned up and kissed him.

He didn't let go of my hand. I squeezed his hand back. Hard. I liked the feel of it in mine.

"I have to go," I said. "I'll talk to you later."

Chapter Forty-five

"How far is it?" I asked.

Neal sat behind the wheel of a surprisingly new Lexus SUV. It didn't seem to match his dirty hair and army jacket, but I didn't point that out. It made me wonder about the kind of clients his father represented.

"You've never been there?" he asked.

"Never."

"Aren't you from Dover?"

"I am. But what would I go to Reston Point for? What's there?"

"Jesus," he said. "They've got Murray's, the best steak place in the state. They've got Fieldstone Farms, where they raise turkeys and serve them in their own restaurant. You never went there for Thanksgiving?"

"We never went anywhere for Thanksgiving."

"You should go this year," Neal said. "Get your boyfriend to take you, unless it's too . . . what would he call it? Beaujolais?"

"Do you mean bourgeois?"

"I guess so." He fumbled around in the glove compartment, reaching across me with his long right arm while he steered the car with his left hand. "We'll be there in about forty-five minutes."

"Is that all?"

The car swerved. "Shit," he said.

"Do you want my help?"

"Got it," he said. He held a shiny CD, which he slipped into the car's player. "Driving music."

I looked out the window. We were on a two-lane road passing through harvested cornfields. In the dying light I could see that everything had been hacked to the roots. A thin band of red glowed along the horizon, but the sky was darkening above. My hands were folded in my lap. I balled my right fist up inside my cupped left hand. I felt nervous and twitchy.

"You like this song?" Neal asked.

"What?"

He pointed to the radio. "The song? You like it?"

I hadn't been paying attention, so I listened. It sounded slightly familiar. A man sang a slightly poppy, slightly country song in a twangy voice.

"Yeah, it's fine," I said.

"Fine? *Fine?* That's Glen fucking Campbell you're listening to. Glen fucking Campbell."

"It sounds good."

"Sheesh, Teach. You need an education. You don't know Ohio. You don't know music. What are you learning in graduate school?" He must have sensed my anxiety. "You know, this woman's probably not dangerous. Most people aren't. And her record says she isn't. It'll be fine."

"Thanks."

"When we get there, I think it's best just to play it straight. Just go up to the door and tell her who you are. None of this sneaking around shit. Like you said, you have a legit reason for showing up."

"And you'll be right there, so that will help."

"Negative, Teach."

"What do you mean?"

"I can't go to the door with you," he said. "A dude—a tall dude—showing up and asking questions? Too intimidating. Best to keep it woman to woman. I'll be around. I'll have your back."

I let out a long breath. Neal's presence brought me comfort, but I had imagined him being right next to me, not waiting in the car. My fears ran deeper than simply the physical. Deeper and, yes, scarier.

Neal must have understood. He asked, "What are you really worried about, Teach?"

I stared out the window. "I guess I'm just scared of what I might find out."

On the outskirts of Reston Point, we turned onto a county road, one that took us west. The sky was fully dark by now. A few stars and a sliver of moon shone above, and at the horizon line I saw the scattered lights of the town. A cluster of bright yellow globes indicated a factory of some kind, and past that the dimmer lights of the downtown. If Elizabeth Yarbrough was really my sister, if we really shared blood and a relationship to Mom, then what was her life like here in Reston Point? Where did she work? What did she do? Was there a damn thing we shared in common besides the woman who gave birth to us?

Neal made a couple of turns, and we ended up in a working-class neighborhood. The houses were small and close together. In the glow of the streetlights, I saw yards full of cars, and people lounging on their small porches smoking and drinking beer from bottles. Neal's car stood out, and the eyes followed us as we passed.

"It's right up here," Neal said.

He made a last turn onto a side street. The sign read CAMELOT LANE, and I wondered whether anyone saw the irony. He slowed the car halfway down the street. He checked his phone, then looked up at the house numbers.

"That's it," he said, pointing to the right.

The house looked the same as all the others. It was white and compact. The yard looked well maintained. There were no cars in the driveway. A dim porch light illuminated the house number.

"It doesn't look like anyone's home," I said. I hoped no one was.

"No, Teach—look." Neal pointed again. "See that glow back there?"

I followed the line of his finger to a window at the back. The blinds were closed, but the glow from a television leaked around the edges. Someone was there, watching TV.

"Shit," I said.

"This is what you've been looking for," Neal said. "Take out your phone."

I did.

"Make sure it's ready to call my number. If you have any trouble, just hit the call button. I'll come running. Okay? I'll be right out here."

I took a deep breath and opened the door.

Chapter Forty-six

I stepped onto the porch. A light wind blew down the street, cool and crisp. It raised goose bumps on my arms and neck, but beneath my clothes I felt hot and clammy. A trickle of sweat ran between my shoulder blades. I lifted my hand and rang the bell.

I waited. I turned and looked back at Neal. I saw the outline of his black SUV in the fading light, but I couldn't see him. I turned to ring the bell again, but before I could, I heard the lock turn on the other side of the door. I swallowed hard again and waited. I felt like an unprepared actor caught in the glow of the stage lights, except my stage light was a grimy little bulb on somebody's porch, the globe filled with the summer's dead bugs.

The door opened, and there she was. If time travel existed, I would have sworn I had gone back twenty years, to the time captured in photos of my childhood. Before me stood a replica of my mother from that time. A little rougher around the edges certainly, a little more worn by whatever life had thrown at her, but a nearly exact version of my mother. I stepped back, so far I almost fell off the porch. I kept my eyes locked on that face. My doubts and questions faded. This woman was certainly related to me. She had to be my half sister.

The woman—*Elizabeth Yarbrough*—raised her hand to her

mouth when she saw me. Even though I was just partially illuminated by the porch light, and even though I hadn't showered
all day and had woken up from my nap only an hour earlier and
must have looked something like a homeless person, she seemed
to understand who I was as well. She probably saw the same
ghost in my face that I saw in hers.

She pushed the screen door open, but didn't speak right away.
I wondered whether she would shoo me away, send me packing
because I had violated her privacy. But when she spoke, her voice
carried a welcoming tone. "Come in," she said. "Come in."

So I shook myself out of the past and moved forward. I
stepped into the small living room. A thick odor hung in the air,
as though something greasy had been cooked recently. The
blinds were all closed, the walls painted dark green. The furniture looked heavy and stained, and children's toys were scattered around the room; I had to look where I stepped.

"Do you have children?" I asked.

Children. My nieces or nephews. More relatives. Who knew
how many people I didn't know about?

"I do," Beth said. "But these belong to my grandchildren."

"Wow," I said. "Grandchildren."

"I'm quite a bit older than you," she said. "A different generation, really."

I didn't know what to say.

Beth didn't offer me a chair or anything. She stared at me
from across the room. Her feet were bare, and she wore tight
jeans and a loose sweater. She was thin, like Mom and like me.
Her hair was colored somewhere between red and brown, with
a hint of gray showing at the roots. She folded her arms across
her chest and shifted her weight from one foot to the other.

"I always knew we'd meet," she said. "I hoped we'd meet. Mom wanted—"

She stopped herself.

Mom. My mom. Before that day I had heard only one other person call my mother by that name. Would I now have to get used to sharing that word with someone else?

"Can I sit?" I asked.

"Yes, please."

We both sat, on opposite ends of the couch. I still held the phone in my hand with Neal's number ready to go.

"I guess you just want to ask me a bunch of questions," Beth said. "I guess you want to know everything."

"Yes. Everything," I said. "You called me on the day of Mom's funeral, didn't you?"

"I did. Yes." Beth nodded. Her voice was a little rough, like a smoker's. "I didn't think it was right for me to go, especially since you didn't know about me. I didn't think that was the time. I almost went anyway. I got dressed. I put on makeup. I was ready to drive down there, but I just couldn't bring myself to do it. Mom was already gone at that point, and it would only make things complicated for you."

"And did you call the lawyer?"

"I'm not trying to chisel money out of anybody," Beth said. "I don't want you to think that."

"But you called him?"

"I just wanted to know where I stood, that's all," she said. "You know, I didn't have anyone else I could ask. I didn't think I could approach you. I wasn't sure."

"How did you know the lawyer's name?"

Beth hesitated, then said, "Mom told me. She told me when

she changed the will. She said if anything ever happened to her, that's who to call. Mr. Allison."

"Did she expect something to happen?"

Beth raised her arms and hugged herself as though a cold breeze had blown through the room. "I don't know," she said. "But there were a few times I talked to her, right before she died, when it seemed like she did think something was about to happen. And then it did."

Then why didn't you do something? I thought to myself. *Why didn't anyone do anything?*

"Okay," I said. "Questions. I guess I'll just start with the big one. Both your father and—"

"My father?" Beth asked. "How do you know him?"

"He came to my apartment," I said. "He told me all about you. About a lot of things. He said you were supposed to be dead, that you disappeared one day when you were fifteen, and you never came back. The police said there was a serial killer in this part of the country then, some guy named . . . Rodney—"

"Rodney Ray Brown," Beth said, her voice thin.

"That's it. Gordon said you were dead. Murdered. But apparently you're not. So what happened?"

"My dad," Beth said. She shuddered; this time it didn't seem to be from the cold, but from the thoughts that were crossing her mind. Thoughts of her father? "I didn't disappear," Beth said. "Disappear makes it sound like I was taken—like someone kidnapped me, you know? It wasn't like that. Not at all."

"Then what did happen?" I asked. "If you weren't kidnapped and you weren't dead, why did you stay away for so many years? Why didn't I know about you until now?"

Beth closed her eyes. She took a long time answering. When she opened her eyes again, she looked right at me. "I chose to stay away all that time," she said. "I wanted to get as far away as possible from that sick, disgusting house. I didn't ever want to go back."

Something wormed around in my gut. It felt like the worm had teeth and was starting to gnaw on my insides. I didn't know how to ask the question. But I pressed on. There was nothing to lose now.

"Did Gordon . . ." I let my voice trail off. "Did he . . . sexually abuse you?"

Beth shook her head. "No, he didn't do that. It was nothing like that." She paused. "I'd like to say it was worse, but when you talk about these things, it's tough to make those comparisons."

"Then what happened?" I had the same feeling then that I'd had in the car during the ride over with Neal. I had to know, but I just didn't want to know.

Beth forced an awkward smile. "This is the time I would reach for a glass of wine or something."

"Do you have some?"

She shook her head. "I quit drinking. I quit all of that stuff. But sometimes I really want it."

"If you don't want to rehash a bunch of stuff, that's okay," I said. But I didn't mean it. I had come all that way for the rehashing.

"That's nice of you to say. But you want to know, don't you? You really don't want me to stop now, do you?"

"No," I said. "I want to hear it."

"And you should hear it," she said. "It all happened before you were born, but it's affected your life, right? It's still affecting your life."

I nodded. "And my brother's."

"Right," Beth said. "I know. And I'm sorry." She licked her lips. "Well, I was kind of a wild kid. Typical in many ways, but maybe even more wild than most."

She then told me the things that Gordon had told me about her wild days in high school. I would have expected Gordon's version to be worse, exaggerated for the sake of proving his own point, but as things went, it seemed that Gordon had been pretty accurate in his description of his daughter. She'd been a trouble-maker. She'd become difficult for her parents to discipline and control. She'd run with an older and wilder crowd. She mentioned the drinking and the drugs.

"Your dad said they found heroin in your room," I said.

"They found heroin *paraphernalia* in my room," she said. "And it really wasn't mine. I know that's the oldest lie in the book, the one every teenager gives when they're caught with something illegal, but it was true in my case. I was holding it for another girl. I've never shot up. I've done a lot of things, but not that. I know it looked bad to them. To Mom and Gordon. Dad, I should say."

"You don't call him Dad?"

"It's hard to think of him as Dad," she said. "You'll see."

She didn't go on right away. She seemed lost in thought. My phone vibrated in my hand. I thought it would be Neal, but I saw Dan's name on the display. Just checking in, I assumed. I wished I'd given his number to Neal so he could stay updated.

"So you were a wild teenager," I said. "And you ran with some wild kids. Wasn't this the seventies? Wasn't everybody wild?"

"Not everybody," Beth said. "I don't think one time is really that different from another. Kids get wild. Parents worry. People didn't always send their kids off to rehab back then. They took a harder line, I guess. Gordon—Dad—threatened me with a lot of stuff. He grounded me. He wouldn't let me use the phone." She shrugged. "Big deal, you know? Kids can find ways around that stuff."

"And Mom?"

Beth paused. She stared at the floor, her eyes fixed on something, some moment in the past I would never see. "Mom did her best. I understand that now. She was hard, you know? She didn't take much crap from me. She even slapped me once when I mouthed off to her."

"Really?"

"Did she ever hit you or Ronnie?"

"Never."

"Different times," Beth said. "I don't blame her. I would have slapped me too. She tried to talk to me as well. She treated me like a human being. I didn't see it all then—I really didn't. But she tried in her own way. I think she was just . . . confused by me. That's all. She was just . . . baffled by my spirit. My strong will. My stubbornness."

"She shouldn't have been," I said. "She had all those things."

"True," Beth said. "I have a daughter, and I see those same things. But it's tough to step back from being the parent. Mom tried. I know she did. I couldn't see that she was doing that, so I couldn't meet her halfway. I just resisted. That was all I knew how to do back then." She sighed. "Sometimes it seems that's all I've ever done with people who wanted to help me. Resist them."

Chapter Forty-seven

"How did you end up . . . leaving or whatever?" I asked.

Beth didn't hesitate. She plunged right into the story. It seemed as though she wanted to get it all out, and I wondered whether she had told anyone else the things she was about to tell me. I guessed she must have told one person. She had likely told Mom the whole story sometime in the past couple of months.

"I snuck out of the house one night when I was fifteen," Beth said. Her voice didn't change much as she spoke, but I saw something in her eyes as she related the story. They looked a little glassy, a little distant. I could see the regret in them.

"I know I was grounded for something at the time, but that never stopped me. I used to go out the window in my room. It was easy. Gordon wasn't home a lot, and sometimes I wore Mom out so much she couldn't keep up with everything I did. She probably felt a great deal of relief every morning when I was still in the house and alive.

"That night I went out alone. Some girls I barely knew had told me there was a party across town. I don't know how they had heard of it, or if they had any idea what was going on there. I doubt they knew what was really happening."

"What was happening?"

"I'm getting there," she said. "I couldn't get any of my usual running mates to go with me because it was a school night and the party was so far away, so I just decided to go out alone. I did that sometimes, and I wasn't afraid to do it. I could handle myself. I had the address. The party was supposed to be thrown by these older guys. I don't think they were in college. This was in Haxton. We didn't have a college there. But there were older guys in their twenties. Guys who worked in the factories and didn't mind chasing after a high school girl every now and then. That was all I needed to hear. A party with older guys? I wouldn't miss it."

"How did you get there if it was across town?"

"I hitched," she said. "Don't look so surprised. People did it a lot more back then. I know it wasn't that safe, but I think it was safer back then. We did it all the time. So I got dropped off on the street where the party was supposed to be, but as I walked up to the house, I could tell there wasn't a party. Parties give off that energy, that vibe that something is happening there. The house was dark. Closed down. I checked the number on a scrap of paper in my pocket. I was in the right place on the right street. Since my ride was gone, I figured I'd walk up to the house and take a closer look. Maybe it was a small party. Maybe it had been busted, and everyone was laying low inside." Beth shrugged. "Shit, I didn't have anything else to do. You know? I didn't want to go home and be locked in my room."

"Sure," I said, although I didn't really agree. I would have rather been home than wandering around town in the middle of the night when I was fifteen.

"I walked around the back of the house. It had a detached garage. The house was dark but I could see that lights were on in the garage. It looked like someone had taped paper or something over the garage windows, but some light came through. I figured the party was back there. Who wouldn't? It might have been safer and less messy to have people trashing your garage than your house. I heard some music playing, so I went up."

She stopped talking, and I wondered whether she was going to go on. She seemed lost deep in her memory of this night, and I knew whatever had happened back then was playing out in her mind's eye. Again.

"To this day, I don't know why they were so stupid as to leave the door to the garage unlocked. Maybe they forgot. Maybe someone had just come in or left. I don't know. I don't know why they didn't have anyone guarding the place. I just walked up. Anyone else could have. Maybe they felt really confident and comfortable."

I swallowed. I wanted to tell her to hurry up, but I couldn't. She had to get the story out in her own time.

"I pulled the door open," she said. "It took me a minute to realize what was going on in there. At first, I thought it was the party. There were a lot of bright lights and the music. It smelled like pot. And there were people standing around. Mostly young people. I don't think they noticed that I had opened the door right away. I tried to see what they were doing, and then it took them a few minutes to see me. About the time they saw me was when I figured out what they were doing in that garage."

She sighed and licked her lips again. "I saw a girl, a young girl. She must have been a few years older than me. She was on the floor, and she wasn't wearing any clothes. She looked . . . vulnerable. Sad, I guess. It might have been drugs or it just might have been the situation. But she was there on the floor. And there were two guys, two older guys—guys in their twenties, like I was talking about. I guess they could have been the guys who lived there, the ones who were supposed to be having the party. But they were on that girl. They were having sex with her. One on the bottom, one on her . . . top. And I only realized it wasn't part of the party because I saw what the lights were there for. They were really bright and on stands. And a camera. They were making some kind of porno movie. And I didn't really think that girl wanted to be there. I don't think she even knew where she was. But once I saw all of that, I couldn't take my eyes off of her. She looked so helpless, so exposed. She was so alone."

Beth stopped talking then. She looked at me and tried to smile, but I knew she wasn't seeing me. She was seeing the face of that girl in that garage. I didn't know what to say or do. Beth was a stranger to me despite our apparent blood relationship. I wasn't the most affectionate person in the world, even with people I knew well, and I wasn't sure if I should reach out and place my hand on hers or lean over and hug her. I stayed in my spot, trying to make the connection between the horrible story she had just told me and the recent events that had brought me to her house.

"Are you okay?" I asked.

She nodded. "I don't think I've ever told anybody all of this," she said. "Not in this much detail."

"It sounds . . ." My voice trailed off. Words didn't seem adequate, but I tried again. "I think it sounds horrifying."

"It was," Beth said. "And I put myself in real danger going in there. People like that—people who do things like that—they don't like it when they get discovered. They might go to great lengths to protect themselves. If it had just been adults, it wouldn't have been as big a deal. But there was a young girl there, a minor. That could have been big trouble for them, and they knew it."

"What did they do?"

"They saw me. And there was a guy there. Not a very big guy and not one of the people in the movie. But he looked like a security type. He was just thick necked, you know. And really stupid looking. He came after me. He took about two steps and it felt like he was right on top of me. He took me by the arm and asked who I was. I said I was in the wrong place and to just let me go and I wouldn't tell anyone what I saw. That was probably a stupid thing to say because then they knew I *had* seen something. But I was scared. Terrified. This guy had me, and he put his hand over my mouth so I couldn't breathe. And then another guy came over. I thought I was going to pee in my pants, I was so afraid. I could feel myself giving up, I guess. The thought went through my head, 'This is how you're going to die. Right here in this garage, you are going to die.'"

"How did you get away?" I asked. *Or did you?*

"I heard someone shout. A man's voice. It said, 'Leave her alone. I'll handle it.' Or something like that. You know, for just a moment, I thought the voice sounded familiar. And then I thought that was crazy. It couldn't be. It couldn't be . . . And then the big guy took his hand off my mouth, so I could breathe a little. Because of the lights, I couldn't see who had said it, but I got the sense he was the guy in charge or something because of the way they all backed off as soon as he spoke. The one guy just held me by the arm so I couldn't run off, I guess. But he loosened his grip. He wasn't rough with me anymore. It took a minute, but then the guy who spoke appeared. He came out from the glow of the lights so I could see him." She swallowed hard. "That was the worst thing of all—seeing him. If I thought I couldn't believe what I had already seen, then I guess I really couldn't believe what I was seeing now."

"Why?" I asked. "Who was it?"

But as soon as I asked the question, I knew. I didn't need her to answer it, but she did.

"It was Gordon," she said. "It was my dad."

Chapter Forty-eight

"He came right over to me," Beth said. "He seemed to loom over me, even though I was as tall as he was. He didn't say anything to me, and he didn't let on that he knew me. He didn't tell anyone that I was his daughter." She laughed a little bit, a dry sound from the back of her throat. "Maybe he wanted to protect me from those people. I don't know. He could get a little violent when I was a kid. He hit me when I was little, and I guess he shook me or shoved me a few times. I felt real fear looking at him. His eyes were vacant in a way that made me afraid of him. It was like there was nothing there. I don't think he was really seeing me. He didn't seem to be angry, just calculating. I was a problem he needed to solve. I'm not sure he saw me as anything more significant than a fly he needed to swat away."

"What did he do to you?" I asked.

"He took me by the arm. He took my arm from the guy who was already holding me, and he pushed me back through the door. As we left, he told the people in the garage to just keep going. 'We need to get that finished,' he said. 'Keep them going.' I assumed he meant the actors in the movie. Then he said to someone else—someone I couldn't see—'I'm going to need your help in a minute.'"

Beth abruptly stood up from the couch. She took a couple of steps to the center of the room and again wrapped her arms around her body as though she was cold. I was worried about her. She seemed upset, and I was bringing it all out. But the story needed to be told.

Beth faced away from me. Then she dropped her arms and said, "This is a hell of an introduction to a long-lost family member, isn't it? I've been thinking about this day for a while now, and I always imagined we'd hug and we'd maybe cry a little. And then we'd tell each other about our lives. I could tell you about my kids and grandkids, and you could tell me all about school and whether you have a boyfriend or not." She turned around. "Hell, I even hoped we'd share girl talk, you know? I thought you could seek my advice about the world, the way sisters do. Instead, we're talking about this. I'm surprised you haven't run away already."

"It's okay," I said. "I want to know. I want to know the truth."

I tried to sound light when I said it. I didn't really care about having someone I could share girl talk with. And I didn't bring my relationship problems to anyone. I simply wanted to understand the past so I could understand the present.

Beth sat back down. She looked a little more relaxed, even though I suspected her story wasn't going to get any easier to hear.

"Dad—*Gordon*—led me by the arm. He practically dragged me down the driveway and out to the street. His car was parked there in the dark. I hadn't noticed it when I walked up to the house, but he led me straight to it. It was raining then. Fat drops of rain. I felt them tapping on my head as he hustled me down the driveway. He unlocked a back door and shoved me inside.

But he didn't close the door. He stood with the door open. The rain came into the car, but Gordon didn't even seem to notice. He leaned against the door frame so I couldn't get past him. 'You don't like me very much, do you?' he said. 'You don't have much respect for your mother or me.'

"I thought it was an odd thing to say to me at a moment like that," Beth continued. "He was the one I had just caught making a pornographic movie with an underage girl. I would think my lack of respect for him would be obvious. He said, 'I don't suppose it would do any good to tell you that you probably don't really understand what was going on back there. That wasn't what it looked like. We're working on a movie project, a *real* movie project. It's not something dirty. I'm helping these people out by producing the movie for them.'

"I had a choice then, I guess. I could have just gone along. That's what he was asking me to do. Play along. Be a good girl. Keep my mouth shut. I'd like to think if I had just said what he wanted to hear he would have taken me home and left me alone."

"Do you really believe that?" I asked. "How could he know you wouldn't ever tell?"

"You're right," she said. "And it didn't really matter. I was never good at just going along with people, and I wasn't going to do it for him. I told him I was going to tell Mom and the police. I didn't back down at all."

"And how did he take that?"

"He played his trump card," she said. "He told me that I could tell Mom all I wanted, and it wouldn't matter to her."

"Why?"

"He said that Mom knew all about the movies. More than that, she didn't just know about them; she had helped him produce them. And if I told the police or anyone else, Mom would suffer the same consequences he would. Maybe worse. And he said that I'd end up in a foster home, living a miserable life without anyone to look out for me."

Her words dropped between us like a heavy stone. I waited for Beth to say more. When she didn't, I said, "That's not true. It can't be true."

Beth's voice was low when she spoke again. "I didn't know what to think back then. I could tell he was threatening me in a way. And I worried that he might hurt Mom."

"Did he ever hit *her*?"

"I don't know," Beth said. "He acted like an asshole around the house. He certainly yelled at her. He tried to intimidate her. But overall, I guess he seemed . . . kind of normal. And that made it all the worse when I found out who he really was."

My phone buzzed again. It was Dan.

"Do you have to get that?" Beth asked.

I sighed. "Maybe I should. Ronnie . . . I guess you don't know what happened to Ronnie today, do you?"

"No."

"But you've met him, haven't you?"

She nodded. "A couple of times. Mom thought it would be easier to meet him first, and then meet you after she'd talked to you more about . . . everything."

"Ronnie has a picture in his room of two little kids. Are they related to you?"

"Two of my grandchildren. You said something happened to Ronnie today?"

I told her about the suicide attempt and the pills, the trip to the emergency room at St. Vincent's and his move to the ICU. Beth listened with her hand to her heart. I watched the fear and anxiety fill her eyes as I gave her the details.

"I think I should take the call—maybe something happened at the hospital."

"Go ahead," Beth said.

I called Dan back and he answered right away. "Are you okay?" he asked, without so much as a hello.

"I'm fine," I said. "Everything is fine. Did something happen there?"

"Yes," he said. "They've moved Ronnie to a regular room. He's doing better."

I felt relief rush through me, like air returning to my lungs after being underwater.

"He's awake?"

"He is. They're going to try to get him to eat something."

I looked at Beth and nodded. *He's okay,* I mouthed.

"And they found out what he took," Dan said. "Apparently it wasn't the sedatives he was on. It was some heart medicine he takes. Digitoxin? No—I don't know. They did a blood test and found a dangerous level in his system. The doctor tried to ask me some questions about Ronnie's heart condition, but I didn't know the answers. I guess people with Down syndrome can have heart problems?"

"Sometimes," I said. "But I didn't think Ronnie was on medication for that anymore. He was when he was a kid. Did they ask Paul these questions?"

"He's not here," Dan said. "He had to leave. I think he was tired."

"You're just there alone?"

"I thought you wanted me to stay here and keep an eye on things."

"Dan, you don't have to," I said. "I'm glad you did, but it's too much."

"It's okay," he said. "I brought a book to read. George Eliot."

"Oh, Dan. Look, I have to go, okay? But thanks for calling me. And please call me if anything else happens. Please."

"I will," he said.

"And, Dan? Thanks. Thanks for everything."

I disconnected and looked at Beth.

"Ronnie's okay," I said. "It looks like he's going to be okay."

I saw more emotion on Beth's face at that moment than at any other time. "Thank God," she said. "I don't think I could handle losing anybody else."

Chapter Forty-nine

Her comment struck me as strange. Someone else, someone besides my mother and my uncle, cared about Ronnie. I wasn't used to that, and I wasn't sure how quickly I could open up and include someone else in my family. I'd mouthed those words to her—*He's okay*—out of instinct. Beth seemed troubled by Ronnie's condition, and I wanted to ease her mind. But would we always be like that, the two of us? Would I have to include her from that moment on?

"Is Dan your boyfriend?" Beth asked.

I hadn't realized I had said his name. "Not really," I said. "We tried that. He's . . . he's just a guy. A pretty decent guy."

"Those can be hard to come by," Beth said.

"I know. I need to appreciate him more."

"Take it from me," Beth said. "Good men are hard to come by."

I didn't want to get sidetracked into relationship talk. She still had a few things to tell me, and it was getting late. Neal was waiting outside in his car, and we had an hour-long drive back to Dover.

"Are you able to finish the story?" I asked.

I didn't want it to be a question, even though I framed it as one. I just wanted her to tell me the rest.

"Sure," she said. "There are only a few things left to tell. Where was I?"

"Gordon said Mom was involved with his illegal activities," I prompted her. "There's no way that was true. Mom would never harm someone. She'd never get involved in anything like that."

"I know that now," Beth said. "I asked Mom about it, when I came back. It hurt her just to know Gordon had ever told me that. But you're right, of course. Mom wouldn't do such a thing. It was just Gordon messing with me."

I let out a deep breath. "How cruel."

"Yes. He was—*is*. But maybe I also believed it a little, when I was fifteen, because it made it easier for me to leave and stay away. I could use it as an excuse, even if it was ridiculous."

"So then what happened?"

"Right. Gordon stared at me for a while, there in the dark and the rain. I could see that his mind was running through all the possibilities. He needed to do something with me, something that would make sure I wouldn't tell what I knew. One possibility was obvious."

She looked at me knowingly.

"Do you think he wanted to kill you?" I asked.

"I bet he did. Looking back, I feel certain it crossed his mind. The only reason he didn't do it was because of Mom. I think some part of him, some tiny, decent part of him, just couldn't go all the way and kill his child. He couldn't kill *Mom's* child."

"So what did he do?"

"He told me he was going to make me very happy."

"How so?"

"He didn't tell me right away. He told me to get down on the floor of the backseat, to duck down and hide my head. He said he didn't want anyone to see me in the car. This was 1975, and cars were big. There was plenty of room. He took off his sport coat and draped it over me. I guess he really wanted to make sure I was hidden."

"I would have been terrified," I said.

"I was. My heart was pounding. I still thought I might die. It was dark, and I was shaking. I told myself he wasn't going to hurt me, that he was my dad and he wouldn't. But I didn't know what was going to happen. I didn't fully trust him. Not really. Pretty soon, I heard someone else come walking up. I heard the footsteps on the driveway. Dad told the other person to drive. Then he got into the backseat with me. He put his hand on my head to keep it down and out of sight. I thought for a moment about trying to jump up and run. But then what would I do? He'd find me, right? I was his daughter. And then the car started and drove off. I couldn't do anything then."

"Jesus."

"We drove a long time. It felt to me like hours. Just hours. Dad didn't say much. He gave the driver a few directions. 'Turn here.' 'Up here.' But otherwise nothing else was said. The driver must have turned on the radio. It was classical music, of all things. Dad never listened to that. I heard that and the beating of the windshield wipers. Back and forth, back and forth. Anyway, we just drove on and on. I felt a little carsick, riding like that. In the dark, not seeing anything outside the car. I wished I could have fallen asleep. We were going fast for most of the time, so I figured we were on the highway, but eventually the car slowed down. We made a few turns with Dad giving the directions again. Finally we stopped."

She shivered a little bit.

"Are you okay?" I asked.

Beth nodded. "Dad told the driver to get out of the car and

wait. He told him—I assume it was a him—to go get a cup of coffee or something. Before the person left, Dad said, 'Do you have it?' Something rustled around, something like paper, and then I guess the other guy was gone. It was just me and Dad. He leaned down close to me and asked me if I knew where we were. I said no. He told me we were in Columbus at the bus station.

"He said, 'I'm going to take this jacket off you, and you can sit up if you'd like. No one's around right now. It's the middle of the night.' I sat up. It was dark, and we were next to some run-down building. The streetlight glowed through the front windshield. I remember the big drops of rain beading on the glass. They looked like clear marbles. And I saw the bus station up the street. A few people stood around outside, smoking and talking. Otherwise, we were the only ones there. Dad held out his hand. He had money, a wad of bills. I couldn't tell how much, but it was more than I had ever seen at one time.

" 'This is five hundred bucks,' he said. 'It's yours. I want you to go into that bus station and buy yourself a ticket.' 'Where?' I asked. 'Far away,' he said. 'It won't cost that much. You'll have enough left over when you get where you're going to start up a new life. Isn't that what you really want? To be away from here, from shitty, small-town Ohio?' "

Beth looked around the little room. She seemed to be taking stock of her surroundings in the dim light from the lamp behind her. I tried to see what she saw—a lower-middle-class home that had seen better days. An old TV, a worn carpet. Ugly curtains.

"I wonder how many people can look at one night—one moment really—and clearly see their life pivot from one place to another. What if I hadn't gone to that party? What if I hadn't opened that garage door? What if I'd had the courage to say no to my dad and just run away? Where would I be?"

"You were afraid, though," I said. "You can't blame yourself."

"That's nice of you to say. But I can blame myself in a lot of ways. I was a snot of a kid."

"All kids are."

"But Dad was right," Beth said. "I did want to get away from little Haxton, Ohio. I'd been counting the days until my eighteenth birthday for a long time."

"All kids do that too. I did."

"He knew which button to push," Beth said. "He knew just what I wanted. I took that money and I walked into that bus station with only the clothes on my back. I bought a ticket to Houston, and I left. I thought I was off on some great adventure. I thought I was being a rebel, some kind of wild and crazy free spirit who managed to leave all the limits of my family and town behind. I didn't even think about Mom and how it would affect her."

She leaned forward and buried her face in her hands. I couldn't tell whether she was crying or not, but I did move forward on the couch and reach out to her. I placed my hand on her shoulder. My own grief over Mom's death was too real for me not to share the experience with her in some way. The idea of leaving Mom—or Mom leaving us—and never seeing each other again was just too real. I held back against my own emotion for fear it would all pour out.

"Thanks," Beth said, lifting her head again. She wasn't crying, but her eyes were full and on the brink of spilling over. "As you can guess, I've been reliving a lot of this over the last week or so."

"I get it," I said. "We can stop. We can talk about this another day."

"It's okay," she said. She rubbed at her eyes, then tried to force a smile. "I bet you're thinking some things are better left unsaid, huh?"

"No," I said. "I'm really not. But your dad's plan doesn't sound like a foolproof one. How did he know you wouldn't just leave the station without getting a ticket? And how did he know you wouldn't just come back and tell what you knew?"

Beth nodded. "He told me that he and his associate would be watching the station. He said I'd never seen his friend before, and that friend was inside the station watching me, so if I didn't get on a bus and leave, they'd know. The rain was still falling, but not as hard. The street was wet, and I had to jump around the puddles. I went inside the bus station and looked around. I didn't recognize anyone, but the station was full of skeevy-looking types. Have you ever been in a bus station?"

I nodded.

"Then you know. As for the other thing . . . I think he was gambling. Like I said, he knew I wanted to leave town. He knew I was going at it with Mom every chance I got. I think he just hoped I'd stay away long enough for there to be no evidence of what he was mixed up in. If I came back and made some wild accusation, he'd just throw up his hands and say, 'What evidence is there of this? The kid's probably on drugs and telling wild stories.' "

"And that was it?" I asked. "You never came back?"

Beth shook her head. "No, I didn't. I did a whole lot of things in a whole lot of places. It certainly wasn't pretty, but it was mine. It was my life."

Chapter Fifty

My phone buzzed again. I looked down and saw Neal's name on the display. I held up my hand.

"I have to take this one too," I said to Beth. "This is my friend outside."

I answered the phone, but no one was there. It didn't sound like a dropped call. It sounded like someone was on the other end of the line but wasn't saying anything.

"Neal?" I said. "Neal?"

The call cut out.

I called right back, expecting Neal to answer. Knowing him, I figured he had grown antsy during the long period of time I'd been inside the house with Beth listening to her story. I should have checked in with him sooner to let him know what was going on, but I'd been so involved with Beth's story, I hadn't thought of it.

Neal was probably ready to go home. Or else he had something else to do.

But when I called back, the phone went right to voice mail. Neal's voice came on instructing any callers to leave their name and, as he put it, "the most pertinent information" and he would call them back.

I didn't leave a message. Something was off. Why wasn't Neal answering his phone?

"Is something wrong?" Beth asked. "Is it Ronnie?"

"No," I said. "It's my friend outside. He's supposed to be out there waiting for me. In fact, we didn't know what would happen when I came in here, so I had his number ready to call in case . . . you know . . ."

"In case I tried to murder you," Beth said.

"Just being safe," I said. "But now he's not answering."

"Maybe he got another call. Maybe he figured you were in here so long everything was okay."

"Sure," I said. "I'm just going to check, though." I stood up and dialed his number again as I walked to the front door. Again it went straight to voice mail. "I'm just going to go out and see."

"Do you think it's safe?" Beth said.

"It should be fine," I said. "Neal knows how to take—"

I had just placed my hand on the doorknob when a gunshot interrupted me.

I froze. Had it really been a gunshot?

Beth was right behind me. "Get away from the door."

Her words jolted me into action. I pulled the door open and stepped out onto the porch. I sensed Beth behind me. She came up and placed her hand on my right arm.

"Come inside," she said.

"Go call 911."

"I will," she said. "But you come in."

"You call," I said. "I have to check on my friend."

I pulled away from her and started down the porch steps. In the wake of the gunshot, the night was quiet. Very quiet. I expected to hear commotion, to see people running outside to give help. But it must not have been that kind of neighborhood. Most of the blinds and doors remained shut tight. Across the street I saw one set of curtains move, but the figure behind the glass disappeared before I could get any kind of look at them.

I turned in the direction of Neal's SUV. The streetlights had just come on, but their glow didn't cover every inch of the street. Some areas remained in darkness and shadow. I saw the figure lying in the street next to Neal's car. I ran forward so fast, I didn't process who it was. But as I came closer, I saw. It was Neal. I recognized the grimy army coat, his tall frame with the long legs splayed.

I saw the blood dripping from his side, staining the pavement.

"Neal!"

When I reached him, he could barely lift his head. But he managed to smile at me, one corner of his mouth lifting. His skin was pale, almost translucent in the half-light. His eyes looked a little glassy. And scared. Even Neal could look scared.

"What happened?" I asked. "The police are coming."

"Some guy . . ."

"Who? What guy?"

He started coughing.

"Just lay here," I said. "Lay back."

I eased Neal's head down against the pavement. He was sweating. I didn't have anything to cushion his head, so I left my hand under there, hoping it brought some comfort.

"A guy," he said. "I saw him . . . He was scoping out the house . . ."

"He shot you?"

"Stabbed me. Fucking stabbed me. Can you believe that?"

"I'm sorry. This is all my fault."

He started shaking his head. "No. Not that." He coughed again. "This guy. He was going for the house. So I got out." He closed his eyes, wincing. "He came over here and we got into it. He just stabbed me. I can't believe he got the drop on me."

I heard them in the distance. Sirens. "Do you hear that, Neal? The police are coming. Just relax."

"He was an old guy," he said. "That's the shittiest thing. Some old fat guy . . ."

"Who fired the gun?" I asked.

"Me." He rolled onto his side a little, and I saw the gun beneath his body. There was blood smeared on the grip. "I think I missed. But it's okay." He winced again. "I have a permit."

I heard footsteps in the street behind me. It was Beth. She had a blanket and she spread it over Neal's body.

"Thanks," he said just before his eyes closed.

"An old fat guy?" I said.

"Old," Neal said. "Fat. He was going to the house where you were . . . He looked like trouble . . . a real asshole . . ."

His voice trailed off. I saw the flashing lights of the police cars as they turned onto the street. I reached out for Neal and held his hand.

It felt even colder than the night air.

Chapter Fifty-one

When the paramedics arrived on Beth's street, they went right to work on Neal. I didn't watch closely, but I saw them slide an IV into his arm and pump a clear liquid into his body. They checked his vital signs and lifted him onto a stretcher and into the ambulance.

The police took over from there. They inundated Beth and me with questions about the stabbing. Who was Neal? What brought all this on? What was my relationship to the victim?

I told them everything I knew, which wasn't very much. But I made sure they understood one thing.

"The man who did this," I said. "His name is Gordon Baxter."

I waited in another hospital, this one in Reston Point. I didn't even know its name. Beth sat beside me. We had no idea what was going on with Neal. They had rushed him into surgery before we arrived in the emergency room waiting area, and since we weren't immediate family members, no one would tell us anything. We made our way to the surgery floor, where the waiting room looked more comfortable. There was coffee brewed and a plate of crumbling pastries and cookies. Maybe I was feeling paranoid or maybe the recent events in my life had diminished my capacity for hope, but I started to think the nurses who hustled through the hallways and the elderly volunteer at the desk were looking at Beth and me with barely disguised pity. I prepared myself for the worst.

A detective from Reston Point took our initial statements and told us to expect a call in the future. I gave him the names of Richland and Post, and he wrote those down with the enthusiasm of someone composing a grocery list.

"Did someone call his family?" I asked.

"We made the notification," the detective said and then left.

A TV played with the sound down, some news show in which two heads argued back and forth. In the harsh hospital light, I saw Beth's face more clearly. I saw the deep lines and the wear. Her eyes lacked any real spark of life. They looked tired instead. But despite all that, I saw the resemblance to Mom. And to me. Beneath the layer of frazzled and harried fear, I saw my mother's steel. This woman—my sister—looked like a survivor, someone who had the scars from battle, but was ready to go another few rounds. No problem.

My phone vibrated in my hand. It was a text from Janie Rader. She and some of her girlfriends were going out for Saturday night drinks—did I want to come? *Oh, Janie,* I thought. *How I wish I could just go out for drinks with the girls. How I wish . . .*

"I guess you still have a lot of questions," Beth said.

I put the phone away. "A few more."

"I'm sorry about your friend," she said. "Is he your—?"

"No," I said. "Neal is one of my students. He helped me find you. My mind was just muddled with all of this stuff, and I thought the police would take too long. I asked him, and he found you for me."

Beth shook her head. Her shoulders drooped. "I get the feeling this is all my fault. None of this would have ever happened if you weren't looking for me."

"I think it goes back a lot further than me trying to find you," I said.

Something beeped above us, and a voice over the loudspeaker summoned a technician to the pediatric wing.

Beth said, "I think it all goes back to my father. He clearly wasn't the man Mom thought she was marrying. He certainly wasn't the man I thought he was when I was growing up. He sent me away. He did those awful things. He tried to kill your friend. And now . . . I can't help thinking about Mom."

"You think he's the one who killed Mom?"

"I'm not sure I can allow my mind to go there," she said, shaking her head. "It's just too much to take in all at once."

I understood what she was saying, but I hadn't had any trouble going where she didn't want to. And I hoped the police saw it the same way once they found out. I looked forward to updating Richland and Post with this piece of the puzzle. They wouldn't be able to conclude anything else—Gordon Baxter killed Mom, just as he tried to kill Neal.

"Can you tell me something else?" I asked. "Can you tell me how you got back in touch with Mom? Did you not see her for a long time? How many years was it before you saw her again?"

"I just saw her again about six months ago," Beth said. "After all those years, we finally reconnected."

"How many years was that?" I asked.

"Thirty-seven," she said.

"Jesus," I said. I couldn't help myself. "Thirty-seven years. Jesus. How did that happen?"

"I want to be clear—it might have been thirty-seven years

before I saw her again. But I thought about her all the time over those years. Every day, in fact. At first, I stayed away because . . . I'm ashamed to admit it, but Gordon was right. I wanted to get out of Ohio. I thought Haxton was too small for me. I was starting some kind of great adventure, I thought. I went away. I found work. I met people, and I partied it up. I picked up the phone more than once, meaning to call Mom. I bought postcards and even started to write them. But I never followed through."

"Why not?"

"I didn't want to go home. And I thought if I started talking to Mom she'd beg me to come back. And then there was Gordon. He made it sound like Mom would be in danger if I made contact with her. I didn't really believe his story that Mom was involved with the movies and whatever else he was doing, but I knew she was there, with Gordon. I didn't know if she knew and turned a blind eye, or if she might really get hurt. I didn't want to risk it. And the more time passed, the easier it was to not make contact. Or I guess I should say, the harder it would have been to *make* contact. You know what I mean?"

"Sure."

"And then after six or seven months of being free and wild, things got worse for me."

"How?"

She looked at the floor.

"If you don't want to get into it—"

"I do," she said. "Remember—" She reached out and placed her hand on mine. I accepted the gesture, but still felt uncomfortable with it. "We're family now. At least to some extent." She took her hand away. "I got into drugs," she said. "Not just a little. And not just holding on to bad things for one of my wild friends. I went all in. For several years, I was a mess. I did things to support my habit, things I really wouldn't want to talk about, but you can guess what they must be. In fact, whatever you can imagine, I did more than that. And worse. You asked me why I went so long without talking to Mom. That was a big part of it."

"What was? The drugs?"

"The shame. I didn't want her to see what I had turned out to be. Everything she warned me about, everything we fought about, I turned into that. And then some. And this happened over and over again. I relapsed many times over the years. I've been to rehab more than once. It finally took the last time, about five years ago. I've been to jail . . . you name it."

"Married?"

She nodded. "Three times. Four kids. Yes, you have four nieces and nephews you didn't even know about. And I'm a grandmother. Six grandchildren, if you can believe that."

"Wow," I said. I didn't know what else to say.

"The grandchildren," she said. "They really helped lead me back to Mom. When I saw them so young, so vulnerable, something kicked in. I guess I realized I was getting older. Time was passing. I'd moved back here, to Reston Point. I'd lived in Ohio once before, about twenty years ago. I lived in Akron. I even thought about coming over and looking for Mom then. I checked the phone book and everything. She'd gotten married by then and had a different name. You couldn't just look on the computer like you can now. And I thought . . . I guess I thought she had a new life and maybe she didn't want me to come back and remind her of all that stuff from the past."

"You know she wouldn't have thought that," I said.

"I know," she said. "I was afraid of Gordon too. I wondered what would happen if I did see him again, so I stayed away. Eventually I realized Mom wouldn't care about any of that. I tracked her down in Dover. I just used one of those services you pay for on the Internet. They found her, and I called her . . . and . . ."

Beth lost it then. She didn't even have time to raise her hands to her face. The tears poured out and her body shook with the sobbing.

I looked around. Only one other family sat in the waiting area with us, an elderly man and a middle-aged couple. They all turned to look when Beth started crying, then looked away again when they saw me scrambling to find tissues. I grabbed a box and brought them to Beth. While she tried to stem the tide of her tears, I placed my hand on her back and gently rubbed. It didn't feel as awkward as I would have thought. I felt for this woman. I didn't want to see her suffer. And I couldn't imagine the pain she was experiencing over first losing her mother as a teenager, then briefly having her back as an adult only to lose her again so suddenly. If we were going to have a grieving contest, I decided Beth won by a mile. It wasn't even close.

She composed herself. She used the tissues to wipe her tears and snot away. The other people in the waiting area had gone back to their own worries and problems. I sank back into my chair. I felt tired, mentally and physically. And I still hadn't been back to Dover to see Ronnie. Maybe Dan was still there, or maybe Paul had returned to the hospital. But maybe Ronnie was there alone, wondering where I was.

"I feel guilty," Beth said. "So very guilty."

"You shouldn't."

"But I should," Beth said. "I should have done something to stop him once I saw him again. More than anyone else, I knew the kinds of things he was capable of. And I should have tried to stop him from hurting Mom."

Chapter Fifty-two

A nurse appeared in the waiting room. She held a clipboard, and she read something off of it. Then she looked up and said, "The family of Neal Nelson. Is the Neal Nelson family here?" The nurse looked around, her eyes bouncing across all the people in the room. I raised my hand.

The nurse came over. She held the clipboard in front of her like a shield, as if she expected someone to attack. "Are you family members?" she asked.

"Yes," I said.

"And what's the relation?"

"I'm his girlfriend," I said.

The nurse wore a stone face. "Are there any *family* members here?"

"I don't know where they are," I said. "But the detective said they were called."

The nurse remained stoic, but some of the sternness eased. "I'm just here to tell you that they're beginning the closing procedures on the surgery. But it looks like everything is going to be fine."

"Oh, thank God," I said. Beth reached out for me. We leaned

in toward each other, our shoulders touching. "He's going to be okay."

"Well," the nurse said, "I didn't say that. I'm just here to tell you it looks like he's going to be okay—so far."

I could live with that. I thanked the nurse. Then she turned on her heel and briskly walked away, still clutching the clipboard.

"I'm so relieved," I said to Beth.

"I know."

We sat there in silence for a few minutes. Then I said, "I hate to go back to this, but I'm wondering why you feel so guilty about Mom's death and Gordon. You're being too hard on yourself."

She paused. I saw that her hands were clenched, the fingernails digging into the fabric of her chair.

"Gordon found me about a year ago," she said. "I don't know how. For all I know he used one of those Internet people finder things. Or else he hired someone to find me. Whatever it was, he found me here in Reston Point. He told me then that he'd been thinking about me a lot and hoped we could reconnect. He gave me a whole line about how sorry he was about the past and everything that happened when he sent me away. He said it was a misunderstanding, that he really didn't mean for me to never come back. I'm ashamed to say I fell for some of it. I guess I was so desperate to connect with someone from my family—this family that had been taken away from me—that I was willing to believe he might be a changed man." She looked at me, her face serious. "People do change, Elizabeth. Take it from me—they really do. I know that better than anyone."

I nodded.

"I asked him about Mom, of course. He told me what he

knew—that she had remarried and had two kids. He said he'd been in touch with her and maybe it was a little soon for me to go rushing back into her life. I found out later, from Mom, that he had only gotten back in touch with her because he knew she had some insurance money from your dad and wanted to try to get something out of her. Gordon hadn't been living in Dover for very long. I still don't know where he'd been living. Columbus maybe. But the money was all he wanted. She said she hadn't seen him in ten or fifteen years, and then he showed up again. Hell, I think he probably wanted money from me, but one look at my life and he'd know the cupboard was bare. But he said he'd help smooth the way and prepare Mom for meeting me if I wanted. I went along with that too."

"Why?"

"Because of what I said before," Beth said. "I still felt that shame, that fear that the life I had led in the past would be . . . difficult for Mom to accept. I wanted to be sure I was ready for anything."

"Did you ever think Mom wanted to send you away?"

Beth paused a long time. "I guess at first I might have. We didn't get along. She was frustrated with me a lot." She shook her head. "But she would never do that. I don't blame her. I never would. And I know she thought I was dead. If she thought there was a chance I was alive somewhere . . . well, I just know she would have tried to find me."

"So how did you meet Mom, then?"

"About six months after Gordon found me, I could tell he was starting to stall a little about getting me and Mom back together. I was getting impatient. I was ready. As ready as I was ever going to be, and I thought if I didn't do it soon I might never do it." She took a deep breath. "He let something slip once. I knew he was seeing Mom somewhere south of Reston Point. I guessed it was Dover because there really isn't much else down here. Even with a town the size of Dover, finding one person when you only know their first name is like finding a needle in a haystack. And I was afraid I'd run across someone I used to know. A kid from school or whatever. I assumed some people might remember me, and I didn't want Mom to find out through someone else that I was around. I wanted to have some control over how it went. Instead, in a roundabout way, it was Ronnie who helped me find her."

"Ronnie?" I asked. "How?"

"Gordon told me once that Mom had a son with Down syndrome. That's all I knew. I didn't even know his name. Or your name. But I did know they had that place in Dover, that center where people with disabilities spend time and get jobs and things like that."

"The Miller Center."

"Right. I worked with a woman who had a nephew who used to go there," Beth said.

"Did she know Mom?"

"No. I just went to that place, the Miller Center, and I asked around. I lied and said my son had Down syndrome, but he had died. And I said there was a woman I met there who had been very kind to me, and I wanted to thank her but I only knew her first name. 'She has a son with Down syndrome,' I said. 'And her name is Leslie.' The volunteer said it must be Leslie Hampton. I had it then. That's how I found Mom."

"Did you just show up at her door?"

"I didn't know what to do. Finally I called. She thought it was a cruel joke at first, but then I told her things no one else could know. How old I was when I got my first period. The name of my stuffed bunny when I was little. That was all it took. We agreed to meet at her house one night. Ronnie wasn't there, but as soon as she saw me, she knew it was me. And I knew it was her. It was like something was completed that night—something clicked inside me that hadn't clicked in a long time."

The nurse with the clipboard came out again and spoke to the other family in the waiting area, using a low voice. The family nodded happily, and I found myself relieved that they appeared to be receiving good news as well.

I turned back to Beth. "How did that mean you led Gordon to Mom? He obviously knew where she was before you did."

"I think there was something else going on," Beth said. "I think Gordon was blackmailing Mom with information about me. He knew where I was, and he knew where she was. And I think he told Mom that if she ever wanted to see me, she'd have to pay up."

I thought of those bank withdrawals over the past year. All that money leaving Mom's account.

"Did Mom say anything about it?" I asked.

"At some point she said it would be a relief to have Gordon off her back. She didn't get specific, but she indicated she'd been helping him out. I didn't know what she meant, but it sounded like money. I think Gordon was telling her that he'd let her know where I was as long as she kept giving him money. He strung her along as much as he could."

"It's hard to believe Mom would put up with that," I said. "Getting strung along that way."

"I agree," Beth said. "Except—"

"She was desperate to see her child again."

"Exactly. And when I found Mom on my own, Gordon lost his leverage over her."

"So you think . . ."

Beth nodded. "I told Mom the whole story about why I went away. I think Gordon tried to get more money out of her, and she told him to get lost—that she knew everything, and not only would there be no money, but she might have even threatened to go to the police. It wouldn't make sense for him to kill her if she was giving him money, would it? But once she knew me again and what he'd done to me, she took a stand. I think she said, 'No more.'" Beth took a long pause. "I think that's when he killed her."

Chapter Fifty-three

"You think he killed her because she wouldn't give him money anymore?"

"She didn't *have* to," Beth said. "And what's more, she also knew it was him who drove me away that night. He probably thought she'd turn him in to the police. Maybe he killed her just to shut her up."

It all made sense to me. And there were other implications that went with it.

"If he might have killed Mom to shut her up, then—"

"Me," Beth said. "I know everything too. My guess is that he was working up to it. Maybe he thought if I was in the will, he might be able to get some money out of me. Who knows what he was coming to the house for tonight? Your friend got in the way, or else who knows what would have happened. To both of us." As she said that, something crossed her face. Some recognition that widened her eyes. "Jesus. Now you're in it too. You know what I know."

"I was in it already," I said. "Hell, I was in it before I was even born."

I stood up and paced around. While I did, a couple came hustling through the waiting room. The man was tall and thin, and except for the nice suit he was wearing he looked a great deal like Neal Nelson. The woman with him was wearing a fur coat, and even from across the room I could see multiple gold rings on her fingers as she patted her helmet of hair into place. They spoke to the volunteer on duty. I saw relief spread through their posture and across their faces. The volunteer made a phone call, and the clipboard-bearing nurse came out and led the couple back through a set of doors, presumably to a post-op recovery area. I took it to mean Neal was doing okay.

And we had done everything we could do at the hospital.

"Do you have somewhere to go?" I asked. "Or do you want to take a drive down to Dover?"

Beth didn't hesitate. "It doesn't look like my house is a very safe place to be, does it?"

"Probably not."

"Then I'm game. What do you have in mind?"

"Would you still recognize Gordon's handwriting?"

Beth and I didn't talk much while we made the one-hour drive to Dover. We were both worn out, exhausted from the evening's events as well as reliving the things that had happened to her over the previous thirty-seven years.

And we both knew something else—there was still more to come. Things weren't over. Not even close.

During the ride, Beth leaned over and turned the radio on low. I didn't recognize the program, but it was a guy giving people advice on all sorts of problems—some financial and some personal. He gave his number at every break, and at one point I said, "We should call him and tell him about us. His head might explode."

Beth smiled a little, but she didn't say anything. Her life had been brutal, and I hadn't even heard the half of it. If I knew all the details, they might make my head spin. I wanted to ask her if she'd gotten help, therapy or something. And I wondered whether she felt she'd managed to beat her addictions once and for all. But I didn't. I gave her space and time to think. I couldn't take anything for granted, but it looked as if the two of us would be getting to know each other even more in the future.

I did ask one question. "Did Mom like to read when she was young?"

"All the time."

"That never changed. She thought every problem could be solved with a book."

Beth didn't say anything else, but I understood why Mom wanted that book from Mrs. Porter. Beth had no doubt told Mom much of the same story—or some sanitized version of it—and I knew Mom would have taken it all to heart. I hated to think how much guilt she would have felt over the life her daughter led when she was sent away. At least she died knowing Beth was still alive.

When we got closer to Dover, Beth said, "You still haven't told me what we're doing. Do you want to see Ronnie?"

"Not exactly," I said. "Although we can do that later if you want."

"Visiting hours are probably over," Beth said. "I kind of figured we weren't seeing him."

"Visiting hours," I said, my voice mocking. "Do you think a little thing like posted visiting hours can stop us? After all we've been through? We're Leslie's daughters, right?"

Some cheer returned to Beth's face and voice. "Right."

Dover Community looked appropriately deserted. We parked

close to the door and stepped out into the cool night. The sodium vapor lights overhead illuminated us, casting our faces and bodies in a half glow. I stopped before we went in.

"You've been here before, right?" I asked.

Beth nodded. "I came to visit Ronnie. Once. It didn't go well."

"You don't have to tell me if you don't want, but what was it that upset him so much about your visit?"

Beth hugged herself against the cool air. We had left her house in a hurry, and she was wearing only a light sweater. It had a dark stain on the front. I thought it might be coffee, then realized it might be Neal's blood. I looked down. I had some on my jeans and shirt as well. We'd make a pretty sight walking into a mental health facility after dark.

"It's stupid, really," she said. "Stupid on my part. I wanted to talk about Mom. I didn't have anyone else I could do that with because I didn't know you yet. I had read in the paper that Ronnie had been taken into custody or whatever, so I wanted to see him."

"What if you'd run into one of us?" I asked. "Me or . . . or Paul."

"I went at an off hour, hoping no one would be there. But you know, I kind of wanted to run into one of you. God . . . Paul. He's my uncle. He was my favorite uncle all those years ago. Such a sweet, sweet man." She shook her head. "It's strange. I never wanted to come back when I was young. But now I kind of just wanted to belong to a family again."

"And it was too much for Ronnie?"

"He was pretty doped up," Beth said. "I think he thought I was Mom. When he started to flip out, I just left. I couldn't handle it. I hated to think I brought him any pain."

"He's tough too," I said. "And understanding."

The door was locked, so I rang the buzzer. A young nurse I had never seen before came to the door and pointed at her watch. She spoke to us through the thick glass. I had hoped to see Janie, but she wasn't in sight—she must have been out having fun with her girlfriends.

"Visiting hours are over," the nurse said. "We open at seven tomorrow."

"We're not here to visit anyone," I said. "We just want to talk to you."

The nurse gave us both the once-over. She took in our tired features and frazzled looks. Who knows if she saw the blood? She stepped away and made a phone call. I knocked again, and when she looked, I made a waving gesture toward the door.

"Come on," I said.

The nurse didn't budge. Instead a trim and fit security guard, a young black man with a razor-thin goatee and a shiny gold badge, came over to the door. He approached us with his thumbs hooked in his belt. He meant business.

"I don't like cops very much," Beth said as he walked up.

"He's a rent-a-cop."

"Those are the worst," she said. "They have the most to prove."

The guard didn't hesitate. He pushed the door open and used his body to block the opening.

"Visiting hours are over, ladies." His voice sounded surprisingly high, almost effeminate. I didn't know whether that put me at ease or gave further support to Beth's theory.

"I know that," I said. I tried to smile, to look harmless and pretty. The guy was about my age. Shouldn't he fall for that stuff? "We just need to talk to the nurse and look at your log-book. You know, the one where guests sign in."

He shook his head. "You have to come back in the morning and talk to the supervisor. Her name is Miss Hicks."

"You know Janie Rader, right?" I asked. "She's a friend of mine."

He shook his head again. "I can't comment on our personnel. But you can speak to Miss Hicks in the morning."

"I don't really have that much time," I said.

"I know," he said. "Everyone has an emergency."

"Yes," I said. "I do."

"Miss Hicks. Seven a.m."

He started to shut the door, so I stuck my hand out, stopping it.

"Now wait—"

"Ma'am—"

"Just listen—"

"Elizabeth," Beth said. "Maybe we should—"

"If he'd just listen," I said. "Just listen. My brother was here. And they say he tried to kill himself, but I don't think it's true. And I need to see—"

"Ma'am," the guard said. "Lots of folks got troubles."

"But my brother—*our* brother—Ronnie, he's in the other hospital because they say he tried to kill himself, but I think someone tried to kill him."

The pressure on the door eased. Something softened in the guard's face. The hard lines and edges of his mouth and jaw relaxed.

"Ronnie?" he asked.

"Yes, Ronald Hampton."

"Your brother is Ronnie Hampton?"

"Yes," I said. "Yes. Do you know him?"

"They told me Ronnie tried to kill himself with pills," the

guard said. There was a long pause. I kept my mouth shut and just waited. "Ronnie's my buddy. We watched the baseball play-offs on TV together."

"Right," I said. "He loves baseball."

The guard looked me over again. His eyes stopped on my pants, the bloodstain. Then he said, "There's no way Ronnie would do himself in." He stepped back. "Come on. What do you need help with?"

Chapter Fifty-four

The security guard told us his name was Edgar. He said he didn't realize Ronnie had two sisters, that Ronnie had only ever mentioned one.

Beth nodded toward me. "Ronnie always liked her best."

As we approached the nurse's station, the nurse who had shooed us away—and had apparently summoned the guard—seemed nervous. She had large brown eyes like polished stones. I didn't say anything to her right away. I looked up and down the counter, trying to find what I needed.

"Can I help you with something?" the nurse said.

"The book where everyone signs in?" I asked. "Where did it go?"

"It's back here," the nurse said.

"Can I see it?" I asked.

"Who are you?" the nurse asked. "Edgar, do you know these people?"

"They're Ronnie Hampton's people," Edgar said.

"Look," I said. "The book isn't a secret. It's usually sitting right here. Every time I've been here, I've been able to see whoever signed in ahead of me. Can I just look at it? We're trying to help someone."

"My father," Beth said. "We need to know if he was here."

The nurse still didn't move. "I just started last week . . ."

I leaned over the counter. "It's right there," I said, pointing. "I could reach over and take it myself."

The nurse eyed the book but stayed firmly in place.

"Would you prefer that?" I asked. "Would you prefer if I just took it? Maybe you stepped down the hall to get a drink of water or a snack, and I came in here and took it."

I didn't wait for her response. I leaned over and grabbed the book. I flipped back a couple of pages and moved closer to Beth. "It must have been sometime this morning."

With Beth by my side, I scanned through the list of signed names and the times. I didn't see Gordon's name, which was no surprise.

"He probably used a fake name," Beth said.

"Do you recognize his handwriting?" I asked.

She took the book and studied the signatures. Her lip curled in frustration as she did. "It's been so long," she said.

"I know."

"Since I was a kid." She pointed at one. "Maybe that. I don't know."

It read, *Stan Smith*.

"Sounds made up," I said. "Do either of you know who Stan Smith is? Is there a patient named Smith?"

The nurse looked confused. "I just started."

Edgar said, "Oh, yeah. Esther Smith. Down the hall. Her husband comes to see her all the time."

"Did you work this morning?" I asked.

"Yes, ma'am. I'm on a double shift."

"Did Ronnie have any visitors in the evening?" I asked.

"Hmm. I'm not sure. There was a lot going on."

"I'll be specific. A fat little white guy with a thick neck. Sort of looks like a giant bullfrog."

Edgar snapped his fingers. "I know."

"What?" Beth asked.

"I got called up to the second floor for about an hour this morning," Edgar said. "There was a disturbance. Somebody stuffed a load of paper in the sink and the toilet and left the water running. Big flood. I had to help get it all cleaned up."

"Oh, yeah," the nurse said. "I heard about that."

"That's rotten," I said.

"Or really convenient," Beth said. "If you're going with this where I think you're going."

I turned back to the nurse. "Okay, I need you to do us another favor."

"Another one?"

"I need you to tell us what medicines my brother was taking."

"No, I can't do that," she said. "That's private information. I can't give that out. I could lose my job."

"We won't tell," I said.

"I just started. I have student loans to pay off." She looked up and down the hallway, then turned back to me. "I can tell you the police already came tonight and took all of your brother's medical records."

"Okay. So give them to me too."

"They're the police."

"Do you know I'm not a cop?" I asked.

The nurse gave me a knowing look. "Edgar just said you're related to Ronnie. You're probably his sister."

"And I'm a cop," I said. "I forgot my uniform."

"Wait a minute," Edgar said. He held up his hand in an authoritarian manner. "What is it you're trying to find out?"

"I need to know if my brother was taking a certain drug."

"The one he OD'd on?" Edgar asked.

"Yes."

"Okay," Edgar said. He leaned over the counter toward the nurse. "Tanya, why don't you just let them ask you if their brother was taking a certain medication. You can just answer yes or no. Then you're not handing over all the records. And then they know what they want to know."

Tanya studied Edgar a long time. "I don't know," she said. "I could still get in trouble."

"Come on, girl," Edgar said. "It will be fine."

Tanya looked back at me. "Okay. What are you looking for?"

"I need to know if Ronnie was on a heart medication. Something called digitoxin or dioxin or something like that."

"Digoxin?" Tanya asked.

"Sure," I said. "I guess."

She turned and started typing on the computer.

Beth looked at Edgar. "Nice job. You're pretty smart."

"I try. I'm taking the exam next week to get into the police academy."

"Too bad," Beth said. "I hate cops."

"Me too," Edgar said. "If I get in, they're going to make me shave my goatee."

Tanya leaned in close to the computer screen and clicked the mouse a few times.

"Well?" I asked.

She shook her head but didn't say anything.

"You're not going to tell me?" I asked.

Tanya shook her head again.

"I think that's your answer about the drug," Beth said.

"Okay," I said. "Is there anything that would deal with the

same problems digoxin deals with? Maybe it's under a generic name."

"Digoxin is primarily used for irregular heartbeats and atrial fib," Tanya said. "Did your brother have a heart problem like that?"

"Not that I know of."

Tanya clicked the mouse a few times again, and the screen went blank. "That's all I can help you with, okay?"

Edgar said, "Are you telling me someone tried to kill Ronnie with some pills? After someone already killed your mother?"

"It looks that way," I said. "And the good news is the police might have finally figured it out as well."

"Damn," Edgar said. "Who would do such a thing?"

I didn't answer. I didn't have to.

Beth said, "Unfortunately, it looks like it was my father who did it."

Chapter Fifty-five

I slept a long time in Dan's bed. Beth and I went there after we left Dover Community, figuring that it was a safe place to spend the night. It was too late for her to drive back to Reston Point anyway, and once Dan got over his initial shock at learning that I suddenly had a half sister, he was willing to accommodate us. Beth slept on the couch, curled up with one of Dan's old blankets pulled up to her chin. We made sure the door was double-locked.

The only thing I could think about before falling asleep was Ronnie. I hadn't been back to St. Vincent's. I hadn't checked in with Paul. Dan reassured me, telling me that when he'd left the hospital Ronnie was content and resting. He already looked healthier.

"I need to see him tomorrow," I said.

And then I faded out.

I don't even think I got out of bed to go to the bathroom during the night. I was deep under, dreaming of Neal Nelson being chased by someone I couldn't see, when the phone started ringing. It took me a long time to surface. Even though the dream scared me, I didn't want to come out of it. I feared that the ringing phone was going to bring me something worse.

Then Dan gently shook me awake. He held the phone in his hand.

"You need to take this," he said. "It's the police. That detective, the one from your mom's case."

I shook the tattered remnants of the dream away and wiped my eyes. I was in Dan's bed. I was safe.

I took the phone, hoping for Post but instead hearing Richland. I had called them the night before and left a message telling them what I had learned at Dover Community.

"Ms. Hampton?"

"Yes?"

"We've been trying to locate you," he said.

"You just did."

"We went by your apartment and you weren't there."

"That's because a fat man with a knife wants to kill me."

"Can you tell us where you are?" he asked. "We need to give you an update on the investigation."

"Did something happen?"

"We'd rather not get into it over the phone."

I sighed. Would the day ever come when I'd be done with the police? "I'm at a friend's house." I gave them the address. "Can you give me half an hour? And then after I talk to you, I need to go see my brother."

"That's probably a good idea," he said. And hung up.

That comment didn't make me nervous. Not at all.

Beth sat up on the couch when I emerged from the bedroom. Her hair was tangled and ragged, her face puffy. Dan must have made coffee, because she held a mug in her hand. She lifted it to her mouth and blew on it gently.

"Did you sleep okay?" I asked.

"Not really."

"It's not a great couch for sleeping, I guess."

"It's not that," she said. "I had a lot on my mind."

"I did too. But that didn't stop me."

Dan disappeared into the kitchen. I heard water running and dishes clanking. He meant to give us our space to talk.

"The police are coming to talk to me," I said. "They have something else to tell me."

"They want to come here?" Beth asked.

"Yes."

"Hmm," she said.

"What's wrong?"

"It's probably nothing, but usually when they have to tell you some bad news, they come to your house and do it in person."

"At this point, I don't know what to expect," I said. "But you're welcome to stay if you want. I'm going to shower since I haven't done that in two days. But if you want to wait . . ."

Beth shook her head. "I have to get back. My granddaughter has a soccer game. I know it's not a big deal, but I agreed to take her. I could call my daughter and arrange something else, but . . ."

"But what?"

"I feel that you might be better off doing this on your own," she said. "I feel like I brought all of this down on you. Maybe you need to be away from me."

"I wasn't thinking that at all," I said. "Are you worried you might be in danger in Reston Point? Gordon knows where you live. He could hurt you or your family. He was already there with a knife. I'm pretty sure he broke into my apartment and trashed it."

"I know," she said. "But I've been taking care of myself for a long time. I've been in tight spots before. Gordon is a son of a bitch, but I've known my share of those as well."

I didn't know what to say. "Well, I'll call you when I know anything else. And if you want to come visit Ronnie in the hospital, you can."

She smiled, but it looked forced. She set the mug of coffee down on Dan's table. I could tell there was something else she wanted to say. I could see her gearing up for it.

"You've been very nice to me. Wonderful, really. And it's great to get to know you like we did yesterday. But I understand that you and I come from very different worlds. If you decide you don't even want to see me or talk to me again, I understand. I have my own family, and you have a nice life here."

"I wasn't thinking those things," I said.

"Well, a lot of time has passed. I don't want to force anything."

She stood up and grabbed her sweater. I stayed in my seat while she gathered her purse and started for the door. The water in the kitchen had stopped running. I suspected Dan was eavesdropping, monitoring my interaction with my half sister. He probably wanted to know whether I'd let her just walk away the way I'd let him go before.

When Beth reached the door, I said, "You know, it was . . . I guess 'fun' isn't really the right word. But I liked being with you last night. I mean, it felt fun to do those things with you, like getting into the hospital and all that."

Beth smiled. "We were like Thelma and Louise or something."

"Right." She didn't open the door. I continued. "I used to ask Mom to have another baby because I wanted a sister. She always told me she was too old. Which she was."

"How old was she when you were born?" Beth asked.

"Forty-three."

"That is too old," Beth said. "I already had grandchildren when I was forty-three."

"Damn," I said. "Well, I know Mom thought Ronnie ended up with Down syndrome because she had him so late. She told me once that the main reason they had me was so that someone could take care of Ronnie after they were gone. It used to really piss me off that she said that."

"She didn't mean that," Beth said. "That's not the only reason she had you."

"I know that now," I said. "In a way, meeting you and every-thing with Ronnie has made some of that clear. I think Mom probably had me and probably would have had more if she could just because she liked having us around. You know?"

"Yeah," Beth said. "I know. That's why I'm off to the soccer game on a Sunday morning."

"I'll call you later, okay?"

"Okay."

She left the apartment, and I went to take my first shower in forty-eight hours.

Chapter Fifty-six

I wanted to stay in the shower for a long time, letting the hot water keep running over my body until I turned into a prune. But I couldn't afford the time. I knew the detectives were coming, and my mind raced with more possibilities. I worried that another shoe had dropped with Ronnie, or that everything we knew about Gordon Baxter wasn't enough to convince them to go after him. I tried to contain the rampaging thoughts.

I toweled off in the bathroom, then stepped into Dan's bedroom. I didn't have much choice but to put most of my dirty clothes back on. I did borrow a T-shirt and sweater from Dan's dresser. I hoped they would keep me from smelling too bad.

When I emerged, Dan was sitting at his desk, his books and laptop opened. But he didn't seem to be doing any work. It looked like he was waiting for me to come out, like he wanted to talk.

"How are you doing?" he asked.

I knew he was probing, hoping to get insight into the deeper regions of my mind and soul. But who had time to go there?

"I'm fine," I said.

"Crazy night," he said.

"Is there more coffee?" I asked. "Or do you have tea?"

He stood up and went to the kitchen. He came back with coffee and two buttered pieces of toast. "I thought you'd be hungry."

I was. I ate the toast so fast the crumbs flew like wood chips out of a chain saw. Dan watched me eat. Ordinarily that bothered me—it bothered me when anyone did. But today I didn't care.

"I can make more," he said. "Or eggs."

"This will do for now," I said. "They'll be here soon." I wiped my face with a napkin. "Thanks for letting us stay here last night. I know it's crazy, me just showing up like that."

"With a half sister I didn't know you had."

"It's not boring around here," I said. "Does that count for anything?"

"Not really."

"Well, I do appreciate it," I said. "You've been great."

I downed the rest of the coffee. I needed the caffeine buzz.

"You seemed to be getting along well with Beth," Dan said.

"Yeah," I said. "We were thrown into the deep end together last night. But I guess being someone's sibling is the same thing. You're just thrown in with that person, and you have to figure out a way to make it work."

"She's going to make your life pretty full," he said.

"It's already full," I said. "I have no idea what I'm doing at school. I have no idea what's going to happen with Ronnie. For all I know, the cops are coming to the door with an indictment against him."

"I understand," he said. "I'm not trying to get you stirred up."

"You've been a champ, Dan. Really. I couldn't have made it through any of this without you."

The doorbell rang. I went and opened it, but only after looking through the peephole first. I wondered whether that paranoia would last the rest of my life.

I let Richland and Post in. They both nodded at me and then at Dan. They looked somber and serious, which only set my mind to racing. I introduced them to Dan, but Richland explained they had met him the night before at the hospital.

"Right," I said.

We all sat down. Richland asked, "Where were you last night?"

"Finding my long-lost half sister in Reston Point." I nodded toward Detective Post. "I'm sure you told him about that, right? Elizabeth Yarbrough. The woman named in the will."

Richland nodded as though he knew all about it, his big head bobbing almost comically. I hoped he appreciated the openness and transparency of his female partner.

"Is this woman around?" he asked. His hand rose in the air. "This half sister of yours?"

"She just left," I said. "She went back to her house."

The two detectives didn't say anything.

"She had a family function," I said. "A soccer game for one of her grandkids."

"Do they play soccer games on Sunday?" Richland asked. "My kids always play on Saturday."

"Hell," I said. "I don't know." I had become more protective of Beth, even though I barely knew her. I didn't want them to suspect her of anything, even though I could tell their detective radar was buzzing.

"We'll have to talk to her soon," Richland said. "And we will. But can you give us an idea of what you found out from her?"

"What I found out from her?" I asked. "Everything. I found out everything. A lifetime of stuff."

"Care to share any of it?" Richland asked. "It might help bring some clarity to things we've been working on."

"Is Ronnie okay?" I asked. "I haven't seen him since yesterday."

Post said, "He's okay. No worries there."

"Really?"

"Really," she said. "Just give us a quick rundown of what you were doing last night. It's important we know this."

So I did. I told them about finding Elizabeth with the help of Neal Nelson. They didn't look happy about that. I went on and told them about Beth's story. The porn movies and her forced exile from Haxton, then coming back and eventually reconnecting with both Gordon and Mom. I shared her theory that Gordon had been blackmailing Mom, and when she cut the money off, he ended up killing her.

"I've seen the bank records," I said. "She was giving money to somebody. And I can assure you it wasn't me."

Post and Richland didn't look surprised by anything I told them. It seemed I was merely confirming what they already suspected.

Richland asked, "So you didn't know this Elizabeth Yarbrough woman existed until your mom died?"

"Not until I saw the will."

"And you believe she's your half sister?" he asked.

"She looks a hell of a lot like Mom. And me. And she knew a lot about Mom. If she's not my half sister, she's doing a good job convincing me."

"Right," Richland said. "And did she indicate the nature of her relationship with Gordon Baxter? Where do they stand now?"

"Just what I told you," I said. "She was trying to get back in touch with Mom, and he was holding them apart to try to get money."

"That's what she said?" Richland asked.

"That's what she told me." I watched their faces. "Gordon knew where Beth—my half sister—was. And he told Mom he knew, but doled out the information in exchange for money. Look, my mom didn't suffer fools gladly. I know that about her. It would be tough to take advantage of her. But this should tell you how much she wanted to see her daughter again. She was desperate. I feel terrible for my mother having to go through that."

They didn't say anything. They seemed to want me to say more.

"Are you wondering if I believe Beth?"

Richland shook his head. "Has she asked *you* for money?"

"No. I just met her yesterday. Besides, she's getting money. A third of the estate. There's life insurance. What are you getting at?"

Richland remained quiet for a moment, as if he was absorbing everything. Then he said, "Okay, we wanted to let you know where everything else stood, especially as it relates to your brother."

"Okay," I said.

I looked at Dan. He was sitting on the arm of the couch, his eyes focused on the cops. I felt alone and scared. I noticed how my hands shook as I tried to tuck a strand of my still damp hair behind my ear. I looked at the front door. I thought about running through it—just get up and go and not hear whatever was about to come.

Richland said, "We spoke to the doctors at the hospital this morning, and they seem to think it's possible your brother could be released in a day or two. His vital signs are back to normal, and they want to get him to eat something today. If that goes well . . ."

He broke his sentence off. I leaned forward, waiting for the rest. What else was there? I looked back and forth between the two detectives.

Post smiled a little. "This is good, Elizabeth," she said. "Our investigation has shifted its focus. We now believe Gordon Baxter is a person of interest in your mother's death. We're actively trying to locate him right now. Your story helps to fill in a few gaps we had."

I wasn't sure what I expected. Ticker tape. A choir of angels. They were telling me the most important news I had ever heard—Ronnie *wasn't* a suspect in Mom's death anymore. And not only that, his health was coming back. He was going to be okay in more ways than one.

I wasn't sure what I felt. It wasn't joy. A touch of relief perhaps?

"Is that it, then?" I asked. "Ronnie is off the hook?"

"Well, it's an open case, an ongoing investigation. And you'll have to talk to the doctors at St. Vincent's," Richland said. He seemed stuck for a moment, not sure what to say next. He pointed at Dan. "I suppose your . . . friend here . . . I guess he told you about the cause of the overdose?"

"This digoxin stuff."

"Right." With something to explain to me, Richland seemed to be on firmer ground. "It turns out it's not a medication that your brother has ever taken. And Dr. Heil, after his examination of Ronnie, reached the conclusion that it was unlikely your brother would harm anyone. Not your mother and not himself.

It seems clear that someone tried to get Ronnie to take that medication, to make it appear as though he killed himself. Perhaps to cover some prior crime and frame your brother for it. At least, that's the working theory. We'll know more when we talk to Gordon Baxter. Like we said, we're trying to find him."

"Is she safe?" Dan asked, his voice full of skepticism. "This guy you're looking for, you think he already killed somebody and tried to kill somebody else."

"Two people," I said. "He tried to kill Neal last night."

"Is Elizabeth safe?" Dan asked again.

"You should certainly be cautious," Post said. "Mr. Baxter knows where you live."

"Can you put her somewhere safe?" Dan asked. "You know, some sort of protection program? What does this guy even want? Do you know, Elizabeth?"

Richland answered for me. "We don't really do that," he said. "Put people in a protection program, unless it's a really dire situation. As far as what he wants . . ." He looked at me. "Didn't you say he wanted money from you? Money from the life insurance policy?"

"That's what he said," I said.

"I don't see how he can expect to get that anymore," Post said. "He may have gone after Ms. Yarbrough because she knew so much about him from the past. But now we all know."

"I think you'll be safe," Richland said. "A guy like Baxter, you have no idea if he's even going to stick around in a town like Dover. His last known address is an hour away in Columbus, and he has an outstanding warrant there. He's not really looking to wait around until the law finds him. Chances are, he's left already, moved on to some other town. He's an old man, and he knows the noose is closing."

If I was supposed to take comfort in that bit of wisdom, I didn't. It made sense that someone might run off when the noose tightened. I knew that better than anyone.

But what about those people who kicked and fought the more the pressure increased? Didn't Gordon Baxter seem more likely to be one of those guys?

Chapter Fifty-seven

They released Ronnie from St. Vincent's two days later. I spent those two days trying to get my life back to normal again. I lived at Dan's house for the most part. We drove to my apartment once, so I could get clothes and toiletries and my laptop. But otherwise I camped out with him. And we talked, mostly about the future. My future, not his and mine. I knew Ronnie was leaving the hospital. I knew he still had some recovering to do, both physical and emotional. He needed as much stability as possible. Frank Allison checked in with me. He told me Ronnie was free and clear, that everything on the legal side was in order. My brother was coming home to live with me.

And I talked to Paul about Ronnie . . . and about everything else. He and I had a long talk the night before Ronnie was discharged. I told him everything that Beth had told me, the whole awful story of why she'd left Haxton and how she'd slowly worked her way back to contact with Mom and Gordon again. Paul listened skeptically, and when I reached the part of the story when Beth said Mom knew about Gordon's crimes, Paul nearly jumped out of his chair.

"No, no, no," he said. "That's not true. No way."

"I know," I said. "I'm with you."

But he didn't hear anything else I had to say.

"No," he said. "This woman is a liar. None of this is possible. None of it."

On the day of Ronnie's discharge, I went to St. Vincent's with Paul. There were papers to sign—lots of papers—and follow-up appointments to arrange. When all of that was finished, we began the long waiting process. Ronnie, like all the other patients, no matter their condition, had to be taken out of the hospital in a wheelchair. Strangely, the hospital didn't have enough wheelchairs to facilitate the release of all its patients. So we waited. And we waited.

At one point, Paul left to use the restroom. I leaned close to Ronnie and said, "You knew we had another sister, didn't you?"

He nodded. His skin looked a little pallid, and he'd lost some weight. But I saw the same life in his eyes he always had.

"Why didn't you tell me?" I asked. "I thought we were buddies."

"Mom told me not to," he said.

"Figures," I said.

"She said she wanted to tell you," he said. "She told me, 'Ronnie, no surprises.' So I kept my mouth shut."

"Right. Mom didn't like surprises. She sure sprung them on us, didn't she?"

Ronnie wouldn't say anything bad about Mom, even as a joke. He changed the subject. "Where is Eliz—I mean, Beth? Where is she?"

"She's coming over tonight," I said. "Once we're home and you're settled in, she wants to see you. She's been worried about you."

"With her family?" Ronnie asked.

"Yes. She has a big one. It's not like our family."

Ronnie seemed to consider this for a moment. "Mom said her family is our family now. Do you think that?"

I'd been thinking about it. And I wasn't sure how I felt about it. *No surprises.* A sister. Nieces and nephews. Their children. It was a lot to take on. "I guess so," I said. "I guess we'll all have to get used to each other."

"A lot of change," Ronnie said.

"Yes. But we'll be in the old house. You can be back in your old room. It's just the way you left it."

Paul came back into the room just then. He told us that he had seen an orderly in the hallway, and Ronnie was the next to go as soon as a wheelchair became available.

Ronnie shrugged, as if to say, *I've heard it all before*. Then his eyes opened wide, as though he just remembered something. "How are you going to go to school and stay with me?" he asked.

"I've worked it all out," I said. "I'm withdrawing from my classes this semester."

"You can't quit," Ronnie said.

"I'm not quitting," I said. "Don't worry. I'm just taking the rest of this semester off while we all try to get back to normal. I'll figure out the next step around the holidays."

"I don't want you to quit school," Ronnie said.

"She won't," Paul said. "Don't worry."

But Ronnie's brow was still furrowed. I knew he tended to worry. He hated to upset people. He obviously felt a lot of guilt about the issues he'd had with Mom. I didn't want anything else added to that.

I put my hand on his arm. "Ronnie, this is the best way. I'm happy about it."

He looked at both of us. Paul and me. His entire support system.

"What is it?" Paul asked.

"Is it safe?" Ronnie asked. "You said the man who killed Mom is still out there. He hasn't been arrested."

I wasn't sure how to respond. It had been two days since the police came to Dan's apartment and explained everything to me, offering their assurances that Gordon Baxter was probably gone. And there had been no sign of him at Dan's apartment or mine. Nor in Reston Point, where Beth lived. No one had seen or heard from him. Neal's wounds were healing, and he too would soon be released from the hospital. Gordon Baxter faced a murder charge as well as two attempted murder charges. Why would he stay? And if he did, what could any of us give him?

"Ronnie, are you sure you don't remember that man coming into your room and giving you some pills?" I asked.

"I don't, "he said. "I don't remember any of that day."

"It's okay Ronnie. And it's safe," I said. I mostly believed it. "The police are going to arrest that man. And we'll be careful. I promise."

"And you can come visit my house anytime you want," Paul said. "We still need to take that fishing trip, right?"

Ronnie looked slightly relieved. Some of the nervousness left his eyes.

I hoped I was managing to hide the nervousness that remained in mine.

Mom's house felt less haunted by her memory when we all arrived. I didn't know whether it was because enough time had passed since I had been there or because I was going with Ronnie and Paul. Did our small little group bring comfort and ward off the bad memories? Would it be a different story in the middle of the night when I was staring at the ceiling cracks at three a.m.?

Ronnie was the calmest of the three of us. He went right to his room and checked all his drawers as well as the closet. He pulled the photo of Mom with Beth's grandchildren out of his bag and put it back on the shelf. Satisfied that everything was in place, he stretched out on the bed and picked up one of his crossword puzzle books and a pencil. When I checked on him again, his eyelids looked heavy and his chin was sinking down to his chest.

"Tired?" I asked.

"Yes," he said.

"You can take a nap," I said. "You probably didn't sleep much in the hospital."

"I didn't."

"Can I ask you something, Ronnie?"

"Sure."

Maybe now wasn't the right time, but I wanted an answer.

"Why did you confess to killing Mom? Why did you say that, when it wasn't true?"

He took a long time to answer. I thought he might not say anything. Finally he spoke. "I felt bad. I did hurt her by not listening to her. I wasn't as good as I should have been. I wasn't as patient. And I wanted the police to go away and leave me alone."

"You *felt* guilty even though you weren't."

He nodded.

"Paul told me something once," I said. "He told me that Mom knew I loved her no matter how we were getting along. That's true of you too."

He looked at me, his eyelids heavy. "Thanks, sis."

"I'm glad you're home," I said.

His eyes closed all the way. I left the door slightly ajar and went out to the living room to talk with Paul. He was sitting on the edge of the couch holding a glass of water. His legs were crossed, his foot bouncing in the air like a man waiting for a delayed flight.

He started to stand when I came into the room.

"Where are you going?" I asked.

He set the water on the coffee table. "I thought I'd let you two get settled," he said. "I'm sure you're both tired."

"I am tired. But it's nice having you around."

He nodded, his face blank.

"Are you okay?" I asked. "Is it difficult for you to be in the house?"

"It's weird," he said. "I associate this place so closely with Leslie. With everything that happened, really."

"I know."

"Can I convince you to come to my house?" he asked. "There's room. We can work something out."

"Do you think it's dangerous here?" I asked. "Really?"

"I've been thinking about it a lot. Gordon Baxter is capable of anything. I don't know that my house is safer than anyplace else."

"Do you think he'd hurt you?" I asked.

"I think he might want to hurt anyone associated with the past. Anyone who knows who he really is."

"I'm going to try to stay," I said. "The detectives promised extra patrols. I'll call 911 if I hear anything strange. A howling cat. A scraping branch."

"Would your friend come over? Dan?"

The question brought me up short. I had enough complications in my life. Enough relationships in need of attention. "He would," I said. "But I don't think I want him to."

"Why not? He seems so nice. So steady."

"I know. But I've got enough here. My plate is full." I left it at that, and Paul let it drop. I shifted gears. "Beth is coming over in a little bit. You'll get to see her."

"Yeah?" His voice sounded distant.

"Thirty-seven years," I said. "Crazy."

"Yes," he said. His eyes glazed a bit, as though seeing something from the past. "A lifetime." He snapped out of it. "How was it with the two of you? Is she . . . okay?"

"Are you asking me that because you said she might be disturbed? You called her a liar."

"I worry about people's motivations. What might have happened to her over all that time."

"The police hinted at the same things."

"Then it's worth heeding their advice, isn't it?"

He was right, of course. I didn't know anything about her. I didn't know what I was getting into. I knew I might end up looking like a fool.

And yet . . .

"I understand," I said. "But all I can think of is Mom."

"You mean she would have wanted this?"

"Yes. That. And that I said no to her. I pushed her away. I pushed her away when she needed me. And Ronnie . . . I don't want to do that again."

Paul fidgeted a little, but seemed to understand. He pressed his lips together into a tight line and scratched his chin. He seemed to be leading up to a pronouncement.

"I think I'm going to let you all get acclimated first. Is it overwhelming for Beth? All of this craziness?"

"I'm sure it is. But she's held it together pretty well. She seems tough."

"Well," he said. "I can see her another time. I think the three of you need to get to know each other. I know Beth. The three of you don't know each other at all. I think it's important that you do. And you and Ronnie have to get used to this new life you're going to be living. It's a different phase for both of you. You know . . . Leslie would have liked this. She would have liked this very much."

Something caught in my throat. I closed my eyes, letting it pass. "I know," I said. "I feel like we're driving you out."

"Not at all," he said. He looked around the house, taking in the door, the walls, the windows. "Do me a favor? Lock the door after me."

"You don't even need to ask."

Chapter Fifty-eight

I woke up in the chair. The sun was down, the house quiet. I had fallen asleep without any lights on, and the whole place was dark. Only an ambient glow leaked through the windows from the streetlights.

I listened. I didn't hear anything. I reached up and turned on the lamp next to me. My back and neck were stiff from the awkward sleeping position. I was hungry too.

I walked down the hallway, stopping at the door to Ronnie's room. I saw no signs of light or life. The door remained ajar, just as I had left it. I gently pushed it open. Ronnie was still in bed, the covers pulled up to his chin. His chest rose and fell. He was worn out. I looked at the large digital clock by his bedside. It was almost seven. I'd slept for an hour and a half.

Wasn't Beth supposed to be at the house?

I walked back out to the living room and found my phone. I sent her a text.

Hey. Are you going to be able to stop by? No big deal if you can't.

I turned on some lights in the kitchen and opened the refrigerator. Nothing there. Mom was long gone, the house long empty. I needed to go to the store, and find out what Ronnie wanted. I'd deal with it when he woke up. I looked through the cabinets, which were pretty well stocked. I found a can of Dinty Moore Beef Stew. Mom usually cooked, but every once in a while she'd take the night off and serve us something like that. I could picture her in the kitchen, working the manual can opener, peeling back the lid, and dumping the contents into a pan. How fascinated Ronnie and I could be just watching her live her routine life.

I did the same thing Mom would have done. I heated the beef stew, then sat at the table spooning it into my mouth. It always tasted better when Mom made it. Even from a can. I checked the phone again. Still no sign of Beth. Maybe her plans had changed. Or maybe . . .

I tried not to let doubts cloud my mind. I knew Paul and the cops were being cautious. Too much crazy stuff had happened not to be. But I meant what I had told Paul. I wanted to do what Mom would have wanted. I wanted to try to be some kind of family.

The phone buzzed. A text from Beth: *B there soon.*

I cleaned up the kitchen, then walked down the hallway to Ronnie's room again and went all the way inside. I gently touched his arm.

"Ronnie?" I whispered.

He opened his eyes. He looked at me for a moment as though he didn't recognize me.

"Do you know where you are?" I asked.

"Home," he said, his voice confident.

"That's right. Do you want to get up? Beth is coming over. She wants to see you."

He groaned and yawned. "I'm tired."

"I know. Do you just want to stay in bed? I can tell her you're resting."

He groaned again. "I'll get up. In a minute."

"Whatever you want."

I knew he'd get up soon enough. He wouldn't want to miss seeing Beth. He wouldn't want to be left out of anything. He hated that.

It wasn't long before the doorbell rang.

"She's here, Ronnie," I called out as I went to the door and opened it.

There was Beth. Eyes red rimmed, her face streaked with tears. She'd been crying. She looked like hell.

"What is it, Beth?" I asked.

I stepped back and she came in past me.

And then Gordon Baxter emerged from the shadows, following her. He stepped right into the house and closed the door behind him.

Chapter Fifty-nine

I backed farther into the room.

My phone was sitting on the kitchen table, far from my reach and any hope of dialing 911. My legs shook. A jittery, rubbery sensation passed down through my body, from my chest to my feet. I concentrated on remaining upright.

I looked at Beth.

She had come into the room and stood about ten feet away from me. She was crying again.

What was going on here? What was she doing bringing Gordon Baxter to my door?

She must have read my thoughts.

"He came to my house right when I was leaving. That's why I'm late."

"I wanted to have all of you together," he said. "It will make everything easier."

Gordon wore a raincoat over a cheap-looking polyester suit. His right hand was buried in the pocket of the raincoat, clutching something, a small, hard object. I didn't need to see it to know he was armed.

"What do you want?" I asked. I hated that my voice quaked,

that it sounded like a scared little girl's. "What do both of you want?"

"Both?" Beth said.

Gordon spoke over her. "I'm offering you an opportunity," he said. "The same one I offered Beth here on that night all those years ago. I know she's shared all of that with you by now, right?"

"You mean how you ran her off," I said. I looked at Beth. "If that's even the truth."

"It is the truth," Beth said.

"You know what I want," Gordon said, taking a step toward me, his hand still in his pocket. "I tried to make a deal with you before, but you wouldn't go for it. Now the price has gone up." He looked at Beth and then back at me. "I want some compensation for the years *I* had to wander in the wilderness. The bad health. The lost jobs. Jail." He gestured toward Beth. "It all started down that way when this one here started making trouble for me. And your mother didn't help. I want that insurance money your mom left to you and your precious and special brother. All of it."

"Why would I give you anything?" I said. "That's ridiculous. You're nothing to me. If Beth wants to give you something, you're her father. I can't stop—"

"I'm not giving him anything," Beth said.

"What leverage do you have over me?" I asked. I pointed to his pocket. "Except for that."

"This," he said, moving it in his pocket a little. "This is nothing compared to other things. I know some truths I could share. I could share them with you. I could share them with the authorities. Your little protected mind would never be the same, would it?"

"He's lying," Beth said.

But her words and her voice weren't convincing to me. I felt as if I was staring into the eyes of a cobra, being mesmerized by his promise of the truth.

"I know things about certain people," Gordon said, moving a little closer. "Your sainted mother, for example."

"If you're talking about the movies, the things Beth discovered, I don't believe it."

"She spilled the beans about all of that, huh?" Gordon said. "And you chose to believe her?" He gestured toward Beth again. "You know, this woman over here, she's a lifelong liar. She lied when she was a kid, and she's been lying her whole life."

"Stop it," Beth said, her voice ragged with tears.

"She's an addict," Gordon said. "An addict will tell you anything to get what they want. If you choose to believe someone like that, then you're the sucker."

"Mom would never—"

"Do you know that?" Gordon asked. "She didn't tell you a lot of things. She didn't tell you about *me*. Or Beth. No one in your family did. And now you want to think the best of *them*?"

"You broke into my apartment. Why?"

He shook his head a little. "I wanted to see the will. I wanted to know who was getting the money from your mom. It was easy to do that. All I needed was a little help."

I opened my mouth to speak again, but my words were cut off by the sound of footsteps from behind me. I turned. It was Ronnie. He was dressed, his hair combed into place. He was red cheeked and looked healthier than before his nap. He looked at Gordon and Beth and then at me. He read my face as he always did, and his brow furrowed.

"It's okay, Ronnie," I said.

"Is this the man?" he asked. "Is this the man who hurt Mom?"

"Yes," I said. "But it's okay." I swallowed hard. "Why don't you let Ronnie leave? He can go to the neighbor's house. He doesn't need to hear all this."

Gordon looked at me, his face dripping with condescension. "Really? He can go? And call someone to help you?" He shook his head. "The little man can stay."

"It won't matter," I said. I nodded toward Ronnie. "*We're* not giving you anything."

"Are you sure that's a deal you're willing to make? Do you want to hear everything I know?"

"I know all I need to know," I said. "You blackmailed Mom. You sucked money out of her and killed her when she threatened to turn you in to the police for kidnapping."

Gordon had taken a couple more steps toward me, bringing him within ten feet of me. But when I said the word "killed," he stopped in his tracks.

"I'm not a killer," he said.

"You killed Mom. You tried to kill my friend Neal."

"That punk. If I wanted to kill him he'd be dead. I defended myself."

"And Ronnie?" I asked. "What about the pills? The heart pills?"

"It needed to be done," Gordon said.

Ronnie darted forward. He lunged at Gordon's face with his hands, clawing and digging. He took Gordon by surprise and sent him stumbling back a couple of steps. But then Gordon regained his balance and pushed back against Ronnie, bringing up both his hands and releasing his grip on whatever was in his pocket.

"Ronnie!"

Ronnie continued to struggle for a moment; then Gordon

regained the upper hand. He shoved against my brother as hard as he could. He sent Ronnie flying backward, where he crashed against a shelving unit. I watched Ronnie's eyes close in pain as he made contact and fell to the floor. The shelves fell on top of him along with the picture frames and other items. I heard glass break, but Ronnie was silent.

"No," I said.

I started forward, my hands up. I swung at Gordon, making contact with the side of his head, feeling my knuckles against his skull.

The blow didn't faze him. He swung back at me, knocking me down. He stepped toward me, reaching for his pocket.

I'm dead, I thought. *I'm dead. This is how I'm going to die.*

Then I saw Beth moving behind Gordon. A quick, blurred movement. Something swinging and a sickening thump of an object against the back of Gordon's head.

I saw the look on his face when the blow connected. His face lost all animation, and his eyes rolled up in their sockets, revealing nothing but white. His mouth formed an oval shape, the beginnings of a cry he never made.

He fell forward, his body limp. He landed at my feet, where I still sat on the floor.

I looked up. Beth held a lamp, a thick glass lamp. The base was cracked but not broken where she had smacked Gordon on the back of the head. Her eyes looked crazed and fearful. She held the lamp in two hands like it was a baseball bat. She looked at the lamp and her hands once. She stepped forward, standing over Gordon.

"Beth," I said.

She swung the lamp again, striking another blow against his head.

Gordon's eyes were open, still showing white. I pushed myself up. Beth prepared to swing again. I put my hands on hers. I tightened my grip, tried to hold her in place.

"Stop," I said, my voice firm. "Stop."

She looked at me, her eyes wide and glazed. She started to pull back, trying to break out of my grip.

"No," I said. "It's over. Drop it. It's over."

She came back to herself slowly. Her eyes regained their focus. She seemed to see me, to recognize me. She dropped the lamp and it crashed to the floor.

"Check him," I said, pointing to Gordon. "I need to see about Ronnie."

I stepped over Gordon's body and ran to my brother. Ronnie was under the shelf, his eyes half open.

"And call 911, for Christ's sake," I said.

She looked down at Gordon. She nudged him with her shoe. He didn't respond. She went to her purse and pulled out a phone.

"Ronnie?" I said. I touched his forehead. A trickle of blood ran down from near his ear. "Are you okay? Ronnie?"

He groaned.

I pushed the shelf off of him, felt the broken glass cutting my fingers.

"Ronnie? Tell me you're okay. Ronnie?"

Beth came to my side, her face white.

"The police are on their way. And an ambulance."

"Good," I said.

"Elizabeth?" she said.

"Yes."

"I think I just killed my father."

Chapter Sixty

A paramedic with a shaved head tended to the cuts on my hands, which I'd suffered when I removed the broken glass covering Ronnie. I sat on the back bumper of the open ambulance, a blanket wrapped around me against the cool autumn night. Ronnie sat next to me, and while my wounds received attention, another paramedic examined Ronnie, asking him to turn his head first one way and then the other. He shined a penlight into Ronnie's eyes and asked him to follow the path of his finger in the air.

"You're looking okay, buddy," the paramedic said to my brother. "You're going to be sore tomorrow, but I don't think you have a concussion."

"He was bleeding," I said.

"I saw that," Ronnie's paramedic said. "It's a small cut. Superficial. He's lucky. With all that glass around him he could have really been sliced up." The man pointed at my hands. "You got it worse, trying to help him."

"She's tough," Ronnie said.

"Is that right?" my paramedic asked.

"*He's* tough," I said. "He saved me." I looked to the house. It glowed with light, and the front door stood open. Richland and Post were inside talking to Beth. "They both did," I said.

The wind picked up, rustling leaves in the street. I shivered.

"Should he go to the emergency room?" I asked.

"He's fine," Ronnie's paramedic said. "He should take some ibuprofen and sleep it off. He'll be back to his old self in a couple of days."

"Thanks," Ronnie said.

"Have they taken the body out?" I asked.

My paramedic turned and looked at the house. "Not yet. Usually the medical examiner and the cops take their sweet time with that stuff."

I knew that well. Two bodies removed from the house in just over a week. Another big night for the neighborhood. They were going to ask us to leave—or turn us into a reality show.

"So she killed him just by smacking him with that lamp?" I asked.

My paramedic nodded. "He was probably gone before he hit the floor. You can do that to someone if you get them in the right spot."

I hoped that was the end of all of it.

Ronnie and I gave our statements to Detective Post. We took turns sitting in the backseat of her warm sedan while Richland remained inside talking to Beth. It didn't take that long. I could recall the events vividly, could still hear the sickening sound of that lamp against the back of Gordon Baxter's skull.

When I finished my statement, Post told me she needed to get back inside to wrap things up.

"Can I ask you something?" I said.

"Sure."

"Beth," I said. "My . . . half sister . . . What do you make of her?"

"She seems like she's been through a lot," Post said. "Hard years. We see a lot of people like that in our business. People whose lives just don't go the way a life is supposed to."

"Yeah," I said.

"Is there something else you want to know?" Post asked.

"I guess I just want to know if you believe her," I said. "If I should believe her."

"I think you know I can't decide that for you," she said. "She's your family, so you have to make up your own mind about her."

"I thought you might say something like that," I said.

"My cop instincts say she's on the level," Post said. "She saved your life and your brother's life tonight. That's not a small thing."

Saved my life. I never thought I'd be the kind of person who would need her life saved.

"And," Post said, "if you want to know something else, we looked into the story she told you about why she disappeared back in 1975. It turns out there's a detective still alive from back then, an old guy named Ron Forest. They broke up a ring of drugs and pornography in Haxton about a year after your sister ran off. The guys who were behind it were involved with a lot of things, and it doesn't look like Mr. Baxter's name ever came up in association with that investigation. But something like that was going on in Haxton back then. It's a little corroboration for her story from a reliable source. And I guess learning something like that about your father when you're fifteen years old could really strip your gears, you know? It might take a long time to get over that."

"Or never," I said.

"Indeed," Post said.

"Maybe thirty-seven years of anger, thirty-seven years of living the wrong kind of life brought that lamp down on his head tonight."

The car started to feel too warm. I still had the blanket wrapped around my body, so I reached up and loosened it from where it rubbed against my neck.

"Are you going to stay here tonight?" Post asked.

"It doesn't sound that appealing. I need to call my uncle and tell him what happened. Maybe Ronnie and I can stay over there until . . . the house is cleaned up."

"Would you like a ride there?" Post asked.

"Is Beth . . . is she finished?"

"Soon. Do you want to talk to her?"

"Yes, I do. I should wait and see where she's going to stay tonight."

Post patted me on the leg. "Sit tight. I'll tell her you're still out here."

She climbed out of the car, leaving me alone with my thoughts in the dark.

Chapter Sixty-one

Uniformed police officers and paramedics remained at the house, milling around and discussing town and work gossip. They took turns showing Ronnie their cruisers and wagons, listening patiently as he asked questions about the most common reasons people dialed 911.

I used the phone while we waited. I called Paul and told him about the events of the night. He offered help immediately, insisting on coming over to the house to make sure we were all okay.

"No, it's all right," I said. "We're almost finished here. In fact, we're going to need a place to stay tonight. I don't think I want to stay in the house after . . . you know, another dead body and everything."

"Of course," he said. "You can stay here."

"We might have to sell this house," I said. "It keeps accumulating bad memories."

"Absolutely. Your mom was never attached to those kinds of things very much. Get a new house."

"Okay," I said. "I'll worry about that tomorrow."

"Are you sure you don't want me to come over there and pick you and Ronnie up?" he asked. "I can."

"I don't think so. I'm going to wait for Beth. She might come along with us. I don't know if she'll be up for driving back to Reston Point."

Paul fell silent for a moment. "Okay," he said. "I just . . . Is she doing okay? Overall. You know?"

"I don't know the answer to that either," I said. "But I guess I have to find out now. She's my sister."

It took another half hour for Detective Post to come back out of the house. Beth walked beside her, wearing a Dover Police Department sweatshirt against the cool night air. I walked up the sidewalk toward them, and the three of us met halfway. Post didn't stay long. She excused herself, saying she needed to consult with someone from the medical examiner's office out in the street.

I immediately wished she would have stayed.

Beth and I faced each other on the narrow sidewalk. It took a moment, but I reached out to her, opening my arms. "I hope you're okay," I said.

We hugged. She felt thin and insubstantial, almost as if she might slip away at any moment. She held to me longer than I held to her. When we let each other go, Beth said, "I think they're going to bring the body out soon. I could tell they were getting ready to move him."

"Would you like to leave?" I asked.

"I guess I should," she said. "There isn't much else to do here. And it's a long drive in the dark."

"I don't mean go home," I said. "I don't think you should go back there alone."

She looked at me, waiting.

"I talked to Paul," I said. "We can go to his house and stay there. He has room, and it looks like it will all be safe now."

"I don't know," she said. "I don't—" She looked around at the night. She looked at the yard and at the sky. Then she turned back to me. "I can't be here with you if there's any chance you believe those things that Gordon said. Either about me or about Mom. I'm a mess—I admit that. But I'm not like him. I'm his daughter, but I'm not him. All I ever wanted was to see Mom again. If you can't understand that or accept it, that's fine. But it's not true. None of those things he said were true."

I looked back at the house. It was still full of light, but it felt farther away than ever. Mom was gone. Dad was gone. At some point, a page had been turned. It was time to move forward, and I could do it alone or with the help of others.

"I know," I said. "Why don't we all go to Paul's house?"

Chapter Sixty-two

Paul opened the door to our ragtag group. A long, awkward moment stretched out as he and Beth stood face-to-face on his front porch. They seemed to be taking each other in, examining and measuring. Ronnie and I stood to the side, watching. My body ached. I was sure Ronnie's did too. But I didn't move. On TV these reunions were always tearful and full of hugs. Seeing all this up close—living it—I could attest there was more awkwardness and uncertainty than anything else.

Paul blinked his eyes a few times and finally said, "Well, I can't really believe what I'm seeing after all this time."

"It's me," Beth said. "It's really me."

Paul finally got ahold of himself and stepped back. He motioned us inside.

"Please come in," he said, his voice turning more somber. "I know you've all had a hell of a night."

We all went in, then settled into Paul's neatly kept living room. Beth sat closest to Paul on the couch, while Ronnie and I were across the room in chairs. I watched Paul watch Beth. His eyes were misted with emotion. His cheeks were flushed. He sat with his hands on his knees, his posture stiff and uncomfortable.

"I just can't get over the way you look," he said. "Just like Leslie. Just like her."

"I know," Beth said. She swallowed and raised her hand to her eye, brushing at it.

I felt it too. The whole thing. I didn't know what happened to us when we were gone, if some part of us was still able to look back on this world and watch over our loved ones. But I wanted to think Mom was somewhere where she knew we were all together. The four of us at long last.

And I couldn't help but think of her absence. She should have been there alongside of us. Her three children. Her only sibling.

Her family.

I couldn't help it. I felt the emotion coming over me as well. I took a deep breath and held it in. But I couldn't hide it all.

Ronnie reached over and rubbed his hand on my back. "You okay, sis?"

"I am," I said. "I'm just thinking about Mom."

"Me too," Ronnie said.

We were all nodding. We were all thinking of her.

"She's here," Beth said. "I can feel her."

"Indeed," Paul said. He seemed to have loosened up just a little. Relaxed. He didn't look at Beth, but he said, "I'm just so sorry for all the time you lost."

Everyone was silent. His words hung in the room like an invisible weight. We all felt the same way. None of us could change it. That was the price Beth had paid for the events of her past: time. She'd lost years of precious time.

Yet she was back. We could all look ahead.

"Sis?" Ronnie said.

I turned to him. He was looking down.

"Your hand," he said.

I looked down as well. A bandage had come undone on one of my fingers. A bright drop of red blood flowed from beneath it, forming a nearly perfectly round bead.

"Shit," I said. And ran to the bathroom.

I peeled the bandage off the ring finger of my right hand. The butterfly strips the paramedic had placed on the cut had worked themselves loose, and the cut had reopened. A smear of blood ran up my finger. I turned the tap on and let the warm water run over my wound. I used a dab of soap to clean the blood.

Paul kept everything so neat. I made sure to drip into the sink and not onto the tile or the carpet. I used a tissue to stem the flow. I applied enough pressure and held tight against the cut until it seemed the blood flow had stopped.

I used my left hand to open the medicine cabinet.

"Band-Aids, Band-Aids," I said to myself.

I didn't see them right away, and I felt anxious to get back to the moment we were sharing in the other room.

I moved some things around and finally found the Band-Aids. I took one out, peeled it open, and managed to wrap it around my finger. It felt tight and secure. I tossed my trash away and tried to put the contents of Paul's medicine cabinet back in order. I righted some bottles, adjusted some creams and pastes.

Then I saw the prescription bottle with Paul's name on it.

My hand shook as I reached out and picked it up.

The cut on my finger became the least of my worries. Whatever blood was in my body turned to rock-solid ice.

Chapter Sixty-three

As I walked down the hallway, the prescription bottle in my hand, I heard faint laughter from the living room. It was Ronnie and Paul laughing. Together.

I came to the end of the hallway and stood in the doorway.

Paul saw the look on my face. So did Beth.

Ronnie noticed something was wrong with me as well. For the second time that night he said, "Sis, are you okay?"

"I stopped the bleeding," I said.

No one said anything else. They were all looking at me, waiting.

Paul's eyes were wide. He looked stiff and nervous again. He cleared his throat and said, "Maybe Ronnie needs to head to bed—"

"No," I said. "He can hear this. He should hear this." I held up the pill bottle and shook it. The pills rattled against the plastic bottle. "Digoxin, Paul? Do you take digoxin for your heart?"

Paul's face remained frozen, a mask showing uncertainty and nervousness. His eyes ticked back and forth. If he tried to lie, if he tried to create some excuse—

But he didn't. The mask crumpled. He lowered his head. His entire body was shriveling into the couch. He raised one hand to his forehead, as if he wanted to shade his eyes from a bright light.

"They're my pills," he said, his voice shaky. "But I didn't give them to Ronnie that day. That was Gordon. *He* took the pills. He went to the hospital and did it. He made a flood upstairs. He had some plan—"

"But you gave Gordon the pills?" I asked. "Why?"

He lowered his hand to cover his eyes. I looked at Beth. She had scooted against the armrest of the couch. Then she stood up. She backed away from the couch. From Paul.

"Why would you cooperate with Gordon on something like that?" I asked, moving toward him. "What did he know about you that would make you do that?"

Paul was sobbing now, his shoulders shaking. He couldn't have spoken even if he wanted to.

I said it for him.

"It wasn't Gordon. It was you. You killed Mom, didn't you?"

He didn't show his face. He kept it hidden from us. He said something, something I couldn't make out. It was muffled by his hand.

"What?" I asked.

He moved his hand aside and said, "She knew."

She knew? What did she know?

"What did she know, Paul? What could Mom have possibly known?"

He said nothing more.

"Paul?" I said. "What? Did Mom know something . . . something about Gordon or you?"

"I was there," he said. "Beth . . . that night . . ."

"Where were you?" I asked.

Beth supplied the answer. "Oh, Jesus. It was you. You drove

the car that night. You were with Gordon, and you were the one who drove me to the bus station."

I came farther into the room. I sat in the chair I had been sitting in before. I looked at Ronnie. He stared at Paul, his mouth open. He looked confused, angry.

"You drove Beth away that night. And Mom found out. And you killed her because . . . she was going to report you? Is that it?"

He didn't respond.

"That's why she changed the will before she died. That's why she removed you as Ronnie's guardian. She knew you drove Beth away. Who told her? Gordon?"

"Yes," he said, his voice feeble.

"Why?" I asked.

"Because she wouldn't give him any more money," he said. "And he was a fucking bastard, and he wanted to make your mom feel rotten about me and everything else in her life. That's why."

"And when Mom found out, she cut you out of her life." I looked at Ronnie again. "And our lives. But why did you have to kill her?"

Paul finally spoke. "She said she wasn't going to, but she changed her mind. She'd been reconnecting with Beth. I guess doing that brought back a lot of the old feelings from when Beth . . . went away. The guilt, mostly. Your mom experienced a lot of guilt. She hadn't fought hard enough to find Beth. She felt she could have pushed the police harder and made something happen. So she wasn't going to let me off the hook. She *was* going to turn me in. Gordon too."

"But after all that time?" Beth asked. "What could they do to you?"

"We'd have faced some trouble," he said. "Real trouble. What do you think the police and the media would think of a story like that? What would people think here in Dover? You know, there's no statute of limitations on kidnapping a child. And that's really what we did. Beth was a minor. She didn't know what she was doing. Children are entrusted to our care. We can't just . . . cast them out. Leslie wanted to send me to jail. I went there that night to talk to her, to try to convince her that she didn't have to do it. She sent Ronnie away so we could talk in private." He wiped at his nose with the back of his hand. "I begged her not to do it. I really did. I told her that her whole family was back together again. She knew Beth. She had the two of you. I was still her brother. I told her that—I was *still* her brother. But she wouldn't budge. Her guilt was so strong, her instinct to do whatever she could for you kids. She just . . . wouldn't listen."

I looked at Paul, the empty shell of the uncle I once knew. I thought that if I opened the front door and the wind blew in, it would turn him into scraps and whisk him away. He was gone. Whatever I once knew in him was gone.

"I was going to tell the police," Paul said. "That day at the hospital, when I asked to talk to the detective alone. I was going to confess. I wanted to. I thought . . . I thought I couldn't live with it all anymore. I wanted to get caught, to have it all over with. But I didn't get my chance to talk to the police—you were there the whole time."

"You didn't have the guts," I said. "You couldn't stand up to Gordon."

"No, I couldn't. You're right. I still can't."

"Still?"

"That night," he said.

"What night?"

"We went to the diner . . ."

He didn't finish his sentence. But I remembered what Gordon had said at Mom's house—that when he broke into my apartment, he'd needed a little help.

"You kept me there at the diner while Gordon broke in and trashed my place. You still let him use you that way. You put all of us in jeopardy."

"It's just—" He stopped. "Once I did live with what I'd done, I realized I'd rather live with the guilt and shame than go to jail. I just couldn't think about going to jail. You needed me. You and Ronnie. When your mom . . . when she was gone, I had a real purpose again. I was an uncle, almost a dad. I thought if I could be out here, I could do more good . . ."

"No," I said. "I'm going to finish the job for Mom."

I took out my phone and dialed Detective Post. As I had hoped, she was still at Mom's house, wrapping up matters there. I told her where to meet us and what she could expect to find. She told me they would be there as soon as possible.

I wasn't really worried about them hurrying. Paul wasn't going anywhere—I'm not even sure he would have been capable of moving off the couch.

Beth remained on the far side of the room, as if afraid to come near Paul. And Ronnie—I turned to look at him. His face was blank, almost expressionless, except for the tears that ran down his cheeks.

I wanted to stop. I wanted it all to stop. But I had to know one more thing.

"How— Why did you ever get mixed up with Gordon in the first place? Why would you make those movies, or do any of those things?"

He didn't respond, but I wasn't going to let it go. I asked him again.

"Why, Paul? Why that?"

Still silence. I stood up and took a step toward him.

"*Why?*" My voice was a ringing shout. Ronnie jumped at the sound of it. But Paul didn't move. He didn't look up as he spoke.

"I was divorced," he said. "My wife left me. You and Ronnie don't remember your aunt Diana. But you do, don't you?"

Beth nodded.

"She left me, Diana. She . . . eviscerated me when she left. She cheated on me. She just . . . gutted me. That's the only way I can describe it." He sniffled.

"So," I said. "What does that have to do with Gordon?"

"I was vulnerable. Weak. Gordon was my brother-in-law. He was older. You have to understand, I knew him and remembered him from high school. That was imprinted on me. But Gordon wasn't the same guy he was in high school. He wasn't the big man anymore. His life was sliding when Beth was a teenager. He lost his sales job. Did you know that, Beth?"

Beth shook her head. "He changed jobs when I was about twelve, I guess."

"He was let go," Paul said. "He was a big talker but not much of a doer. A blowhard, and his bosses could see it. But I couldn't really. I still saw him as that guy from high school. I fell for that memory. I was swayed by it. He took me down a dark path I shouldn't have gone down."

"What dark path?" I asked.

"It started small," Paul said. "Gordon was receiving stolen property. I knew that. I let him store things at my house for a while, and he gave me a cut of the proceeds. I knew it was illegal, but I went along. Something about the sense of danger and recklessness made me feel alive again. Hell, I didn't really care if I got caught or not. I didn't care about anything then. I told myself I wasn't hurting anyone, that I was a passive participant in those things. It was an excuse and a poor one at that."

"I agree," I said.

He smiled a little. "You sound just like your mother when you say that."

"How did this lead to the night you drove Beth away?" I asked.

"Like I said, the things I did were small. Mostly. Once I helped Gordon with a stolen car." He shook his head. "He didn't tell me it was stolen. But I knew. I drove it for him, and another guy picked it up. By that point, I was starting to get worried about myself. I knew I needed to snap out of it. I had a job. I needed to get back to having a real life again. That car thing, it was a turning point in my mind. I told myself that I wouldn't do that anymore, any of it. But then Gordon contacted me and asked for one more favor."

"The movies?"

He nodded. "I didn't know that's what they were going to be doing that night. Gordon told me we were just going to be hanging out and drinking, that there would be women there. He dangled that in front of me. Women. I guess he knew what I desired deep down. Maybe I did need that."

"Sex?" I asked.

"I was *alone* when Diana left. We didn't have kids. I didn't think I'd ever have kids. Being alone that way . . . I was lost. Empty. Believe it or not, Gordon's suggestion of sex helped. It brought me along. I went along. I needed to. I wanted to feel . . . I don't know . . ."

"Like a man again?" Beth asked. "Desirable?"

Paul looked at Beth. He seemed to be seeing her for the first time. "That's right."

"I've been there," Beth said. "I didn't respond to it the way you did. But I know how that feels."

"I didn't know they were going to be making a movie like that. I wouldn't have gone along with it. I showed up and walked into the middle of that. That was . . . across the line. Disgusting. I took a stand, believe it or not. I told Gordon I was going to leave."

"Why didn't you?" I asked.

"He asked me to do one more thing," Paul said. "He told me one of the girls needed a ride to the bus station, and he asked me to drive the car. I didn't know it was Beth at first. I thought it was strange. Gordon rode in the back with the girl. He had her down low, a coat or something over her. I didn't ask questions. I didn't want to know. I just turned the radio on and drove, kept my eyes on the road."

"Classical music," Beth said, her voice small and hollow. "You were listening to classical music."

"You didn't know it was Beth at first," I said. "When did you find out?"

"When she was gone," Paul said. "Right after that, she was gone. I put it together. Gordon's secrecy that night. The girl hidden in the backseat. I was an accessory to Beth's disappearance. Or her running away. Whatever it was, I had played a big role. I'd helped it happen."

"So why didn't you come clean?" I asked. "Tell Mom? Tell the police?"

"I went to Gordon and told him what I knew," Paul said. "I asked him where Beth had gone and told him we needed to make it right." Paul sighed. "He had leverage over me. The crimes I'd been involved in. Even driving Beth away. He knew those things, and he threatened to use them against me."

"You gave your niece away," I said. "She was a kid. You couldn't stand up to him?"

He didn't answer me.

"Well?"

There was a long silence. When at last he spoke, he looked at Beth. "I'm sorry, Beth. But the truth is . . . it sometimes seemed Leslie would have been happier with you gone. And you seemed like you might be happier as well."

Beth kept her composure, but I could see the hurt and regret in her eyes. Her top teeth bit down on her lower lip.

"That's such bullshit, Paul," I said. "You're making excuses for your pathetic life."

He turned to me. "It was pathetic. Is pathetic. I agree. I just hope you never get to find out how bad a life can get, Elizabeth. I hope you don't find anything like that out at all."

.

Epilogue

Five months after Paul's confession, the three of us—my siblings and I—go to the cemetery to visit Mom's grave. It is mid-March, and the sky is the color of steel wool. In the corners of the cemetery, in the shadow of the stone walls, snow remains on the ground. The grass is soggy and springy as we walk across it, our shoes squishing in the soaked earth.

What can I say about our lives? They move forward.

I am back in school, arranging my schedule around Ronnie's needs. Ronnie is working at his part-time job and going to speech therapy. He spends fifteen hours a week or so at the Miller Center, interacting with other adults with Down syndrome, learning the new skills he may need to live on his own—away from me—someday. Although when that day will come, I cannot say. But it is the goal, a goal Ronnie understands and pursues.

During the times when keeping up with school and Ronnie becomes too much, Dan helps me out. Our relationship has continued to progress. Slowly, but it's progressing. I've tried to keep the door open wide enough to let him in.

Beth is harder to read. She lives her life in Reston Point. She sees her children and grandchildren and works in a local clothing store. We visit and talk as often as we can, although not as much as we did in the immediate aftermath of Gordon's death and Paul's confession. Back then, we all three clung to one another, survivors of the same wreckage. We spent many a late night talking through the things on our minds, sharing the images from our nightmares.

I used some of the insurance money to install a security system in Mom's house. And, yes, Ronnie and I did move back in there. It seems like the only place to be, bad memories and all.

But over time, we all started to recognize the differences in our lives. If siblings grow up in very different circumstances, in very different times, and for all intents and purposes in very different families, are they still siblings? Can they ever feel the way other siblings feel?

We reach Mom's grave. The grass has grown in and covered her plot. I stare at the headstone. Mom's dates have been etched in next to Dad's. I think about that, the two of them lying side by side for eternity. I've thought about it many times over the past five months, and I can only guess that Dad must have known about all of it before he married Mom. Gordon, Beth, the disappearance. How could he not? But the only person I could ask— Paul—is not someone I am willing to speak to. He sits in his prison cell, alone. I am finished with him. Once and for all. I'd like to say he is no longer my uncle, but I know that isn't true. He is my uncle and always will be. He is part of the story.

I knew my dad well enough to guess how those things about Mom must have made him feel. It wouldn't have mattered one bit to him. He would have taken her on—her life and whatever came with it—without a second thought. He loved her. For Dad, it was always that simple.

The three of us line up at the foot of the grave in a little half circle. Beth has brought flowers, and she lays them in the grass. We all stand there for a moment, alone with our thoughts.

Then Ronnie says, "Sis?"

I look over at him. He wears a winter coat and earmuffs. Beth looks too, and Ronnie notices.

"Sis and sis?" he says, his voice uncertain.

"What is it, Ronnie?" I ask.

"We're not normal, are we?" he asks. "I mean, everything that's happened. This family. It's not really normal."

I don't know what to say to that. Mom lived her whole life making sure Ronnie felt and acted normal, and I am trying to carry that on. Not just because Mom wanted it, but also because I love my brother. I want a normal life for him.

Before I can formulate a response, Beth says, "I've been in a lot of families. A *lot* of them. Marriages, in-laws, kids, grandkids. Not one of them is normal. As far as I can tell, there's no such thing, Ronnie."

This seems to satisfy him. He even laughs a little and nods his head.

"Okay," he says. "Who wants to be normal?"

The breeze picks up. It moves the clouds, allowing a little sliver of sun to peek through. The wind chills me as well, and I shiver. My brother and sister move closer to me, one from each side.

And that's the way we stand in the cemetery:

Together.

Acknowledgments

Thanks to all my friends and colleagues in the Western Kentucky University English Department and the Potter College of Arts and Letters for a great work environment. Thanks to Lanna Kilgore for legal advice about wills and other matters. (Any mistakes are mine and not hers.) Thanks to Jim Weems, Glen Rose, Jeff Weems, Barrett Griffin, the McMichael family, and the folks at Lost River Cave in Bowling Green, Kentucky, for the book trailer. Thanks to Marianne Hale and Samantha "Super" Starr for assistance and support. Thanks to Kara Thurmond for the Web site. And, once again, I owe a huge debt to my friends and family.

Major thanks to the booksellers, librarians, bloggers, reviewers, book club members, and readers who love books and keep them alive in all their forms. And a special thanks to the Warren County Public Library in Bowling Green and Barnes & Noble in Bowling Green for all of your help and support over the past few years.

None of this would be possible without the efforts of everyone at New American Library/Penguin, including my splendid publicist, Heather Connor, her amazing team, and all the folks in sales and marketing.

ACKNOWLEDGMENTS

Danielle Perez is the best editor on the planet. She knows the right questions to ask, when and how to ask them, and always pushes me to be a better writer. Thanks, Danielle.

Laney Katz Becker is the best literary agent, guide, and advocate I could wish for. Thanks for always demanding the best and getting the best, Laney. And thanks to everyone at Lippincott Massie McQuilkin Literary Agents for their support.

And finally, special thanks to the one and only Molly McCaffrey for love, advice, and support, for tolerating my habit of watching the Reds and for walking in the cemetery with me even on Halloween. What more could I ask for?

David Bell is currently an associate professor of English at Western Kentucky University in Bowling Green, Kentucky. He received an MA in creative writing from Miami University in Oxford, Ohio, and a PhD in American literature and creative writing from the University of Cincinnati. He has been nominated for the Pushcart Prize twice. His previous novels are *Cemetery Girl* and *The Hiding Place*.

CONNECT ONLINE

www.davidbellnovels.com
www.facebook.com/davidbellnovels
www.twitter.com/davidbellnovels

NEVER COME BACK

David Bell

QUESTIONS
FOR DISCUSSION

1. Like all mothers and daughters, Elizabeth and Leslie have a complicated relationship. Is the conflict between them heightened because of Leslie's determination to give Ronnie the best life possible and Elizabeth's drive for education and independence?

2. Elizabeth is reluctant to commit to caring for Ronnie. Can you understand why she feels this reluctance? Or do you think she has an obligation to care for her brother no matter what? What do you think you would do in a similar situation?

3. Having a family member with special needs places an extra strain on a family. How do you think Leslie, Elizabeth, and Paul handle Ronnie's special needs?

4. Elizabeth has chosen to come home to attend graduate school. Do relationships between parents and children change for the better as the child becomes an adult?

5. Elizabeth and Dan have a complicated relationship. How do you feel about the way they get along? Is Elizabeth always fair to Dan?

6. When Elizabeth finally meets Beth, they obviously have a lot of catching up to do. What do you think of the way the two sisters try to get to know each other under these difficult and unusual circumstances?

7. Elizabeth relies on her student Neal Nelson for help. What do you think of Neal and his role in the book? Have you ever dealt with someone like him in your life?

8. Gordon Baxter plays a key role in the book. What did you think of him when he first showed up at Elizabeth's apartment and told her he had been married to Leslie? Did you initially feel any empathy for him? At what point did you realize he was a truly dangerous man?

9. Paul seems like a caring and loving uncle at the beginning of the book. What was your reaction when you found out his secrets in the final chapters? Why do you think he did the things he did? Do you think he should receive any sympathy?

10. Beth wanted to get away from her town and her family. Is this a natural desire that a lot of children have? Is it

understandable that she felt so ashamed of the direction her life had taken that she had a hard time reestablishing contact with her mother?

11. In the end, Elizabeth decides to take on the role of caring for Ronnie. Does it surprise you that she decides to do this? Do you think she's going to make this work and still have the life she wants to have?

12. The novel closes with Leslie's three children visiting her grave. Are the three of them a family now? Will they have an easy time adjusting to being in one another's lives, or have the real challenges of being a family just begun?

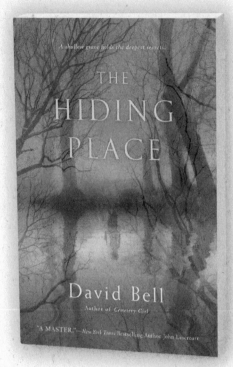

Prologue

What do you remember from that day, Janet?

Janet remembered the heat. The way it shimmered in waves in the distance, making the edges of the trees, the cars in the parking lot blurry and indistinct. Wherever she stepped, the grass crackled or the dirt puffed. The heat rose from the ground and scorched her feet through the soles of her cheap plastic shoes.

She was seven years old and in charge of her baby brother for the first time ever.

Janet watched Justin. She thought of him as a dumb four-year-old, a silly kid with a bowl of blond hair and a goofy smile. He sat with the other kids in the sandbox, scooping piles of sand into mounds with his hands, then smoothing them over. Back and forth like that. Sand up, sand down. Dumb and pointless. Something little kids would do. She watched him. Carefully.

But no, that wasn't right. That wasn't right at all . . .

Justin wasn't silly. And he didn't smile all the time. He was a quiet kid. A loner. He sat in the sandbox alone that day. And he didn't smile much. Not much at all. No one in her family smiled much, not when she looked back on her childhood . . . or even her life now.

What did she remember from that day? What did she really remember? It was so hard to—

Michael showed up.

She remembered that.

Michael showed up, her seven-year-old playmate, the boy from the neighborhood and school. Their parents were friends. They played together all the time. Her boyfriend, she liked to think and giggle to herself, although they never touched each other. Never hugged or kissed or held hands. They were too young for that, too young for a lot of things.

But Michael showed up wearing denim shorts with a belt like a long rope and sneakers with holes in them. His hair hung in his face, and he brushed it out of his eyes constantly. He lived on the other side of the park. And so Michael called her name, and when he did her heart jumped and she turned away from the sandbox and the swings and the other kids. And she followed Michael wherever he went. Across the playground, over the baseball diamond, over by the trees. She followed him.

Is that all she did? Run across the playground?

It was enough. She let Justin out of her sight. Dad was at work and Mom was at home, and Mom let them go to the playground alone that day for the first time ever, but it didn't seem like a big deal. The park was near the school and the church and the other kids would be there, other kids they knew and even some parents. And all Mom said on that day when they left the house was, "Janet, don't let Justin out of your sight. He's a little boy . . ."

But she did. She let Justin out of her sight.

Did she see the man?

Janet can't say anymore. She's seen his face so many times. At the trial. In the newspaper. The mug shot. His face stoic, his eyes round, the whites prominent. His full lips, his black face. Not really a man. Now when she looks at the face, she sees a kid. Seventeen when he was arrested, but tried as an adult. He would have looked like an adult back then, that hot day in the park . . .

But she doesn't know if she saw him.

Other people did. Adults and kids. He was in the park, talking to kids at the sandbox and the swings. He carried Justin, according to some of the witnesses. He paid special attention to her brother, they said. Walked around with him. Talked to him. Lifted him on his shoulders.

For years, Janet thought she saw that, thought she remembered that. The young black man with the frizzy hair and the dirty clothes carrying her brother on his shoulders. Justin's blond head up high, almost as high as the top of the swing set. Justin parading around like a champion. Being tricked by this man. And then being taken away.

But she doesn't really remember that, does she?

She thought there was a dog. A puppy. It ran through the park, and Justin ran after it.

Is that what happened? Is that how Justin got away?

What do you remember from that day, Janet?

She can't be sure anymore. Not after twenty-five years.

She isn't sure she saw the man that day. But she wishes she had. She wishes she knew.

And she really wishes she had kept her eye on Justin, like she was supposed to.

She didn't see the man and she didn't see Justin.

And when it was time to go home, when Janet finally did look around and try to find her brother, he wasn't there. The adults became hysterical and the police arrived and people asked a lot of questions, but none of it mattered.

Justin was gone. Long gone.

Chapter One

Janet hid the morning paper from her father. She saw it when she'd come downstairs, and even though she knew it was coming— knew for close to a week that an interview with her brother's murderer would be on the front page—the sight of it, the sight of his face, hit her with the force of a slap. And then she thought of her dad. His anger, his roiling emotions at the mere mention of Dante Rogers. She folded the front page in half, with Rogers's face inside the fold, and slipped it beneath a chair cushion.

Janet heard water running in the bathroom down the hall, then her father's feet on the hard wood. She was breaking her own rule. When she'd moved back in with her father after he'd lost his job, she'd made a silent vow not to be his household servant. She wouldn't become some version of a substitute wife to him—cooking, cleaning, laundry. But on certain days, she made exceptions. She took out eggs, cracked them into a skillet, and watched them sizzle. Summer work hours at the college left her just enough time to do it—and it might take the old man's mind off his troubles.

"Where is it?"

Janet turned. Her father, Bill Manning, filled the entrance to the kitchen. He was still tall—over six feet—but since being laid off he had gained about twenty pounds, mostly in the stomach and the face. He'd been out of work for nearly two years, ever since the recession had hit and his company, Strand Manufacturing, "went in a different direction," which meant laying off anyone over the age of fifty. Twenty-seven years working in product development and then an unceremonious good-bye.

Janet recognized the foolishness of trying to hide the paper. She pointed to the chair. Bill picked up the paper and sat down. Janet put the eggs in front of him.

"I thought you said you wouldn't wait on me," he said.

"I felt like it."

"You felt sorry for me," he said.

Janet didn't answer, but there was some truth in what her father said. Years ago, he'd lost his son and then his wife. Then came the recent job loss, and Janet moved in to help make sure he didn't lose the house. Her father might be reserved and distant—difficult even—but she never outgrew the desire to protect and help him. And that desire only became stronger as her father grew older. He was sixty-two and starting to look his age.

"Jesus," he said. He folded the paper, snapping the pages into place with a flick of his wrists, and leaned close to read the story. "Not even at the top . . ."

Janet knew what the story said. Her brother had disappeared twenty-five years ago that day, and the local paper was running a couple of stories to commemorate the anniversary. The first one detailed the life of Dante Rogers, the man convicted of killing her brother. Paroled three years earlier, slowly adjusting to life back on the outside, working part-time at a church on the east side of Dove Point, Ohio . . .

While her dad read the article and cursed under his breath, Janet turned to the sink. She ran a rag over some dishes from the night before. "Today's our day, remember?" she said. "The re-porter is coming over at two. I'm leaving work early—"

The paper rustled and fell to the floor. When Janet turned, her dad was cutting into his eggs, shoveling them toward his mouth with machinelike quickness. He paused long enough to ask a question. "Do you know what I think of all this?" he asked.

"I can guess."

He pointed to the floor where the paper rested, the article about Dante Rogers facing up. "This article—it's like they want me to feel sorry for this guy. It reads like he got some kind of a bum rap be-cause he went to jail for twenty-two years for killing a kid—"

"Did you read the whole story?" Janet asked.

Her dad kept chewing. "I already lived it."

Janet leaned back against the counter and folded her arms across her chest. "He still says he's innocent," Janet said.

Her father's eyes moved back and forth, giving him the look of a caged animal. His cheeks flushed. "So?" He looked down at his plate, pushed the remains of the egg around, making a runny yellow smear. He didn't look back up.

"He says—"

"I don't want to hear it," he said, dropping his fork. "He just wants sympathy from people. Probably living on welfare."

Janet took hold of the belt of her robe. She worked it in her hands, fingering it, using it almost like rosary beads. "If it makes you feel any better, I don't really want to tell my story to the reporter either," she said.

"I know the story. Rogers killed my boy. That's it." He pushed away his plate and rose to his feet. The first year after being laid off, her dad dressed just like he did when he went to work—shirt and tie, neatly pressed pants. The past year had seen a change. He no longer dressed first thing in the morning and went days on end without shaving. He stopped reading the classifieds a few months earlier.

"Then I guess it's silly for me to ask if you want to do anything special today?" Janet asked.

"Anything special?"

"For the anniversary of Justin's death."

"Have I ever before?" he asked. "Have you?"

Janet shook her head. She hadn't. Every year, she tried to treat the day like any other day. She tried to live her life, work her job, and raise her daughter.

"Then there's your answer, I guess," he said. "What time's that reporter coming over?"

"I just said. Two o'clock. So, are you going to talk to her?"

He left his dirty dishes on the table. "I've got nothing to say to any of them," he said. "Nothing at all."

Chapter Two

Ashleigh sent Kevin a text: *Where R U?*

She waited near the swings, the sun high overhead prickling the back of her neck. It was just eight thirty and already hot enough to send sweat trickling down her back. Ashleigh scuffed her sneakers in the dirt and checked her phone.

No response yet.

Where was he?

She watched the little kids scream and play. They ran around like monkeys, their mouths open, their hair flying. They never tired or stopped. Ashleigh felt something swell in her throat, an emotion she couldn't identify. She took a deep breath, like she needed to cry, but swallowed back against it, choking it down. She turned away. She couldn't watch the kids anymore. They looked so vulnerable, so fragile, like little glass creatures.

This is the park, she thought. *This is where it happened.*

Kevin came out of the trees. She recognized his loping gait, his broad shoulders. He wore his work uniform—black pants and a goofy McDonald's smock. He'd decided to grow his Afro out over the summer, and it made him seem even taller. Ashleigh took another deep breath, collected herself before Kevin arrived.

"Hey, girl," he said.

"Thanks for writing back."

"I got called in." He pointed at his shirt. "I have to be there at ten."

"That's bullshit."

Kevin shrugged, casual as could be. "I have to earn my keep."

"Let's get going then. These kids bug the shit out of me."

They didn't talk much. Ashleigh imagined that the parents on the playground—the ones who always came to watch their kids, whether they knew what had happened there twenty-five years ago or not—had noticed the two of them: a tall black boy and a short white girl, walking side by side. She'd known Kevin for three years, ever since the first day of junior high, when they'd sat next to each other in history class. At first she thought he was dumb, maybe even retarded. He was so big, so quiet. Then she noticed the jokes he cracked at the teacher's expense, his voice so low only she could hear.

"What's your plan?" he asked.

They came out into the neighborhood that bordered the park. It was opposite where she lived with her mom and grandfather, and a little nicer too. She supposed it was upper middle class as opposed to simply middle class. Bigger houses, nicer cars. A neighborhood where no one got laid off.

They walked past older homes with nice yards. Retirees lived there, old people who spent their days digging in their gardens and sweeping their walks. If a piece of trash ended up in the yard, they'd probably call the police.

"I don't have one yet," Ashleigh said.

"You usually have a plan for everything."

"I don't for this."

They reached Hamilton Avenue, a major road dotted with strip malls and gas stations.

Kevin said, "So you're just going to go up to this dude and say, 'Hey, what do you know about my dead uncle?'"

"Be quiet."

Ashleigh looked down the road. She saw the bus.

"If I go with you . . ." Kevin sounded uncertain. "I'm going to be late for work. I'll get written up."

"Then don't go," she said. "Make hamburgers for strangers. Forget about all those football games I went to with you."

"Come on, Ash. My dad says if I don't have a job this summer, he's going to kick me out of the house."

"And remember how I helped you proofread your history term paper? Heck, I proofread all of your papers last year."

"You're going to throw that back at me?"

"I'll go alone. The guy's probably not dangerous."

"You know how my dad is," Kevin said. "He's old-school. He worked his way through college, so he thinks I need to earn my keep."

The bus pulled up, air brakes exhaling. The diesel stank, burned Ashleigh's eyes. When the door rattled open, she didn't even look at Kevin. She just climbed on and dropped her coins into the slot, where they rattled like loose teeth. She moved down the aisle and took a seat, staring out the window and watching the traffic go by.

She picked up movement at the front of the bus, something in her peripheral vision.

"Hey," the bus driver called.

It was Kevin. He ignored the driver and walked right back to Ashleigh's seat.

She looked up into Kevin's face. A cute face, she had to admit. Beautiful eyes. A little puppyish.

"What?" she said, trying to sound mad.

"You really want to do this?" he asked.

"Yes."

"Come on, goddamn it," someone yelled from the back of the bus.

"I have one problem," Kevin said to her.

"What?"

"Can I borrow fifty cents?" he asked, smiling.

She reached into her pocket and handed him the coins.

Chapter Three

Janet tapped lightly on Ashleigh's door. Nothing. Then she knocked again, using more force.

"Ash?"

The knob gave as she turned. Janet stepped into the darkened room and saw that Ashleigh was already gone, so she pushed the door open all the way. It wasn't unusual for Ashleigh to leave the house early. Not unusual at all. She'd be with Kevin most likely, or sitting at the library thumbing through books and magazines. Kevin. Ashleigh didn't bring him around much anymore, not since they'd moved in with Bill. But the two spent all their time together. Janet tried not to pry, tried not to be a nosy mother, but she wondered sometimes. Did her moody daughter have a boyfriend? That at least was a normal concern for a mother to have, worrying about her daughter's dating life. The other things Janet worried about were a product of her own childhood, and they made her heart flutter . . .

It's okay, she told herself. It's okay to let her out of the house. She's not a child—she's fifteen. She won't get taken and it'll be okay.

Janet reminded herself to breathe. She'd half entertained the notion of taking Ashleigh out to lunch or shopping, something to break the usual routine and mark the importance of the day. But Ashleigh was living her life, just the way Janet wanted her to. Why burden her or anyone else?

Janet turned her attention to the things in the room. She had to give Ashleigh credit for something else—the girl knew how to keep order. No teenage mess in that room. The bed was made, the closet closed. Janet went over and opened the blinds. The light fell across a neat row of photographs on the shelf above Ashleigh's bed. The photos were all familiar. Janet and Ashleigh at a school awards ceremony. A portrait of Janet's mother—high school graduation?—the grandmother Ashleigh never knew. And on the end, facing the light, the last portrait of Justin ever taken, the one that ran in the newspaper and on TV during the summer he disappeared. Janet picked the photo up, ran her hand across the dust-free glass.

Janet had once asked Ashleigh why she kept a portrait of her dead uncle above her bed. The girl just shrugged.

"It's the past," she said. "Our past. And isn't the past always with us?"

Janet shivered. Out of the mouths of babes . . .

She went to get dressed for work.

Janet had begun working at Cronin College fourteen years earlier. She'd started in the mailroom just after high school, sorting packages alongside work-study college students from all over the country. Ashleigh was a year old then. Janet didn't think she could work, raise a baby, and attend college, but she took the job at Cronin with an eye toward bigger things. She knew—*knew*— her daughter would go to college someday, and employees of the college received a huge tuition break. Janet even planned on getting a degree herself and had taken classes over the years as she worked her way from the mail processing center to the copy and print center to the chemistry department and finally to her current position working for the dean as office manager, overseeing a staff of five. She loved her job. She loved supporting herself and her daughter with her own work. She even enjoyed knowing that her job and salary helped her dad hold on to her childhood home.

But she didn't love her job the day the story about Dante Rogers ran in the paper.

As soon as Janet walked into the office, she knew everyone had read about it. Nobody said anything—at least not right away. But she could tell by the looks on their faces. Her coworkers smiled at her, but they weren't happy smiles. They were forced, toothless, the heads cocked to the side a little, the lips pressed tight. *Oh, you poor thing*, the smiles said. *The tragedy. You were there that day* . . .

You were supposed to be watching him . . .

In the break room during lunch, Madeline Hamilton, the office's resident busybody, approached Janet, sitting down next to her and casually removing a soggy sandwich from a plastic bag. Madeline had known Janet's mother, had landed the job in the dean's office with Janet's help. Janet knew Madeline's interest wasn't casual, and Janet even found herself happy to see the older woman cozying up next to her. She hoped someone would break the tension, pop the black balloon that seemed to be hovering over her head.

"So," Madeline said, drawing out the *O*, her tiny mouth formed into a similar, circular shape. Madeline didn't bite into her food. She raised her right hand and fussed with the pile of bright red hair on the top of her head. "Crazy day for you, huh?"

"Do you want to ask me something about the story?" Janet said.

Madeline took a bite of the sandwich and gestured with her free hand. "If you need someone to talk to . . . ," she said, the free hand floating in the air, a heavy, fleshy butterfly. "I've always thought of you as family. And I know today's that awful anniversary. Are you going to the cemetery or anything?"

Janet shook her head. She had a Diet Coke and a bag of pretzels in front of her. She'd eaten two pretzels and barely touched the drink. "They're interviewing me today."

"Oh, really," Madeline said. She wiped her mouth and set the food aside, shifting to all-business mode. "But you read that story? The one today?"

"Yes."

"Can you believe he's still here in Dove Point? Just living here? Among all of us?"

"Where is he supposed to go?" Janet asked.

"I'd think he'd want to live anywhere but here."

"His parents are dead. He lived with his aunt . . . back then. But she's dead, too."

"See," Madeline said. "No ties here. He could just pick up and move anywhere."

"You make it sound so glamorous. He's an ex-con. What's he going to do? Besides, I don't think he's going to hurt anybody."

"He's already killed two people," Madeline said. "First Justin and then your mother. She'd still be with us if not for the grief."

Janet didn't disagree. Her mother never recovered from her brother's death. Diabetes-related complications, they'd written on the death certificate nearly eighteen years ago. Janet knew the truth—her mother had died of a broken heart. But Janet just couldn't summon the same anger toward Dante Rogers that everybody else did.

"Don't you feel sorry for him?" Janet asked. "Even a little? He looks so pathetic, so empty."

"Sorry for him?" Madeline fanned herself with both hands. She looked like she was choking. "Sorry? For a killer? He better hope he doesn't come my way or cross my path. I can't be held responsible."

Janet checked the clock. She needed to get back to her desk. The dean's office didn't rest in the summer, despite the shorter hours. In fact, summer brought more work. Annual reports, budgets, faculty travel arrangements. But she wasn't ready to go back.

"Do you ever wonder?" Janet said. She knew her voice sounded dreamy, distracted. She didn't know what she wanted to say. She didn't know if she should even give voice to her thoughts.

"Wonder what?" Madeline asked.

"The way he maintains his innocence, even after all this time. He has no reason to. He's already done his time."

"Remember what was lost," Madeline said. "Your mother never had the life she wanted because of that man. And neither did you. You've been without a mother for eighteen years because of that man."

"I'll see you later, Madeline."

"You call me and tell me how it went when you're finished."

Janet left without agreeing to make the call.

But Janet didn't go back to work. She took the back stairs down to the parking lot. She stepped out into the hot day, felt the wave of humidity wash over her. The trees just beyond the parking lot were a rich summer green and the traffic on Mason Street just off campus hummed back and forth, the steady rhythm of Dove

Point's life. When she needed a break from work, a moment alone or a moment to think, she came to the back of the building. No one else ever went there unless they were coming or going from their cars. Janet knew she could steal a quiet moment.

She noticed the man almost immediately. He stood by a parked car, watching her as she stepped outside. The man was tall and lean like a runner. He looked to be the same age as Janet, and despite the heat, he wore jeans and a long-sleeve button-down shirt. Even though about two hundred feet separated them, Janet could sense the piercing nature of his eyes. Was he a faculty member, perhaps someone newly hired she had never met? She thought of turning away, of simply stepping back inside Wilson Hall and going back to work, but something about the man's posture and the way he held his head looked familiar to her. She had seen this man before—hadn't she?—but not for a long time.

And then he raised his hand and made a waving gesture, beckoning her to him.

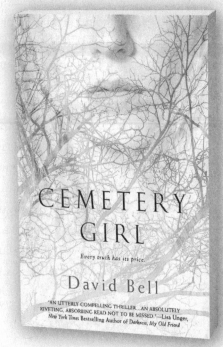